Latakia

JF SMITH

ISBN: 1974443876
ISBN-13: 978-1974443871

<010110>

CONTENTS

LATAKIA

Chapter 1 - The Promise

I'll be a better boyfriend. I swear to God, I promise.

Matt's thoughts had been playing this over and over for a while now. He was lying on his side and reviewing how he could be better. The petty doubts and itching suspicions he had allowed to seep in seemed silly and minor now. He wanted to deserve Brian. He certainly appreciated Brian, and had from day one, but maybe he could appreciate him even more. He should. He should appreciate him more. He was lucky to have a guy like Brian and should appreciate him much more. All he wanted was a chance. Dear God, just a chance.

Matt shifted on his side, trying to get comfortable, and thought back to the first time he ever laid eyes on Brian. He had gone out for drinks to the new upscale bar, Clover, with a few friends, the few really good friends he had managed to make after moving to Richmond. He had noticed Brian across the way, in a small group, drinking and laughing and chatting. Brian was so good looking. Masculine, with light brown hair, fair complexion, and absolutely killer eyes. Clearly well-built. Clearly out of his league. Matt couldn't help it though; he kept getting distracted and looking over at Brian.

Brian eventually caught Matt looking at him, which embarrassed Matt terribly. But Brian had nodded and smiled, acknowledging Matt's attention. Matt was certain that this handsome guy was just being polite.

As usual, he had been just a little too shy to actually go talk to him. Bret and Jim, the friends whose company he was supposed to be enjoying at Clover, finally noticed how distracted he was, and started to rag him mercilessly. In the end, they really did want him to go talk to the guy, and agreed he was extremely good looking. And, as Bret pointed out (in the way only Bret could), the worst, most disastrous thing that could happen would be that they would click and fuck. And Jim, as he had pointed out to Matt in the past, reminded him that anybody that didn't fall for those green eyes of his was blind, or straight, or stupid, or some pathetic combination of the three. Neither Bret nor Jim was surprised, though, when Matt had no intention of doing something so reckless as saying hello to the guy.

Normally, after the missed opportunity, Matt would have regretted not trying something. But thinking back on it now, it worked out better that way.

What had made it ok was that the following weekend, Matt, Chiliburger (as Bret Chilbergh hated to be called), and Jimmy Bob (as Jim Bobson similarly hated to be called) had decided to go back to Clover, and Brian was there again. Matt was infatuated and distracted by Brian's presence, just as he had been the week before. But this time, as they were getting ready to leave (with Matt too unwilling to make a move yet again), Brian stopped him on his way out and said, "I think you left something over there on the bar." Bret and Jim, hoping that Matt would finally get laid, said goodbye and walked on out without him.

Matt hadn't brought anything with him that he could have left. "I did? I don't see anything over there."

"Yeah, the drink. Your drink," said Brian, smiling and nodding his head back over towards the corner of the carefully illuminated bar. Matt felt like Brian's smile could charm the stars from the sky so he could put them in his pocket.

Matt was confused. "There's no drink there."

"I haven't bought it for you yet."

And that broke the ice. Matt and Brian wound up talking, and an hour later Brian told him, "You know, you look like you could use a good date. Will you go out on a date with me?"

That was how they started dating. And maybe it hadn't been perfect in the year since they had met, but Matt hated how he had been alone prior to meeting Brian, and Brian was really good looking, and he was lucky to have Brian. Matt just needed to resolve to appreciate what he had even more.

The angle of Matt's head on the cold floor while lying on his side got uncomfortable, so he turned to lie on his back instead. He had started thinking about Brian to keep the panic and dread away. And this had worked since he hadn't heard the voices outside the room in a while. But he knew if he heard anything outside the door, the naked, trembling fear would return.

And as soon as he even thought about that, he regretted it. The fear and panic *did* return. His eyes watered as the tears started to flow and he cried to himself silently. He hated that he was crying, if for no

2

other reason than he couldn't spare the water. He was already terribly thirsty and very hungry from being in the room for what felt like well over a day now.

He lay on the cold floor in the completely empty room, except for the bucket in the corner. He was stripped completely naked and bound with zip ties at the hands and feet. The tears slipped from his eyes for the fear and mortal dread of what was probably going to happen to him.

He looked up, but in the darkness of the room he couldn't even see the ceiling. All he saw was the black emptiness. The only light that came in was the thin strip of light under the door that led out of the room. Were it not for that thin strip of light, Matt felt he could easily be buried alive, except in a coffin that was ten by ten, but a coffin no matter what the size.

Matt vowed as the tears dropped from his eyes, draining moisture from his body, *Please God, let me get out of here. I'll never doubt Brian again. I'll deserve him, I promise. Please. Just let me get out of this room alive.*

Chapter 2 — Three Weeks Earlier

Matt spotted a parking spot opening up, so he stopped for it and put his blinker on, the wipers beating rapidly to slough off the hard rain. He looked up through the sunroof at the heavy drops pouring down from the black night sky. He had already driven around the parking lot twice looking for an open spot, along with everyone else arriving at the movie theater, and this was the first one he had finally come across that was freeing up.

"Don't grab this one, there's got to be one a little closer up to the theater than this," whined Brian.

Matt said, "C'mon Brian, this place is packed. We'll drive around for another fifteen minutes before we find another spot any closer than this one! You can have the umbrella."

Brian grumbled a little and Matt pulled into the spot after the car occupying it finally pulled out.

The two of them made their way up towards the movie theater, dodging cars and puddles along the way, and Matt finally just made a dash for it over the last thirty yards or so since Brian had the majority of the umbrella coverage anyway. It was easier to let Brian have it than to try and get him to share a little more. He had to make his way around the crowd waiting at the edge of the cover of the theater. They were exiting from a recently-ended film and were all trying to decide how to deal with the rain that had started while they had been inside.

Under the shelter of the overhang in front of the theater, Matt ran his hands through his hair and then across his chestnut brown goatee to help shake off some of the rainwater. While he waited a few seconds for Brian to catch up to him, he saw Tommy and Sal, a couple that were friends of his from the gay softball team he played on, walking out of the theater. He waved at them and they came over, giving him a quick hug.

4

Matt pulled at the wet clothes clinging to his skin and said through an embarrassed smile, "Sorry, I'm getting you guys wet, and I probably look about as good as a drowned cat!"

Sal thumbed the tip of Matt's chin and said with a giggle, "You and your wet pussy jokes!" Matt had really missed seeing them over the last month or so. They always made him laugh when he was around them.

Tommy ran his hand along Matt's arm and said, "Oh stop it, we're about to get soaking wet on our own mad run out to our car, and you'd still be adorable even if you had fallen face first in a mud puddle out there!"

Matt asked about the movie they had just seen, which, it turned out, was the one he had been interested in seeing. That was, before Brian had convinced him to see a different one instead.

Brian finally made his way over to where they were, closed the umbrella and shook the rain off of it while nodding a quick hello to Tommy and Sal. But instead of joining the conversation, he started to pull on Matt's elbow. "Let's go, baby. I don't want to get in there late and get a bad seat."

Matt dug his heels in, though. One minute ago, Brian had been willing to spend probably another ten minutes driving around for a marginally better parking spot. Now, all of sudden, he didn't have a minute or two to speak to Matt's friends.

Matt said, trying to ignore Brian, who was still pulling on his arm, "Yeah, that's the one that I'd really like to see. But Brian really wants to see *Stark Starless Sky* instead, so we'll be seeing that one tonight."

"Ooooh... yeah," said Sal. "I've heard that one's ok. Maybe next time, Matt!" He gave him a sympathetic look.

Brian put his arm around Matt's shoulder, pulled him close, and gave him a quick peck on the nearest cheek. He said to Tommy and Sal, smiling that mischievous smile he was so very good at, "Oh, he'll get his reward for seeing the movie I want to see tonight. I'll get him home later and let him sit down on the ol' smokestack for some quality time. That'll make him forget all about any movies."

Tommy and Sal laughed, and so did Matt even while rolling his eyes a little. This kind of talk didn't embarrass any of them; on the contrary, he and most of his friends comfortably teased each other with talk like this all the time.

What it did do, however, was re-open a mildly irritating wound of Matt's.

He ignored it for the moment because he wanted to make sure that both Tommy and Sal were going to be playing softball this year, especially since practice was starting up the following week. They chatted about the upcoming season until Matt couldn't ignore Brian's antsy behavior anymore. He bid Tommy and Sal farewell, and turned to Brian.

"Why didn't you just go ahead and get the tickets while I was talking to them?" he asked. "You didn't have to stand here waiting on me."

"You said you'd put the movie tickets on your card tonight, remember?"

Matt frowned a little. Yes, he had promised that. But making that promise was the only way to get Brian to go out and do something. And Matt wanted to get out and do something with Brian since in a few weeks he'd be going away on the trip. It felt weird to Matt that Brian had made it clear earlier that evening that Matt was "getting what he wanted," but they were going to see the movie that Brian wanted to see and Matt was paying for it. How, exactly, was that "getting what he wanted?"

Matt nodded and acquiesced, "Yeah, I did. I know." This path was easier than arguing with Brian about it.

They, or rather Matt, paid for the tickets, and the two of them made their way into the theater. Matt followed along behind Brian as he led the way to the theater where *Stark Starless Sky* was playing. He loved watching Brian's ass in motion. He loved watching *Brian* in motion, actually. He still felt very lucky to have someone like Brian as his boyfriend. He was masculine and handsome all the time, but could also be very charming, when he wanted to. And, he could have a great sense of humor, when he wanted to.

Matt would miss Brian while gone on the trip for two weeks. He wasn't the clingy type, but he had definitely gotten very used to having Brian around since they had started dating a year earlier. Brian had made a big point of how he would be sitting around lonely and miserable until Matt got back. Matt somewhat doubted it, but it was nice of Brian to say it.

As they walked into the theater, Matt dreaded seeing a large crowd, because he'd catch hell for making them late and getting bad seats. Fortunately, Brian's concern about that was completely unfounded, as the theater was only about a quarter full. Brian found seats about midway back and they settled in to wait for the movie to start.

While Brian checked his phone for any text messages, Matt finally decided to address the issue that had come up while talking to Tommy and Sal. "So, seriously," he said, putting his hand on Brian's knee, "are you going to top me after the movie? You know I'd really like that. I even have witnesses that heard you promise!"

Brian immediately looked up from his phone and whipped his head around to make sure no one was within listening distance of their conversation. Satisfied that no one was, he said, "Oh, baby, you know I say that just because everyone pretty much expects it of me. What we do behind closed doors is our business."

"But that's just it…" started Matt. He thought better of continuing down this path, though, and stopped. Instead he said, "Well, you know I'd like to bottom some. I'd think that you'd like to switch it up sometimes, too."

Brian reached over and ran his hand along Matt's arm, brushing the hair on it. "Matt, you know you're the only person I've ever bottomed for. Between you and me, you're a good top! You think about it, Matt. Think of all the guys that would kill to be you, to be the one that gets to plug Brian Crimp's bootie!"

"It's not that I don't like being the top, I just…"

"Sometimes," interrupted Brian, "I get the feeling that you don't really appreciate what you've got, Matt."

Matt got flustered. "That's not it at all, Brian." He really didn't want Brian to feel like he didn't appreciate him. "You know I love you. But that's why I thought that maybe you'd like to be on top for a change."

Brian looked sideways at Matt. "You want me to sit down on it, don't you?"

Matt said, trying to not sound exasperated, "You sitting down on my dick doesn't make you the top, Brian."

Brian flipped his phone back on and started checking his text messages again. He said, "Baby, if it doesn't matter what I'm willing to give up for you, then, sure, I'll be the top later tonight."

The movie screen lit up with the start of the previews. Matt sat there, mostly ignoring them. He had heard exactly this promise, delivered almost exactly this same way, enough times before. But the truth was that in their year together, despite what Brian always told other people and despite his promises to top Matt, Brian had been the bottom every single time. And it wasn't that Matt was a screaming bottom and hated being the one doing the driving, so to speak. He actually liked it a lot. He just wanted to experience the other side of it as well, with Brian. He wanted Brian to have the chance to be inside of him. He wanted to feel Brian's presence that way.

He'd heard this promise from Brian enough times to know that it wouldn't happen. But Brian was right that there were plenty of people that would love to be in Matt's shoes given a chance. Matt reached over and took Brian's hand on the armrest between their seats, allowing their fingers to lace together, and settled in to watch the movie.

Chapter 3 — Two Dollar Balls

The Saturday a full week after going out to the movie, Matt sat with Bret and Jim in the bleachers at one of the softball fields in Byrd Park. Bret had watched while Matt and Jim had been through some of the initial training exercises with the rest of the Shockoe Sliders, the gay softball team that the two of them played on. It was now mid-March, so softball practice was starting up even though it was still cool weather in Richmond, but their coach always liked to get in a few easy practices to start off with.

With the basic drills done, the coach was now having each of the team members take turns at bat so he could get an idea as to where they stood, as he dramatically put it, "after a winter of seasonal affective disorder and martinis."

Bret, sitting behind Matt and Jim, pouted, "I was hoping to see you guys in tight softball pants today. I want my money back."

"Keep your eager little dick in your pants, Chiliburger," warned Jim. "You'll get your chance. It's our first practice session. Thank God we don't have to do any serious running or sliding today, or we'd be wearing them."

Bret wasn't to be deterred. "My time is valuable. And you guys are wasting it! So either I get tight, bouncy, athletic asses right now, or I demand a full refund!"

Matt sighed, stood up, and pulled his sweat pants down just enough in back to show a few inches of butt crack.

Bret rolled his eyes and said loudly, "Not *yours*!"

Matt feigned disappointment and said, "I can't even give it away!"

"Not to Chiliburger, you can't!" said Jim. "But if you feel like giving it away, I know a few people that would probably take you up on it."

Matt asked, "Bret, seriously, why don't you join up and play this year? You spend enough time out here with us on the field. You might as well do more than watch."

Bret said, "No way! I'm not a jock and you two know it. I'm far happier…" he wafted his hands up towards his nose and inhaled very deeply, "just breathing in the testosterone-thick air instead."

"Jimmy Bob, he's talking about you. You must be giving off that musk again," said Matt, grinning.

Jim lifted his right arm and gave his underarm a sniff. "Yeah, maybe."

Bret turned to face away from Matt and Jim with a flourish. "I don't know why I hang out with you Neanderthals. Aside from the raw, sexual ener… oh, forget it. I don't even get *that* from you two."

Despite Bret's teasing to the contrary, Jim actually did exude a raw, sexual, jock energy. He was probably six feet tall and about 205 pounds. A fair amount of that was muscle, but at 27, he was starting to have a little bit of stomach show up on him. Jim had wavy brown hair and dark hazel eyes. Mostly, though, he was self-conscious about his legs, which were skinnier than he wanted. They just weren't quite in proportion to the upper body strength he had.

Bret was a very slight five foot nine inches, and only weighed about 170 pounds, even when wearing heavy shoes. His proportions were just right from top to bottom, though, a testament to his gym regimen, and his spiky, dark hair set off his blue eyes very well. Bret had one of those very clean, chiseled faces that framed his eyes perfectly. He had already turned thirty, but had the complexion of a guy still in his early twenties.

Matt, for his part, was a little bit in-between. Like Jim, he was right at six feet tall, but probably only about 190 pounds. He didn't quite have the upper body strength that Jim had, but he had good strong legs that fit his upper body well. He didn't have the paunch that Jim had, either, although he always felt like he should be trying to lose another ten pounds. Most of the time, he was unselfconscious about his looks, but was wary of getting love handles now that he was less than a year away from turning thirty. His full head of dark chestnut hair, a shade shy of being outright black, was accented below with his perennial goatee. But his favorite feature, the one everyone noticed immediately, was his deep green eyes.

Matt clapped his hands as the coach called the next Slider up to bat. He yelled, "C'mon Lane, let's see what you've got!" Jim and Matt, during the previous season, had always felt like Lane had been holding back a little for some reason, and that if he'd throw himself into it a little more, would really be a great player on the team.

Lane waved at Matt and Jim and stepped up to the plate. He fidgeted with the bat, trying to get it into a comfortable position in his hands.

Matt turned to Jim and said, "Look at the way he's choking up on the bat. You think he jacks off like that?"

Jim grinned, but so did Lane as he turned back to face towards them. He said, "I heard that!"

Matt tossed back through a smile, "Well? Do you?"

Lane put his hands on his hips, the bat hanging loosely at his side. "I just do it the way your mom showed me, Matt!"

Several team members started laughing out loud at this point.

Bret stood up and yelled at Lane, "Sir, you offend him! There's no way you could afford his mother!" which set off a fresh round of laughter from everyone within earshot.

The coach yelled, "Ok, ladies, if we can please get back to practice here!!"

Matt reached back and tried to poke his finger at Bret, who quickly started slapping his hands away. Jim leaned over to Matt and said, "I always thought your mom was pretty cheap, myself."

On the first pitch, Lane managed to hit a really good line drive out just inside the foul line along third base, and turned to give a formal bow to Matt, Bret and Jim and the others sitting near them. They all clapped for him as it was one of the better hits so far during practice.

Jim yelled out to Lane, "It's good to see you haven't forgotten how to handle those balls, Lane!"

All the Shockoe Sliders up in the stands started screaming and Jim groaned when he realized what he had said. He yelled and beat his hand on his knees, "Shit! Dammit! Fuck! I'm such an *idiot*!"

Matt laughed and started pushing him down off the bleachers towards the field and yelled, "Pay up, motherfucker!"

The coach held out a jar labeled "Balls Jar" towards Jim. Jim fished a couple of dollar bills out of his wallet and put them in the jar, the very first of the season. He turned to go back to his seat and did a victory jump for the benefit of everyone watching him.

The coach turned back to the rest of the team in the stands, "And we're off to a good start! At this rate, by the end of the season, we'll be able to afford something extra special for our end-of-season party! Maybe we'll be able to hire a stripper this year!"

From somewhere in the stands came a faint "Maybe we can hire Matt's mom!"

The coach referred to the roster he carried on his clipboard for a moment, then called out, "Goodass, you're up!"

Matt groaned and said, "Very funny, Blake. It's Goodend! It never gets old, does it?"

The coach shook his head gleefully and said, "Nope, it never gets old!"

Matt took his turn at bat, fouling once before hitting a pop fly.

On his way back to his seat in the bleachers, he could see Bret and Jim in an animated conversation that ended abruptly as he got near.

Bret asked Matt, "So I guess we won't see much of Mr. Wonderful at these games, just like last year?"

"Probably not. He's never given a hoot about any kind of sports."

"Well," retorted Bret, his tone very staccato, "you know how I feel about that!"

Bret then asked, "So, does Brian ever hang out with Greg at all? I mean, they really broke it completely off, right?"

Matt wondered where this conversation was about to go. "No, he had broken up with Greg before I even met him. He hasn't seen Greg since we started going out."

"Polly said he saw them out having drinks a few weeks ago."

"Where?" asked Matt.

"I think he said it was at Kremlin, that new vodka bar."

Matt thought to himself that this sounded just like Polly, whose name was actually Paul, which had turned into Pauly, which had then turned into Polly. Polly loved to stir shit up if at all possible. Matt wasn't sure if he trusted information from that source or not. Besides, even Bret had on occasion tried to turn him into a jealous and suspicious boyfriend.

"Brian didn't mention meeting up with Greg to me," said Matt. "But I didn't necessarily mean that he literally had not seen Greg. Maybe they have kept in touch some. Besides, you know how Polly is."

Jim seemed a little uncomfortable and stayed quiet, but Bret pushed a little harder, "Polly said he saw them leave together."

Matt exhaled and started to feel a little defensive, "See! Stir it up! Chili, you're turning into Polly."

Bret and Jim exchanged a quick glance.

"We just don't want you to get hurt," said Bret, his tone noticeably softer.

"I know you guys are just looking out for me," said Matt, adding more jovially, "just like a couple of mother hens."

He looked down at his hands. "But, I think you guys are totally overreacting. I'm lucky to have Brian. He's the hottest guy in Richmond!"

Jim said, "Well, yeah, he's good-looking, but looks only go so far, Matt."

Matt turned his attention to Jim. "Brian is really good to me, guys, and you know it."

"Remind me again when was the last time he took you out to dinner?" asked Bret, his question dripping with faux innocence.

"Taking someone to dinner," explained Matt, "is not the same thing as being good to them, Bret."

Bret pursed his lips and thought for a moment. "I give up. Matt, you are too sweet for your own good, darling."

"You guys sometimes don't seem to acknowledge how lucky I am to have Brian. I could easily do a lot worse."

Jim looked like he was about to say something, but before he could, Matt heard Tommy calling to him while he and Sal were walking over their way.

"Matt! Hey, Matt!" called Tommy.

Tommy and Sal made it over to where they were sitting.

"What's this Blake says about you being gone for two weeks, Matt?" demanded Tommy.

"Yeah," replied Matt, "I'm going to miss a couple of practices starting next week."

Sal hit Matt in the chest playfully. "No one cares about that, dummy!! Syria, though? You're going to *Syria* for two weeks?"

Matt blushed and nodded that Tommy and Sal were correct as they sat down on the bleachers in front of him and Jim.

He explained, "So, I've been volunteering with *Doctors Without Borders* for a little while, mostly administrative stuff here in the US, but this time they have some actual field work I can help with."

"But you're not actually a doctor, right? Or, we didn't think you were..." said Sal.

"No, I'm not a doctor. But what I do for the state of Virginia, the health policy stuff for childhood immunizations, efficacy tracking programs, metrics, and the like, matches up with an initiative in part of Syria right now. So, I'm going over there to help them set it up based on what we've already learned here in the States."

"Get the fuck out of here!" said Tommy.

Bret cut in, "He's going to get him some of that forbidden Arabic peter while he's over there!"

Matt rolled his eyes. "Christ, Bret, can't you *not* think with your crotch for thirty minutes?"

"I made it ten minutes once!" lamented Bret. "It was horrible!"

Matt quipped to Tommy and Sal, "Just ignore him, please."

Those two glanced at Bret, grinning. They replied in unison, "We do."

Bret put his hands on his hips and his face lit up. He gasped and said, "Have I just been issued a *challenge*?! I LOVE a challenge!" Fire danced in his eyes at the thought.

"Doesn't this kind of scare you? With all the shit going on over there? Isn't Syria, like over near Iraq, or something?" asked Sal, turning his attention back to Matt.

"The Department of State just lifted the travel advisory for Syria," said Matt, "which means they feel it's pretty safe there now. And yes, Syria borders up against Iraq. But I'll be in Latakia, which is on the west coast, as far away from Iraq as possible."

"And you're really not scared?" asked Tommy.

"Well, I'm a little bit apprehensive, but way more excited about it than I am nervous. *Doctors Without Borders* has me set up with some good people there, and I'll be spending most of my time at Tishreen University, which is a pretty large school. I'll be working with some of the faculty and government people from their health department. I'm not that worried about it."

Coach Blake waved at everyone to get their attention. "Ok, guys, thanks for coming out to the first practice. I think that 2010 is going to be our year and we're going to have a great season! See you at the next practice and please be on time!"

Tommy and Sal both congratulated Matt on going somewhere so very exotic like that, and for a good cause to boot.

Chapter 4 – Text Message

Matt glanced down at his phone to read the text message that had just arrived from Bret.

Thx for the oj, fruit and soup. No note, but I kno it was u. Have a good trip and send emails/pix!

Matt smiled at the note. Bret had been sick the last two days, and Matt had taken a few things over to his place earlier in the afternoon so he wouldn't have to go out to get it himself. He had let himself into Bret's apartment with the key he had and dropped the items off without waking him up.

Brian flashed that evil smile of his at Matt and winked at him across the table while he picked at his salad.

"You'd better not come back and tell me you've been swept off your feet by some Syrian prince while you're over there!" Brian warned Matt, his eyes sparkling. "Man, that'd be just my luck! There'll be some big, strong, swarthy prince with houses and yachts all over the world just looking for some American cutie to make his kept boy. Shit, how am I going to compete with that, huh? Just promise you'll write every once in a while and let me know how things are in your new life as a harem boy, ok?"

Matt laughed out loud. "Yeah, I'm pretty sure that's *exactly* what's going to happen! We might as well just split up now. As of tomorrow, I'm sure as soon as I land in Syria, there will be a line of them waiting for me to pick from, right there in the airport! I promise I'll have my standards, though. They'd better have a big dick and a Bentley convertible waiting for me."

Then he added, "Not necessarily in that order," which actually got a laugh from Brian.

Brian picked at his salad some more while Matt finished the last few bites of his. His mood turned more serious and Brian said, "Man, I don't even like joking around about this. I know I get jealous too easily, but it's just because I care so much about you."

Matt said, reassuringly, like the suggestion was completely preposterous, "Brian, you've got even less to worry about with me over there than you do with me here."

"So, are you saying I've got something to worry about with you here?"

"Don't be ridiculous. You know I love you."

Brian asked, "And you know you're lucky to have me, right?"

"The luckiest guy in Richmond!" confirmed Matt.

The waiter arrived and swapped out the salads for the entrees they had ordered for dinner. Brian turned away from Matt a little to glance up at the waiter, but Matt still just managed to catch a wink of the eye pass from Brian to their server, followed by a subtle smile creep across the waiter's face.

Matt gave Brian the evil eye, but accompanied it with a smile. "I saw that! Am *I* maybe going to need to be worried about *you* while I'm gone?"

Brian froze for a moment, but then said, "Oh, I wasn't even sure what you were talking about!" He started in on the steak the waiter had placed before him. "I'm just trying to make sure we get good service here. He's been a little attitudey since we sat down, so I'm just trying to loosen him up some, baby!"

Matt was already chewing on his first bite of pork chop, but said, "Mmm hmmm," laced with a teasing suspicion. The waiter *had* been dishing up a little bit of an attitude along with the food and drinks since they sat down. Matt wasn't drinking any alcohol at dinner because he had to be up at 4am to get to the airport for his flight, and he assumed this was part of the reason that the waiter wasn't paying much attention to them.

But at the same time, Matt had started to wonder about stuff like this. Ever since Bret had mentioned that Polly had seen Brian out with his ex-boyfriend, Greg, Matt had been a little more sensitive to any little signs like this from Brian. But even if Brian had met up with Greg for drinks one night, that didn't mean anything, did it? Brian and Greg had dated for quite a while; why couldn't they be friends?

But over the last week, his mind kept nagging at him about it, and he kept resolving to not be that way. He really didn't like being suspicious or constantly watching for signs that Brian was cheating on him. He didn't like being that kind of a person at all. He resolved once again to stop being that way.

Besides, Brian had been nice enough to splurge and take him out to Bookbinder's in Richmond for a nice going-away dinner.

Through the rest of their dinner, Matt felt bad about having any suspicions about Brian. Brian absently glanced at his phone to check for any messages before putting it down next to his plate. He asked Matt, "Hey, you did remember to pack your passport and the visa for Syria, right?"

Matt nodded. "Yeah, those were some of the first things I pulled together."

Brian quizzed him on a few other things Matt needed to remember to pack as the waiter swung by again to clear their plates off the table.

Before the waiter came back to ask about dessert, Brian excused himself to run to the bathroom for a moment. Matt watched as Brian turned down the short hallway where the restrooms were and took notice that their waiter headed down the same hallway a moment later. Matt tried to decide if he should go to the bathroom as well, then felt bad for even thinking like that. Did he really expect that Brian was going to be getting a blowjob from this waiter in the men's room? It was silly, of course. But before he could even think much more about it, Brian's phone beeped and the screen flashed to indicate a text message had come in. Matt had never snooped on Brian's phone and had no intention of starting now. But he couldn't help but lean over and notice the screen announcing the arrival of the text message. He frowned to himself when he saw that the phone said there was a message from Greg.

He felt a slight pang to realize that Brian, at the very least, *was* keeping in some kind of touch with Greg. When Matt had started dating Brian, Brian had gone on and on about how awful Greg was and how bad things had gotten between them. Matt tried to shake it off by telling himself that maybe it wasn't even *that* Greg.

When Brian got back to the table, he had a huge smile on his face.

He said, "You're going to have such a great time while you're over there!" He paused for a moment, distracted while he read the text message that had come in on his phone, before adding, "Just remember me every once in a while, miserable and lonely until you get back!"

Matt laughed and verbally poked at Brian, "Oh please! You're not going to be miserable or lonely while I'm gone at all!" Brian had a few of his own friends that he liked to go out with, just like Matt went out with Bret and Jim without Brian quite frequently, especially since Brian really didn't care for them a whole lot.

Brian frowned though, and drummed his fingers on the table for a few seconds. He didn't seem amused by Matt's comment.

Matt wondered if he had said the wrong thing somehow.

Brian said, "I wish you'd just say it."

"Say what?" asked Matt, confused.

"That you don't trust me."

Matt was now dumbfounded. That wasn't what he meant by his comment at all. "I didn't say that."

"But you've been hinting at it all night long," said Brian through a scowl.

"No, Brian. We've both joked..."

Brian cut him off, "And I know how easy it is for you to be suspicious, but it's wearing me down, Matt."

Matt didn't know what to say. Where the hell was all of this coming from all of a sudden? Had Brian really interpreted their joking around earlier this way? Brian had joked about being suspicious of Matt as well. None of this felt like it made any sense to Matt. It felt like it was coming out of the blue sky.

Brian heaved a sigh and said, "Look, I've never been anything but totally true to you, but your insecurity about being with me is getting to be a lot to deal with. It wouldn't be fair for me to not be honest with you about this, so I want to make sure you know how I feel. I've tried to ignore it, but you're making it harder and harder for me to do that."

Matt sat there, his face flush with this sudden disclosure from Brian. It took him so off guard that he didn't even know what to think. The last week or so, after Bret's grilling at the softball practice, he had internally questioned if maybe Brian might be cheating, but he hadn't said anything to Brian about it at all, even obliquely. He wasn't about to accuse Brian or insinuate anything like that without being very sure of the truth.

Matt started to protest, but Brian stopped him again. "Matt, you know what you mean to me. But I can't handle this right now. Before this turns into an ugly fight right before you go off for a few weeks, we need to stop it."

Brian stood up and said, "I'm getting upset about all this and need to stop before I say something I regret."

Matt sat there in shock and complete confusion before he could pull himself together enough to say, "Brian, I'm not sure at all what I've done to make you think any of this, but..."

"Matt, no. Please." Brian started picking at his earlobe, which Matt knew all too well he did when he was upset. Brian closed his eyes and took a deep breath. "This is a terrible time and place to get into this, and you've got to be up really early. So baby, just go on home tonight and get ready for your trip. I need to cool off a little myself. Send me a note or call me as soon as you've made it safely to Latakia. I'll be anxious to hear how your trip is going, and when you get back, maybe you'll feel a little less insecure about us. In fact, a few weeks away will probably be a great thing to remind you of how much I mean to you. Ok?"

Matt didn't know what to say without potentially upsetting Brian any more. So he just said, "Ok. But you know how much I love you, Brian, right?"

Brian walked over and stood next to him. He said, "Of course I do," and kissed Matt on the top of his head. "Send me a note when you get there and have a good trip, baby!"

Brian walked out of the restaurant. Matt sat, in his chair, completely motionless and staring vacantly for a long while. How could something like that have come completely out of nowhere? Was Matt giving off subtle vibes to Brian that he didn't even realize, but that Brian was picking up on? He couldn't remember doing or saying anything that could vaguely be construed to be what Brian was accusing him of.

And then a small nagging thought popped into his head. And he hated himself for it, especially before he'd be going off for a few weeks. It almost felt like Brian was maybe picking a fight. Maybe he wanted to be mad at Matt and not go home with him that evening.

God, how he hated having that thought creep up in his mind. And he really wanted Brian with him in bed, next to him, before he went away. He had really looked forward to that before being gone for two weeks.

The waiter stopped back by and put the bill down on the table. And then Matt's only thought was, *Shit, now I'm the one paying for dinner!*

Outside the restaurant, as he walked to his car, Matt's mind reviewed how he had behaved towards Brian at dinner. He looked up at the cloudy night sky of mid-March and couldn't decide if he was an asshole, or a fool.

Chapter 5 — Tishreen

Matt finished typing a few notes into his laptop from the morning session with the Syrian health department staff, and as he reviewed the last of what he had typed up, he finally started nibbling at the manaeesh he had gotten for his lunch. He had had the manaeesh, a small pizza made with cheese, onion and usually some minced meat, earlier in the week and found that he really liked them. He also had some of the polo, or lemonade with mint, which had become one of his favorite things since arriving in Syria.

So far, everyone he had worked with had been really great and very appreciative of the fact that he had come to help them on the childhood immunization initiative. Several of them were usually delighted to accompany Matt to lunch to help explain the food to him so he felt comfortable with it, but after several days of this, Matt liked having the time to himself to catch up on his notes and send some emails. Plus, once he found out that a lot of the food in Syria was typical Mediterranean, he was much more at ease with it. Things like hummus, falafel, stuffed grape leaves, and tabbouleh were all widespread in Syria, and were familiar to Matt from Mediterranean restaurants back in Richmond. But he had ventured out and found some of the other dishes that were new to him, but that he liked very much, like the manaeesh and polo and others as well.

Doctors Without Borders had made an interpreter available to Matt outside of his time at the university if he needed one to get around, but after the first three days, Matt decided he really didn't even need that. In the central city, particularly the places frequented by tourists like himself, there was always someone around that spoke at least passable English and was willing to help out.

Matt finished sending his emails out to Brian, Bret and Jim and closed down the lid on his laptop. He had been sending them an email or two every day telling them about what he was doing and what Syria was like. Bret and Jim were fascinated and replied to every one, asking all kinds of questions about Syria and Latakia. Brian focused more on either teasing Matt about finding a rich Syrian prince that would steal him away, or telling him that he missed him and couldn't wait for him to get back to Richmond. The email that he was sending today told about his dinner the night before at a nice restaurant called The View. The View was in the Southern Corniche part of the city, but right on a point overlooking the Mediterranean Sea. The meal was excellent, and so was the view of the water, but it was a little expensive. That dinner and his trip late one afternoon up to the Cote d'Azur north of town had pretty much blown his personal sightseeing budget for the trip. He also sent a note to his volunteer coordinator back in the States letting her know how everything was going now that he was halfway through his stay.

He glanced at the stickers that had accumulated on the lid of his laptop over the last two years — a Shockoe Sliders sticker, several from bands and video games he liked, even a small rainbow flag sticker and one with the familiar yellow equal sign of the Human Rights Campaign. Matt decided he really needed to try and find a Syrian sticker of some kind to add to his collection, maybe one from Tishreen University. He put his laptop away when done with his notes and emails, and turned back to finish his manaeesh.

As he ate, he started thinking about Brian again. He had only called Brian one time since getting to Latakia because the phone calls were expensive, and that was right when he arrived to let him know he had made it there safely. He was worried about the call, of course, afraid that Brian was still going to be mad about what had happened at their dinner right before he left, and he hated that he had left while there was still the tension between them.

Fortunately, Brian seemed to have forgotten all about it when he talked to him. In one way, Matt was very relieved that he wasn't dwelling on it, but at the same time, the whole thing was puzzling. If Brian was truly upset and felt like he didn't trust him and it was starting to impact their relationship, why did it just seem to evaporate like that? Plus, he was still feeling a little guilty about thinking that maybe Brian was just inventing a fight that evening.

He didn't want to screw up what he had with Brian. It had been hard to find someone that he fit with since moving to Richmond. Bret and Jim kept trying to say it was simply that he was a little shy and needed to be just a little more confident. Before Brian, Matt had gone on dates, but the guys never felt right, or only wanted sex, or only wanted to do drugs, or the hundred other things people did that made them a bad match. Brian, though, had a stable job, was very attractive to Matt, and wanted to be a part of Matt's life. Matt was lucky to have him.

He decided to go ahead and give Brian another call to check in with him and let him know how things were going and to see how Brian was doing. He wanted Brian to know that he really cared.

He dialed Brian's number and it finally started ringing. On about the third ring, though, Matt realized that it would be early, before 6am, in Richmond. But since it had already rang several times, he decided to let it go.

A moment later, Brian answered with a groggy "hello."

Matt said cheerfully, "Hey Brian! It's me, Matt."

As he said it, though, he could have sworn he heard someone else in the background mumbling something. It was a guy, but it definitely wasn't Brian's voice.

Matt continued, "I know it's early, but I thought I'd give you a quick call before you started getting ready for work."

Matt very much wanted to ask Brian if someone was with him, but absolutely did not want to instigate a repeat of the fight they had the night before he left for Syria. Instead, Matt asked, "What was that? Is the TV on?"

There was a pause on the other end of the phone. "Yeah, umm, the TV's on," replied Brian, sounding fully awake at this point. Matt could hear Brian getting out of bed and walking down his hallway.

Brian asked brightly, "How's the trip? You having a good time? Do you miss me?"

Matt smiled and said, "Yeah, I do. I miss you a lot! But I'm having a great time. The guys here I'm working with have been really good to me and I've gotten to do some really neat things. I may try and copy over some of the photos I took earlier in the week to my laptop and send those to you in an email, the ones when I went to the Cote d'Azur north of here."

"That'd be great! I've really liked getting the emails from you so I can hear about the trip as it happens. Are you doing something exciting later today?" asked Brian.

"I've blown the money I felt comfortable spending doing my own sightseeing, so it'll be less exciting stuff the rest of the trip. Tonight, the guys here at Tishreen recommended a good outdoor café in town that a lot of expats go to, especially Americans and people from the British consulate here in Latakia. I'll probably go check it out."

"So you really miss me, baby? Do you miss having my arms around you at night?" asked Brian.

Matt grinned warmly to himself. "Yeah, I really do. It's been cool being over here, but it'll be good to come home, too."

Brian said, "That's good! That's what I want to hear!"

"Ok, I'd better go since these calls are so expensive. I love you, Brian!"

Brian closed with, "You'll be home before you know it, baby! Keep sending the emails!" He yawned and hung up.

As soon as he put the handset down, Matt felt like it had to have merely been his imagination making him think he heard another guy's voice at Brian's place. It felt so good to hear Brian's voice, though.

Matt scratched at his goatee and got amused when he remembered Brian's comment about missing his arms around him at night. When they slept together, Brian usually got hot and went to the other side of the bed from Matt. Actually having contact with Brian while sleeping was a rare treat.

~~~~~

That evening, Matt sat at the café and finished up his coffee. The café was a nice place, but had far fewer patrons than he was hoping for. He had expected it to have more people there based on the recommendation from his friends at the university, but he had gotten there later than he intended. The slim crowd seemed to have started out with a few Americans and British customers, but they had left pretty early and all that was left was a few Syrian and other Middle Eastern customers, mostly men at this time of night. Some were wearing more westernized clothes including jeans and collared shirts, but the rest were wearing the more traditional didashahs and kuffiyahs. He was a little disappointed that his plans to maybe find some compatriots from the US or Britain to chat with didn't pan out, so he instead spent his time having a late dinner and copying over the photographs from his camera's memory card to his laptop.

He paid his bill and left to find a taxi back to his hotel near the university. The waiter had told him there were usually some taxis waiting a block over to the east of the café, so he set off in that direction and enjoyed the cool air of the late evening.

Matt made his way to where the waiter had indicated, hoping he wasn't getting the directions wrong. The roads in much of Latakia were very old, and were almost always narrow and twisty, forming a confusing maze of buildings, roads, and alleys. Just when he thought he had gotten lost, he looked through an alleyway and finally saw some taxis one street over.

He started down the alley to get to where the taxis were waiting, but a van came up behind him and he had to push to the side to get out of the way so it could pass. But just as the van passed him and got in front of him, it stopped. And before Matt had any time to react at all, two guys jumped out of the van just a few feet away and turned towards him. That's when Matt saw that one of them had a gun in his hand. The blood ran out of his body and he started to back away.

But just as soon as he turned around to try and run back the way he had come, he was violently hit in the back of the head with the gun and a black sack was pulled over his head. He was seeing stars and felt dizzy and was having trouble standing upright. Instantly, the assailant pulled a rope in the neck of the sack, tightening it around his throat. Matt felt totally disoriented, and had trouble concentrating enough to know he needed to resist, but he started to fight and he started to yell as best he could.

That strategy only lasted for a fraction of a second before he was hit in the head again and he was knocked completely unconscious.

Chapter 6 — Log In

Matt sat naked and bound on the cold tile floor in the empty room, and tried his best to understand what they wanted from him. It was hard to concentrate and think about it given how hungry and thirsty he was getting. He felt like he'd do anything for a drink of water at this point, after having been locked up in the room now for what felt like several days. His mouth was sticky and dry, and the hunger was giving him constant cramps. It felt like he had been there a little more than two days, but with no light from outside, it was hard to say for sure.

Earlier, about what felt like a day after being abducted, his captors had come into the room for the first time. They turned the lights on before they entered, which blinded Matt. Of course, Matt was terrified of what might happen when they came in, and he felt utterly defenseless given that his hands and feet were bound and he was completely naked. He did what he could to back into the corner and curl up into a ball.

There were two men that entered, and both were wearing the more traditional Syrian clothing - didashahs and kuffiyahs. One was younger and had a full, dark black beard and was carrying a gun, and obviously wanted to make sure Matt didn't try anything stupid. The other one was older and had a longer beard with two pronounced streaks of white running through it. He was carrying Matt's laptop.

Matt's heart beat furiously from the fear of what they might do, and he would have been crying, but the dehydration and bright light made his eyes just sting instead. His imagination ran wild with the horrible things that were going to happen to him. He would give anything to not have come to Syria at this point.

But as he sat, curled up in a ball in the corner of the room, trembling, the two men did nothing for a moment. Matt ventured a furtive glance at them to see what they were doing, but they just seemed to be looking at him. He also finally could see the room he was in. It was just a small room, about ten by ten, with a bare, brown tile floor and plain beige walls. There was nothing else in the room and no other door or window. The man with the streaked beard studied him silently for a moment. It might have been just his eyes stinging him, but he felt sure the look on the man's face was that of a deep, burning hatred.

Finally, the older one spoke and held out Matt's laptop to him. It was in English, but through a very thick Arabic accent that made it difficult to understand what he was saying. He held out Matt's laptop to him and said, "Log in."

Matt didn't understand why they wanted this. What could they possibly want with his laptop? There couldn't be anything of value on it that they'd want.

Unfortunately, his confusion made him pause long enough that the one holding the laptop said something in Arabic to the other one with the gun. The younger one leaped forward and struck Matt on the side of his head with the butt of the gun, hard.

The older man shouted at him, "Log in!"

Matt didn't hesitate this time, despite the horrible ringing in his ear and shooting pain in the side of his head. He reached out to the laptop and tried to still his shaking hands and fingers so he could type. It was difficult, and he had to move slowly given that his hands were tied together, but he logged in and quickly resumed his semi-fetal position in the corner of the room. He prayed they would just go away.

But rather than leave immediately, the bearded man started looking at his laptop and browsing around on it, searching for something. Matt wanted desperately to ask for something to drink, but didn't dare. His ear continued to ring and felt like it might be bleeding, too. He was starting to not care how this nightmare ended. As long as it ended.

The man wasn't done with Matt yet, though.

He held the laptop back out to Matt and said to him a word that didn't make any sense. The man said, "Ayeedeentel!" and tried to push the laptop back into Matt's hands. He repeated "Ayeedeentel!" more angrily when Matt didn't seem to comprehend.

Before Matt could make it clear that he didn't understand, another younger captor came into the room from outside and called out to them. The older one that had been getting angry at Matt for not understanding turned back and said something to the new man standing in the doorway, who then held out a cell phone to him.

The man with the white-streaked beard looked back at Matt with piercing, furious eyes while he listened on the cell phone for a few moments. He hung up the cell phone, stood up quickly and swept out of the room with Matt's laptop, followed by the other captors. As they left Matt alone in the room, they locked the door behind them, and then the light went out again.

Matt's eyes stung and he was developing a terrible headache from where he had been hit in the head. If he could understand what they wanted from he would have given it to them instantly. He would have done anything at that point to make this all end.

Since that point, his captors had not come back in the room, but he did hear what he thought was the older captor yelling at the others outside the room a few minutes after they had left. Then it had gotten quiet again. All he could figure was that the person that had come into the room and made Matt give him access to his laptop must be the one in charge. But beyond that, he couldn't understand what they wanted from him or why they had kidnapped him.

What felt like five or six hours later, Matt heard some more noises from outside the room. There was more yelling in Arabic, but it didn't sound quite like the guy in charge. Matt decided that maybe it was the others instead of the leader. And this time, he thought he heard another voice. A new voice. A voice speaking in clear English. And this voice sounded like he was pleading. Through the door, it was hard to make it out, but it sounded like he was pleading with the kidnappers.

Matt wondered if they were conducting a series of kidnappings of Americans for some reason. Was it a new terror tactic, now spreading to Syria? Was it a for-profit kidnapping? That didn't quite make sense to Matt since they were clearly interested in something on his laptop.

After the brief burst of voices outside the room, it grew quiet again and he didn't hear anything else for a while. Matt wanted Brian so much it hurt. He'd never take sunlight or friends or food and water for granted ever again. But he'd definitely never take Brian for granted.

Please just get me back to Brian.

Eventually, even with the ringing in his ears and the headache and the hunger cramps, the exhaustion in his body from being on edge for so long took over. He dozed off for a little bit in a fitful sleep of horrible dreams, and then jerked awake at some point after that when his body realized it had fallen asleep. The ringing in his ear was now less, and he could faintly hear something else now. He heard what sounded like shouting again, but it was farther away and fainter than when it had been just outside the door. He wasn't sure if it involved what he thought of as the new victim or not.

And very suddenly, with the faint shouting still going on, Matt heard the sound that made his blood turn ice cold.

He heard a single, clear gunshot from another room in the building, followed by perfect silence.

Chapter 7 — Incursion

Matt stayed locked up in the empty room, in the dark, for a long period after the gunshot. His immediate fear that he would be next to be shot didn't seem to be what was going to happen to him, though. In fact, nothing had happened since he heard the gunshot. Hours and hours had dragged by in a slow, repetitive parade of fear and exhaustion in the dark. If he had to guess, he would say at least two days had passed after hearing it. None of the people keeping him locked up came in the room, and no one brought him any food or water, which was quickly becoming a far bigger fear than a gunshot. No one asked him any more about his laptop.

He still occasionally heard faint voices outside, so he knew they were there. At one point, when it was quiet for an extended period, he did get up and try the door, only to find that it was a very solid door and was locked from the outside. In his weakened state, he knew that throwing himself against the door to try and knock it down would do no good.

Matt had not had to use the bucket in over a day now to relieve himself. With no food or water for at least three days, there was nothing to go into it.

The headaches from the dehydration were getting bad, his mouth was dry and sticky, and his tongue felt like it was swelling. Even more worrisome than that, he had had a few spells where he had woken up, but felt more like he had lost consciousness rather than fallen asleep. His abdomen was cramping constantly now and the thirst was maddening.

Matt, finding few other options and with almost nothing to lose, had tried another tactic. He chose a moment when he heard the men talking somewhere outside the room. He went to the door, knocked on it, and yelled as best he could through a very weak and cracked voice that he wanted some water. He literally begged for even just a sip of water.

Almost immediately, the light in the room came on, blinding and burning his eyes and making him step back, and one of the men burst in and waved a gun at him angrily. It wasn't the man in charge, but one of the other captors. The man yelled at him in some incomprehensible Arabic language, but clearly wanted Matt to be quiet and to get away from the door. He tried to indicate to the man that he just wanted something to drink, making drinking motions with his bound hands while standing naked before him. When the captor raised the butt of the gun to beat Matt with it, Matt shrunk back and cowered in the corner again. Worse, the captor stepped into the room next to Matt and spat on him before laughing as he walked back out. He was once again left with nothing when the door was closed and locked.

He tried to take his mind off of things, to focus on something hopeful. Surely someone had noticed he was missing. His friends at Tishreen University, maybe. Or maybe Brian had realized he hadn't emailed and was calling people to look for him. He thought about getting home to Brian, holding onto him and never letting him go. Never doubting him again and never ever taking him for granted again, not even for a moment. God, what he wouldn't give to see Brian's handsome face again, just one more time.

But the thirst continued to get worse, and it eventually drove all other thoughts from his mind. The thing that started making him feel truly hopeless, that he was just waiting for an inevitable finish, was that he felt like maybe a gunshot would be better than the slow, tortuous agony of dying of thirst. He managed to wonder just how much longer he'd last before he would welcome a gunshot to the head to make the burning, rabid, all-consuming thirst go away.

~~~~~

Matt awoke with a start, looking straight up into the dark, blank nothing that was the ceiling of the small room he was in. The thirst and cramps hit him immediately and he wished he had just stayed asleep or unconscious — he didn't care which any more. And for just a second that's all he focused on.

But then something caught his attention that drove even the thoughts of his thirst from his mind. He heard noises outside the room. Noises completely unlike those he had heard before. There was yelling again. But while he had heard what felt like angry yelling before the gunshot earlier, this time sounded more like panicked yelling, coming from multiple people at the same time. But there was a new noise, too. An occasional, odd, thud-like punching sound.

He heard it a few times and things immediately got very quiet outside the room. The silence made Matt very nervous. Nervous enough to almost forget about his body's cries for water. He forced himself to sit up, dragging his bound feet around him across the cold floor so he could put his bound wrists around his knees and wrap himself up into a ball.

Without warning, there was shouting again somewhere outside. But this time it was a single person shouting in Arabic, and farther away. Like before, it only lasted a brief moment. He heard one sudden loud gunshot, followed by another couple of the faint punching sounds, ending in an utter, terminal silence. In his delirious state, Matt would not have thought he could be any more afraid than he had been in the last few days. But there was something about the silence that made his dehydrated blood run ice cold. He pushed himself with his feet back farther in the room, into the far corner, as far away from the door as he could get. He didn't want to be anywhere near the door now.

He waited and concentrated all of his strength into his hearing, listening for anything outside the door. But he heard nothing. Matt kept his eyes glued to the strip of light under the door for any sign of what might be happening, but he could see no movement.

A few moments later, and silently, causing a dread in Matt that made him want to crawl through the wall, he saw something moving. A shadow moved across the crack along the bottom of the door, but there was no sound to go with it. There was still only the harrowing silence. Matt started shaking uncontrollably and crouched into the corner of the room, now even facing away from the door.

Matt closed his eyes in the dark and thought of Brian. He thought of the night Brian had asked him out the first time. He thought of the time he and Brian had gone to Sky Meadow State Park and had a picnic out in the middle of a field with no one around for what felt like miles, just the two of them. He thought of the weekend trip they had taken up to DC back in January to see the museums, the trip where they got locked out of the car and Brian got so pissed off. He thought about the last time Brian had kissed him and looked into his eyes, brushing Matt's unruly shock of hair out of his face and back to where it was supposed to be. He wished he could be a better boyfriend for Brian. He wished he had been. There were so many things he could have done better.

Finally, what he knew was going to happen, happened. The door to his room burst open with a deafening crack, making him jerk reflexively and try to push into the corner even farther than he already was. He didn't dare look. He just wanted it to be over.

In the moments of silence that followed, he couldn't help himself. He held out his bound hands towards the light pouring in from the open doorway and sobbed in abject fear of whatever horrifying violence was about to come down on him.

"Please... no..." he begged.

He waited for a moment, for the gunshot, for the blade, for whatever had forced its way into the room was going to do. But nothing happened. He started to turn to face whatever had forced its way into the room just as the overhead light came on, blinding him and burning his eyes. He blinked and squinted anyway and tried to see whatever was now in the room with him.

Matt saw a person squatting in the doorway, pointing a large handgun directly at him. He turned away again, his body shaking violently. He pleaded again, his voice dry and barely more than a parched whisper, "Don't..."

Matt waited, trembling, for whatever would happen. But what happened was that he heard a voice, low and deep, like thunder in the distance.

It asked, "Are you American?"

The voice disoriented Matt. He wondered where it had come from. Was someone actually speaking in English?

Matt turned nervously to face the person in the room pointing the gun at him. He ventured a terrified glance through his stinging eyes and said shakily, "Yes... American."

What Matt could see was a man — he thought it was a man — squatting, but no longer pointing the gun at him. He was covered in tan and brown. But he had no face. There was just a helmet, and goggles over his eyes and a black nothing where the bottom half of his face should be. At least he wasn't pointing the gun at Matt anymore. He suddenly realized the man wasn't alone, though. There was now another, dressed just like him and also with no face, standing in the doorway behind him. He was holding a much larger gun, a rifle, in front of him, and it *was* pointed at Matt.

Matt blinked a few times, trying to get the image to clear. His mind tried to understand. Why didn't they have faces? It was terrifying, not being able to see any part of the actual person in the room with him. He wanted to look away, but couldn't. He'd be looking at the rifle when it was fired, finally killing him, ending all of this.

Matt watched as the one squatting holstered his handgun and pulled a large knife instead, rolling it very deftly in his hand. Matt's breath hitched in his throat. In his fear, he turned away and faced into the corner again. Why did it have to be a knife? Why couldn't it be quick and painless with the rifle instead?

He heard the voice again. The voice said carefully, "It's ok. It's ok. I'm just going to cut the zip ties off your hands and feet, alright?"

Matt looked back over at the figure squatting in the door and blinked again, trying to get his eyes used to the light.

The figure with no face nodded at Matt and said, "Hold out your hands, ok?"

Matt wasn't sure what to believe any more, so he did as he was told. The man stood up and stepped over to Matt slowly before crouching back down. Matt's hands were shaking, and he felt a gloved hand grab them to hold them steady, pause for a moment, and then in a split second, the zip tie that had bound his hands since he had been in that room was gone.

The voice asked, "What's your name?"

After what he had been through, it felt like he had to remember who he was in a past life. "M... Matt..." he said, almost more as a question than a statement.

"Ok, Matt, let me get your feet for you, too. Hold steady." In a flash of the large knife, Matt's feet were free as well.

For the first time, Matt dared to hope that maybe he would leave the room alive.

"Where you from, Matt?" said the deep voice.

"From... from Richmond. Virginia."

The figure put his hand gently on Matt's shoulder for a moment. He glanced back over his shoulder briefly, and the other faceless man that was standing there lowered his rifle and left the room.

As Matt's eyes adjusted more, he got a closer look. But even with the person right next to him, he still couldn't see any of the man that was squatting there with his hand on his shoulder. The man was covered in a desert camouflage uniform, loaded up with packs, pockets, and gear all over it. He had a helmet on his head and peculiar goggles perched on the brim, plus goggles over his eyes. And there was the strange black void where his nose and mouth should be. There was just nothing there.

He had to be a soldier of some sort, Matt assumed. He stayed next to Matt, squatting down, but took his hand off Matt's shoulder while he put his knife back into its sheath on his thigh.

The voice then said something to Matt that would have made him cry if his eyes could. "It's going to be ok, Matt. We're going to get you out of here."

Matt's heart jumped up into his throat and he felt dizzy, like he was going to pass out. The room swayed around him, but the gloved hand reached out to his shoulder again to steady him.

Matt said feebly, "Water... do you have water?"

The soldier stood up and started taking a pack off of his back. He asked as he did so, "How long have you been in here, Matt?"

Matt had trouble making his tongue work it was so thick and dry. "Not sure... since Friday night, I think."

The soldier pulled a flask out of his pack and took the top off. "That'd be about three days, then. No water the whole time?"

"No..." said Matt.

"Ok, drink very small sips, and only a little for right now. I'll give you some more in a minute. Too much and you'll get sick."

Matt started to take the flask in his shaking hands, but the soldier held it for him. The first few sips of water he had had in three days tasted better than anything he had ever tasted in his entire life, even as it burned his throat.

The other soldier appeared in the doorway with a blanket in his hands. He came on into the room.

"Can you stand up, Matt?"

Matt was already feeling better from even the few sips of water he was allowed to have. He went to stand up, but felt dizzy again and almost lost his balance.

Both of the soldiers reached out to keep him steady and help him stand up the rest of the way. They wrapped the blanket around him so he was no longer naked.

The two soldiers looked at each other and made a few gestures between them, but Matt heard no words. Now that he was almost totally used to the light again, he could see their mouths moving slightly under the black fabric masks they wore, but he heard nothing.

The second soldier left the room again as the first soldier offered Matt a few more sips of water.

"We're getting ready to bug out of here, but you have to listen to me. We're not supposed to be here, and we've got to be quiet, ok?"

Matt nodded.

"Quiet like our lives depend on it. You understand?"

He nodded again.

The soldier explained, "We're going to have to walk a little bit, though, but you're going to be safe, you hear me?"

Matt said, his voice shaking, "Thank you."

The soldier lifted Matt's arm and directed, "Put your arm around my shoulder and support yourself. You're still pretty weak."

Matt did as he was told and they started out of the room. Matt walked through a doorway that he didn't think he'd pass through alive. He looked around, for the first time seeing what was outside of the room he had been held in. There was a short hallway that led past another room next to the one he had been kept in. They walked beyond that, Matt supporting himself on the soldier next to him.

The hall lead to a small, dirty kitchen area, and Matt almost became nauseous when he saw the scene. One of his captors was dead in the corner of the kitchen, a large, gaping hole where his heart should have been. Blood was sprayed everywhere... all over the poorly stocked shelves, walls, refrigerator and cooktop in the kitchen. The smell in the kitchen overwhelmed Matt; it was like corroded, rusted iron, pulled from the depths of the sea. Matt felt sick, but couldn't look away from it. He had never seen anything like it in real life, and he hoped to never again.

There were three other soldiers in the kitchen, all dressed the same as the first. One, a few inches taller than the others, was packing up some items on the kitchen table into a rucksack; another was peeking out of the small window that led outside from the kitchen area. The third had a large something wrapped up in a blanket and thrown over his shoulder.

As Matt got a better look at the soldiers, he felt like maybe he should be as scared of them as he was of men that had kidnapped him. And if it weren't that he felt like he had nothing to lose, he probably would have been. The fact that he couldn't see them at all, the fact that they were covered with guns, knives, and who knew what other kinds of equipment, made them terrifying. At least with his captors, he could see their eyes on the few rare occasions they had come into the room. Looking at their eyes, he knew where he stood with them, and felt appropriately scared. With these men, they were blanks, armed to the hilt. They seemed inhuman, like there could be anything

36

underneath the camo, boots, helmets, gloves and masks for all he knew. They had been kind to him, but, they looked so frightening and he wasn't totally sure he wouldn't still wind up like the body on the kitchen floor with a hole in its chest.

Matt glanced in the room beyond the kitchen and saw more blood splattered all over the furniture and carpet. Thankfully, this time, he couldn't see any more bodies, but he knew they were there, somewhere.

There seemed to be more coordination among the soldiers, but without any words passing between them. The one at the door cracked it open slightly to see if the coast was clear outside.

Matt happened to glance down at the things the tall soldier was putting into the rucksack. He noticed something of his and said, "That's my laptop."

The soldier held it up and looked at it briefly. This soldier had a brighter voice coming from behind the mask. "This yours?" he asked.

Matt nodded, and the soldier looked at it again. He held it out for the others to see the stickers on the lid of the laptop, "Check it out! We got us a pole smoker here! You got pics of all the assholes you've eaten filling up the hard drive on here? Huh, cockbreath?"

Matt was too weak to respond. What would he say if he could? He didn't get a good feeling, though.

The soldier at the door opened it fully and they started to make their way down a flight of steps on the outside of the building. The two soldiers in front had their rifles out and pointed in case they encountered anyone else that might give them trouble. It was dark outside, with only a little light from the moon and a weak floodlight several buildings over. Matt's eyes were able to relax a little getting back into dimmer light, and he was glad to be away from the bloody and gored body in the kitchen.

But as he took just a few steps down the stairs, even leaning on the soldier that had helped him, his vision started to gray and he felt his legs start to give way. He gripped the soldier's shoulder a little harder, and despite his fierce attempt to stay conscious, Matt blacked out.

~~~~~

When Matt came to, he was lying down and staring straight up. And what he saw when he looked up was a night sky dotted with stars and the faint, ghostly outline of a few clouds. For a moment, he forgot everything about what had happened and just looked at the stars. So beautiful in the night sky. So peaceful. Except... for that sound.

Matt became aware of an annoying sound in his ears, one that sounded like some kind of steady roar nearby. Then he felt the bouncing.

He looked to the side slightly and saw the four soldiers seated around him, their blank void faces looking down at him. They were all bouncing up and down with him. He didn't understand the bouncing.

He could feel the large object next to him, the thing that one of the other soldiers had carried, pressed up against his side. And he realized he was practically lying on the boots of the soldiers in the tight space. Suddenly, Matt felt that his entire back was soaking wet and he could now feel the occasional spray of water.

Matt started to panic when he realized he was lying in the bottom of a tiny rubber boat, the soldiers sitting up on the sides around him. Matt tried to sit up, ignoring how his head was trying to sweep him into unconsciousness again. He couldn't be in a boat. Not like this. Not in the water. Anywhere else would be fine, but not in the water.

He grabbed at the nearest leg in a panic and tried to pull himself up. He had to get out. He tried to yell over the sound of the motor, "I can't be in here. Not here! Let me out!"

His frenzied attempts to get out of the boat, to somehow get back on land, ended very quickly, however. One of the soldiers put his boot squarely down on Matt's chest and said, "Yeah, you probably don't want to jump out right now, buddy." The boot pushed firmly down on Matt's chest, forcing him back into the bottom of the boat. Matt clawed at the foot holding him down. He had to get out. And even then his vision started to unfocus and turn gray. And a moment later, Matt slipped into unconsciousness yet again. Somewhere in a tiny boat. Somewhere in the water.

Chapter 8 – Haze Gray And Underway

The next time Matt woke up, it was much more slowly. It was much more comfortable. There was a mattress under him, and a sheet over his body, and his head was resting on a pillow.

He sat up a little and looked around. The room he was in had about ten beds in it, all lined up in a row along one wall. Looking at them, he could tell they were hospital beds. A couple of them had other people in them, but the rest were empty. For an infirmary, it seemed a little cramped to Matt.

He looked down at his arm and noticed the IV needle stuck into his wrist. But aside from feeling a little groggy, he didn't feel too bad. He wouldn't mind having something to drink, but he didn't feel the burning thirst any more.

Matt noticed a young kid nearby. He was probably only 20 or 21 years old, skinny, and still with a little bit of acne on his face. He had a shaved head and was dressed in olive green pants and a khaki t-shirt and he came over when he realized Matt was awake. Matt thought the kid seemed oddly dressed for an infirmary.

The kid said, "Hey, you're waking up! Don't try to get up yet. Lemme get the doc over here to talk to you some."

He turned and yelled at a curtain that had been pulled across the far end of the room, "Hey Lieut, the rider has come to!"

Matt heard an impatient and half-shouted "Ok, hang on!" come from behind the curtain.

The kid turned back to Matt and said, "You feeling ok?"

Matt nodded and actually felt relieved to be able to honestly say, "Yeah. Actually, I do."

The kid leaned in a little closer and asked him quietly, looking around furtively to make sure no one was listening, "Is it true? Were you kidnapped? Were they going to kill you?"

Matt's voice caught in his throat and he suddenly felt lost and disoriented again. He knew that it was true. But to hear it spoken by another person somehow made it almost more real than having experienced it. His mind swarmed with the thoughts. He had been halfway around the world, kidnapped, and who knew how close to being murdered there. Naked and in an unlit room.

Before Matt could pull himself together to answer, a more senior looking soldier made his way over and warned the kid off, "Koski! You know what you were told. Go get me a cuff and the oto."

Koski nodded and went to get the items the doctor asked for.

"You Matt?" the doctor asked when he got to Matt's bed.

The doctor looked to be in his late thirties but had a good head start on a receding hair line. He was actually wearing a khaki shirt with a name tag sewn on that read "Ehlert".

Matt said, "Yes, sir."

Doctor Ehlert pulled a pen light out of his pocket and held Matt's chin with a free hand, shining the light in Matt's eyes to check his pupils.

"Call me Ron. How are you feeling? Thirsty? Hungry? Are you feeling faint?"

"Uh, I'm actually feeling pretty good, considering..." replied Matt. "I'm not thirsty. Not like I was. I am hungry, a little. I don't feel faint or woozy, though."

"Good. When you got here, you were pretty dehydrated. We've kept you sedated and on just an IV drip of saline and glucose to get you back where you should be. If you're not hungry right now, you will be soon enough. Just to check since you've got a couple of bumps on the head here... how many fingers am I holding up?"

"Four?"

"Ok. Do you know what year it is?"

"Uh, 2010?"

"Yeah. Who's the president?"

"Obama."

"Good. Now, who's the Undersecretary for Personnel and Readiness at the Department of Defense?"

"Uh..."

Dr. Ehlert smiled. "Bah. Three out of four is close enough."

Matt's forehead creased and he asked, "How long have I been here?" He ran his free hand across his goatee and realized he must look like a scuzzball. He had no idea how long it had been since he had shaved, or even had a shower, for that matter.

"You got here about a day ago. Like I said, we kept you sedated because you really needed the rest and you needed the fluids."

Matt noticed that as other people, he assumed soldiers, came in and out of the infirmary, they all glanced over at him curiously. He wondered if any of these people were the ones that rescued him.

Koski walked back up with a blood pressure cuff and one of the small scopes doctors used to look into ears. He handed the otoscope to the doctor and grabbed Matt's left arm to take his blood pressure.

The doctor took a look in Matt's right ear, the one that his kidnapper had hit pretty hard with the butt of his gun.

"You got something of a knock here on your ear, Matt. It's looking pretty good, though. You're probably lucky... there doesn't look like there's any permanent damage."

Doctor Ehlert handed the otoscope back to Koski as he finished taking Matt's blood pressure reading.

"I think you're good to go, Matt. We've got you a rack set up and Wickland's going to probably want to talk to you pretty soon. Before all that, I guess I should ask if you want a shower first, or something to eat?"

Matt was hungry, but not terribly so. He felt gross, though, and knew he had to smell like crazy. He was still feeling a little lost about what was happening to him, but he just replied, "A shower, I guess."

Dr. Ehlert nodded, "Koski, go ahead and take Matt to his rack and get him settled a little." Koski smiled at the idea of the duty he was asked to do, hoping to be able to ask Matt about his ordeal again.

Dr. Ehlert took the IV needle out of Matt's wrist and put a little gauze and tape where it had been. He reminded Koski, "And you know what we were told. No questions." Koski's smile deflated.

Koski brought over clothes for Matt to wear, things that would make him look like Koski... a khaki t-shirt, some desert camo cargo pants, tan boots, socks and a pair of white boxer shorts.

Matt started to get dressed and Dr. Ehlert looked around to make sure no one other than Koski was within hearing distance. He put his hand on Matt's shoulder sympathetically and said, "It's good to see you made it through ok."

Dr. Ehlert started to turn around, but Matt called out to him, "Hey, Ron, where am I?"

Dr. Ehlert grabbed a chart off another bed and called out to Matt as he walked back down to the end of the room, "Iwo Jima."

Matt almost did a double take as he finished putting his boots on. They were a little tight for him, but better than nothing.

He started to follow Koski to the other end of the room and asked, incredulously, "Iwo Jima?! As in the island? Like in the south Pacific?"

Koski looked back at him and laughed, "Hell, no! Not the island! The *USS Iwo Jima*! Haze gray and underway, my man!"

~~~~~

It turned out that the "rack" thing Dr. Ehlert had mentioned to Matt was, in fact, a bunk. Barely. It was narrower than a single bed and had about twenty-four inches of clearance above it. As soon as Matt saw it, and realized he was expected to sleep there, he decided he had been stupid to not ask the most obvious question of all so far - *how soon can I get out of this... whatever?*

Koski had grabbed a few towels and toiletries for him on the way to his rack while following a confounding maze of narrow halls, turns, hatches, and stairs that were practically ladders between decks (he was pretty sure that was supposed to be the right word). On the way there, Matt had gotten a few curious glances, which he wondered about since he was dressed the same now as just about everybody else he passed. When they arrived at the cabin where Matt's bed was located, Koski pointed out to him where the "head" and shower were, just a little further down the "passageway" from where his "rack" was.

There was so much that was totally foreign to Matt in this place that he immediately got hopelessly turned around. And the whole time they had walked, Koski was talking a mile a minute in a language that was all slang, numbers and abbreviations that meant nothing to Matt.

As soon as Koski left him alone, Matt realized he had no idea what he was supposed to be doing, how he could get home, where he could get some lunch. (Or breakfast or dinner... he had no idea what time it actually was.)

He decided to take his shower first since he at least knew where *that* was. Koski had warned him to go ahead and get out of his clothes in the cabin and just wear the towel down to the shower as there was not much space for changing in or out of clothes there.

He felt very self-conscious walking down the passage to where Koski had said the shower was wearing nothing but a towel and carrying a few toiletries. He passed one very built guy with a stern look on his face, but this guy didn't give Matt a second glance, so Matt felt like maybe somehow he was actually less conspicuous in just the towel.

Matt pulled at the towel to stop it from riding up his butt any more than it already had when he ran across two more men coming along the passageway. Unlike the first, these two didn't ignore him.

The first guy was tall and had extremely fair skin to go with his flaming red hair. It had to be the brightest, reddest hair Matt had ever seen. The guy's t-shirt was tight and Matt could tell he had a really lean, muscular body. Absolutely chiseled. The one right behind him was about Matt's height, but with very thick black hair cut short and coming down to a point in the center of his forehead. He had dark, penetrating eyes and an olive complexion that made Matt nervous. Matt decided that what made him nervous was that the guy looked vaguely Middle Eastern. But he was in the same fatigue-type pants and white t-shirt that the red-headed guy was in, so he had to belong there.

The red-headed guy was laughing, but then did a slight double-take when he saw Matt. He grinned and said, "Hey hey, look here! The doc was able to pull him through after all! You feelin' better after your nap?"

Apparently, this guy knew something about what had happened. Matt nodded and said, "Yeah, I'm ok."

The red-head glanced back over his shoulder and realized where Matt was headed. He grinned again and said, "Actually, you know what? That head has been without water for two days now. C'mon, I'll show you another one so you can actually clean up."

The dark headed guy said, "Petey..."

Red-headed Petey jerked his head so that Matt would follow him. "It's not far. You won't get lost," he said, interrupting the dark headed one. He made sure Matt was following, turned down one passage, went a short distance, and then turned down another before stopping in front of a closed door.

Petey asked, "Think you can find your way back from here?"

Matt felt very discouraged. He wasn't lost and he could find his way back to his bed or bunk or rack or whatever the hell they insisted on calling it, but he did feel totally lost in general. He was completely out of his element here. He had no idea who any of these people were, what they knew or didn't know about him, what was supposed to happen next, and he really just wanted to get into the shower and clean off.

Matt sighed and said dejectedly, "Yeah, right right here, then the next left and the room with my bed is there."

Petey corrected him, "Your berth with your rack."

Matt scratched at the heavy growth of scruff on his face. "Yeah, ok, whatever."

Petey opened the door and motioned for Matt to go on in. As soon as Matt stepped in, Petey grabbed the towel around Matt's waist and yanked it off. He immediately pulled the door closed behind Matt.

Before Matt even realized what had happened, he heard the one called Petey laughing and yelling from outside, "Hey Mope, here's the little ass pirate! He said he wanted to give you a knob job!"

Matt realized the very cramped bathroom space was already occupied. There was one shower in it with nothing surrounding it, and there was a guy already under the spray of water, less than two feet away from him.

Matt's eyes locked onto the guy under the water just as he, Mope, looked at him. All Matt managed to see was dark hair and a pair of ears that stood out from the guy's head before he realized what Petey had yelled.

Several harsh things hit Matt at the same time; he was standing naked in front of this person; he had just been referred to as an ass pirate; he no longer had a towel and a long walk back to his *fucking* "rack". Matt felt beaten and humiliated. He turned to face the wall, away from the guy in the shower.

It took a second to pull himself together before he could say, "I'm sorry. I didn't know... That guy... said I should use... I'm not in here trying... to... uh..." Matt stopped and exhaled heavily. What was the point, he wondered? He leaned his forearm against the wall he was facing, lay his head against it, and closed his eyes. Matt really wanted off this *Iwo Jima* thing.

He vaguely heard the guy behind him say, over the spray of the water, "Whatever. Didn't think you were. Besides, I don't have anything you haven't seen before. And forget Colorado. He's just being himself." His voice reverberated in the enclosed shower area.

Matt wasn't really paying attention at this point, though, even as the water behind him turned off. It finally hit him that the red-headed guy knew he was gay. It was hard for him to imagine, but that guy *had* to be the one that had referred to him as the "pole smoker" when he was being rescued. Why did he have to be rescued by a complete asshole? A homophobic asshole.

He stood there, naked and leaning up against the wall, eyes closed and trying to hold himself together. Matt wanted to go home more than anything in the world. If he had been rescued, why did this feel almost as bad as being in the empty room? Why couldn't he just be with Brian? Why couldn't he be away from these people? Why couldn't he be home? Familiar and safe.

Matt heard the door open and then close again, almost like it was in the distance, while he was lost in his thoughts.

A few moments later, he stood back up and looked around to find he was alone in the shower. He didn't have a towel, but he could go ahead and get cleaned up. He forced himself to shave, and then got under the water. He had to admit, a shower for the first time in who knew how many days felt like being reborn. He didn't think a shower had ever felt that good.

While he was feeling the water wash off everything from the last few days, he heard a quiet knock at the door and someone say something from outside. Before he could respond, the door cracked open and a hand tossed in a towel over on the lavatory.

Chapter 9 — Next Question

Once done showering, Matt felt much better, although food was definitely his next order of business.

But as he got back to his rack, he found a black girl waiting on him. She introduced herself as Keisha and said she was there to take him to go see the fellow named Wickland. Matt asked who this Wickland person was, but Keisha replied that she didn't know anything about it, she wasn't supposed to know anything about it, and didn't care to know anything about it. She just needed to get Matt to the cabin where Wickland was waiting for him.

Matt changed back into the clothes they had given him while she waited outside, then they headed off on another bewildering tour of passages, hatches, twists and turns.

Along the way, they actually did pass a dining area, and Matt smelled food for the first time in days. It made him a lot hungrier suddenly.

"Can I get something to eat first, Keisha?" he asked.

"Nope. This guy's waiting on you right now. But you've seen where the chow hall is now, so you can come back and get whatever you want."

She added, "I think they got the red death in there today. Stay away from that."

"Uhh..." said Matt, wrinkling up his nose.

"Corned beef and cabbage," she explained.

They walked a little further, Matt finding out quickly that the narrow passageways meant he had to duck under pipes and conduits pretty often or flatten up against the wall to allow others to pass. Matt asked Keisha, "So, are you curious about why I'm here?"

Keisha didn't seem too impressed with his question. "I heard they brought someone in yesterday. You, I guess. We get riders occasionally for whatever reason. Other than that, why you're here is above my pay grade. Lot of times, there's some rumors, but they've kept this one pretty tight, which ain't usual. But I've been around long enough to know that curiosity just gets you more work on your plate."

Matt was hoping maybe she had heard some rumors about what had happened and would tell him since he himself understood so little about it.

"How about the Marine guys that brought me here... do you know anything about them?" he asked.

Keisha stopped suddenly and turned around to face Matt. Her complacency and boredom replaced by a little more fire in her eyes.

"Those guys weren't no dumb-ass *jarheads*!" she replied, derisively. "Seabags can't handle anything that requires an IQ of more than dip-squat! All that 'ooo-rah' bullshit all the time! Those guys that brought you in were SEALs."

Matt realized he obviously had hit a nerve. But it still didn't really mean anything to him, other than it clearly *wasn't* Marines that rescued him.

"So," he tried again, "the tall guy named Petey, with the really bright red hair... he's not a Marine?"

"Hell no!" Keisha scoffed.

"Uh, I don't know anything about the military... what's a SEAL, then?"

Keisha stopped again and looked back at Matt like he was the stupidest two-year-old child she had ever run across.

"SEALs? Shit! That's what those dumb ass jarheads *dream* of being! SEALs are pure Navy, all the way. They're the cream of the bad-ass crop! The toughest and smartest of all the Spec-Ops guys. They'll take a mission that other teams wouldn't touch with a ten foot pole attached to a remote controlled Predator, and they'll make it look easy. Those guys that brought you in? They are the deadly serious shit, man."

She led Matt a little further to a door and stopped again in front of it. She smiled a huge smile at Matt, only barely tinged by sarcasm, and said, "You have arrived at your destination! Thank you for flying Air Keisha, y'all!" before she walked off back down the way she had come with Matt.

Matt stood there for a moment, thinking about how Keisha had referred to the guys that rescued him. The words "deadly serious shit" raced around in his head. He finally took a deep breath and knocked lightly on the door and heard a man's voice say "Come!" from inside.

Matt walked in. The man inside was short, much shorter than Matt, probably somewhere in his fifties, with silver hair parted neatly on the side. What struck him was that he wasn't in any kind of military uniform — he was wearing plain khaki casual pants with a white knit polo shirt and had what looked like a fairly expensive steel wristwatch on his left wrist.

The man stood up and introduced himself to Matt as Randall Wickland, with no title or rank preceding it. Matt shook his hand and Randall gestured to the chair for Matt to sit in.

For some reason, Matt was expecting something like an office or a conference room. A conference room like he was used to in an office building. This wasn't like that at all. It was tiny and could barely fit four people comfortably. But unlike the bland gray and steel that he had seen everywhere else, this room was finished with a more "decorative" fake wood paneling. In front of Randall's chair were a few folders filled with papers and printouts.

They both sat down and Randall started looking through one of his folders for a moment while Matt continued to examine the room he was in. He also noticed the room didn't have any windows in it. Matt realized he had not seen a single window since he woke up in the infirmary.

He asked Randall, "Are you assigned to this boat?"

Randall glanced up and corrected him, "Ship. It's a ship. No, I'm not." He flipped through a few more papers and offered no more information than that.

Randall got his papers in the order he wanted them and began, "Ok, so let's start by getting…"

Randall paused a minute and cocked his head slightly before he started over. "Sorry. The docs got you fixed up ok?"

"Yeah, I'm doing ok. Glad to be out… of… uh… you know." Matt suddenly realized that thinking back to being in the room, naked and captive, made him feel nervous and shaky. He started bouncing his leg nervously under the table. It was only barely more than a day since he had been held captive and in mortal peril, and barely mentioning it here made the memories flood his mind and start to drown him.

Randall watched him closely. Matt got the feeling that Randall was busy studying his face and not really listening to anything Matt said.

Randall finally nodded before continuing. "Matt, if you would, I'd like to cover two areas with you. First, I'd like to hear about you and about what you were doing in Syria. Then I'd like to get into the details about your abduction, and I'll ask a *lot* of questions about that. Please help me with this... I want every detail you can possibly remember. Nothing is too small to leave out. So, let's start with the easy part. Just tell me all about you, please. Your name, where you live, where you work, why you were in Syria, who you were there meeting with... all that."

This *was* the easy part, so Matt focused on it. He told Randall his full name, that he lived in Richmond, Virginia and about his job at the Virginia Department of Health. He explained all about his volunteering for *Doctors Without Borders* and his project at Tishreen University. Randall stopped him at several places along the way and asked additional questions, but Matt thought it odd that he never bothered to write anything down.

After ten minutes or so of going over Matt's background, Randall shifted the conversation. "Alright, so let's talk about what happened to you. Again, I need as much detail as you can give me, no matter how unimportant you might think it is."

Matt started to feel a little queasy and asked, "So, uh, would it be possible to have some water? I'm still a little thirsty after... everything." Randall looked at him with a tinge of impatience, but then he relented. He reached back behind his chair and pulled out a bottled water from his briefcase and handed it to Matt.

Matt opened the bottle immediately and downed almost half of it. "Thanks," he said through a weak smile. The water wasn't really making the anxiety go away.

Randall led the conversation this time, and took Matt through what had happened step by step. Randall's questions were blunt and very thorough. As they went through the events, Matt became more and more jittery. Having to relive it had an effect on him he had never felt before, and it wasn't pleasant. It got harder and harder to respond to Randall's questions, and Matt felt like Randall was having a hard time controlling his impatience towards Matt's answers. And unlike the earlier questions, Randall took copious notes on everything he said.

Randall focused for a while on the café where Matt was captured, including the people that had suggested Matt go there. The insinuation of that question was not something that Matt had even thought about before, and it made him visibly upset. Would someone that he had been working with set him up to be abducted?

Then Randall spent a lengthy amount of time on the one that Matt described as the leader and tried over and over to get Matt to give a name to go with the person, but Matt had heard no one call the person by name. As a backup, Randall asked for an extremely detailed description of the person. How tall was he? What kind of clothes did he wear? What color were they? What about his hair and beard? Did he wear a watch? Did he have any moles or visible scars? What were his eyes like?

Then Randall wanted to know about Matt's laptop. Specifically, he wanted to know what the lead abductor wanted for Matt to show him on the laptop. But Matt couldn't remember. It sounded like a nonsense word to Matt when spoken with the guy's thick accent. He wasn't even sure it was English, for that matter.

When he got to the point where Matt described hearing the yelling followed by the gunshot in the other room, Matt had problems. His mouth dried up and his mind played the sound over and over in his head, along with the feeling of utter despair that he would be next. He could feel himself back in that coffin of a room, bound and naked, waiting for his turn to be shot.

Matt finally snapped back to the room he was in with Randall smacking his hand on the table in front of him to get his attention.

Matt forced himself to breathe deeply a few times and said, "Can you just… give me a second here. This is hard. It's just… hard. I felt like I was… already dead, but… was just waiting for the act… of being killed to… catch up… to where I was." Matt wiped at his eye and took another sip of water. Why was everyone so completely indifferent to what he had been through? Did no one care? Matt sank down in his chair a little when he realized that what had happened didn't seem to matter to anyone. He felt small, and tired, and alone. And hopeless.

Randall finally ran through his patience, cleared his throat, and said, "Ok, let's continue. I bet you're hungry, and the sooner we finish, the sooner you can eat."

Matt didn't really feel hungry any more, but he did want to get away from Randall Wickland sooner rather than later.

Randall finished getting Matt to walk him through the remaining details, including everything he remembered about the SEALs rescuing him.

When Randall finished scribbling out his notes on the last few details Matt was able to give him, he finally looked up at Matt with a smile. "Good! This helps a lot! Thanks! So, you're probably starving. You want to go get yourself some lunch and relax a little bit?"

Matt looked at Randall dumbly.

"No," said Matt.

"No?"

"I've got some questions, too, if you don't mind," insisted Matt.

"Oh. Yeah, you probably do. Go ahead, I'll answer what I can." Randall leaned back in his chair casually.

"When can I go home?"

Randall replied, "We're working on that. We'll get you home soon, though."

"How soon is soon?"

"Mmmm... Not totally sure just yet."

Matt started to feel trapped. "Am I being held here, then?"

Randall smiled, amused. "No, Matt. Believe me, there's nothing about you that is even the slightest bit fishy in any of this. It just doesn't happen instantly, though. For one thing, we're already working on getting you a replacement passport from the Department of State. For another, we'll probably have an additional conversation at some point. We may have some photos to show you, based on your descriptions, to see if you recognize any of the people that grabbed you."

Matt relaxed a little bit. "Who are you? Are you one of the guys that rescued me?"

Randall smiled and said, "No. Next question."

"Are you with the military at all?"

Randall didn't seem put off by the question. He leaned back some more and put his hands behind his head and replied through a sly smile, "Next question, Matt."

Matt thought a second before asking, "Do you have my laptop?"

Randall sat up and said, "Oh yeah, about that... we do have it. We're going over it now. Sorry, but this is a national security thing. And while we checked for anything they might be looking for, we're also looking to make sure they didn't *add* anything to your laptop."

Matt never thought that maybe the people that had held him might actually be looking to *put something* on his laptop. He had no idea what they might put on it, but he had to acknowledge the possibility.

Randall added, "You'll get it back, Matt."

"How can you even access it without me logging into it?"

Again, a smirk from Randall. "Next question."

"Who were these people? Why did they grab me? Were they going to kill me?" Matt's voice was suddenly more emotional than it had been in the entire interview.

And for the first time, Randall actually looked somewhat sympathetically at Matt. "We don't know who they are. We're hoping that some of the information you gave us will help us figure out what's going on here. As for why they grabbed you specifically, we have a theory, but I can't discuss it just yet. Give us a little more time on that, though."

Matt felt frustrated by this. He wanted some kind of understanding about what happened to him. The who and the why. He wanted some kind of closure. He hated to say it, but even if they were just extremists looking to kill a Westerner, at least then he'd have some kind of paper thin understanding. But he wasn't even getting that.

And Randall conspicuously hadn't answered the final part of the question. Matt repeated, quietly, "Were they going to kill me?"

Randall looked down at the table so he didn't have to make eye contact with Matt. He shifted in his seat and cleared his throat uneasily. "Yes, you almost certainly would have been killed were it not for the team that rescued you. Probably, uh... pretty quickly."

It was one thing for Matt to fear that that would have been his fate, but to hear it spoken with that kind of certainty from someone else drove a blade into his soul. He hadn't done anything to any of these people. He came here with the best intentions to help them. Why would they want this?

Why?

Matt sat limply in his chair. By all accounts, he should be dead by now. He looked at his own hands, resting on the table. He should be dead.

He thought about the fight with Brian the night he left. That should have been the last time he saw Brian. He thought about stopping by Bret's to take him some food and peeking in at him sleeping. That should have been the last time he saw him. He thought about two nights prior to that when he had met Bret and Jim out at a Thai restaurant. That should have been the last night he would have seen Jim. All these things in his life should have been bluntly cut off and permanently interrupted. But by some unbelievable miracle, they weren't. He had somehow cheated death halfway around the world.

Matt heard a noise and realized that Randall was calling his name.

He asked Randall suddenly, "How did the SEALs find me?"

Randall leaned forward in his chair, challenging Matt. "Who said they were SEALs?"

"C'mon, Randall. Who else?" bluffed Matt.

Randall considered this for a moment, and then leaned back in his chair again.

"Next question," he said.

"Can I at least call some people back home? Send an email? I actually do have some people that might be a little worried about me, you know?"

Randall clapped and pointed at Matt with both hands. "Yes, definitely! That I can absolutely make happen for you! But... there's a few rules. You can't tell anyone any specifics about what happened. Not yet."

Matt looked at Randall like he was insane. He sniped, "I can't tell anyone?! After what I've been through? What the hell is that? You can't be serious!"

Randall shook his head. "No, I said 'no specifics'. For now, just tell your friends that you ran into a little problem and the US Navy wound up helping you out. When they want details, just tell them you've been asked to not say anything else. And reassure them that you're fine and will be coming home soon."

Matt grumbled, "That's a lot easier said than done."

"I'm serious, Matt," said Randall. "This is still an open issue of national security. You are not to risk what might be our next steps by discussing any of this yet in any more detail than that. With anyone."

Randall locked his eyes on Matt's and asked, "Will you promise me, Matt?"

Matt frowned. He didn't like this. He wasn't sure if he believed this guy and the line about this being an issue of national security. How could he be wrapped up in something like that? But, at the same time, the important thing was just to let Brian know he was safe and not to worry.

Matt caved. "Yeah. Okay. I promise."

Randall took Matt to a communications room where he could email or call anyone he wanted to. Matt just wanted to hear Brian's voice. He wanted something familiar in his life back. Something to remind him of home.

Brian answered the phone, yawning. "Hey! I haven't heard from you in a couple of days! How's the trip going? You ready to come home?"

Matt felt a little twinge that Brian didn't seem to notice anything amiss in his lack of communication, but then he dismissed it since Brian was always pretty unobservant that way. Besides, just hearing Brian's voice almost made Matt break down.

"Hey, Brian." Matt had to compose himself before continuing. "Yeah, I'm really ready to come home. You... you have no idea."

"You ok, baby?" asked Brian, waking up a little more. "You sound a little upset. Is everything ok?"

Matt took a deep breath and said, "Yeah, now. I'm fine. I'll be home soon."

"What's wrong? You sound a little funny..."

"I, uh... just had a... small problem over here. Aaaaaand I couldn't, uh, email or call for a few days. But I'm ok now."

Brian still wasn't fully coherent. "Ok, you still getting back on Saturday?"

Matt wasn't sure if he was happy or not that Brian didn't probe much further than he did. He decided to just let it go for right now since he couldn't give any specifics anyway.

"I'm not sure right now. I'll let you know if that changes."

Brian stifled another yawn. "Ok, baby. I'll be glad to see you. I've missed you!"

When he hung up, Matt closed his eyes and savored the sleepy sound of Brian's voice for a moment. He was so ready to be home.

Matt called Bret next, and as soon as Bret heard Matt's voice, he freaked out. "MATT! Holy shit! Are you ok? Where the hell have you been? Why haven't you emailed in, like, five days now? Jim and I are totally shitting bricks over here!!"

Matt said, "I'm fine, Bret. Really. I just had a little problem that I had to get some help with before I could get back to you or Brian or Jim."

"What kind of problem? Help from who? Where have you been?!"

Matt sighed. Bret was going to be much more persistent than Brian. "I just ran into an issue and the US Navy had to help..."

Bret practically screamed at Matt, "An 'issue'?! The fucking NAVY?! Are you ok? Do I need to come get you? What the hell do you

54

mean by the Navy? What kind of trouble did you get in that requires the goddamned Navy?!"

"Bret! Shut up a second! First of all, I'm fine. I'll be coming home soon, so just relax."

Bret wasn't to be totally allayed, though. "Coming home when, specifically? Where are you? Are you still in Syria? TELL ME WHAT HAPPENED!!"

Matt said, "Not sure exactly when yet, but they're working on that. Hang on..."

Matt looked over at the person in the communications room with him and asked, "Where are we?"

The communications officer said, "I can't say exactly..."

"I'm not asking for the coordinates or whatever. Just where are we in general? The Mediterranean? South China Sea? The Las Vegas strip?"

"Oh," said the officer. "Yeah. Still in the Mediterranean, off the coast of Syria."

Matt turned his attention back to Bret. "I'm on a Navy ship, right off of Syria. I can't really talk about what happened right now, though. Just listen to me a minute. I need to go. I'm going to call Jimmy, too, and let him know I'm ok. But I'm fine. I'll call or send an email when I can, alright?"

It did no good. "On a *ship*? You can't talk about it?! This is insane, Matt, and you..."

Matt interrupted him, almost shouting, "Chiliburger!! I'm fine! Go take a Xanax or something, ok? I'll call back soon!" Matt hung up, knowing that would be the only way he was going to be able to end that conversation. In spite of everything, he had to smile to himself at Bret's reaction. Over the top, like everything.

He finally called Jim, who was worried, but not nearly as wildly panicky as Bret.

"Matt! Is everything ok? You just disappeared on us there!"

"Yeah, Jimmy. It's good to hear your voice, though. I had a little problem and the Navy had to step in and help, but I'm fine. I'll be coming home pretty soon."

"Whoa... back up a second. The Navy? Like in the *US* Navy?! What happened, Matt?"

"Jim, I actually can't talk about it right now or go into any details. Ok? But everything's fine."

"Seriously, though, the US Navy?" pressed Jim. "If you're joking around, it's not funny, Matt. We've been really worried."

"Yes, the US Navy. And no, I'm not joking around. I know you guys have been worried. You guys are the best, you know? I just talked to Bret a moment ago, so you'll probably start getting text messages any minute now."

"Is there anything I can do, Matt? Do you want us to come over there and get you?"

Matt smiled and felt better. Jim was the calm rock in his life. It felt good to have friends like that. He wondered if he had subconsciously saved his call to Jim for last.

"No, Jimmy. Thanks, but that definitely isn't necessary. I'll get back in touch when I know exactly when I'll be coming home. It shouldn't be long."

"Ok, Matt. It's good to hear your voice and to know you're ok. Call back and let me or Chili know if there's anything at all we can do."

Once he hung up, Matt felt much better. Just hearing Brian's, Bret's and Jim's voices made him feel like everything had turned out alright. He just had to wait until he got to go home now.

Chapter 10 — The Rider

Given the tiny amount of clearance between his bunk and the one above it, it took a moment for Matt to figure out how to get into it so he could lie down. But despite his careful attempts, he wound up hitting his head twice anyway getting settled in. The pillow was thin and the mattress might as well have been stuffed with a couple of shredded up Sunday newspapers, but it was a far cry better than a cold tile floor, that was for sure.

He turned on his side and wondered if anyone else was sharing the small cabin he was in since there were other racks besides his. He assumed not since they looked empty. The berth itself was a very narrow walkway, hardly wide enough for a single person, with the racks built in on either side. At the end were a couple of narrow lockers and a single shared desk. Everything was painted the same disheartening gray that had been everywhere except for the room that Wickland had been in.

At least he felt much better after having had a rather large lunch. After finishing with his calls, Matt got the guy in the communications room to tell him how to get back to the chow hall so he could eat. He wandered around some, wound up in a room some large and intimidating Marine told him he shouldn't be in, but pointed him back in the right direction to the chow hall he was looking for.

They were serving lunch, so Matt loaded up. Out of curiosity, he asked one of the people keeping the food lines stocked if they had the corned beef and cabbage. The guy told him they did, but then warned him to not "be stupid enough to actually eat it."

He wound up getting a lot of vegetables and something that looked like it was supposed to be chicken and dumplings. He settled in at a small table by himself to eat. It might have been terrible, but after five days of nothing, it tasted just fine to Matt. It also occurred to him that the last meal he had prior to this one was the one he had at the café before being kidnapped.

He also noticed for the first time that he could occasionally hear a loud rumbling that actually shook the boat a little. The first time he heard it, he thought it might have been a bomb going off of onboard somewhere and started to panic at the thought of the thing sinking with him on it. But he watched the other people and no one else in the chow hall seemed to even notice it.

He had to ask several people how to get back to his rack, complicated by the fact that he didn't know how to tell them which cabin was his. Fortunately, most everyone seemed to pick up on the fact that he was "the rider" as they referred to him and knew where to direct him. At one point again, he wound up trying to go through a locked passageway that he thought he was supposed to go down. As he tried to open the hatch a few times, another Marine came along and told him that, unless he wanted to be responsible for the Sidewinder missiles in there, he probably ought to go around. Matt turned a little pale and backed off from the door slowly and the Marine started laughing. Matt explained where he was trying to go and this Marine took the time to walk him most of the way back to where he was going.

On his way back to his rack, Matt's mind played back part of the conversation with Randall Wickland. Randall had specifically said he realized Matt would want to call his friends back home. He didn't say "friends and family". He knew that Matt didn't actually have any family since his dad passed away while he was in college and his mother passed away two years ago. He felt sure Randall already knew this. And that explained why he didn't write anything down when Matt was talking about his background. He already knew all of it, or had access to it. Matt guessed that Randall was in the CIA or something like that. He had been dealing with a "spook". A real live spook. He wasn't sure what it meant, other than the fact that this was probably more than just some rescue mission for a kidnapped American.

As Matt lay in his bunk, he let his mind drift back to his call with Brian earlier that morning. He was a little disappointed that Brian didn't seem to hardly notice or be concerned that Matt hadn't called or emailed in days. Especially when he compared that reaction to both Bret's and Jim's. But he also knew that Brian was never very alert first thing in the morning, and he wasn't a very clingy boyfriend that needed to talk to Matt five times a day. Well, he could be a little clingy in other odd ways, but not that way.

Rather than let his mind go down that path too far, Matt reminded himself of his commitment to be better than that and to appreciate Brian more. He forced his attention back on how good it was to hear Brian's voice and how glad he'd be to get home and see him.

Even with another momentary roar that he could hear off somewhere in the ship, Matt's mind drifted off rapidly, letting him sleep off his lunch.

Chapter 11 — Bait

Why do they have to start banging like that now? Don't they know people are trying to sleep?

The sound intruded into Matt's mind, forcing him out of his sleep. Then he vaguely heard, "Yo, rider! Matt Goodend!"

He sat up with a start, inevitably banging his head on the rack above him and causing him to curse. He rolled over and saw yet another very young Marine — the one that had been trying to wake him up.

"You Matt Goodend?"

"Yeah, that's me."

"You know a guy named Wickland?"

"Yeah."

"He needs to see you again. Now."

Matt followed the Marine back to the same small conference room that he had met Randall before. After this second trip there, Matt was starting to feel like he'd be able to find his own way.

Like earlier, Randall was mostly all business. He wanted Matt to look through about fifty digital photographs on a laptop of people that more or less matched his description of the leader of the group that kidnapped him. They weren't mug shots like in a police department, though. There were shots of these various people (Terrorists? Insurgents? Enemies? Allies?) from candid or surreptitious situations that they had in their possession.

Unfortunately, since they all roughly matched Matt's memory of the leader, he couldn't pick out one that he felt like was definitely his kidnapper. He narrowed it down to five or six that he felt were possibilities, but it might have been any of them. Or maybe none of them at all.

Randall seemed a little put out with Matt that he couldn't pick the guy out, but Matt told him that he simply wasn't sure. Then Matt told Randall that he could pick one at random and insist that that was the guy with absolute certainty, but he didn't really think that would be what Randall wanted in the end. Randall backed off and agreed that that would be worse.

Randall took the laptop back and fiddled around on it some. Then he sat quietly and studied Matt for a moment, like he was trying to make a decision. Matt sat and waited for him to make the next move.

When none came, Matt asked, "So, do you know when you can get me back home yet?"

Randall took a deep breath and said, "Let's talk about something else first."

He turned around the laptop so Matt could look at one more photograph on the screen.

Randall asked, "Do you know this person?"

Matt looked at the screen and immediately almost got angry. He said hotly, "Is this some kind of a joke?"

Randall said bluntly, "No."

Matt narrowed his eyes slightly and looked directly at Randall. What the fuck was up with all of these games? "You and I both know that that's me. But it's not me, either."

Randall agreed, "It's not you. But do you know this person?"

"No, Randall, I don't know that person."

It was a clear face picture of someone that looked very similar to Matt. Same dark hair in the same style. Almost the same green eyes, but not quite. Similar style goatee. The chin was a little different than Matt's, but the mouth was a pretty close match.

Randall sat up in his chair and said, "This is Eric Stillman."

Matt shrugged his shoulders. He still had the feeling that this was some kind of ugly joke or something.

"This is the person that was killed in the room next door to yours, Matt. The body the team brought back with them? It was Eric."

The confusion swept over Matt. He looked at the photograph again. That person had been in the room next to him? That was the person he heard pleading? That was who was killed by the single gunshot?

"Matt, the situation is such that we need to trust you with some information that we normally would never give outside the intelligence or military communities. In fact, we've already started the process of giving you a provisional security clearance and because of the extremely limited amount of time, I'm even jumping ahead of that, but the consensus is that you can be trusted with this."

Matt heard the words, but his mind was caught on the fact that the person in the picture was the body lying in the boat next to him. The guy, Eric, looked so much like him. And Eric was dead. And Matt wasn't.

Matt interrupted Randall and demanded, "Why did they kill him?"

Randall paused for a second and answered, "Based on what we can tell, we think it was an accident. A sloppy job at pistol-whipping him."

Matt remembered how he had been hit in the head with a gun, too.

Randall said, "Let me back up a little, and I'll explain. But you've got to understand, Matt, that what I'm about to get into is a matter of national security. You are not at liberty to discuss this with *anyone* not directly involved in it. Is that perfectly clear? No one. Under *any* circumstance."

Matt nodded. Why did this guy have to be such an asshole?

Randall said, "Eric Stillman worked for the US Embassy in Damascus. But he liked to go over to Latakia every so often for some beach time. We believe that these people had every intention of grabbing Eric while he was there. But you were in the wrong place at the wrong time, and happened to really look like him. You were just a mistake, Matt. They thought you were Eric. You mentioned that while the leader was asking you for information on your laptop, which they probably thought was Eric's, he got a phone call and seemed to leave you alone after that. We think that he found out at that point that you weren't who they thought you were. Apparently, they tried again and got the right Eric Stillman on the next try. That was the guy you heard them bring in. We also think that the leader guy wasn't around at this point, probably busy with something else. The other guys, the flackies guarding you, decided to try to get access to Eric's laptop and tried to beat it out of him, but killed him accidentally in the process. After that, they were probably just waiting for the guy in charge to get back to decide what to do. And by that point, we had already pinpointed where we needed to go in and were able to get to the scene before the leader got back. He wasn't one of the ones the team eliminated when they went in. We've identified some information on Eric's laptop, part of a project he was helping on, that we're pretty sure they wanted."

Matt had a hard time believing all of this. But it seemed to fit as far as he could tell.

Matt was hit by a question he wasn't sure he wanted to know the answer to. But he needed to know. "How did you find me there?" As soon as he asked it, he wished he hadn't.

Randall said softly, "We didn't locate you, Matt. We found Eric. Well, Eric's laptop."

Matt's breathing got shallower. His hands were clenched together so tightly his fingernails were digging into his own flesh. They weren't there to rescue him. He was just a lucky find. An accident. If the extremists, or whatever they were, hadn't gotten the right person, he probably never would have been found. No one would have known what happened to him. He would have just disappeared. Just like that.

Randall added, "The SEALs, being the way they are, aren't going to leave an American in harm's way, Matt, if there's anything they can do about it."

Matt reeled. *But still. They weren't there for me.* His skin felt clammy.

It took a few seconds, but Matt pulled himself together a little bit and said, "Well, I'm sorry about what happened to this Eric guy. I don't know how I got to be the lucky one to make it through all this."

He unconsciously pushed the lock of hair out of his forehead. As terrible as it was to understand now more about what had happened, he genuinely did appreciate getting at least this explanation for it.

Matt asked, "Was he... Eric... did he have a family?"

Randall replied, "No. Well, he wasn't married. We are going to have to notify his parents, though, soon. For the moment, though, all information regarding this is on a stronger lockdown than usual."

Matt nodded, but he was feeling a little weak. This was a lot to take in. He asked, "Thanks for telling me this. Can I go back to my rack now?" He just wanted to lie down.

Randall said, "No, not yet, Matt. I mentioned we have a limited period here. And we normally wouldn't even have told you *this* information. But your involvement presents us with an opportunity. We need your help with something."

Matt had no idea what else he could tell them that he hadn't already. Even hearing the explanation didn't jog his memory to any other details that might be important.

He said, "I don't remember anything else that might be important to tell you."

"No," said Randall. "Some of these guys are still out there. They know by this point that you and Eric are gone, but there's a good chance they don't know Eric is actually dead. If we make them think Eric is still alive and that they have another chance to try and grab him, we may be able to actually get some of these guys. This is important. You don't have any idea what we might be able to get if we could get some of these guys. This is *really* important, Matt."

Matt wasn't sure what this had to do with him. He couldn't fit this together. "I don't understand," he said, his mind fogged.

"We want to set a trap, Matt," explained Randall, his gaze fixed on Matt.

Shit, thought Matt.

Shit, shit, shit!

"You want me to be the bait?!"

Randall clenched his teeth slightly and nodded slowly to Matt.

Matt sat there for a second. The fact that he had been kidnapped at all was pure chance. The fact that he had been rescued was also pure chance. He was scared shitless of leaving any more of his life to chance.

Matt's chest heaved. He felt cold and yet felt a drop of sweat rolling down the back of his neck. He said, "Hell. No." He was supposed to be done with this and going home. Not dangling back out in front of these people so they'd have *another* chance to kill him. Hell. No.

"Look," replied Randall, "I can't... we can't... force you to do this, obviously. But believe me when I say, if some of our other conjectures are correct, this would be very important for us, Matt."

Matt shook his head. There was no way this was going to happen. He spat at Randall, "You asshole! You have no idea what I went through! I was bound hand and foot for three days and left naked in a dark room! Do you know what it's like to go without water for three days, Randall? Do you?"

His skin was clammy and his eyes stung and he wiped at them at even the thought of winding back up in that situation ever again. Matt's voice got steadily louder. "It burns! I actually *wanted* them to come in and shoot me to end the burning thirst! I was ready to *die* just to end it! *You* try it, Randall, and tell me if *you'd* be willing to risk something like that again!"

Randall actually pushed back in his chair and he was clearly uncomfortable dealing with the raw emotional reaction that Matt was having to this.

Matt put his head in his hands and tried to get the images out of his head that had reared up in the last few seconds, making him relive the most terrifying three days he had never even imagined someone could have.

Randall finally said, "Matt, if it weren't for us, where would you be right now? Huh? You'd be dead, Matt. Think about that! You're on borrowed time the *rest of your life* because of us! You owe us something, Matt!"

Matt jumped up out of his chair. He couldn't stand to be in that room any more. He screamed "Fuck you!" at Randall and pushed his way out of the room as fast as he could, his heart beating furiously and his ears ringing.

He ran down the hallway, pushing past a couple of people in red shirts coming his way, his mind spinning, trying to remember how to get back to his berth.

As he turned another corner, though, on his way, he saw four guys coming towards him. The one in front was the very last person he wanted see right now. Of all the fucking people to run into, it was Petey with the fire-red hair sauntering his way down the passage.

Petey lit up when he saw Matt and his face twisted up into a cruel smile. He said, "Hey little lady bug! You look upset! What's the matter? Is your butt-plug all twisted up?"

Matt stopped a few feet in front of Petey and he boiled over in a way that was extremely rare for him. He practically exploded at Petey, "Fuck you, you god damn asshole! Fuck you! You have no idea what I've been through! And now I have to deal with you bunch of homophobic shitheads!"

Petey's smile immediately evaporated and it was obvious he wasn't expecting this kind of a vicious reply. The scowl that replaced his smile made it clear he didn't particularly like it, either.

"What? Lighten up, man! And we saved your *fucking* ass, you know?" he replied angrily. He took a menacing step forward towards Matt, which made Matt unconsciously back up a step. "You dipshit! *We were there*, remember?" Petey pointed at the four of them in a row in the passage.

Matt finally glanced at the other three. The second one behind Petey was the vaguely Middle Eastern looking guy he had seen with Petey before. The third guy was a little shorter than Matt, but much thicker and far more muscular, and looked Hispanic. The fourth guy, to Matt's sudden realization and surprise, was the guy with the dark hair that he had been thrown into the shower with.

Matt stood dumbfounded as he took this in and realized he was now face to face with the group of guys that had saved him, and been so horrible to him, too.

Petey took another step towards Matt, who matched it by backing up another step. Petey continued, practically spitting he was so mad, "We were the ones that *found you,* right? You do *remember* us, right? You didn't just walk out of there by yourself, you know. Christ! This is the thanks we get! I guess it doesn't mean anything to you, but you know Travis *carried you on his back for a fucking half mile* to get you out of there. Shit! And now you're all rainbow-gay-flag fired up at *us?!*"

Matt's head was spinning. He was furious at this guy, and confused, and a lot scared. He was angry at how Randall had said he owed them all. He was pissed at how they were treating him. He was terrified of what they wanted from him. But they had gotten him out of that building alive, and been fucking assholes. He felt like the entire boat was capsizing violently around him and about to pull him down to the bottom of the ocean, drowning him. Why didn't anyone else feel this? Why didn't these SEAL people seem to notice this? He needed, absolutely needed, to be away from these people and everything right then. He pushed his way forward and past all four of the Navy SEALs, not even looking at them.

Even with his head spinning, Matt managed to get back to his cabin and clumsily collapsed into his rack again and faced the back wall. He broke down this time and the tears flowed out of his eyes. He just didn't know what to think. How could they ask him to risk himself like that, like he was the property of the US military now because they had saved him? Why did they have to be so fucking juvenile about the fact that he was gay?

He just wanted to be home and away from all of this.

Chapter 12 — Vulture's Row

Matt dreamt about being back in the empty room, alone and bound and scared. In this dream, though, the door to the room was open, and nothing was stopping him from going out through it. But he stayed in the room anyway, paralyzed by what might be on the other side. As bad as he wanted out, the fear of what was outside seemed worse. He also noticed there was a whispering sound from long ago, but he couldn't understand what the whispering was trying to tell him to do. He didn't know what to do, and so he just stayed. The dream then shifted, became more real, and yet not as uncomfortable. He was still in the room, but it felt more... immediate. He could hear a voice, more clearly than the whispers had been. It sounded like the one that had stayed with him in the room and helped him. In his dream he could hear the low voice saying his name, making him feel less afraid.

And for the second time that day, Matt realized there really was someone saying his name. He sat up, cracking his head on the rack above him yet again.

"Damn it!" he cussed to himself while rubbing his head. "I swear to God, these things are like a cruel joke!"

When he turned to his side to see who was calling him, he was surprised to see a person squatting right next to him.

The guy made a pained face when he saw Matt hit his head and said, "Ohh, ouch! You ok?" in a deep voice.

Matt looked at the guy blankly for a moment as things fell into place. Crouching next to him was the SEAL with the dark hair and ears that stuck out. But he recognized the squatting position, and the familiar voice, too, and it finally came together for Matt. This guy, this one, the one next to him right now... he was the one that Matt knew. He was the one that cut the ties off of him and helped him out of the room that he had assumed he would die in. This was the one that he had been thrown in the shower with briefly. He tried to remember what Petey had called him when he threw him in there. Mope? Was that it?

He took a moment to get a slightly better look at the guy. The dark blue t-shirt he was wearing showed that he was well-built, just like Petey and the others had been. His face had a strength and intensity to it, but not the severe, almost pissed-off look that Petey's had. His ears did stick out a little too far, and his nose was a little bit crooked and probably had been broken at some point. Mope, or whatever his name was, had deeply etched smile lines forming parentheses around his mouth, but he wasn't smiling. Mostly right now, he looked a little concerned about Matt hitting his head.

Matt finally replied, "I'm ok. I'm getting used to hitting my damn head on this thing. You're uh... Mope? Was that it?"

Mope nodded. His dark eyebrows arched slightly and he said, "I didn't want to wake you up, but I need to talk to you for a minute."

Matt lay back in his rack, turning a little stubborn in the process. "You came to poke some more fun at the queer?"

"No," said Mope simply. "I want to talk to you a little about what you and Randall Wickland discussed."

That was worse. Matt pulled himself out of his rack, very clumsily, and stood to face Mope, who rose from his crouching position. Matt realized the guy was probably an inch or two taller than himself. His forehead creased in anger and he said, "I've got nothing to say about that. I can't believe that Wickland guy even asked me to go back through that. I just want off this boat!"

He quickly corrected himself before this Mope character had a chance to, "Or ship! Or submarine, or whatever the *fuck* this thing is that we're on! There's no windows anywhere, so how the hell am I supposed to know?"

Mope looked surprised for a second. "Mmm... you really have no idea where you are?" he asked with genuine curiosity.

"It's the *USS Iwo Jima*, which means absolutely zip to me! I'm not in the military."

Mope looked thoughtful for a few seconds and said, "Come on. I'll show you Vulture's Row."

Matt looked at Mope doubtfully. Why couldn't anyone speak plain English around here? If Vulture's Row had anything to do with food, it didn't sound like he wanted to see it.

"C'mon, I promise you'll like this," Mope repeated.

He wasn't sure he wanted to go. One, Vulture's Row didn't sound like anything he wanted to see. And two, he didn't particularly want to be around any of these guys. But against his better judgment, Matt followed Mope out of the cabin and they started through a new route he had not been along before.

While they were walking, Matt cooled off enough to ask quietly, "It was you, wasn't it? You were the first one that came in the room where I was. You were the one that cut my hands and feet free..."

Mope glanced back over his shoulder and gave Matt the most authentically sympathetic look he had gotten yet since arriving on the *Iwo Jima*. He confirmed, "Yeah, that was me." They continued to wind through the ship.

"I think I should tell you thanks... for what you did for me," said Matt.

Mope nodded while leading him farther along. Eventually, Matt realized they were going up. A lot farther up than he had been before. They finally got to a metal doorway, secured shut. Mope cranked the handle to open the door and stepped through.

When Matt followed through, the first thing he noticed was blinding, beautiful sunshine, the first he had seen in days. He looked around and stepped up to the railing while Mope secured the door again.

Mope swept his hands from one side to the other across the whole view. "This," he said, "is the *USS Iwo Jima LHD-7*."

And for a while, Matt forgot everything else that had been on his mind. He and Mope were standing on something of a balcony, several levels up in the air, looking out over the massive flight deck of the *USS Iwo Jima*. The sun was brilliant outside and the sky was blue. Down at one end of the flight deck, Matt watched as a large helicopter with huge rotors in the front and back was taking off and heading somewhere out over the Mediterranean Sea. There were several more helicopters secured out on the flight deck, as well as an odd-looking jet aircraft. Below them were a bunch of busy crew members wearing various colored shirts — red, yellow, blue and purple. The scene boggled Matt's mind.

"I've been on an aircraft carrier this whole time?" he asked, shouting over the sound of the retreating helicopter.

"Actually, no," replied Mope. "This isn't an aircraft carrier. Aircraft carriers are even bigger than this thing. This is actually what's called an amphibious assault ship. It can still launch helos and fighters, as you can see. But what this can do that aircraft carriers can't is open its entire ass up so other boats and hovercraft can be deployed from the well deck."

Matt wasn't sure he totally understood the distinction, or really cared. The sight and size of the ship was extremely impressive, though. He felt the breeze against his face, and he inhaled deeply, finally taking a moment to savor the fact that he was outside again, able to breathe fresh air. It was tinged with the smell of aircraft fuel, but fresh nonetheless.

But finally, his mind dragged him back to what he knew was coming up. He turned to Mope and said, "Randall sent you to try and convince me to be bait for you guys, didn't he?"

Mope continued to look out over the ship and the Mediterranean all around it. "No, he didn't. He told me about the conversation he had with you, and I know about what they want to do, though. I offered to talk to you about it on my own."

Matt wasn't in the mood to be pressured again. "You can save your breath. I'm not doing it. I find it a little unbelievable that you guys would even ask me to risk something like that again."

"No one's going to make you do anything, Matt. I promise you that. I saw what you were like in that room when I found you. I saw the pain and fear in you, naked… exposed… crouched in a corner and trying to hide in a room that offered nowhere to hide. I know you'll do anything to make sure you never go through anything like that again. I don't blame you at all."

"But… there would be a fundamental difference this time around, Matt," continued Mope. "We'd be there with you. We'd be there with the one critical task of making sure you're kept safe. You saw what happened when we stormed into that apartment with no knowledge of who or what we'd find in it. They barely got one sloppy shot off at us. I don't like bragging, but we're really good at what we do, Matt. Fucking good at it. And I don't know all the details about what they think they may get out of this, and Wickland won't tell even us just yet, but it smells pretty important."

Matt frowned. "Randall's an asshole. And why should I help you guys? You've been a bunch of homophobic jerks to me."

Mope shook his head a little, "Randall's just not good with people. Hell, I'm not either, but I'm better than him. And as for Petey, he's not really homophobic."

Matt looked at Mope, fully insulted. "Are you kidding me? Do you even know what the fucking term means?"

"I know what it means, Matt," said Mope, patiently. He tried to explain, "Petey's a good guy. He just plays a little rough. But that's all it is, Matt... he's just playing with you."

Matt cut Mope an angry look. This was getting offensive.

Mope exhaled deeply. "I know it's hard for you to see it that way, and Petey probably could stand some sensitivity training, but he's just having some fun. Actually, he's hoping you'll give it back to him. Give him some of what he's dishing out, and he'll love it."

Matt continued to look at Mope like he had tapped a special bullshit reserve to feed him.

"None of this matters," said Matt. "I don't have the training you guys have. I'll cause more problems than helping."

"Nobody is asking you to do anything you're not trained for. That's what we're there for."

Matt started to get desperate to fend this off.

"I just don't think I can, Mope. You guys... you're, like, fearless. I don't have the courage you guys do. I can't do something like this."

As a hasty afterthought, Matt added, "It's a gay thing. I'm too afraid to get mixed up in something like this." Matt knew that it was a cheap, pathetic shot if there ever was one, but he was terrified of where this conversation might lead if he didn't put a hard stop to it.

Mope leaned way over so he could rest his forearms on the railing. He put his head down on his arms and looked out over the sea, thinking. He stayed like this for an eternity before standing back up and leaning against the wall behind him. Matt watched him carefully and saw the firm, fixed look on Mope's face.

Mope clenched his lips together for a second before looking at Matt and responding. "So, I'm going to have to call bullshit on you for that statement, Matt. And it is - it's total bullshit."

Matt was defiant. "You don't know."

Mope looked back out over the water. "Yeah, I do."

Mope scratched at his chin for a second, then admitted levelly, "I'm gay, Matt. Just like you."

The words made the anger boil up in Matt again, and overflow him. This was going too far. "You'd *fucking lie to me* like that just so you guys could use me like bait?! This is *worse* than being bigoted assholes to my face." He was livid at Mope at this point. Were they really this low? Matt was astonished at these people.

Mope didn't respond. He didn't even look at Matt. He leaned over on the railing and put his head down on his arms again. Matt waited for Mope to give in, to exhibit some sign that it was all bullshit. He wanted to see the lie in Mope's eyes. But as he watched Mope looking out over the water, he couldn't find the lie anywhere. All he could see was someone that had taken a step that he had no idea he'd be taking when he woke up that morning. Someone that hoped he wouldn't regret that step.

As Matt watched the Navy SEAL next to him, the anger ebbed back away.

"Oh my God, you're serious…" said Matt. "You really are! Holy shit! Do those other guys know?"

Mope stood up suddenly and shot a very stern look at him. "No! They don't! And it needs to stay that way! I'm trusting you with something very personal, Matt. I've got good reason to believe you can be trusted, but I need to know you'll keep this between you and me."

Matt was floored. He mind raced around the scene at the apartment. The dead bodies and blood. He thought about how they had gone in there with no direct knowledge of what they would face, and came out without a scratch. This guy standing next to him had done that. Matt wasn't one to play into stereotypes, but he had to admit that reconciling that image with the fact that Mope was gay took a little effort. All that aside, though, it wasn't in his nature to betray someone that trusted him with something like that. Matt just wasn't that kind of person.

He said, sincerely, "You don't need to worry, Mope. It'll stay between you and me, I promise. Wait, what did you mean by that, when you said you had *reason* to believe I could be trusted?"

"Not just me, really. Randall, too. He wouldn't have explained *anything* to you without some concrete evidence that you could be trusted. Before he let you call your friends back home, all he did was ask that you not tell them anything. He didn't threaten you or use any strong arm tactics. They listened to your calls, Matt, just to make sure…"

Matt interrupted angrily, "They *what*?! Who the *hell* do they…"

"Sorry, Matt. Navy ship, Navy rules," said Mope, interrupting.

Matt glared at Mope, still extremely pissed about being eavesdropped on.

"No one's snooping, Matt," said Mope. "They wanted to see how well you could be trusted when you're being led *only* by your own principles. You didn't say anything you shouldn't have. We can trust you, Matt. *I* can trust you."

It took a moment, but Matt's anger melted away enough to where he could move on from it.

Mope said, "And that's a huge part of it. Trust. Do you know where courage comes from, Matt? The courage you say you don't have?"

Matt didn't know how to answer.

"A large part of courage comes from trust. Trust in yourself. But also trust in your brothers that they're there backing you up. Having faith in knowing that there are those that will do anything, absolutely anything, to support you and help you gives you a courage you could never have otherwise. Courage *is* faith and trust, Matt."

"I couldn't do what I did to help you out by myself. Not just that it was too much for one person physically, but psychologically, too. But knowing I had three highly trained men, that I trust absolutely, that are practically extensions of myself, there supporting me, gives me a courage I can't have alone. And I in turn give them that same courage. It's not just the training and the skills that are important. It's the bond. Trust and faith in one another makes us more than what we could be without it. The missions we're assigned - recon, demolition work, sniper missions, rescues, stuff that's almost always way behind enemy lines - would be pretty much impossible without it. Including going into that apartment where you were held."

It started to sink into Matt just how fundamentally different these guys' lives were from his own. The kinds of things they did, what they faced as a part of their profession, wasn't some artificial movie scene. The body of his captor with the huge hole in his chest, lying in a pool of his own blood, wasn't fake. These guys willingly put themselves into these situations. Suddenly the words "deadly serious shit" had a slightly different meaning to him.

Listening to Mope made Matt start to feel something. Words like 'courage', 'faith', and 'trust' didn't form much of his own day to day life, certainly not in the sense that Mope was using them. But for these men, he began to understand, these concepts were a crucial, elemental part of their life. They literally lived and died by these words.

"You say you don't have any courage, Matt. That's probably true right now. You don't have faith and trust in yourself in a situation like this, and you definitely don't really have faith or trust in us. Yet."

Matt listened closely to Mope, and the truth of what Mope was saying surfaced. Mope was right.

Mope said, "I see what you came through, Matt, and I think you have it in you to help us. But it's understandable that you don't see it for yourself. That's ok. And as for us, I'll make a deal with you. But don't decide one way or the other yet."

Matt looked over at Mope. "Instead," continued Mope, "come have dinner with us tonight. Spend some time with us. Get to know us a little bit better. See if you think you can have some faith in us and can trust us to back you up. That we would support you just like we would each other. That we won't let you fail."

Matt found that the conversation had gone exactly where he had originally had no intention of letting it go. He found himself responding to the things that Mope had said. He didn't know about faith and trust just yet, but he now found he respected Mope. His words dug deeply into Matt, beyond just trying to convince him to help them. Mope had him thinking about deep things that he had spent precious little time in his life thinking about.

Matt looked out over the water. Somewhere out there was the port city of Latakia. Somewhere out there was an empty room.

He looked over at Mope, whose dark eyes were pinned expectantly on Matt. Matt nodded and said, "Ok." He pushed the hair out of his forehead and repeated, "Yeah, ok."

Mope added, "One other thing, and this will be critically important for you to remember. If, and I understand this is still an 'if' for you... *if* you wind up doing this with us... you're the mission, Matt. You."

Chapter 13 — Any Of Us Would Have

The closer Matt got to the mess hall for dinner, the colder his feet got. He may have promised Mope earlier to meet them for dinner, but now that the time had come, he wasn't sure he wanted to go through with it. The other two guys that he hadn't really even spoken to, he didn't know about. It would have been easy to assume they were jerks like that Petey guy, but honestly, Matt hadn't had much chance to interact with them at all. What it really came down to was that guy, Petey. Despite Mope's assurances otherwise, Petey still seemed like a queer-hating bigot to Matt.

And on top of that, there were now the troubling doubts about Mope. Matt's conversation with Mope earlier had made him feel much better, and finding out that Mope was gay made him see him in a different light. He wasn't sure why it *would* make a difference. Shouldn't a gay guy be capable of doing what these guys did? Maybe it was really just learning a little more about the person behind the guns, goggles and face mask. Mope became a little more humanized in Matt's mind and Matt could relate to him some now. Maybe that was it.

But when he had gone back to his rack, and reflected on it, a doubt snuck up on him. What if Mope was lying after all? What if he had just said he was gay to try and gain some kind of "affinity" from Matt? What if Randall Wickland had put him up to it just to try and convince Matt to be their bait? He hated having that thought. He fucking hated it. Deep down in his heart, he wanted to believe that Mope was a really good, gay guy, but his head was still mistrustful of Randall and scared of being turned into a lure, and it was messing with him.

As he reached the top of the steps to the deck where the chow hall was, Matt decided this wasn't going to work. His head was too all over the place for him to deal with these guys at dinner. He stopped, briefly blocking a couple of Marines also trying to get to the chow hall for dinner. But just as he was about to go back down and go to the berth where his rack was, he heard Mope's voice calling him from the passage behind him. He knew he was stuck with them now.

He turned and saw Mope walking towards him with the Hispanic-looking SEAL. Petey and the other SEAL weren't with them. Matt thought that maybe, at least, he'd get lucky and Petey wasn't coming. And just seeing Mope again made Matt want to believe him. He wanted to believe that the face he saw, with the dark eyes, misaligned nose, sloppy ears and smile lines was the face of a fundamentally sincere person and he wanted to believe in the things that Mope had said to him. Why did he always seem to have to have these creeping doubts?

Mope greeted Matt and said, "And I don't know if you've really had a chance to meet Tony yet, or Desantos as we pretty much always call him."

Matt said "hi" and shook Tony's hand. Tony Desantos was about Matt's height, maybe a hair shorter, but was built like a tank and had huge arms, a broad chest, and a broad, round face to go with it. Desantos didn't really smile and had the same serious look that he had seen on Mope.

To Matt's disappointment, Mope said, "Let's go before the line gets too long. Petey and Baya are going to have to wait in line once they catch up."

They got into the mess hall and Matt made the mistake of treating it more like a buffet, with choices. He stood out of the line to look the selections over before he realized the two lines had exactly the same items, none of it well-presented.

Mope called to Matt and said, "Yeah, it's not going to look any better from a distance, I promise you!" Matt got back in line a few people behind where Mope and Desantos were.

Just as he got back in line, he heard the voice immediately behind him that he was dreading.

"Hey, Pink Petunia!" called Petey, plenty loud enough for every Marine and sailor in the immediate area to hear him. "I heard you're eatin' with the men tonight! Did you finally get your panties all out of a twist?"

Matt gritted his teeth, his face turned as red as Petey's hair, and he closed his eyes for a moment without looking back. How could Mope make any kind of a believable claim that this guy wasn't an asshole? And if he was full of shit about this, what else was he full of shit regarding?

Before he knew it, he had turned around and said, "No, not with *men*. I'm eating with *you guys* tonight."

Shit, thought Matt. He hadn't intended to say something like that. It just came out before he realized his mouth was moving. He wondered if he was going to get belted clear across the chow line even as he heard the sailor in line in front of him chuckle at his comment.

Matt turned back to look at Petey behind him, and Petey looked pissed. Jesus, the guy was big, and downright frightening when he was pissed. Matt thought to himself, here it comes.

Petey said, "The fuck are you laughing at, squid? Huh? You got somethin' to say to me?" For a second, Matt thought Petey was talking to him, but then realized his comment was directed at the sailor in front of Matt that had laughed.

The sailor stopped laughing immediately and didn't even look back. Instead, he just stepped out of line and took what food he had on his tray over to the table where his buddies were as fast as his feet would carry him.

Petey looked back down at Matt and nodded at him to keep the line moving. He asked Matt, "Is it really true?"

"Is what true?" asked Matt, dreading wherever Petey was about to take this.

Petey started laughing and asked, "Is it true that your last name is Goodend? Are you really a *gay guy* with the last name Goodend? Because if it is, man, that's like, totally fucking *awesome!*"

Matt put the mashed potatoes on his plate and smacked his hand against his forehead. He wondered what fucker had told Petey his last name. Dear God, he'd never hear the end of this. He tried to wiggle out of it. He started to rush off over to where Desantos and Mope were sitting, saying "No. Not me. Don't know where you got that from!" This was going to be the most miserable dinner ever.

Matt sat down, but Petey and Baya were right behind him. Before Petey had a chance to push any further on the subject of Matt's last name, Mope interjected and said, "Colorado, shut up for one minute, man. Matt, you know Petey there. You see what we have to deal with on a daily basis, so... welcome to our world." Mope nodded over to the remaining person Matt had not met. "And this guy's Skander Baya."

Baya shoveled a forkful of food into his mouth and reached over to shake Matt's hand. Baya was also about Matt's height, but much more slender than Desantos. His black hair was grown out just barely enough to where Matt could see the natural wave in it.

Petey couldn't hold back any more, though. He said, "Careful shaking that hand, Baya, he's been digging around in his back door trying to adjust that buttplug all day!"

Matt flushed red, yet again, and said, "I have not!"

"So, you've just been sticking your finger up your ass all day? Is that what you've been doing?"

Matt glanced briefly over at Mope, giving him a split-second plea for help. Mope gave him a quick nod, trying to encourage Matt to give it back to Petey.

Fine, thought Matt. What the hell did he have to lose?

"What? You sound like you don't like the idea of that," said Matt, issuing the challenge.

"Hell, pink..." started Petey.

Matt interrupted him, "You think that's nasty?"

"Damn nasty..."

"You think that's offensive?"

"Hell, yeah," agreed Petey.

"And yet, you just *had* to steal the towel that had been riding up my ass crack so you could huff it all afternoon. Was it ripe enough for you? Huh? You gonna sleep with it under your pillow tonight?"

Baya busted out laughing, as well as a few of the Marines sitting closest to them in the crowded chow hall. Desantos barely grinned, and didn't seem to find it quite as funny as Baya did.

Petey scowled at the chuckling Marines and said, "Don't you punks ever mind your own goddamn business?" but they just kept laughing to themselves as they ate.

Petey started to get up out of his chair and the two Marines stopped laughing very suddenly and looked everywhere other than at Petey.

Petey said, "Yeah, that's what I thought," and sat back down.

Petey looked back at Matt and nodded at him as a smirk started to spread across his face. Matt finally relaxed a tiny bit. He stole a quick glance at Mope, who gave him an impressed nod of approval.

Matt didn't leave well enough alone, though. He reached back to scratch his ass casually a few times with everyone at the table watching. He held his finger out to Petey and said, "You want a fresh round, Petey? If you like the towel, you'll love this!"

Petey said through his widening grin, despite the new round of laughs from Baya and the Marines sitting close by, "Okay, I see how it's going to be. You're on, Fingers Goodend!" Even Matt had to admit he hadn't heard that one before and smiled back.

With the ice fully broken at this point, Matt decided he had something he needed to say while all four of them were there, seated around him.

He got very serious and said, "So, all the PMS'ing I did at you guys earlier today aside, I really should say thanks."

He looked at each of them, but they gave him a chance to say what he had to say, even Petey. "You never expect to have to tell people 'thanks for saving my life', and... and you sure as *hell* don't expect it to have been under the circumstances that you saved mine. When you guys found me, I was so scared and the thirst had gotten so bad, I wanted to die. I wanted them to come in and shoot me in the head to end it. I had lost hope at that point and was ready for it to be done with." Matt paused a moment before continuing, "What you guys did for me was unimaginable. Every day of my life from now on is something that *you* guys gave me, and I'll take that with me. I'm sitting here trying... to... trying to figure out how to say it in a way that measures up to what you guys did for me. And I honestly don't know how. I don't know that the words even exist, you know? As pathetic as it is, all I know to say is thanks. Thank you. Thank you for saving my life when I thought it was already over."

Matt looked down at the table and the enormity of it hit him like a softball bat. What he said was true, in that room he had lost hope and fully expected to die. Wanted to die. And these people that he was sitting with and having dinner with, men that he probably wasn't even supposed to know existed, had busted into a building with armed kidnappers and pulled him from the empty room that was to be his coffin. Matt's lips turned down, frowning in an effort to hold back the sheer emotion of it, and losing the battle.

The table was silent, even amidst the general noise of the rest of the chow hall. And then, without warning, Petey asked hopefully, "Sooooo... does this mean you're going to give us all blowjobs?"

And relief washed over Matt. God bless that asshole, he thought. It was exactly what he needed to break the emotion and not start crying like a baby at a table full of Navy SEALs.

With barely a missed beat, Matt looked up at Petey and said, matter-of-factly, "Sure, but I've got my standards. It's gotta be bigger than a squirrel's dick, Petey, and I'm willing to bet good money that leaves you out of the running."

From that point on, Matt was much more relaxed, and the conversation was much lighter.

To Matt's surprise, the guys showed a lot of curiosity, asking him about what he was doing in Syria, his volunteer work with *Doctors*

Without Borders, and his job back in Richmond. They also wanted to know if he had a boyfriend or not (a "butt buddy" as Petey insisted on putting it), how long he and Brian had been together, and how they met. Then they found out he played softball and Petey had to give him a hard time about being on a gay softball team. He wanted to know where they managed to find dildos big enough to use as softball bats, but then reflected, "Never mind, if there's anybody that could sniff out a dildo that big, it'd have to be you, Glitterballs."

Matt, for his part, asked them if they had families, but none of them did. Neither did they really have steady girlfriends. Desantos mentioned that what they did for a living made relationships a little difficult since they travelled a lot and couldn't say much about what they were doing. Actually, Petey said he did have a "steady girlfriend" and then explained it was a "steady stream of girlfriends, a different one every time he got drunk and horny."

He found out from them that the four of them formed what was called a fire team, which was a part of a platoon of SEALs, which was in turn part of SEAL Team 8.

Matt learned that Petey was Peter Tuttle and was from the small town of Parsons, Tennessee (which the others referred to as Possums, Tennessee). Matt was surprised at this and had assumed he was from Colorado since he had heard them call him that several times. Desantos pointed out they called him that just because "Colorado" meant "the color red". Petey had been in the Navy three years prior to trying out to become a SEAL and was therefore the only one with Navy experience prior to making it into SpecOps.

Skander Baya was from New Jersey and his parents were both Tunisians who had moved to the US and gotten their citizenship even before he was born. But his background meant that, in addition to English, he could also speak French and Arabic fairly well. Granted, he admitted with a grin, it was Arabic with a New Jersey accent, but Arabic nonetheless.

Antonio Desantos was born in Mesa, Arizona, but had grown up in San Diego, California since his family moved there when he was four. He had also gotten a degree in structural engineering from the University of California in San Diego, and then pissed his family off by becoming a SEAL instead of doing something with it. Tony found this funny because his degree often came in pretty handy with the demolition work they sometimes got called on to do.

As the dinner progressed, Matt noticed that Mope seemed to hang out of the conversation. And even with the joking that went on, Mope rarely smiled. Matt started to wonder if he was doing the wrong things with the other guys and it was bothering Mope, so he started to hold back some. Mope had been really good to him, and he didn't want to do anything that would piss him off or upset him. It puzzled Matt since he felt like he had actually gotten on a decent footing with them. Even Colorado.

When they had finally finished eating, Petey grabbed his tray and said, "Alright, gentlemen, and lady, I need to go see if I can figure out why that sight is sticking on my M4. It's been driving me nuts."

Mope stood up with him and asked, "Which one?"

"The Trijicon."

Mope said, "I'll come help with it. Matt, I'll find you in the morning, ok?"

Matt agreed, and as Petey and Mope left, Baya turned to Matt and asked "I don't suppose you ever play any video games, do you?"

Matt said that, actually, he did, and told Baya about the game system setup he had at home. They talked about which games they each had for a moment before Desantos stood up to head out, too, and said, "I'm going to go make a phone call back home and check email."

Baya asked Matt, "So, you up for a game or two?"

"Absolutely!" said Matt. "There's nothing else for me to do here."

The put their trays away and Matt followed Baya off through the ship.

As they walked, Matt asked, "So, uh, Skander, if your parents are from Tunisia, does that mean you're Muslim?"

"Yeah, well, not hardcore, though. And just call me Baya... everybody else does. I grew up about as Muslim as you probably grew up Christian. We didn't even keep halal, except in a few rare instances. We weren't really ever very observant about Ramadan, either, but we did usually celebrate Eid when it was over. So, all the fun parts and none of the tough stuff."

Matt was curious, but didn't want to offend Baya, either. He finally decided to ask. "Is it hard? Being Muslim and doing what you do? I'm assuming those guys that had kidnapped me were Muslim."

Baya shook his head, "Not really. Most of that extremist stuff I don't consider to be really true to Islam at all. These people are just extremists and use Islam as an excuse for their own crazy agendas. I'm sure you'd feel the same way about Christian extremists killing random Muslim people in Richmond."

"Is it hard being Muslim in the US military? Do you get treated differently?"

Baya stopped for a minute and looked at Matt. "Yeah, well that's the heart of it. It can be tough. So many people in the military want to lump me in with the extremists, and it starts right when they first see me. It's pretty discouraging. But usually, once they get to know me and see what I'm really like, they see we're really on the same side. I've just got to work that much harder to earn people's trust, though. BUD/S training was tough because I was really an outsider there. But by the time I got through it, I had bonded with the other guys pretty well. Coming into SEAL Team 8 raised eyebrows again some, but once they got to know me, they trusted me as much as anyone. Now that I'm settled in, it's not an issue any more. Desantos was probably the toughest one to overcome. He's pretty down and dirty Catholic, and it took a while for him to get past me being Muslim, but even he was willing to move past it. And being a SEAL earns me a lot of immediate respect from the rest of the Navy and the Marines."

He added, "It's probably a lot like for the gays in the military. They assume the worst about them so quickly, but once they get to know them a little bit, they see it's a bunch of bullshit — being a good or bad soldier has nothing to do with being gay or straight. Of course, I can't be thrown out of the Navy for being Muslim, but a gay guy can get booted even if he's done nothing but be a good soldier. So anyway, I've got plenty of reason to not apply stupid prejudices against other people."

Matt said, "Yeah, I'm having a hard time deciding if Petey really means what he says or is just joking around."

Baya said, "Shit, I've had Petey call me raghead and Sheik Abdullah so many times I've lost count. By the way, Matt, you held up well against Petey at dinner. He's going to like you. And that's the thing with Petey. He only rides rough on the people he actually likes. And as long as you can hold your own, he'll like you that much more. In the end, he's just having fun. Petey can be pretty scary to people that don't know him, but he's a good guy. You'll see. You keep giving it back to him and you'll wind up wishing he *didn't* like you."

Matt decided that he liked Baya very much.

Matt changed the subject and asked where they had a video game system set up. Baya said that the ready room they were borrowing for the mission had a game system set up in it, but that Petey was the only one that really liked to play against him.

When they got to the ready room being used by the SEALs, Baya started getting the game system ready and Matt looked around a little. The room looked like it was normally set up with a few rows of comfortable, high-backed seats, like there were presentations given in there, but these seats had been pushed around some to clear out a space in the middle with the seats facing in. Along one of the walls behind the seats, he spotted five or six large duffel bags piled up. In addition to the large flatscreen monitor that Baya was switching over to show the game system, there were a lot of checklists on the walls with acronyms that Matt didn't understand, whiteboards with notes, helicopter diagrams, plus some cabinets along the back wall. Taped over one of the boards, though, was a large satellite map.

Just as he was about to get a closer look at the map, Baya said, "You know, Matt, thanks for what you said at dinner earlier."

Matt looked over at Baya, not quite following what he was saying.

"Some of the things we do are pretty tough, and it's not often that we get to really help someone like we did you, aside from other soldiers, I mean. And when we do, we rarely get to actually meet or talk to the people afterwards. Usually, after a mission like this, we would have been gone immediately and we're not even supposed to see or talk to the people we helped. But there's something still going on here. We're waiting for further instructions, which is really unusual. And this time, we get to actually get to know the person we helped. It's kinda nice, you know, to hear someone say the things you said."

Matt nodded thoughtfully and pointed at the map. He asked Baya, "Is this your map?"

Baya glanced at it as he walked over to where Matt was standing. He said, "Yeah. You probably don't even know where you were the whole time you were being held, do you?"

Matt got quiet. It was true. He had no idea where he had been. He whispered, "No, I don't."

Baya showed Matt on the map a canal that went from the Mediterranean Sea inland along the south edge of Latakia. He explained that this is where they took their boat. Then he pointed to a compound of buildings in a less dense area, about a half a mile off the canal.

Baya said, "There. The building you were in was there."

Matt was more than a little fascinated with seeing this. It was probably only a few miles from Tishreen University where he had been staying.

"I don't remember leaving. I passed out just as we got out of the building," he said. "How did you get me to the boat?"

Baya shrugged and said, "Same way we got Stillman's body to the boat. We carried you. Well, Desantos carried Stillman."

Matt remembered now. "Petey mentioned this. I guess I wasn't really listening. It was a guy named Travis, he said."

A voice behind them said, "Any of us would have done it, Peaches."

They turned and Matt saw Mope and Petey coming in the door. Petey had another duffel bag in one hand, a small rifle in the other, and a larger, much more frightening rifle with some kind of complicated scope system on it across his chest. Mope was carrying a smaller bag and another one of the small rifles. Matt wasn't used to seeing people walk around armed to the teeth like this.

It had been Petey that made the comment while walking in. And Matt was on the verge of being impressed with Petey's newfound sincerity, until Petey added sarcastically, "Or, at least I would have if I had thought I might get my knob polished in return."

Petey started setting up in a few of the seats to work on their weapons while Mope put the duffel bags with the others.

Mope reassured Matt, "*Any* of us would have done it, Matt."

Matt asked, "So, wait… who's Travis, then?"

Baya laughed, "That's Mope!"

"A half mile? How did he carry me a *half mile*?" he asked. Matt was incredulous at the thought. He repeated the question to Mope, who was locking up one of the duffel bags in the cabinets in the back of the room, "How did you carry me a half mile?"

Baya seemed almost amused by Matt's questions. "On his back. Desantos already had Stillman. Mope's probably got more endurance than me or Petey, so he carried you while Petey and me leapfrogged in case we ran into hostiles on the way back to the CRRC."

Matt had that odd feeling again, like he didn't deserve what these guys put themselves through to save him. He had to repeat the statement to himself to try and make it really sink in. "Mope carried me a half mile on his back?"

Mope looked over from the duffel bags and repeated, "Any of us would have done it, Matt."

"C'mon, Matt! None of us would have left you there!" said Baya, almost casually, like Matt was being astonished that someone held a door open for him.

Matt stood there, starting to fully understand the extent to which these guys had gone to get him to safety, and what Mope had said earlier in the day up on Vulture's Row came back and haunted him. His doubts about Mope's message and motivation earlier seemed like a horrible, shallow betrayal of the man. He was determined to not let those kinds of paranoid doubts cloud his mind again.

And he never would have imagined having the other thought that started to creep into his mind at that moment. And in fact, he had been dead set against it earlier that day. But the thought was there, nonetheless; if there was going to be another part to this mission, and if there was anything at all Matt could do to help these guys, he'd never be able to live with himself if he didn't. Not after what they had done for him, and then made it sound like it was nothing.

Baya flopped down in one of the seats in front of the flatscreen and said, "Now get your ass over here so I can kick it from here to Saudi Arabia."

While Mope and Petey worked on the scope on one of the rifles, Matt and Baya played the video game for a while. It turned out they were pretty well matched against each other as the car racing game they were playing was one of Matt's favorites. Brian always disliked how much time Matt spent playing video games, but he hadn't been able to shake him of the habit.

When they got tired of that game, Baya went to look for another one of his favorites, and started digging around in one of the duffel bags lying around the ready room. Petey came over to where Baya was and started digging around with him. Mope continued trying to get the scope unstuck from Petey's rifle and cussed at it.

Petey glanced back over at Mope and said, "Better figure it out, Mope, or it'll be just one more thing for your dad to be disappointed in you about."

Matt saw a pronounced scowl pass over Mope's face as he started trying that much harder to fix the scope on the rifle.

Petey pointed down in the bag and told Baya, "Gimme that one, it's my turn to rip off a piece of Tinkerbell's ass now. God knows what I'll catch from that ass, but I want a piece."

Matt slapped his butt a few times for Petey's benefit. "I knew you'd come around. They all do sooner or later."

Chapter 14 – The Bond

Mope said, "Man, you gotta learn not to jerk up like that. How many times will you need to hit your head to learn?"

It took a moment for Matt to shake the sleep off and realize where he was. He finally said foggily, "Dunno." The top of his head was throbbing where he had banged it.

He had been dreaming again about being in the empty room. It started to worry him that maybe he was going to have this dream every time he fell asleep. But, for some reason, it didn't feel like a nightmare, which struck Matt as being a little odd. He would dream he was in the room, alone, but the door would be open. He could sometimes hear a faint whisper, but not like there was someone outside the room waiting to hurt him. If anything, he felt like there was no one there. But he never was quite willing to leave the room. In one way, having the dream bothered him, but then again, since it wasn't scary and didn't feel like a nightmare, he felt like the side-effects of his abduction could be much worse.

"Most people only hit their head once," said Mope.

"I'm not most people, I guess."

Mope was squatting down next to Matt's rack, a serious expression on his face. Matt wondered if he ever smiled.

He asked Mope, "Is something wrong?"

"Nah, nothing's wrong. I just wanted to have a chance to have a talk with you today. Plus there's something else cool we can go do this morning."

Matt knew what he probably wanted to talk about, but he wasn't above being bribed. "What kind of cool thing?"

Mope said, "You'll see. I've got something to go do for a little bit. Go ahead and get your shower and I'll meet you in the mess hall. But if

I'm not there right away, go ahead and eat since you need to be done in thirty minutes. I ate a while ago."

"Ugh, thirty minutes? I don't move that fast in the morning."

"Thirty minutes, Matt. You don't want to miss it. Get moving, sleeping beauty!"

Matt called out to Mope as he left, "You'd better not be turning into Petey!"

~~~~~

Matt and Mope, plus a few other Marines and sailors, stood on the deck of the huge elevator lift as it slowly raised them from the hangar deck of the USS Iwo Jima up to the flight deck.

Mope had taken Matt through the ship's hangar deck, surprising him again by the sheer size of it, given that the hangar deck ran almost its full length, and served as the hangar space for the helicopters, planes, and other equipment. He explained that the planes were vertical liftoff aircraft — mostly Harriers, plus some Ospreys. He took Matt over to the big elevator on the exterior of the ship that was used to lift aircraft from the hangar deck up to the flight deck and said they were going up top for the FOD walk. Matt gave him a blank stare and Mope explained that they stopped all flight ops periodically and got personnel to go topside to look for any stray debris, or foreign object debris, on the flight deck. Mope said it was just a good excuse to get out in the open air a little bit.

As the elevator neared the flight deck, Matt asked "Were those actual missiles I saw down there?"

"Yeah, they are. Navy ships tend to carry a few of those around. They come in handy sometimes."

"Actual missiles? Like explosives? As in bombs?"

Mope nodded. "Yeah, real live bombs. I guess it's probably good I didn't show you what was in the duffel bag Petey carried into the ready room last night."

"Why?" asked Matt, "What was in it?"

"A bunch of fragmentation grenades. Well, that and a lot of ammo for the rifles."

"Yeah, I think I am glad I didn't know," remarked Matt.

It was a beautiful morning, with the sun already up over the horizon, and the water an impossibly sparkling blue. Matt and Mope stepped off the deck of the elevator and onto the flight deck proper. Matt was shocked at how large the space was when he was down on it, as opposed to viewing it from up high in the Vulture's Row.

A crowd of personnel had already gathered to help with the FOD walk, but Mope headed past them towards the very end of the flight deck with Matt right next to him. But the closer he and Matt got to it, the slower Matt walked until he refused to go any further, about ten feet away.

"I don't think I want to get that close to the edge. There's nothing keeping me from falling off."

Mope said, "You're not going to fall off. You'll get a kick out of seeing how high up over the water we are here."

"Uh uh!" said Matt, shaking his head. Even the thought of looking over the edge of the ship to the water below when there was no railing made him dizzy.

Mope said, "Ok, chicken little, let's go over here instead. There's a railing on the starboard side behind the island."

They walked over to the part of the ship that rose up above the flight deck, where the two of them had been up in Vulture's Row the day before. Behind that, along the edge of the deck, was a railing that Matt was only slightly more willing to get close to.

He looked over the edge of the railing and immediately felt queasy at how high up they were. He felt much better when he didn't look directly down at the water far below slipping along the hull of the ship.

He had to admit, the breeze and the morning air felt great, though, and just being outside again was very welcome.

Mope put his boot up on the lower rung and leaned on the railing. "You seemed to settle in pretty good with the guys last night."

Matt nodded in agreement. He had actually wound up having a really good time with them, at dinner and after.

"Petey really likes you, by the way," said Mope. "He was pretty skeptical of you at first, but once you started pushing back, all that changed."

Matt said, "The guy kind of freaks me out. He comes across so intimidating, well all of you are that, but Petey even more so because he's kind of antagonistic."

Mope nodded. "Oh, yeah. And he has that semi-permanent pissed-off look on his ugly mug. The funny thing is, Petey comes across antagonistic and like he doesn't give a shit about anyone. But once he's on your side, he's *really* on your side. He's one of the most loyal people I know."

Matt immediately noticed the rare smile creep across Mope's face as he added, "Just don't get into a wrestling match with him. He's deadly when it comes to hand to hand combat, and ridiculously fast. Probably better than anybody else on SEAL Team 8 at hand-to-hand."

They stood at the railing in silence for a moment before Mope started to shift the conversation and said, "I hope..."

Matt took a deep breath and immediately interrupted him. "Was all that, last night... was all that *just* to get me to help you guys? I need to know, Mope. Was it all just put on?"

Mope looked Matt squarely in the eye. "It's important to you that it be real, isn't it?"

Matt just watched Mope, waiting on an answer to his question.

Mope said, "I give you my word as a SEAL, Matt. Nothing about last night was arranged or put on to convince you of anything. The guys like you. You're an easy guy to like. We don't wind up in this situation often, where we get to know someone that we've helped out of a bad spot. We all wish we could, actually, but it's the nature of what we do that we can't. Normally, we would have already left long before now and someone like you would never know our names, or even see us. But this time, given the opportunity we have, we've been ordered to stay put."

"The guys appreciated hearing you thank them directly, too," continued Mope. "Hell, it even got Petey to shut his yap for a minute, and we're *all* grateful for that, any way we can get it. I appreciated what you said, too, by the way. A lot."

Mope set his jaw firmly, and Matt could tell he was thinking intensely about something. He watched Mope, and for the first time noticed the scar over his right eye, cutting a little more than an inch through his eyebrow.

"We, uh... we don't often... I, mmm... never mind," said Mope, scratching at his nose a little.

Matt asked, "Mope, do you mind if I ask you a question?"

"Anything."

"Does it bother you being gay and being a SEAL? I mean, the bond between you guys has to be really deep. Like you said, faith and trust are fundamentally important. Life and death important. Does hiding who you are bother you?"

Mope thought about it a little bit. "I'm a SEAL, Matt. And I'm gay. But the two things don't really have much to do with one another. As a SEAL, training and real missions are treated the same. We give the same discipline, focus, and complete dedication on both. The bond that needs to exist between me and Petey, Baya and Desantos, or the rest of the platoon, or the rest of my SEAL team, would be the same whether I was straight or gay. Actually, that bond is deeper than gay or straight. It's survival. I would give my life, without hesitation, to protect or save any other member of my SEAL team, just as they would do for me. Do I think that they'd care if they knew about me? Probably not. But is it worth risking that bond over? No. Especially when it's not relevant."

Matt said, "But still, don't you feel like you're hiding from them, especially since being gay *is* an important part?"

Mope frowned for a moment. "I look at it this way... I'm not hiding anything from them that really matters. As a person, I may be gay, and that may be an intrinsic part of me as a person. But as a SEAL, it's just irrelevant. I may have become a SEAL for the wrong reason seven years ago, Matt, but I'm good at it. And I love doing it, and I'm really proud of it. It may seem sappy to some people, but it's an honor and a privilege to serve my country and my team in a way that very few others can. But being a SEAL means a lot of personal sacrifices, and *one* of those sacrifices, for me, is the personal choice to leave the gay aspect of myself out of it entirely and to focus on the things that I consider to be far more important."

Mope reflected, then added wryly, "Besides, I suck at being gay. I'm a really good SEAL, but I stink at being gay."

Matt laughed out loud. "What do you mean?"

Mope let a tiny smile escape. "What Desantos said last night was true. Being a SEAL makes having a relationship pretty difficult. SEALs can and do have relationships, even get married, but it's really tough. So I've already got that working against me. Next," said Mope, thumping his ear with his forefinger, "C'mon... look at these ears sticking out from my head. My dad always said I looked like a taxi driving around with the doors wide open. And my nose looks like a twisty mountain road. I'm not exactly the pretty boy in the bar. And then, if I *can* manage to get someone's attention, I don't know how to talk to them. I mean, I'm not a total loser, but it's hard to relate. And I can't talk much about me, so guys find it hard to relate to me."

Matt felt there were so many things wrong with what Mope had said that he didn't know where to start. Sure, Mope didn't have the pretty, magazine-cover model looks that someone like Brian might have, but that definitely didn't mean he wasn't good looking. He was built like a rock-solid wrestler, and his face was naturally masculine. Frankly, Matt believed that if guys were put off by his appearance, it was far more likely because they were intimidated by him than finding him unattractive. And if guys didn't feel comfortable approaching him because of that, then it was their loss.

Rather than start arguing all this with Mope right then, though, Matt asked, "So, do you never get to be with guys?"

"No, I do. I manage to get the occasional date here and there, or I'll just trick out with someone, but other than the physical sex part, it's rarely been very satisfying. Sometimes, the guys think I'm an idiot for being gay and in the military at all, which I personally find insulting. I fucking hate when guys are like that. Some guys want to bitch at me about US foreign policy, like I'm the one making those decisions somehow. Others just want me to have sex with them while I'm wearing the sailor uniform. It's not encouraging when that's the majority of the experiences I've had."

"You've never had an actual boyfriend, then? Maybe before you became a SEAL?"

"I did, but it was brief. About five years ago... this was after I'd been a SEAL for a couple of years... I met this guy at a bar and we started going out. He was just a regular guy type, and I really liked that. But I couldn't tell him what I did, other than just to say I was in the Navy. And then I'd have to go off for periods of time. Sometimes it was training and I could tell him where it was, but if it was a mission, I couldn't say anything. Half the time, I couldn't even tell him when I'd be back. He had this suspicious and jealous side that started showing itself and assumed I was sleeping around on him everywhere I went. I guess I don't blame him. I just couldn't tell him the things that would help him understand. We broke up after trying to make it work for about four or five months. The second half of that time got pretty painful, but the first half was good, and I liked it... I liked having someone."

"No one before that, though?"

Mope shrugged. "Nah, he was pretty much the only one. Up until exactly one week before I went into SEAL training, when I was twenty-three, I had no idea I even *might* be gay. I dated girls through high school and college without a second thought, and I thought all that was fine. But then the week before BUD/S training started, I got wasted drunk. Totally trashed. I wound up waking up next to a person that I didn't know. All I remembered was that it had been really great. Better than anything before. Imagine my surprise when I realized that the person next to me was a guy. I kind of freaked out about it. Then I went into BUD/S and had to push all that out of my mind. Well, for the most part, at least. BUD/S training is pretty excruciating, by the way, but in the occasional moments I had to myself, I thought about it and realized the truth. And I accepted it. I came out of BUD/S training a fundamentally different person than I was when I went in, in more ways than one."

They both were silent for a long while, each lost in their own thoughts. After listening to his story, Matt could not think of a single person he admired more than Mope.

These men didn't have to open the door that they found him behind. They already had what they had come to that building for. They had Eric Stillman and his laptop. They didn't need to add any risk by opening another door that they had no knowledge of what was behind it. But they did. And on top of what they already had to get back to the ship, they took him, too. They carried his unconscious body a half a mile through country they weren't supposed to be in to get him to safety.

Matt took a few deep breaths. Something inside him felt different, and his absolute conviction from the prior morning, to get home as fast as possible and away from all this, had done a one hundred and eighty degree turn. If Mope was bullshitting about the things he had said about faith and trust, then he was the best liar in the world. But Matt didn't think he was lying. In the span of a day, he had come to see Mope as one of the most principled people he knew. And now Matt felt himself about to take a leap of faith based on this, even as the thought of taking that leap of faith scared the bejeezus out of him. Almost more frightening, Matt realized that the leap of faith in front of him wasn't just in these men, it was a leap of faith in himself, too.

It would be so easy to walk away from this, to take the easy road out. But everything that had happened to him had been so extraordinary, these people he found himself with for even a few days were so extraordinary, that deep down he knew it would be a terrible thing to turn his back on them. It would be terrible to turn his back on the change he was feeling down inside of himself. He felt like he would perhaps regret what he was about to say, but he knew he'd surely regret *not* saying it far more. He looked up into the clear sky of the sunlit morning off the coast of Syria, forcing himself to find a kind of resolve he had never needed before.

Mope finally prompted him, "So, what're you thinking about, Matt?"

Matt looked Mope in the eye with an odd mix of resignation and resolve. He took a deep breath. "I'm in, Mope," he said. "I don't know what you want me to do, but I'm in."

Mope nodded. He said, "You'll do good and it'll be fine. You *are* the mission, Matt. Don't forget that."

Chapter 15 — Creed

Petey, Desantos, and Baya sat on the floor of the hangar deck while Mope squatted in his preferred crouching position. Together, they discussed aspects of the mission — strategies, failure points, contingencies, weapons choices, and so on. Matt, having heard the plan, sat with them but could only manage to stare at the floor in front of him.

Earlier that morning with Mope, he had signed on, so the mission was officially a go for the following night. Randall had joined them in a staging area on the hangar deck now reserved for them and reviewed key aspects of what the mission was to be. Randall had spent time with them, talked them through the "snag-n-bag" as they all referred to it, and had left to take care of his own preparations. Now, with that initial briefing over, the reality of what Matt was being asked to do began to hit him. And it was hitting him hard. Matt stared at the floor, wondering if he was really ready for this after all, no matter how good his intentions.

Matt wasn't even really listening to the SEALs, but Mope, who was right next to him, at some point put his hand on Matt's back to get his attention. He leaned over and whispered into Matt's ear, "Remember what I said about you being this mission, Matt. Listen carefully to what you're about to hear..."

Mope stood up and snapped into a rigid posture, his eyes fixed determinedly ahead. To Matt, it looked like a two-ton cement truck could hit Mope head on and he wouldn't budge an inch. Mope barked loudly, "Fire team!" It made Matt jump it was so sudden.

Immediately, with no arguments, discussion, confused looks, or hesitation, the other three team members jumped up and into the same rock-like position of attention as Mope.

Mope boomed again, his deep voice reverberating through the hangar deck, "Fire team! Who are we?"

All four of them responded in exact unison, "We are SEAL Team 8!"

Mope shouted, his deep voice drawing the attention of almost everyone on the hangar deck, "Fire team! SEAL Team 8 has a creed! What is that creed?"

Again, all four shouted the response in the same practiced unison, "We are SEAL Team 8! We exist to serve our mission, to fight for our brothers, and to defend our country! Even with our last bullet! Even with our last breath! *We do not fail!*"

Even when finished, all four of them stood stock still, eyes locked straight ahead. Matt watched this and felt strange. He felt almost uncomfortable by what he saw. There wasn't the slightest hint of sarcasm or irony or complacency in their words or their faces. They meant each word that came out of their mouths. Matt was feeling the same way he felt the day before when Mope had talked about courage, and faith, and trust. What was making him uncomfortable was that he realized that he had never been committed to anything in his life to the degree this team was. He had that luxury, and he felt the poorer for it. It made him feel ashamed, but it inspired him, too.

Suddenly, the words "we exist to serve our mission" reverberated through him. He understood the message Mope was sending him through this. If Matt couldn't have confidence in these men around him right now, then would there ever be *anything* in his life that he *could* believe in?

Matt desperately wanted to not let these guys down. He wanted to be worthy of the risk that they had already put themselves at to save his life, and the risk they were about to put themselves at again. He never wanted anything so badly in his entire life.

Mope finally said to the team, "As you were, men," and all four relaxed out of their rigid poses and looked over at Matt.

"Mope, Colorado, Baya, Desantos..." said Matt, quietly, "I swear to God, I'll do everything I can to not disappoint you guys."

Baya was the one that spoke and said, "You'll do fine, Matt. And we'll be there."

That was the key, though. That was what actually made this tough for Matt. The plan that Randall had laid out didn't require Matt to hardly do anything. He just had to be at a specific café for a while, and then leave. The thing that hadn't hit Matt until he heard Randall describe the plan was that he'd be alone.

The SEALs would be there, somewhere, but invisible, and Matt would not see them. If Matt could see them, then the targets could, too, and that would be failure. Matt would have to have a faith that he had never had before. But after listening to them recite their team creed, the thought reverberated through him again — if he couldn't have that faith in these guys, then what could he?

Petey, as was usual for him, managed to break up the seriousness, though. He said, "Hey, Skip Chicks, how about this for some motivation... when this is over tomorrow night, I'll let you blow me like you've been begging to do. Huh?"

Matt smiled in spite of himself. He pushed the hair out of his forehead and said to Petey, "Colorado, I'd have to get a tetanus shot before going down on that tiny, rusty thumbtack of a dick you've got."

Petey laughed and shook his head, "Ok, we're going to settle this once and for all. You keep accusing me of having a tiny dick. Let's see who has the tiny dick."

So right there, in the wide open space of the hangar deck of the USS Iwo Jima, Petey reached down and pulled his pants and boxers shorts down so that his dick, with its scorching red bush, was fully exposed for everyone to see. Even the nearby flight ops personnel and maintenance guys started clapping and whistling at Petey.

Petey issued the challenge, "Okay, you big bag of homo, let's see how *you* measure up to this here prime Navy cannon!"

Baya and Desantos started laughing, and even Mope had a slight grin. Matt groaned and mumbled, "Shit, I can't believe I'm doing this." He stood up, unbuttoned his pants, and pulled them down in front of everyone. Both Desantos and Baya started laughing hysterically and Matt spun around with his arms out so all the flight ops and maintenance guys within eyesight could get a good look as well. Anybody that was near enough to watch stopped what they were doing and started hooting and yelling.

What was clear to everyone was that Matt had Petey beat, easily. Even soft, Matt's dick was probably twice as big.

Mope held out his hands and shrugged in sympathy for Petey. He said, "Sorry, Colorado, you lose. You know what this means..."

Petey cursed, "Goddammit!" He glared at Matt, "Mary Fagdalene, this is all your fault!" Petey looked over at Mope, clearly disgusted. "How many?" he asked.

Mope said, "Give me ten, Colorado!"

Matt and Petey both pulled their pants up, but Matt was completely lost and had no idea what Petey and Mope were talking about.

96

Mope and Petey walked a few feet away to where the bulkhead of the hangar deck was. Matt looked over at Desantos, confused. Desantos said, "Petey's gotta do ten v-ups. They're vertical push-ups. If you've never seen them... watch this."

Petey got next to the wall and did a handstand with Mope helping him to find his balance. Once Petey was reasonably balanced and his feet only barely touched the wall to keep him upright, they all counted off as he performed ten push-ups in a row this way. Matt stared in disbelief, his mouth hanging open stupidly. He had never seen anyone perform push-ups while in a completely vertical handstand.

When Petey was done and had stood back up, Matt said, "That was... amazing, Petey!"

But Desantos said, "C'mon Mope! Why don't you show off a little! Show him the real thing!"

Petey frowned and said, "Yeah, no reason for *me* to be the only one doing this shit!"

Mope looked around, rubbed his hands together, and said, "Okay, five each."

Unlike Petey, no one helped Mope and he didn't use the wall to keep his balance.

Mope flipped up into the handstand position and held for a second until he was sure he had the proper balance. And to Matt's utter amazement, Mope shifted his center of gravity slightly and lifted his left arm off the ground so his entire body was supported on his right arm. In this position, and with one arm, he proceeded to lower and lift his entire body five times. When he finished those, he carefully shifted over to his left arm and performed five more repetitions with just that arm. Mope stood back up, and for the first time, Matt saw a broad smile across Mope's face. The crowd of hangar personnel and even Marines that had gathered to watch the demonstration all talked amongst themselves and shook their heads in amazement. Matt thought to himself that if Mope would just smile like that in a bar, he'd have no problems meeting plenty of guys.

Petey yelled at him, "Mope, you fucking ham!"

Mope said, "Alright, alright, enough goofing-off. We've got a mission to prepare for. I need to go get some detailed sat images pulled so we can plan. Matt, why don't you go relax. We'll grab you later when it's time for chow."

"Hey, would it be ok if I went and made some calls back home?" asked Matt.

Petey said, "I'll take him and catch up with you guys in the ready room in a little bit."

Petey and Matt headed off forward, towards the bow of the ship, where the comm room that Matt had used the day before was. Petey asked, "So, Princess Buttery Goodend, does that butt buddy of yours let you stick that big thing you've got up his ass?"

Matt pushed on Petey's shoulder playfully and said, "Jesus, Petey, do you sit up at night thinking these names up?"

Petey shrugged and said, "Hey, don't get all uppity at me. That's the name I saw on the nameplate outside your cabin."

Matt pushed the hair out of his forehead and replied, "Fuck you. And it's none of your business what me and my boyfriend do."

Petey made a sour face at Matt and said, "I'll take that as a yes."

To Matt's surprise, Petey didn't just drop him off at the comm room. While the comm officer "set it up" so he could call back to the states (which Matt now had a good idea what that really meant), Petey settled into a spare chair to wait. Matt wasn't sure he wanted Petey listening to his conversation, but hell, who knew how many other people were listening to it anyway.

With the time difference, Brian had just gotten into work for his morning when he answered the phone.

Brian said, "Hey, baby! I'm glad you called. I sent you an email, but you don't seem to think I'm worth returning emails to now."

"Yeah, I want to. I just haven't been able to send emails right now." Matt closed his eyes so he could focus entirely on the sound of Brian's voice. He missed him and he missed home so much.

"So, I was still half asleep when you called yesterday, but you sounded a little funny and upset. Are you sure everything's ok?"

Matt said, "I can't go into it much. I tried to explain a little yesterday, but I don't think you were able to focus very well. I ran into a little problem while over here and... the Navy happened to be there and helped me out. I'm with them right now." Matt glanced over at Petey, who was sitting there listening to every word he said.

There was a pregnant pause, then Brian said, alarmed, "Wait... what?! I don't remember any of this from your call yesterday! Are you sure you're ok? When are you coming home?"

"I'm fine, Brian, I promise. I think I'll be coming home in a couple of days. I'll have to let you know when they've scheduled a way to get me home."

"Ok, but tell me what happened. What kind of trouble?"

"I'm sorry, Brian, I really can't talk about it right now."

"What do you mean you can't talk about it right now? I'm your fucking boyfriend, Matt! You'd better tell me! What happened?"

"Brian, I want to, but I can't. I've been specifically asked to not discuss it. With anyone. Just give me some slack on this right now, ok?"

Brian sounded hurt and pissed all at the same time. "I can't believe you don't trust me. Is all this just you trying to pick some kind of fight with me for some reason?" The tone in Brian's voice upset Matt. He didn't like being accused of not trusting him, not right now. And how the hell could Brian think this was all just about picking a fight with him?

Matt said, his voice cracking, "Brian, I'm not trying to pick a fight with you! And this isn't about trusting you or not trusting you!"

Matt caught a glimpse of Petey out of the corner of his eye, who could hear that the conversation wasn't going well. Petey looked mad, like he was about to grab the handset from Matt and give this Brian guy something to think about. Matt held out his hand to stop him. That would be the last thing he needed right then.

Brian's voice rose on the phone and Matt had to almost shout to interrupt him. He said to Brian, "Brian! *Brian!* Listen to me! I've got to go right now. I'll call you when I know more about when I'm coming home. I love you, Brian!"

Brian said angrily, "Wait, I'm not done talking..."

Matt interrupted again, "I have to go *now*, Brian. I love you."

Brian replied, "Fine," and hung up.

Matt looked over at Petey, embarrassed by the call, but Petey didn't say anything. Instead, Petey sat next to him, fighting to keep his anger in check.

Matt couldn't face Petey at that moment, so he looked the other way while he called Jim next.

Jim was glad to hear from him again, and asked if Matt knew yet when he'd be coming home. He wanted to know if Matt could tell him more about what had happened now, but Matt reminded him he still couldn't talk about it, and Jim didn't press it. Jim did mention that Matt still sounded a little upset, but Matt explained about the call he had just made to Brian. Jim's reply was that Brian's reaction didn't surprise him. Jim ended by saying that he and Bret were still worried about Matt, and that it was good to hear from him.

Finally, Matt called Bret, who immediately wanted to know what all was going on. Matt explained yet again that he couldn't talk about it, to which Bret said Matt was going to have some heavy explaining to do once he did get home. Next, Bret wanted to know what ship Matt was on, and Matt wasn't sure he was allowed to say, so he demurred on that question as well. Matt asked if Bret had gone to watch Jim at softball practice, trying to distract him from a lot of other questions, which actually worked pretty well. Bret told Matt he wanted him home soon, and to call him or Jim anytime day or night if there was anything they could do.

When Matt ended the call, he looked blankly at the handset for a moment. He really hoped that he would indeed see them all again. What he had committed himself to doing inserted itself into his mind again, and he hoped he was making the right decision.

He turned around to see Petey staring a hole in his back, his arms still crossed across his chest, and a look on his face that could blister paint off a car.

Matt said, "I'm going back to my rack."

Petey stood up and said harshly, "Your boyfriend, Brian, did he say he loved you?"

"Relax, Colorado, he's just wound up right now. He was mostly asleep when I talked to him yesterday." Matt called him Colorado and tried to brush it all off as unimportant. But Matt felt a slight pang when he remembered that he was almost certain he heard another voice in the room with Brian when he talked to him before he had been abducted.

Petey's expression didn't change. He asked insistently, "Did that jerkoff say he loved you, Matt?"

Matt didn't answer.

"What about the other two guys you called... they friends of yours?"

Matt was happy enough to change the subject. "Yeah, Bret and Jim. My two best friends."

Petey nodded in approval. "Good. They seem like good friends."

Petey left Matt to go to the ready room while Matt went back to his rack. When he got back to his cabin, taped right on the door was a sign that had been printed up that said "Princess Buttery Goodend". Matt pulled the sign down and crumpled it up, but he couldn't help but chuckle to himself. He wondered how long it had been there. Two Marines coming down the passageway saw Matt at the door and both bowed slightly as they passed him. One said, "Your Majesty" in deference to Matt, followed by snickers as they continued on their way. They had obviously been down the passage at some point already.

Matt got in his bunk and started thinking over the plan for the next night. It made him nervous, but he needed to have it down.

Randall had said there were actually two parts to the mission, but the first part was really for the embassy in Damascus. They felt that someone in the embassy was leaking information, which is how the targets knew that there was information on Eric's laptop that they wanted. Randall said they had an idea who was leaking the information, so they had already made sure this person knew Eric was still alive, still in Latakia, and that he'd be at a specific restaurant the next night before heading back to the embassy in Damascus the following day. If they had the right leak, then this would give the bad guys the information they needed to try again.

The second part of the mission was for Matt and the SEALs. They'd get Matt back into Latakia, and all he had to do was to go to that café at 9pm, have a leisurely dinner and leave at 11pm. The key was that he needed to leave a certain way. Hopefully, like the previous time, the targets would try and grab Matt after he left the café, but this time the SEALs would be there to grab them, instead. Matt had asked what would happen if they tried to grab him while at the café. Randall didn't think they would, as that would be too brazen for them. Mope assured Matt, though, that Baya would be acting as a sniper, keeping an eye on Matt while he was at the restaurant, and if anyone tried anything there, they would simply get shot.

Randall had admitted that the entire plan might result in nothing, in which case Matt was to get back to the *Iwo Jima*. From there, Randall would see to it that he got home.

Matt hoped that it really would be that easy. All he had to do was have dinner and then leave. The rest was out of his hands. What scared him was that he would not see the SEALs. He would just have to trust that they were actually there.

He just had to have faith that Mope, Petey, Desantos and Baya were actually there, somewhere, when the shit hit the fan.

Chapter 16 — It Doesn't Have To Be Like This

After dinner that evening, Matt went to the ready room to hang out while the team made a few arrangements in the staging area. Baya had told Matt to dig around in his bag and grab whatever video games he wanted and crank them up. He found a few that he liked and had started playing one by himself for about thirty minutes before Desantos showed up to grab a duffel bag out of one of the locked cabinets in the back.

Matt paused the game. He had wanted to catch Desantos alone for a moment anyway. A subtle vibe he had gotten from him and then something Baya had said left him with something he wanted to talk about.

He asked, "Hey, Desantos, you got a second?"

Desantos finished locking up the cabinet. He put the bag down on one of the seats and said, "Sure."

Matt wasn't sure how to approach this. He decided direct was best. "Look, I know that I'm the outsider here, but are you uncomfortable with me being gay?"

He didn't ask it accusingly. He just wanted to know. Desantos hadn't seemed quite as comfortable around Matt as Mope, Petey and Baya had, and on top of that Baya had said Desantos was pretty Catholic.

Desantos flopped down in one of the seats next to the duffel bag and said, "Let me guess... you've been talking to Baya, haven't you? The short answer is that yes, I'm a Christian and yes, I'm a Catholic. But I don't really have a problem with you being gay. I think all of us need to be right with God in the end, and I think that people that insist on being gay aren't right with God. But, unlike a lot of people, I know it's not my place to sit in judgment of anyone. In the end, it's between you and God."

Matt wasn't sure what to think of this answer. He would have expected a Catholic person to pretty much demonize him like so many Christians seem so bent on doing.

Desantos sat forward in the seat a little and regarded Matt carefully. "To be honest, I haven't been around that many people that were openly gay, so it hasn't come up that much. If it makes you feel any better, I think it's good you're willing to help on this mission. A lot of people wouldn't, especially after what happened to you already."

He added, "And frankly, I don't know what Mope did to convince you. None of us expected you to sign up for this. Not even close. But Mope seems to have a knack for bringing out the best in people. I guess that's why he's an obvious person to be one of the leaders in Team 8 and leader of this fire team when we're put together."

Matt nodded. He laughed and said, "Yeah, Mope was really good at appealing to whatever latent principles I had laying around being unused. I guess there's no sense in letting them go completely to waste."

"So, this is kind of an awkward question," asked Matt, "but are you really willing to help make sure I'm okay on a mission like this? I mean, a lot of people with strong religious convictions wouldn't be too happy about having someone gay around that they have to look out for in this situation."

"I said it's not my place to sit in judgment of you, Matt," said Desantos, "and I meant it. As much as other Christians feel like it's their place to do that, I don't. And I don't think it's theirs, either."

"You heard our creed today," he continued, "and Wickland has made it clear to us that our top priority is to ensure your safety. After that, if we can grab some of these guys, then we grab them. When I repeat that creed, I mean it without reservation every single time. All of us do. So in answer to the question that you may not even realize you're asking — I will ensure your safety on this mission, or die trying. I would do the same for Baya and Colorado, and I don't really think they're all that right with God, either. But that doesn't mean I can be less than one hundred percent committed to my mission and my team. I mean that, Matt."

Matt felt better hearing this, but still couldn't quite get a handle on Desantos' attitude. Maybe he just wasn't used to someone that seemed to have a strong religious faith, but did what he did for a living. Someone that could see people going to hell, and yet be willing to lay down his life for those people. Actually, when he thought about it like that, it didn't seem totally incompatible with the Christian faith; it actually seemed kind of central to it. It just made so many other

Christians seem to be the ones that didn't quite get it. At any rate, Matt felt reassured that Desantos didn't seem to resent him, and he felt reassured that he would still be there to help if it came to that.

Matt asked, "I wonder why it is that you and Baya, given your backgrounds, can trust each other so completely, be willing to die for each other, and yet so many Muslims and Christians seem to only be able to assume the worst about each other."

Desantos looked thoughtful as he considered Matt and what he had said. "I don't know, Matt. I wish I did. I'm glad you see it. God knows Baya and I have talked about it a lot."

Baya had walked into the ready room as Desantos was speaking, and sat down in the chair across from them. He said, "What's crazy is that it doesn't have to be like this. Christians and Muslims and even Jews have lived side by side in the past with no problem. It seems like a lot of religion, on all sides, has shifted from being about a person's own relationship with their God to more about blaming and vilifying others. And what we get is the world we see today. Living together isn't that hard and yet the human race seems to suck at it. I'm glad Tony here has a more open mind than most. I'd hate to have to get all jihad on him." He grinned when he said the last sentence and Desantos flipped him a good-natured bird with his middle finger.

Desantos said, "Listen to that BS coming out of his mouth! Mostly, it's us against Petey, anyway. Me, Baya, and Mope all have to band together a lot just to keep Petey on some kind of a leash. Yesterday afternoon when you two blew up at each other in the passage, I thought we were going to wind up having to pull Petey off of you. And you really don't want Petey going after you in an enclosed space. It's a good way to get killed."

Everyone seemed to think Petey was so dangerous and Matt wondered if they were serious or just joking around. He had a hard time thinking of Petey that way now. But that scene after lunch also felt like a long time ago to Matt at this point.

Petey warned, "Dicklips isn't out of the woods yet." He walked in and sat down in one of the other chairs in the ready room. He gave Matt a silent, acidic stare through narrow eyes and his chin jutted out. "You think you can go a round against me, faggot? You wanna try?"

Matt knew better than to back down. Not against Petey. Without hesitating and without warning, he pretended to suddenly lunge out of his chair and at Petey, which took *all* of them off guard. Petey actually flinched before he realized Matt was standing there and laughing at him. Baya and Desantos both started laughing, enjoying the rare sight of Petey being caught off-guard like that.

Even Petey grinned and shook his head. He jumped up and chased Matt around some of the chairs shouting, "You've got some stainless steel balls to try that kind of bullshit around me, you little ass-biter!!" It took barely a second for Petey to catch Matt and put him in a headlock and to get his legs around Matt's, totally immobilizing him. For a moment, Matt got worried, but then Petey just wound up giving him an Indian rub on his head, which made Matt laugh that much harder.

When Petey let go, Matt said through his laughter, "Ouch, asshole! That actually hurt!"

Petey raised his voice a few octaves and mocked Matt, "Ow! Stop It! You're making my tampon get all wadded up!"

Matt said, "Eat my ass, Colorado. If you guys are done for the night, get over here, and we'll take this fight up onto the flatscreen and see who the wadded up tampon is!"

Petey came over and sat down next to Matt so they could play the video games.

Matt said, "Yeah, that's what I thought. Petey wants his spanking. Baya... you're up next, so don't go anywhere!"

Chapter 17 – The Accidents

Matt sat in the staging area on the hangar deck with the SEALs, going over some of the remaining details that applied to him. The hangar deck was much quieter than usual that afternoon as there weren't any planned flights for the next five hours or so and the flight deck above them was inactive. Talking through things, the team constantly re-assured Matt that this would go off without a hitch, and that was only if anything happened at all. If the person Randall had fed information to at the embassy wasn't the leak, or if the targets smelled any kind of a trap, then nothing would happen. Still, the anxiety level in Matt increased the closer they got to the time for everything to be put into motion.

In a few hours, he'd get on a boat, a CRRC as they called it, but which was nothing more than a small rubber boat as far as Matt was concerned, and they'd go to a pre-arranged meeting place off the coast of Latakia. Randall had worked with the British consulate in Latakia to have them charter a small boat for the day and take a few consulate employees out for an afternoon of fishing. Matt would transfer to their boat and when they got back to Latakia, he would simply be one of the consulate employees that had been out for the afternoon. He would stay with them and be a welcome guest of the British consulate until time for him to go to the café later that evening.

Matt dreaded the boat ride. Why did it have to be such a small boat? Surrounded by water? He wasn't sure if he'd be able to handle even the first simple step in this whole plan.

He did everything he could to distract himself from the idea of the little boat. He thought about softball. He thought about Bret and Jim. Then he thought about Brian, which made him think of the last phone call he had made to him, the day before, that had turned very frustrating. Instead, he tried to focus on his promise to himself, the promise he had made just a few days before, to be a better boyfriend and to appreciate Brian more. Despite their quarrel on the phone call, he couldn't wait to get home to Brian, warm and familiar and safe. His mind drifted back to the moment Mope and Baya had busted into the room where he had been kept and how terrifying they were, probably more so than the men that were going to wind up killing him. This triggered a memory in Matt, something he had wondered about but hadn't asked yet.

"Hey, how do you guys talk to one another without talking?"

Mope looked over at Matt and asked, "Huh?"

"When you guys broke into the room to get me out, I remember thinking that you were talking to each other, but I never heard you say anything."

Mope nodded in understanding, "Oh, yeah. The AARDVAARCs. That's what you're asking about."

"AARDVAARCs?" asked Matt.

Mope started digging around in a duffel bag. "Yeah. It stands for Acoustic Relay Something Something. Uh, Baya, what does that stand for again? I can never really remember it."

"Antipodal Attenuation Relay Device for Voice Analysis And Realtime Communication," said Baya. He tilted his head and then snarked, "You know, I should get an extra hundred bucks every time I remember that for you."

Mope waved at Baya impatiently, "Yeah, yeah. Starting next paycheck. I swear."

Mope looked back over to Matt and added, "It's a specialized comm system we use. It can take barely audible whispers and amplify them so they sound like a regular voice. We're all tied in to each other while on the mission. We can have conversations that sound like our normal speaking voices while never actually talking in anything more than the slightest whisper."

Mope found what he was looking for and showed Matt. There was a small pack attached to a wire than ran up to an earpiece, which in turn had a tiny microphone boom hanging down from it. The microphone boom, though, was bent into an odd hook at the mouth end. Mope showed him by hooking the mic boom inside his mouth, then putting the earpiece on.

"The mic actually goes inside your mouth, like this," he explained. He handed another one to Matt and said, "Here, you can try it. Put it on like I did. I'm assuming you don't mind getting Desantos' nasty slobber in your mouth."

Matt was curious and said, "Sacrifices, you know," before putting it on.

Desantos scowled at them and said, "Hey, I'm right here, guys. You're not whispering yet, assholes! And now I'm going to need to bleach that thing before I use it. I notice you're not at all sympathetic about that, Mope."

Mope turned on his AARDVAARC unit and Matt's and then said in a normal voice, "You should be able to hear me at a normal volume in your ear, right?"

Matt nodded.

Next, Mope whispered in a voice that normally even he wouldn't be able to hear, "And you can still hear me and it sounds just like I'm speaking in a normal voice, right?"

Matt's eyes got huge and he said, "Holy shit!" Then he said more softly, "Sorry, didn't mean to yell like that."

Mope whispered, "Doesn't matter, the system amplifies or attenuates so that what comes out in the earpiece is always perfectly audible. It takes into account ambient noise levels as well, so gunfire, explosions, whatever, won't drown out the voices. These things came along about the same time I joined the SEALs, and man, do they help."

Matt and Mope tried it a few times and Matt was very impressed with the technology. It made perfect sense now how he would see them make hand gestures like they were talking, but never hear anything. And with the fact that they wore the black masks over the bottom half of their faces, he couldn't see their mouths moving.

He handed the AARDVAARC back to Mope and said, "I've never heard of anything like this!"

Mope said, "Yeah, classified stuff. This will be yet one more of those things you won't ever be able to talk about."

Mope put the two AARDVAARCs up and said, "Ok, Matt, I need to take you with me to go get the clothes Randall pulled together for you to wear tonight. The BDU you have on now clearly won't work."

They headed off, but when they got out of the hangar deck, Mope took a path that didn't lead towards where Randall was usually set up.

"Where're we going?" Matt asked.

"I wanted a chance to talk to you a minute first."

Mope led Matt up, back out onto the flight deck. Since there was no planned flight ops, personnel were allowed out on it, and there was even some people running laps around the deck. It was another brilliantly sunny day, and getting a little warm in the afternoon, but Matt still liked getting out in the open again.

Rather than going to the railing they had spoke at the day before, they found a spot at the base of the island and sat down looking out across the massive flight deck.

Mope studied Matt gravely and asked, "You ok, Matt? Seriously. I don't want a pat answer."

Matt said, "Yeah. I'm ok. I mean, I'm nervous, but I'll be ok. I just need to focus on how little I really need to do."

"I guarantee you, Matt, we'll be there. There's no way we're going to leave you dangling there alone."

Matt nodded, exhaled deeply, and looked off in the distance. He chuckled once, weakly and said, "I know. I can count on you guys more than I can count on myself."

Mope's baritone voice replied, quiet, but authoritative, "You're more capable than you give yourself credit for."

Matt nodded and certainly hoped that was the case.

Mope asked, "The boat part bothers you, doesn't it?"

Matt nodded again.

"What happened? Why are you so afraid of the water, Matt?"

"I was eight and me and my mom and dad had gone out west for a trip, to see the Grand Canyon and all that. Another family that was friends with my parents went, too, with their four kids, all about my age. I didn't get along with them very much, though, and they didn't really like me. Well, one afternoon, we all went out on a rented boat in Lake Powell. My parents and their friends had been drinking some, and they weren't wasted, but they weren't totally together, either. At some point, I was leaning over the side of the boat, and fell out. I hit my head as I fell out, but I fortunately had a life jacket on. I didn't pass out, but I was woozy for a minute or two. When I looked around, they were just gone and I was in the middle of a huge lake. I was there for four hours before they realized I was missing and found me again. Turns out the other kids realized I was gone, but they didn't say anything because they didn't like me. I didn't know how to swim, and for four hours my imagination went wild with all kinds of terrible things swimming around under me, waiting to eat me. That and, since the sun started to go down, I imagined being out there at night, which freaked me out even more. So after that, I've never liked boats or the water very much. My parents couldn't even get me into so much as a bathtub for weeks afterwards. I went to see a kiddie shrink for months and months for the abandonment issues I had as a result."

"Your parents didn't go for help?" asked Mope.

"No, they said they didn't want to go any further away from where I got lost than they already were. I think part of it, too, though was that they were afraid to ask for help since they had been drinking a little."

Mope said, genuinely sympathetic, "I'm sorry that happened. It's hard for me to understand what it would be like to be so afraid of the water. I've always loved being in the water. I'm probably more comfortable in the water than I am out of it. You sure you'll be ok on the CRRC?"

"As long as you guys are there."

Mope nodded.

"Mope, can I ask you a question?"

"Shoot."

"Yesterday, when we were talking, you mentioned that you joined the SEALs for the wrong reasons. Do you mind telling me why you said that?" The statement had run through Matt's mind several times, and he wasn't sure if he was prying by asking about it.

Mope sat, his dark eyes locked on the horizon of the Mediterranean Sea.

Matt felt like he had asked about something he shouldn't have. "Never mind, Mope. I'm not trying..."

Mope said, "No. I want to tell you, Matt. I don't talk about it much except with people I trust, but you're one of those people now."

"I had a brother, three years older than me," began Mope. "Christopher Tyler Thomason. Actually, Christopher Tyler Thomason, Jr. And he was the son my father, Dr. Christopher Tyler Thomason, Sr. always wanted. I was, on the other hand, an accident. I spent my entire life dealing with a father that doted on my older brother, and always seemed to regard me as a distraction. At best, in his eyes, I was just a sad imitation of my brother, Chris."

Mope scratch at his ear. "No matter what I did, no matter how hard I tried, no matter what I accomplished, I wasn't Chris. At Christmas, birthdays, sports, school, college, nothing ever seemed to carry any weight with my father. And I was a glutton for the indifference; I spent my entire life doing everything I possibly could to get even a tiny amount of the approval that my older brother got so easily."

"The proudest day of my father's life was when Chris announced he was going to go to BUD/S training and become a Navy SEAL. And he could have. He had it in him. But in the physical exam he went through prior to BUD/S, they found out he had leukemia. Aggressive leukemia that had been asymptomatic prior to that. Chris, God bless him, was a fighter and fought hard, but only lasted a year in the end. Losing Chris devastated the family, Matt. My mom became an alcoholic after that. All my dad had left was me, the disappointment of the family."

"So, I convinced myself that I'd do it. I'd become the Navy SEAL to honor Chris. And I did. We lived in Baltimore, and after graduating from the University of Baltimore, I went into BUD/S training. And I made it through. Out of three hundred that started in BUD/S training, five of us made it through and became SEALs. It didn't seem to matter much to my dad, though. It wasn't Chris that had made it in, so it just didn't seem to matter."

"I think that the saddest day of my life was about a year after I had become a SEAL. I was visiting my mom and dad, right before she passed away, and I was trying everything I could to get my dad to acknowledge that I had done something special and that it meant something to him. My dad looked at me and said, 'You're not Chris, Travis, and you never will be. Stop trying to be Chris.'"

Mope paused a moment, but his voice had not wavered while telling the story.

"What hit me at that moment was that what my dad had said... he was right. I was fooling myself, Matt. I didn't do it to honor Chris, as much as I had loved him and wanted to. I did it to try and be Chris in my dad's eyes, and he wasn't having any of it. Even now I find myself trying to believe that I did it for Chris. But, the truth is, I did it to try and replace him in my dad's eyes. To get the approval and love than accidents don't seem to ever get. Even just a little. All I want is a little."

Matt listened to the story and felt terrible. How could anybody lucky enough to have Mope, Travis, in their life not feel incredibly blessed? This was the person that Matt had come to admire more than probably anybody he had ever known. How could his own father be so... indifferent? How could he not see what he had in his son, the one that survived? How could he not appreciate everything that his son had accomplished?

Mope said, "I got the nickname Mope because that's what I tend to do a lot of, and now you know why."

Matt felt miserable for having asked Mope the question, but kind of glad he understood, too. But mostly he felt sad that Mope had grown up like that. He was unable to speak, which was probably good because words utterly failed him. He remembered Petey making a comment now about Mope's dad being disappointed in him. A few tears started to leak out of Matt's eyes. He was at a complete loss for words for what to say to Mope.

"That's why hearing you thank us the other night means a lot to me, personally, Matt. You have no idea what it means to me."

Matt finally pulled himself together enough to ask, "Do you still speak to your father?"

"Oh, yeah. He's all the family I've got now. But it's hard to be around him, for me and for him, I think. For him, I'm just a reminder of what he lost. For me, he's a reminder of what I never got growing up."

"Anyway," said Mope, trying to cheer up some, "I focus instead on all of this, on the team, on being a SEAL."

Matt thought to himself how Mope found the bond he never had with his father instead in a team of men in whose hands he placed his life. Men whose lives in turn he carried in his. Matt pitied Mope's father.

Matt said quietly, "I'm sorry, Mope."

"Don't be. Every so often, I get... reminded... that my dad isn't everything. Kind of like getting your first sip of water after not having any for three days. It's a huge relief to get it. But it also reminds you of how thirsty you are."

Their conversation couldn't continue, though, as Petey's voice interrupted, "Hey, losers! Get your asses up!"

Mope stood up suddenly, a little off guard at being caught this way.

Petey was carrying a rather large rifle of some kind and a large orange ball.

Mope asked as Petey, Baya, and Desantos walked up to them, "What are you doing with the MP5, Colorado?"

"It's for Ladypants here. Nothing takes your mind off things like a little target practice with a submachine gun!"

Matt's face turned pale. "I'm not shooting that thing! Are you crazy? I'll shoot a hole in the boat."

Petey said, "Ship. It's a ship for the millionth time. And yes, you're going to man up and shoot this motherfucker!"

With Matt continuing to protest, they took him over to the edge of the stern of the ship, as close as Matt was willing to go. They threw the orange floating target out into the water, and demonstrated the use of the weapon for Matt. Baya fired off a few three-round bursts, hitting the orange target every single time, even with it bobbing around in the water. Mope took a turn as well and did almost as good as Baya, missing only one single time.

Then they made Matt take his turn. They showed Matt how to hold the gun, how to aim it, and explained how to fire the three round bursts. Matt tried it a few times, but he didn't even get close to the orange target. Petey came up close behind Matt, putting his arms around him, and helped him hold and aim the weapon so that on the next few rounds, he managed to hit the target, even if it was just one time.

Petey said, "See there, sparkles? You *can* do it after all! Even with me pushing up against your back door and distracting you!"

Matt turned around and said, "Sparkles? Ok, Colorado, I've had it. Can you *please* come up with one name for me and stick with it?" As soon as he said it, he regretted it.

The grin that Petey got was positively evil. "Cornhole it is!"

Matt groaned, "Fuck! I can't believe I set myself up for that!"

After they finished their target practice, and were walking back in, Petey hung back and trailed behind the rest of the team with Matt.

He asked, "Cornhole, you want to go make some calls today, before we suit up for this thing?"

Matt decided he would just have to resign himself to being called "Cornhole". He said, "Nah, not much point in calling them until I know for sure when I get to go home."

They walked along a few more seconds when Petey asked, "So this Brian dude, you really love him?"

"Yeah," replied Matt casually.

"Really?"

Matt took a second before he replied, "Yeah, I do."

"You hesitated there. When was the last time he did something nice for you? Took you to dinner or made breakfast for you... something queer."

Matt replied, "The night before I left to come to Syria."

Petey nodded, "Good. That's better."

"But, I guess, actually... I wound up paying that night," said Matt, remembering what happened that night and correcting himself.

"Did he at least let you take a ride on his pink pony before you left?"

Matt flushed red in the face from the double embarrassment of having a Navy SEAL wearing a submachine gun around his chest asking these kinds of blunt questions about his sex life, and from the knowledge that he had never managed to get Brian to be the top.

"The answer is obviously no," decided Petey.

Petey tried a different approach and asked a more sincere question. "When was the last time this shithead made you feel like you were walking on air?"

The questions started to make Matt feel very uncomfortable. He said, "Mmmm..." but never managed to answer the question.

"Ok, so when, exactly, *was* the last time he said he loved you?"

Matt thought back, and realized he honestly couldn't remember. Brian definitely had, but it was back far enough that Matt had trouble remembering the specific time. But so what if it wasn't every single day? It just reaffirmed for Matt that his promise to himself to be a better boyfriend to Brian was the right thing.

Petey said, "You know what, Cornhole? Ahhhh, never mind..." Petey forgot about giving his assessment to Matt as they turned into the ready room. Randall was there waiting with some civilian clothes for Eric Stillman to wear to Café Lucien in Latakia that night, along with Matt's laptop and Eric's laptop.

Randall explained, "We've wiped everything off of Eric's laptop that might be sensitive, so don't worry about losing it if it comes to that. Your laptop is fine, too, by the way. We didn't find anything on it. And before you ask, we didn't add anything of our own on there, either."

Randall asked, "Ok, Matt, you ready to suit up in a little bit?"

Matt felt his knees start to get a little weak at the thought, but nodded anyway.

~~~~~

The CRRC bounced in the water as it sped to the meeting point, but Matt kept his eyes tightly closed and gripped the handle on the rubber boat tightly with one hand and his life preserver with the other one. God, how he hated being surrounded by this much water.

Petey and Desantos were in the boat with him, along with a pilot, and Petey was talking casually to Desantos, like they were just spending a Sunday afternoon drinking beer out on a lake. They weren't wearing their AARDVAARCs, so they had to shout over the sound of the boat motor.

Desantos said, "I thought you didn't like that chick."

Petey replied, "No, you're thinking of the one that had the long brown hair. Now she was carrying around some sushi-grade pussy in her shorts, but she was a bitch. That girl shit fudgesicles she was so frigid. No, I'm talking about the other one with the brown hair, not as long and a little curlier, from three weeks ago."

Desantos asked, "Yeah, ok, what was her name? Jane?"

"Jamie," replied Petey.

"Yeah, Jamie, I remember now."

Petey said, "Yeah, that other girl was a disaster, but Jamie's hot! And, Christ, is she tight! You could stick a blue and a yellow crayon up her twat and pull a green one out, man!" Petey started laughing at the thought.

Normally, Matt would have loved to give Petey a hard time about all this, but at the moment he was holding on for dear life with his eyes tightly shut and trying desperately to not think about being out in the middle of the Mediterranean Sea with no land in sight.

The CRRC slowed suddenly and Matt opened his eyes. He could see a charter fishing boat about a quarter of a mile away.

Desantos took a look all around with binoculars and Petey asked, "We all clear?"

Desantos confirmed, "Yeah, we're good."

They pulled up to the fishing boat and Desantos confirmed that it was indeed the people from the British consulate helping out with the mission.

Before Matt transferred over to the fishing boat, Desantos put his arm on his shoulder and said, "It's gonna be fine, Matt. You're gonna do just fine. Baya's gonna have you covered the whole time."

And then Petey put his hand behind Matt's neck and whispered in his ear, "I swear to you personally, Cornhole, I won't let anything happen to you, ok? Anybody comes near you, and they're gonna pay, I promise." Petey locked his pale blue eyes onto Matt's until Matt nodded his understanding. It dawned on Matt just how much Petey had come to mean to him in only a few days. Mope had been right. If it weren't for hearing this from Petey and Desantos, he didn't think he'd be able to go through with it. Every little bit of reassurance helped.

They helped Matt step over onto to fishing boat, and without waiting, the pilot of the CRRC took off at top speed back in the direction of the *Iwo Jima*.

Matt watched nervously as they sped off towards the horizon. There was no turning back now.

Chapter 18 — Café Lucien

Café Lucien sat in an older part of Latakia, an area less visited by tourists. Still, the fact that it had a reputation for good French food with a Mediterranean influence meant that it wasn't completely unheard of for Westerners to be seen there. For the purposes of the mission, the SEALs felt they could access it and set up a trap there with stealth and confidence. It would be appealing to the targets because it would provide them with a good opportunity to grab Eric Stillman. And in that sleepier part of town, at 11pm on a Friday evening, there would be very little activity on the streets to interfere with or disrupt the plans.

The people at the British consulate in Latakia had been extremely gracious hosts while he stayed with them that evening until it was time for Matt to go to the café, but they had also peppered him with questions about exactly what he was up to. Matt had to repeatedly refuse to answer their questions, per Randall's instructions. Randall had also made sure Matt knew to go to the café thirty minutes earlier than the time he had leaked back in the US Embassy in Damascus just to ensure no one tried to grab him on the way to café. Getting there early forced the targets to wait until he was leaving, when the SEALs would be fully in place and prepared.

Matt had chosen a table outside on the spacious patio area and took his time ordering food and eating. Normally, he would have very much enjoyed a place like Café Lucien on such a beautiful, clear evening, but his stomach was in knots over the whole situation and so the night, the location, and the food made virtually no impression on him at all. His pulse was racing as he sat at the table, and he had to force himself to eat food he didn't want, and make it look comfortable and leisurely at the same time. He consoled himself with the idea that, somewhere around there, Baya had a sniper rifle trained on him. Even just two days before this, he wouldn't have trusted any of these guys any farther than he could throw them. But now, it was a genuine comfort to know they were there. So much had changed in such a short span of days.

As much as he was tempted to study the buildings, alleys, and rooftops around the café to see if he could see them, Randall and Mope both had told him very strictly to not do this. Any kind of tipoff like that could put himself and the team in extreme danger. So he fought the strong urge to search for them. He did glance over at the corner where he would need to walk to when he left. It was the corner with some kind of shop and large glass windows displaying brightly colored fabrics inside. At 11pm, he would pay, walk to that corner, turn down the quiet side street that led down the side of the shop and see what happened.

Matt picked some more at the Cornish hen dish he had ordered and sipped at the polo drink that he had come to like so much, even though it all tasted bad tonight.

It had only been a week now since he had been kidnapped, but Matt felt like it was a lifetime ago. He wasn't quite sure if it was due to his mind actively working to block off the traumatic memory, or if it was due to the emotionally charged days that followed. In a blink of an eye, it felt like Matt had gone from being afraid of the team that rescued him, to thinking they were bigoted jerks, to deeply respecting them. And now caring about them. Mope always referred to his team as his brothers, and Matt got it now. It wasn't just some superficial label applied to teamwork. After spending two days with them and hearing what they did for him, and how they regarded each other, Matt himself felt that bond as deeply as he had felt anything before. Matt had been an only child, but if he could have had a blood brother, he couldn't imagine being any more deeply tied to him than he was to these men.

Mope was right about something else, too. It had nothing to do with being gay or straight. Trust and faith were what mattered and those were very elemental things. And honor, too — following through on the commitment no matter what the personal cost was. What Matt felt as a result of all this was a courage he had never experienced before. He trusted these men with his life, and it was that trust that gave him the courage to calmly sit in that chair rather than run away in a wild, goose-eyed panic. It was like he might have known the meaning of the word before, but never really understood it until now. He had Mope to thank for this — the man that had made him understand these things and given him the chance to experience this bond. Mope had done more than save his life; he had changed him.

Matt roused himself from his reverie about these things and picked at his food some more. He opened up Eric's laptop to check the time and browse around on it to pass a few minutes while trying to finish his food. The clock on the laptop said it was a little after 10pm. Matt could feel the seconds ticking by and he started to get nervous again.

To take his mind off of it, he reminded himself that he'd be going home, probably even tomorrow, no matter what happened tonight. Well, he thought, as long as the worst case scenario didn't happen. That thought didn't help his nerves at all, so he tried to put it out of his mind.

He focused instead on getting home and being with Brian, seeing Bret and Jim again, getting back into softball practice, getting caught back up at work. He thought about all the things that, well, felt like they were now a part of someone else's life. He thought about the odd, uncomfortable fight that he and Brian had at dinner the night before he left for Syria. He thought about the ways he could be better. If there was good that came out of the abduction, it was that it reinforced for Matt the things that were important in life and it put that much more force and conviction behind his promise to be a better partner for Brian. He would move past the petty suspicions that caused him to doubt his partner and everything would be better.

But, try as he might to focus on home and Brian, his mind kept taking him back to Mope. He had never met anyone like him, and he had a deep suspicion he'd never meet another. It seemed like there was nothing that Mope couldn't do. The images of the blood and bodies from the apartment where he had been held came to mind, and for someone that could exhibit such violent force when called to, Mope had shown Matt more about basic human values and convictions than anyone. How could Mope's father not see the rare gift he had in his son? How could he be so indifferent to the son that had done so much, all for just a little recognition and acceptance? Matt wondered if Mope's father knew he was gay or not; maybe that was part of the problem. Mope had not said one way or the other, though. In so many ways, it broke Matt's heart to see someone so deserving left to thirst for these things. Mope deserved so much more than he got.

Matt looked again at the clock on the laptop. It was a little past 10:30pm at this point. The waiter came over and Matt ordered a coffee to finish out the evening before he would need to leave. His hands were clammy feeling and he was nervously bouncing his leg under the table and he had to force himself to stop doing that.

A minute later, just as the waiter brought Matt the coffee he had ordered, a slight motion out of the corner of his eye caught his attention.

He glanced up just in time to see the fabric shop on the corner violently explode into a ball of fire and shattered glass. The force of the explosion knocked the waiter off of his feet and blinded Matt momentarily. When his eyes adjusted, the shop was engulfed in flames and Matt could feel the heat even across the street and twenty-five yards away. His ears were ringing like a bitch and the sounds of screams seemed distant and muffled. Matt stared at the scene in utter shock. He glanced down at the table and saw bits of shattered glass lying on it. He looked back at the fire, and a split-second later, Matt saw a small object fly through the air, propelled directly into the burning shop, followed by a second explosion, this one literally demolishing part of the building where the shop was, which collapsed into a heap of concrete and plaster and glass onto the sidewalk and street.

To Matt's horror, he knew this was meant for him.

And without even realizing he was doing it, he grabbed the laptop and ran — in the opposite direction.

Chapter 19 – Last Bullet Last Breath

Matt fled, but rather than run down along the more prominent road in front of the café away from the explosions, he turned and ran down a narrower road that ran along the south side of Café Lucien. He could hear screaming and yelling behind him from people still at the café, possibly hurt, but he ran anyway, his heart beating like a snare drum.

The road he ran down doglegged to his right and he turned and followed it. A few yards later, he slowed down and tried to calm the shaking of his hands and heart, and the heaving of his lungs. The instant his own panic ebbed the slightest bit, though, his immediate thought was of the team. He didn't know if they were in that building or on top of it or even just near it, but he prayed desperately that they weren't. He glanced down and realized there was blood running down his arm. He followed it up and found a three-inch shard of glass sticking out of his arm, lodged near his elbow. He winced at the sharp pain as he pulled the glass out, then felt around his head and face to see if there were any more flying shards sticking out of him. He didn't feel any and couldn't find any more blood, to his relief.

Matt glanced behind him, back towards the horror scene, but he was far enough away that he couldn't see anything more than the light and smoke from the fire over the tops of the buildings between him and the café. He could hear fresh screams in the distance, though. A white van turned down the narrow street that Matt was on, and he noticed that one headlight was dim, about half the brightness of the other. Suddenly, recognition dawned in Matt as he looked at the rest of the box-shaped van. He remembered one like that before, if only briefly. His blood turned cold and he stood frozen in the mismatched headlights. Fear was a hooded figure behind Matt, whispering things in his ear. Terrible things.

The van stopped about fifteen feet away from Matt, and he saw a man get out of the passenger side. The fear whispering things in his ear now took out an ice cold blade and drove it deep into the base of his spine. The person that had gotten out of the van was an older Arabic man with a white-streaked beard. It might have felt like a lifetime ago to Matt earlier in the evening, but it was all too recent for him to not recognize the leader of the people that would have killed him less than a week ago.

The man with the beard pulled a gun and Matt finally forced himself to act. He darted and ran. He spotted a narrow alley, too narrow for the van, which split off to the left from the street he was on, so he ran down it as fast as he could. It dead-ended into another alleyway. To the right was a dead end, but to the left, he could see where it emptied out onto a larger road with a park on the other side. He prayed he could get to the end of the alley before the men behind him could follow him and start shooting. Matt could hear sirens in the distance now, heading towards the scene. If he could just get to one of those sirens, maybe the Syrian police would help him.

Matt burst out of the alley into the larger road and turned right to continue running, when he was suddenly tackled from behind and fell to the ground.

He started to fight, but the man that had tackled him pulled a gun from his didashah and held it to Matt's throat, putting a quick end to Matt's resistance. Another assailant came running up and the two of them yanked Matt up off the sidewalk and threw him into the back seat of a waiting white van. They shoved Matt to the passenger side of the back seat and the one with the gun got in with him, keeping the weapon pointed directly at him. The other assailant got in the front seat, in front of Matt, and then the driver of the van took off. The three captors were yelling at each other, and all at the same time, but the one in the back seat with Matt never took his eyes or the gun off of him.

The one in the front seat, in front of Matt, had also pulled a gun at this point, but the one in back with Matt waved at him to put it away. Instead, the one in front reached back and grabbed the laptop out of Matt's hands. He hadn't even realized how tightly he was gripping it at this point and had forgotten all about it.

The fear was so overwhelming that Matt was seeing stars. He didn't know what else to do. He closed his eyes and the image of the empty room screamed at him, the burning thirst already gnawing at him. How could things have gone so wrong so easily? The leader wasn't here, which meant there must be two vans. Was all of this just a way to drive Matt to a certain capture? He was just a pig being herded to a certain slaughter.

The driver made his way away from the scene, but didn't speed or drive erratically, and Matt watched helplessly as the van passed several police cars heading towards the cafe and the explosions while they headed away from the heart of Latakia.

Time ticked away, and the farther they got from the main part of the city, the more the kidnappers seemed to relax and the more Matt's hopes that something would happen faded. He had no idea what *could* happen, but he knew the idea of leaving the city made him far more afraid than staying in it.

The farther they went, the more hopeless Matt felt. He didn't necessarily feel panicked... just helpless. And hopeless. He had taken a chance on this mission, and now what these people had attempted the first time around would finally be completed. He had managed to cheat death, but probably for only a week before the Old Reaper had caught up to him, dressed in a didashah. Matt's heart sank. He thought to himself — I've been on borrowed time, but only one week's worth... just one small week. Matt barely noticed how easily he resigned himself to what was going to happen as the urban structures began to thin out.

They drove for several minutes on a major road that then hit the edge of town. Here, they passed fewer and fewer cars and motorcycles, and the buildings and development stopped entirely. They were out of the city and Matt fully despaired of where he was being taken and what would happen to him.

Out of the city by several miles, there was no traffic, save for one motorcycle that whizzed past the van on its way out of the city, too, leaving the van behind. There were no buildings any more, just crops of various kinds on either side, along with large cement irrigation pipes laid out next to the road waiting to be buried.

Matt wished he had told Brian he loved him more often than he did. He wished he had told Bret and Jim how much he loved them, too. He couldn't have ever hoped for better friends. He wished he had told Baya, Desantos, Petey and Mope how much they had come to mean to him. Life seemed to be too many missed opportunities. And when on borrowed time, you ran out of those opportunities all too soon.

Matt looked out the windshield towards whatever was waiting for him at the end of this trip.

Then Matt and the two assailants in the front seat seemed to see it at the same time. At the very farthest reach of the van's headlights, there was something in the middle of the road. The driver slowed the van slightly trying to understand what it was and the two in front started speaking to each other in puzzled voices.

Matt couldn't believe his eyes, but even at this distance and in only the light of the headlights, he instantly recognized the familiar desert camouflage pattern of the battle dress uniform, and the now very familiar crouching position that the figure directly in the path of the van had assumed.

A second later, the two in the front seat started yelling and pointing as they realized that what was in their path was a person. At the exact same time, the windshield of the van shattered, causing the driver to swerve slightly before he regained control. The driver sped up and intentionally aimed the van at the figure now only about forty yards ahead.

And one more second later, without any other warning, the head of the gunman in the backseat with Matt completely exploded.

The driver of the van did lose control this time and the van careened off the right side of the road and smashed obliquely into the large concrete pipe section resting there. The van slid along the side of the pipe for a distance before coming to a rest.

Matt had been thrown against the seat in front of him during the crash, but wasn't hurt. He looked in horror over at the body in the seat next to him, half of the head had disintegrated, the hand with the gun in it hung limply at its side. Matt looked at his hands and arms and realized he was covered in blood, bits of brain, and bone. He heard the gunman in the seat in front of him groan, disoriented from the impact. The gunman in front recovered quickly and started scrambling madly, looking for the gun he had in his own didashah.

With no conscious thought, Matt slid over and grabbed the gun from the lifeless hand of the body next to him. His shaking hand pointed it at the gunman in the seat in front of him, and just as the gunman turned to point his gun at Matt, Matt pulled the trigger with it two inches from the man's face. There was a flash and a deafening crack from the gunshot, and the kidnapper's face split into two, his head twisted around horrifically, and his body flew back against the dash of the van.

Matt stared at the body, bent unnaturally against the dash, almost pushed out through the smashed windshield from the force of the gun. Matt was completely numb and in disbelief at what had just happened. His head slowly turned and he now noticed the driver of the van screaming in terror and frantically grasping for any kind of weapon.

The driver didn't have a chance, though. Just as he went to grab the gun that had fallen out of the hand of the kidnapper in the front seat, his head exploded as well. Matt sat, going into shock at the scene, splattered with blood and skin and bone, along with the rest of the interior of the van.

He sat in a fog. Somewhere in the distance, he heard yelling, but the yelling didn't matter. He just stared at the stump where the driver's head had once been, blood pouring out and down the seat of the van. Even hearing his name in the distant yelling didn't matter. He just looked at all the blood. The smell filled his nose, just like it had at the apartment. The smell of rusted iron.

"MATT!!!"

He finally realized the voice wasn't in the distance. It was right outside. He managed to pull himself out of the fugue state, but only a little. He could see Mope ten yards outside of the van, his rifle raised, the scope against his eye, and pointed at Matt.

Matt said vaguely, "Mope?"

"ARE THERE ANY MORE?!" Mope screamed.

He finally understood the question. "No, they're all dead," he replied indistinctly.

Mope lowered his rifle and ran up to the van, tearing open the door to the backseat. He yanked the dead body next to Matt out and boomed, "Get out of the van, Matt! Look at me, Matt. LOOK AT ME, MATT!! Come on, get out! We've got to get you out of there!"

Matt slid over and Mope helped him get out of the van. Mope frantically grabbed the goggles covering his eyes and pulled them up over the edge of his helmet to get them out of the way.

"Look at my eyes, Matt. Look at me, okay! You're ok, Matt! You're fine. I'm here, and you're fine. Ok? Alright, Matt?" Mope was pleading with him.

Matt finally came back to himself entirely. He looked at the one part of Mope that he could actually see. He looked at Mope's eyes and realized it was true. He was ok. It was over. Mope continued to hold his rifle in his right hand, but his other was on Matt's shoulder.

Matt exhaled deeply. "You... you came after me."

Matt couldn't see the bottom half of Mope's face, but he could tell he was smiling in relief.

Mope said, "Yeah, well, I didn't have a whole lot else going on tonight, so... ehh, why not?"

Mope put his hand behind Matt's neck and shook him gently. Matt heard Mope's deep voice, completely earnest, say, "Last bullet. Last breath. You heard the pledge, Matt."

But Matt's shoulders slumped. He said, sadly, "I killed someone, Mope. I put a gun an inch from his face, and... and I... I... A fucking gun,

Mope! I... I didn't... even hesitate." Matt's face contorted and the tears started flowing out of his eyes. He started breathing rapidly and his hands started to shake.

Mope let the rifle drop so that it hung in front of his chest. He pulled the black mask down to expose the rest of his face, and then grabbed Matt's head with both hands.

"Look at me, Matt. I want you to breathe with me. Slowly, we're going to breathe slowly. Don't think about anything else but matching my breaths. Look at my face and breathe with me."

Mope started to breathe slowly and deliberately, his eyes locked with Matt's, making Matt slow his breathing down and making him not think about shooting the kidnapper. Mope got Matt's breathing back under control and comforted him, "You did good, Matt. You had to. You had no choice. He would have killed you if you hadn't killed him, Matt. You had no choice. You did what you had to do."

Matt sniffled and nodded slightly. He felt for sure he would have already gone insane were it not for Mope.

"Actually, you did amazing, Matt. Fucking incredible comes to mind. You have more in you than you can possibly imagine. Right here, Matt. Right here," said Mope, beating his fist lightly on Matt's chest as he said these words.

Matt couldn't help but think that if that was what 'fucking incredible' was, he wasn't sure he wanted it.

But then Matt suddenly shot a torrent of questions at Mope, "Where did you come from? How did you find me? How did you get here? Are the other guys ok? Did they get hurt? Where are they?"

And then Matt actually got a little testy. "Hey, you SHOT at me! I was *in* that van that you were shooting at!"

Mope smiled one of his rare smiles, the mic of the AARDVAARC still hooked into the corner of his mouth. He chuckled and patted Matt on his shoulder.

"That's more like it. You may have been in the van, Matt," said Mope through a lopsided grin, his smile lines deeper than ever. "But I'm a good shot. Even among SEALs, I'm a really, *really* good shot. Especially with moving targets."

Matt repeated, "Are the other guys ok? Where are they?"

"They're fine, Matt. No one was immediately by the explosion. Actually, Baya was on that roof, but he was on the south end of the building. I was closer over to the park. Petey saw you run and saw the van follow you and was about to go after you. When you popped out of the alley by the park, I saw the guys grab you. I couldn't get a clear shot because you were fighting them. As soon as the van drove off with you, a guy on a motorcycle came by and I knocked him off and took his bike. I followed behind you guys, and when we got out of the city, I raced ahead and set up in the road. I told Petey, Desantos and Baya to all get back to the extraction point and start arranging a new extraction for us, farther inland."

Words could not describe the relief Matt felt to hear that they were all safe.

Mope said, "Ok, I've got to clean up the van just a little. I want you to go sit against the pipe over there. Don't look inside the van, ok? Just don't even look at it at all."

Matt nodded. He went and sat in the dry dirt against the pipe a few yards away. Mope dug around, doing whatever he needed to do inside the van. Matt looked back towards the city and thought he could see lights in the sky over it. A few minutes later Mope came back and handed Matt a clean rag to wipe the blood off of his face with.

"Did you manage to grab any of the bad guys?" asked Matt.

"No, the explosions and the fact that you ran shot those plans to hell," said Mope, sitting down next to Matt. He pulled out a bottled water from his pack and handed it to Matt. "We'll rest a minute, then take the motorcycle and go a little further away from town and away from this van. With the explosion, there's a lot of Syrian helos over the city, so we'll have to wait for that to die down some before we try another extraction."

Matt drank some of the water and handed the bottle back to Mope, who drank some as well. He tried to not look at the van, but felt his eyes inexorably drawn back to it at the same time. Every glance he couldn't prevent made him feel a little sick.

Mope said, "You had to do it, Matt. You understand that, right?"

Matt sighed and said, "I know. I know I did. Even with no choice, even knowing what would happen if I didn't... I just don't have to... like it."

Matt started to relax a little, and the silence of the Syrian countryside east of Latakia surrounded them. He looked back down the road leading back into the city and noticed headlights headed their way. It was bad enough to see a car approaching, but it got much worse when he realized one headlight was noticeably dimmer than the other.

Chapter 20 — Look Up

Matt should have felt the terror rise up in him again. But it didn't this time. He was nervous at the sight of the approaching headlights, but not scared. Mope had noticed the headlights as well.

Matt felt it then, down inside of himself. Through faith and trust came the courage. It felt like nothing Matt had experienced before. When the approaching lights were almost illuminating their spot, Matt asked Mope, "You swear to God you're a really good shot, right? Will you promise me you are?"

Mope said, alarmed, "What are you..."

"The one on the passenger side is the one you really want alive," interrupted Matt and he jumped up. Just as the headlights started to illuminate their position and the wrecked van that they were hidden behind, Matt paused one more second so they'd get a good look. Mope started to try and grab him, but Matt dashed across the highway, fully illuminated by the approaching headlights. He jumped behind the concrete pipe lying along the far side, then ran a little farther down and hid behind it as best he could. He hoped and prayed that Mope could handle however many were in the van.

The van pulled up just short of where the other crashed van was and stopped. Immediately, the driver of the van and the leader with the white-streaked beard jumped out, shouting at each other in Arabic. They both ignored the crashed van and ran across the road to where they had seen Matt disappear behind the irrigation pipes.

Matt waited with his eyes closed, praying for the dull thump sound of Mope's rifle with the suppressor on it, but he didn't hear it. Matt really started to panic when he heard the two men immediately on the other side of the pipe talking to each other.

He looked up just in time to see the terrible grin of the man with the beard looking down at him triumphantly. Just as Matt was about to turn away from the face he had learned to hate and fear so much, the face changed suddenly. The smile faded and the leader's eyes rolled back in his head. He collapsed on the side of the pipe and fell down to the ground off of it.

Matt heard that voice, the deep bass of gentle thunder in the distance that had become the most comforting sound in the world to him, "It's done, Matt."

Matt stood up and saw Mope looking right at him, the goggles and mask obscuring his face. At Mope's feet was the body of the driver, a knife buried to the hilt in the side of his neck and a pool of blood spreading out from it. In a heap next to the pipe was the body of the leader. Mope put his boot on the head of the driver and leaned over to pull the knife out of his neck, first twisting it and digging it in to make very sure he was dead. He wiped the blood off the knife on the driver's didashah before putting it back in its sheath on his thigh.

Mope asked, "Are there going to be any more of these fucking vans?"

Matt couldn't help but smile at Mope's question. He shook his head no and climbed back over the pipe. He said through his smile, "Were you just waiting to make me sweat over here?"

He heard Mope's voice from behind the mask, "Maybe I should have! But, I had to sneak up on their van and make sure there were no others in there. Once I knew that was clear, I could deal with these two more easily."

Mope walked over to the body of the leader and kicked at him gently with his boot.

Matt asked, "Is he dead?"

Mope held up the handgun Matt now noticed in his hand. "Nah. Randall gave us these dart guns to use. These things don't shoot worth a shit, though. Needed to be up close to make sure I got him. That bastard there is going to wake up in about ten hours to the worst nightmare he'll ever imagine."

Mope walked up to Matt, put his hand on Matt's head and playfully messed his hair. He exhaled and said, "We got one, Matt. *You* got one. You have no idea how much you've done. No idea."

Mope took the dead body of the driver, dragged it from the middle of the road and put it in the crashed van. He wouldn't let Matt help because he didn't want Matt anywhere near that van and the grisly scene inside, the scene that Matt had been in the middle of. He did let Matt help him lift the unconscious body of the leader and put it into the good van. Mope put zip ties on the hands and feet of their prize, just in case he woke up unexpectedly.

Mope decided they needed to get farther out of town, find somewhere off the main road, and wait until another extraction could be safely made. They loaded up in the van and Mope drove another five miles out of town, then turned off the highway, driving along the edge of a large, orderly grove of olive trees. On the far side of the field, they stopped the van. Mope and Matt got out and walked a few feet away to where a thick and gnarled olive tree trunk was lying. They sat down on the ground and leaned against it in the cool Syrian night air to wait. There was a light, delicate, almost fruity smell in the air that Matt assumed was the olive trees.

"We're really far from the sea. How are we going to get back?" asked Matt. His eyes started to get used to the faint moonlight that night and could see Mope barely illuminated next to him.

"Already working on it," said Mope. "It'll probably be yet another thing you won't ever be able to talk about, though. The 'when' depends on air traffic over Latakia dying down some."

"How will they know where we are? I don't even know where we are."

"They know exactly where we are already. I'm GPS'ed out the ass and sending the coordinates back to the *Iwo Jima* constantly, as well as still transmitting on the AARDVAARC. The guys have been listening to everything that's happened."

Matt sat silently for a moment. So much had happened so fast tonight. Try as he might to not see the images in his mind, they inserted themselves into his consciousness. He saw a human head three feet away from him explode. Felt the blood and bits of brain and skull hitting him in the face. He himself had held a gun within a few inches of another human being's head and pulled the trigger. He could smell the awful stench of spilled blood. Lots of it. He saw the face of the leader leering over the concrete pipe at him, with evil, angry triumph in his eyes.

It overwhelmed Matt and he felt himself choking up, and his body started to shake as the tears began to flow. He started crying with the fear and pain and brutality of everything he had just experienced. And once it started, he couldn't stop it, so he let it out and blubbered like a baby.

Mope said, "Jesus, Petey, just butt out! Just let me know when the Nosferatu is on its way. Until then, I'm cutting the audio feed to you guys."

Mope opened up a tightly velcroed pocket under his left arm, pulled out the AARDVAARC box and flipped a switch.

He reached around Matt, putting his arm around his shoulders and pulling him close. He moved the goggles back up onto the brim of his helmet and pulled the black mask back down.

Rather than try to get Matt to stop, though, he said gently, "Let it out, Matt. Let it out. You've been through hell tonight, so let it go." He squeezed Matt to him tightly and let him cry.

Matt finally asked through his heaving and crying, "What did Petey say?"

"You really don't want…"

"What, Mope?"

Mope sighed and said, "Petey said, 'Tell him to stop all that damn crying! Tell that bitch to stop menstruating himself into an early menopause! He still has plenty of time to take it up the ass and have a bunch of little faggot babies.'"

Matt sobbed a few more times, which then turned into a chuckle. He couldn't help himself. Petey took offensiveness to an Olympic gold-medal level.

Matt's chuckle then turned into a laugh and Mope started laughing, too.

Matt said, "That motherfucker!" and laughed some more.

"It's killing him that he couldn't be out here with you, you know," said Mope. "There's nothing he wouldn't do for you. He would have literally ripped these guys apart with his bare hands if he could have been here."

Mope paused and gave Matt another squeeze with his arm. Matt very much liked being with Mope like this. Despite the terrible things that had happened, Mope made him feel safe, and like everything was ok. He liked Mope holding onto him like this.

"But I got to be the lucky one tonight," added Mope. "I know it's hard for you to see it, Matt, but what you did tonight was amazing… I think you're amazing."

Matt blushed, grateful it was invisible in the feeble moonlight.

"That boyfriend of yours is really lucky to have you. One lucky son of a bitch."

Matt looked over at Mope, giving his usual automatic response. "No, I'm lucky to have Brian."

"I guarantee you," insisted Mope, "Brian is the goddamn lucky one."

He added, "And I feel safer just knowing I've got a bad-ass motherfucker like you here next to me."

Matt laughed wistfully again. He felt something towards Mope he had never felt towards anyone before. It was respect, and admiration, and comfort, and trust, and faith, and... and... and what, exactly, he wondered.

Mope said, "I'm sorry for what you've gone through tonight, Matt. All this that's happened... it's not like some bullshit Michael Bay movie. Seeing and feeling a building get hit by a rocket propelled grenade, seeing two guys get their heads blown off by hollow points, a knife in a guy's throat. The reality is very different from the Hollywood crap. None of us would have gone through with tonight if we thought this was how it was going to go."

Matt thought sadly, truer words were never spoken. Somehow Mope always knew exactly what to say.

Matt looked up at the night sky and felt humbled by what he suddenly realized was above him. For Matt, it was a rare sight, and it took his mind off of everything that had happened. He said to Mope, "Look up."

Mope looked at Matt, then looked up in the sky and saw what Matt did, and it took his breath away.

There, stretched above them, from one end of the Syrian night sky to the other, the dazzling beauty and complexity of the Milky Way galaxy hung silently above them. Far enough away that the city lights of Latakia couldn't drown out the magnificent view, Matt and Mope sat and stared at it, feeling dwarfed and awed by it.

Matt heard Mope whisper the word "amazing". He looked down from the sky in time to see Mope looking at him.

Matt looked back up at the stars twinkling in the sky.

"Mope, those guys that you went out with were stupid assholes," Matt whispered. "You deserve a lot better than them."

For some reason, after Matt had made the statement, he felt like he had crossed some unidentified line that he probably shouldn't have, and he felt bad for crossing it.

He heard Mope breathing in the dark next to him. Mope said, almost daring Matt, "Oh, really? So, are you saying to me that, if you didn't have that lucky bastard Brian waiting on you back home in Richmond, you'd go out with me?"

"Are you kidding me? You've saved my life, like, two or three times now! I've lost fucking count! I'd do anything for you!" said Matt.

As soon as he said it, Matt understood why he felt like he had crossed a line. It had nothing to do with Mope, but with Brian. As soon as he said it, he knew it was true. The thought of going out with Mope made him feel like he was walking on air. Which in turn made him wonder if what he had with Brian was really all that great, after all. He had crossed a line he had not crossed since he met Brian, and now the guilt of it started pulling at him. Especially after he had made a promise to himself to really appreciate Brian and remember how lucky he was to have him. Matt had sworn as he lay dying of thirst in an empty room to be better to Brian. And this was the sad way he was keeping that promise.

But Matt couldn't help it. Even as the guilt burned him like acid, he dreamt of having Mope turn to him and kiss him right then. He imagined leaning back against Mope, being held in his arms as they sat and looked at the stars overhead. He felt awful for wanting it.

"Yeah. Good. That's good. Thanks, Matt," said Mope.

To Matt's extreme disappointment, Mope took his arm from around him and turned his AARDVAARC mic back on.

"C'mon guys! Are you going to make us wait all night? We could have walked back to the *Iwo* by now!"

Matt was only halfway listening. For a moment, it felt like there was something between him and Mope. It seemed like maybe Mope felt the same way towards Matt that Matt felt towards him. But he guessed not. Maybe it had just been wishful thinking. Matt was left with the guilt that if Mope had kissed him right then, he probably would have kissed him back.

Mope continued, "No, we're clear here. The ground isn't any good for a landing, though. Too rocky and too many scrubby trees. You can get down to about ten feet and hold it." There was another pause, then Mope said, "Ok, got it."

Mope turned to Matt and said, "They're on the way. This is going to be pretty good because they're in a Nosferatu."

"Is that supposed to mean something to me?" asked Matt.

"It better not. This thing's really classified. I've seen one, but this'll be my first time actually using one on a mission. It's a new helo. It scatters radar like a banshee, so the Syrians won't even know it's here, even if they're looking for it. And you'll barely be able to see or hear it until it's right on top of us," said Mope, excitedly.

"It's not going to land," he continued. "Baya will drop down, and we'll get you lifted up into the helo first. I've got goggles, but you don't, so keep your eyes closed with all the sand blowing around. Then we'll get our little party favor and lift him up next. Then we'll be on our way. Once we're back over water, we're pretty much home free!"

Mope stood up and looked around, selecting the clearest area nearby to use. Matt helped him get their captive out of the van, and Mope carried him over to the area he had chosen and unceremoniously dumped his body on the ground.

Matt kept looking towards town to see if he could see the helicopter approaching, but couldn't see or hear anything.

Mope said, "Yeah, we're ready. You see me? Alright, let's get out of here."

Mope looked around, too, and clearly couldn't see the helicopter, either.

He laughed and said, "Fuck you guys! Shit, that thing is invisible!"

They both finally heard a slight whine, like nothing more than a hair dryer in the distance, and immediately felt the blast of air as the Nosferatu lowered towards them. Despite wanting to look up at it, Matt had to close his eyes due to the sand and dirt flying around.

A second later, he heard something drop to the ground right next to him, followed by two hands on his shoulders. He heard Baya say, "Good to see you, Matt!"

Matt felt Baya slip a pair of goggles over his eyes so he could see. When he turned, all he saw was a SEAL in battle dress with goggles and mask, but he could tell it was Baya from his build. He looked up and could only see the outline of the helicopter over him where it blocked the light of the stars. Other than that, it just appeared to be a void in the starry sky. Baya and Mope got Matt safely attached to the rigging to get him up in the helo and he immediately felt himself lifting up in the air. When he was even with the opening in the side of the helo, a hand reached out and grabbed him and pulled him inside. Matt tripped getting his foot out of the rigging and fell into Petey, knocking him down onto one of the seats. Matt's face shoved right into Petey's groin.

Petey said, "God damn! You greedy little cocksucker! Can't even wait one *fucking* minute before you're pushing your face in my crotch!"

Matt stood up, embarrassed, and Petey grabbed his shoulders, turned him around and pointed at a seat. He kicked Matt playfully in the ass with his boot and said, "That's your seat, Cornhole. You'll have to wait until we get back to the ship for me to teabag you."

Matt sat down and said with a stupid grin on his face, "It's good to see you, too, Petey!"

Petey knelt down in front of Matt to make sure he was buckled in securely. Matt couldn't help but grin wildly the whole time and Petey said through the black mask, "Wipe that dumb-ass grin off your face, asshole!" He slapped Matt against the chest and handed him a helmet to put on.

In the meantime, Desantos had gotten the lead kidnapper up in the helicopter as well. Petey went to help him get the body in a seat and buckled in.

Finally, they helped get Mope and Baya back up into the Nosferatu, and the instant they were in, the helicopter canted and flew off at a dizzying pace. The SEALs sat down and buckled in like it was standing still, completely at ease with the wild motions of the helicopter.

Matt should have been interested in looking out the window and watching everything. Or at least looking to make sure they would get back to the *Iwo Jima* safely. Instead, he found himself staring at Mope. Despite the fact that the SEALs all still had their goggles and masks on, Matt could now easily identify them just by size and mannerisms.

He had mixed emotions about what he felt towards Mope. The thought of Mope touching him or kissing him was wonderful, even if it now felt like a silly and impossible daydream. He'd be going home very soon and Mope would go his own way and that would be that. Matt hoped he would be able to remain friends with all of them, but especially Mope. But he also imagined the crazy parallel world where Mope felt the same towards him and there was something more between them.

Matt shook the thoughts off and glanced at his kidnapper in the seat across from him, hands and feet bound the way Matt's had been. The sight instantly reminded Matt that these thoughts towards Mope were already a betrayal of Brian. Did the sacred promise he made to himself mean so little that he was willing to imagine tossing it aside even a few days later? Matt didn't like that thought. Mope had shown him what faith and trust were about. He had made him understand that honor was a real thing. He couldn't have these thoughts about Mope without violating his commitment to Brian. And he wanted to be a better person than that. Matt felt caught between something in his heart towards Mope, and the honor that the same person had made so important to him.

He consoled himself by thinking that soon he'd be home. His life would get back to normal. He would have Brian waiting on him, and it would be good to hold him and kiss him and feel him by his side. But he'd be looking at normal through different eyes now.

There finally came a point where the SEAL team relaxed a little and they all moved their goggles up onto their helmets and pulled their black face masks down. Matt realized the Nosferatu had just crossed from being over land to being over the Mediterranean Sea.

Petey slapped his hand on Matt's knee excitedly a few times and shouted at him, a crazy and exuberant look on his face, "Fuck! You are a hardcore badass, motherfucker!! You shot one of those fuckers WITH HIS OWN GUN!! That is... Christ, that is THE SHIT!!! In his FACE, motherfucker!! With his own FUCKING gun!! They better bring a sack lunch if they're gonna mix it up with this here butthole bandit!"

Matt was very uncomfortable being forced to remember doing that. Maybe Mope was right that he didn't have any choice, but it still wasn't something he was prepared to see himself doing so easily. He was clearly capable of doing something like that, but did he *want* to be capable of something like that? Matt slumped in his seat a little bit and tried to tell himself that he just wasn't used to being in such a primal fight for survival.

Mope said, knowing Matt needed the support, "Might as well get used to it, Matt. There's gonna be quite a few people wanting to talk about it and a lot of people wanting to congratulate you. Remember what I said."

Matt was once again hit with how much Mope meant to him. Why did Mope keep doing this to him? Even now, Mope was trying to protect him and prepare him for what was still to come. Mope had made the most terrifying moments of life, the most difficult things he had ever done, easier. And that made Matt feel the guilt.

Baya said, "After the explosion, I watched you through the scope. I saw your arm start bleeding. You ok?"

Matt looked at the dried blood that had run down his arm. "I'm fine. It was just a small piece of glass."

"When you ran, I almost took a shot in front of you to try and get you to realize you needed to go back the other way, but you turned down the side of the café too fast."

They all talked about everything that had happened the rest of the way back to the ship, but they already knew all the details as Mope had been feeding them audio and describing things to them the whole time through his AARDVAARC. Matt felt downright embarrassed by how they described what he had done that evening. They made it sound like he was a hero.

~~~~~

The hot shower after everything that had happened that evening felt extremely good, but had its own disturbing consequence, too. The sight of just how bloody the clothes he had been wearing were made him feel nauseous before he ever walked down to the shower. When he got under the spray and saw how much more blood washed off of his body, very little of it his own, he had to stop and lean against the wall with his eyes closed to keep from throwing up. It took a long time to let the tension and anxiety from the night wash down the drain. The rule about short "Navy" showers while onboard could go to hell.

The ship ran 24/7 and he had expected there to be a fair amount of activity on the flight deck when the Nosferatu landed, but instead it was deserted save for two Marines to take their captive into custody and then two flight deck crew. That was it. Mope explained that all other flight ops were delayed and everyone cleared off the deck and out of the hangar until the Nosferatu was stowed and secured below. It was that highly classified.

Matt was glad for the peace and quiet on the deck, and in the shower. Back safely on board the *Iwo Jima*, he now realized just how tired and drained he was. He felt empty. Worse, he knew he felt empty for multiple reasons. He had experienced terrible things he never expected to experience in his lifetime. And he had a feeling towards Mope that didn't seem to be returned. Which made him feel bad about his promise to Brian. Matt felt empty.

When he eventually pulled himself out of the shower and made his way back to his rack, he was more than ready for bed. Of course, when he got back, his clothes, his sheets and his pillow were all gone.

Matt was tired and his nerves were shot and he didn't feel like having Petey fuck with him right then. Just when he was about to go make the angry trek all the way over to their cabin, Petey and Baya walked in.

Matt scowled at Petey. "Petey, goddammit, I'm exhausted and can't fight back tonight with you screwing around, man. I just want..."

Petey smiled and held up his hand, "Slow down, Cornhole. After tonight, there's no way you're staying in here by yourself. You're one of us now, man."

Matt looked at him stupidly. He didn't understand.

"You're staying with us tonight, Matt," said Baya. "C'mon, we're all ready to crash."

Maybe it was a stupid thing, but Matt felt like it was an honor to be invited to bunk with them. He relented and started to follow them to their cabin.

"Oh, and Petey?" said Matt, trying to make amends for snapping at him.

"What?"

"It's *Mr.* Cornhole now, dumbass!"

When he got to their cabin, Mope and Desantos were already crawling into their racks. Baya took the upper rack so Matt wouldn't have to climb up to it. Matt climbed into the middle rack, facing across to Mope's. Mope lay in his rack, in his boxers and t-shirt, watching Matt silently.

When Matt was about to turn over to go to sleep, he heard Desantos say, "You made the SEALs look good tonight, Matt."

Petey echoed immediately, stifling a yawn, "Not bad for an ass-muncher! Next thing you know, they'll be wanting to adopt kids and serve in the military!"

Matt felt warm hearing this, even the sideways moment of praise and sincerity from Petey. But his eyes never left Mope. Mope's expression remained stolid as he watched Matt and he didn't seem to hear Petey's comment. He looked at Mope's arm, his bicep stretching the t-shirt, the fine black hair on it getting denser towards the wrist, and thought how that arm had been around his shoulder earlier. It hadn't been much, but he'd take it gladly. He and Mope watched each other silently across the space between them, Mope finally offering a small, crooked smile before he nodded at Matt and closed the curtain on his rack to go to sleep.

Matt lay there, staring at the curtain over Mope's rack for a full minute before he closed his own curtain and rolled over to try to go to sleep.

Chapter 21 — Twenty-Four Karat Gold-Plated Bullshit

Keisha finally had to yell, "Yo, Riii-derrrr! Rider! Matt!" to get him to wake up. Matt, lying on his stomach, lifted up and hit the back of his head on Baya's rack above him. He rubbed it a few times before he realized Keisha was standing in the berth next to him.

He had been having the dream again. There was something weird about it. It should have been a nightmare, being in the empty room with the door open, but unable to leave for some reason. But it didn't feel like that. What he remembered was feeling sad in the dream. All he had to do was get up and leave the room. Why wouldn't he just leave if nothing was keeping him there?

He rubbed his eyes a few times and Keisha said, "You're a heavy sleeper, you know that? Anyway, Wickland wants to see you."

Matt pushed his face back down in his pillow and said, "Now?"

"As soon as you can. You can clean up if you want. I'll wait."

"Ok, ok."

He rolled over and got out of his rack. He looked around and noticed that the rest of the team was gone. He wondered where they were. Then he wondered how they left without waking him up. They weren't gone completely as their stuff was still lying around, but they weren't in their racks.

Matt said, "Lemme wash my face. You don't need to wait. If Randall's in the same room he's been set up in, I know where that is."

"I'll wait."

Matt went down to wash his face and found Keisha still waiting on him when he got back.

As they walked, Keisha asked, "Why are you in with the SEALs now?"

Matt answered, "They're big babies and scared of the dark."

Keisha looked at Matt like he was crazy. She asked, "Were you part of all that shit going on in the middle of the night?"

For someone that showed precious little interest in Matt the last time, she seemed much more curious now. But at least he understood why she wanted to wait and walk with him.

Matt was pretty sure he shouldn't talk about it, so he asked, "What shit?"

She looked at him a little suspiciously, like she knew that he knew exactly what shit she was talking about. "They locked this ship down. Locked it down tight. No one on the flight deck. No one on the hangar deck. No one in the passageways except for essential crew. Everyone else was confined to their berths until notified."

Matt said, "Huh. I had no idea." It was true, sort of. Then he said, "I thought you didn't care about asking these kinds of questions."

She glanced at Matt out of the corner of her eyes. Matt could tell she was picking up on the fact that she wasn't going to get any information out of him.

As they arrived at the door to the cabin Randall had been using, she said, "Whatever went down, it's not run-of-the-mill stuff."

"Maybe you can ask Randall. Maybe he'll be able to tell you."

She rolled her eyes and walked off since she knew she wasn't going to be able to pump any gossip out of him.

Matt entered and Randall asked him to sit down.

"Matt, first of all, thank you for your help with this mission. I speak for a lot of people when I say this couldn't have happened without you," started Randall, a little stiffly. Matt immediately wondered why he was still being a formal prick. Didn't he help give him exactly what he was after?

Randall continued, "The provisional security clearance we granted to you is still in place, so I'd like to more fully explain exactly what you helped us accomplish last night. Plus, psych studies have shown that closure and understanding in these circumstances actually help minimize the violation of rules regarding classified information down the road."

Matt was happy to get a better understanding of what he had helped do, even if he had to sit through Randall being a patronizing jerk to hear it. He shrugged and said, "Ok."

"Matt, please understand that what you've helped with is big, and the fallout from what happened last night is continuing even now. The person that you helped capture last night is Shahrokh Al-Hashim. He is an Iranian by birth, but his mother is Syrian. He is, for lack of any better way to describe it, the father of the use of IEDs, improvised explosive devices, in Iraq. This man more or less introduced the use of these weapons in Iraq, helped establish supply chains to provide a steady flow of materials for them to insurgents, helped them adapt these weapons to be more effective over time, and coordinated efforts among Iraqi insurgents. This man used his family ties in Syria to establish a supply chain to get explosives and materials for IEDs from the port of Latakia and into Iraq. Eric Stillman was helping us identify these supply chains here. Al-Hashim found out and wanted to understand exactly how much we knew so he could alter the supply chains appropriately. That's why you and Eric wound up being kidnapped."

"The instant last night we knew the information we leaked to the embassy in Damascus had been acted upon, we knew we had identified the correct leak there. That person has already been dealt with. Today, we're keeping word of Al-Hashim's capture as quiet as possible until we can work with the Syrian government to disrupt the supply chains that we know about. We're just having to act a little sooner on this than we wanted to, but we have to before the supply chains are abandoned."

Randall paused, then said sadly, "If you were to ask how many deaths Shahrokh Al-Hashim was directly responsible for, it would probably be a handful. But the number he is indirectly responsible for is staggering, for both Iraqi civilians and coalition forces."

Matt didn't know what to say. All he could do was sit and look dumbly at Randall. This was the person that kept Matt bound in an empty room for three days? Had beaten him to get access to his laptop? That even last night had looked down in evil delight as Matt cowered behind a cement pipe? Matt's mind couldn't even comprehend this. This was the kind of person that Matt heard about on the evening news, not stared directly into the malicious eyes of.

Randall waited to see if Matt had any questions, but when Matt didn't seem to have any, he continued, "This information, these events, the people, the techniques we've used, the equipment you've seen in use, is all highly classified Matt, and will be for a long time."

Randall went on to step Matt through exactly what he could say and what he couldn't say when he got home. He explained how hard his friends would press him for information, and how Matt was required to never answer, positively or negatively, these questions. What it amounted to was that Matt had been abducted, the Navy was in a position to secure his release and get him to the *Iwo Jima*, and then see to it that he got home safely. Any more than that was off-limits.

Randall looked uncomfortable for a moment. "Matt, the consequences for discussing this under any circumstance and with anyone other than those directly involved in it are extremely severe. It is an act of treason against the United States of America to discuss this in any way other than I've described, and will be prosecuted as such, do you understand?"

Matt was shocked. Why was Randall being like this? After what he had done, did Randall really think that Matt needed to be threatened like this?

Matt started to say, sourly, "Randall, do you really..."

"Do you understand, Matt?" interjected Randall sharply.

"Yes, Randall, I fucking get it," said Matt, sullenly.

Randall softened a bit and said, "The government of the United States does appreciate your help, Matt."

Matt wanted to say, "Fuck you," but instead, he just shrugged and stood up to leave. He didn't even want to waste that much effort on Randall.

Before he could turn to leave, Randall stood up as well and put his forefinger against his lips. He walked over to a small panel on the wall and flipped a switch that Matt had not paid any attention to the other times he had been in the room.

Randall said, the tone in his voice suddenly very different, "Matt, can I talk to you a little more privately? If you don't mind?"

Understanding dawned on Matt like a new day.

Randall said, "Actually, let's go up to Vulture's Row, if that's ok."

Matt followed Randall up to Vulture's Row, his mind seeing the conversation he had just had in a very different light once he understood that it was between more people than just himself and Randall.

When they stepped out and looked out over the flight deck, Matt asked, "Who was listening to all that, Randall?"

"Probably a lot more people than even I realize."

Randall continued, "All those threats about treason and prosecution and whatever are the official line, Matt, but I want to talk to you unofficially. I had my doubts about you prior to last night, but you came through, and I'm glad to be wrong. The crap about treason and prison, is, unfortunately, required for us to cover in an odd situation like this and is unfortunately true. But you're not going to talk, Matt, and I know that. You're a far better person than that and deserve better than to be treated like this. Even with the very real temptation to talk about this when you get home, I've seen how you are with the SEALs. There's no way in the world you'd put them at risk by talking about their methods or missions. After all, you're going home, but they'll still be involved over here as the need arises."

The difference in Randall's demeanor was remarkable, and it made all the difference in the world to Matt.

"Keep in touch with them, Matt. With them, you can talk about it openly and freely, and you'll need to. So do just that. It'll make it a lot easier to carry this around. Just not on the phone and not through emails, please."

Randall laughed gently and said, "Actually, based on what they've got planned for you, I think you'll have a hard time shaking them off if you wanted to. What you did was remarkably brave, Matt. It's rare to have a mission fail so completely so quickly and then two guys turn it around and pull a spectacular win out of it the way you did. You should be incredibly proud of what you did for your country."

Randall held out his hand for Matt to shake, sincere admiration in his eyes.

He said, "There's one other person that's specifically asked to speak to you. I'll go get him if you'll wait here just a moment. And when you're done, head on down to the staging area on the hangar deck. The guys want to see you." Randall left, leaving Matt alone with his thoughts.

He looked out over the USS Iwo Jima, watching the various colored shirts going about their work — flight ops, refuelers, aircraft handling, ordnance, and more. He wasn't sure how to handle the way people were reacting to what had happened the night before. To him, it felt like it had been mostly uncontrolled panic and one moment of desperation to distract that Al-Hashim person long enough for Mope to do his thing. Was that bravery? He thought about the split-second decision to run across the road in full view of Al-Hashim's van. He had done it only because he had absolute trust and faith in Mope. Through faith and trust came courage. Maybe it was a little bit brave, then.

The door out to Vulture's Row opened a few minutes later, and a more formally uniformed officer stepped out to join Matt. Matt still didn't know ranks to save his life, but this guy had a lot more stuff on his sleeves and shirt than he had seen before. He was probably in his late fifties, with brown hair gone mostly gray where it hadn't receded, and a weathered skin that betrayed what was probably a lifetime out at sea.

He said, "Matt, thanks for waiting for me."

Matt nodded and shook the man's hand.

The officer asked, "Do you know who I am?"

Matt felt like he probably should have, but answered honestly, "No, sir, I don't."

The man smiled warmly and said, "I'm Navy Captain Warren McHaffie. I'm the commanding officer of the *USS Iwo Jima.*"

Matt said, "Oh," unsure of the protocol for meeting the captain of a Navy ship.

"My rank on this ship means I'm included in a lot of information most others on board aren't. For example, I know that below the flight deck, locked off, is a Nosferatu helicopter, the one you got to ride in last night. I've never gotten to ride in one myself, Matt, and I think I'd give my left nut *and* a buck fifty to be able to, so I'm a little jealous."

Matt laughed and finally was able to relax around the captain.

The captain turned more serious. "I wanted to personally thank you, Matt. You killed one of those bastards last night, and then brought the worst one to us."

Captain McHaffie looked across his ship. "This is a big ship, Matt. There are 1,800 in the Marine Expeditionary Unit on board this vessel, plus a complement of about another thousand in Navy crew. Since the war in Iraq started, IED's have killed more US service people than are on this entire ship right now. And IED's have wounded many times over the number on board. It's not easy for me to see the men and women of the *USS Iwo Jima* and think about what could happen to them every time they leave this ship. I don't like thinking about it, but I *do* think about it. Quite a bit. Thank you for getting that bastard out of the game he's been playing. You and I both know it won't stop it, but you've helped put a fine fucking dent in it."

Matt was having a hard time knowing how to respond to this. He fumbled around and said, "I mostly kind of screwed it all up, I think. If it weren't for Mope, I mean, Travis, and the other SEALs, none of this would have..."

"Bullshit!" said Captain McHaffie. He smiled a genuine smile and his gray eyes danced. "With all due respect, Matt Goodend, that is twenty-four karat gold-plated bullshit, and I get plenty enough of that each and every day already."

Matt had to laugh and the Captain did, too. "What you did took a lot of courage, Matt. In fact, I was going to invite you to dinner with me, my XO, and a few other officers tonight. But, I was told in no uncertain terms by the SEALs to back off, that your ass was theirs the rest of the day until you left! And I know when I've been outranked, Matt. Believe me when I say it's no small feat to earn the respect of the Navy SEALs. Think about that. So instead, I'll just say thanks. From me, personally, thank you for making me rest a little easier at night. Matthew Goodend, you are welcome on board my ship any time!"

Chapter 22 — Slut

Matt twisted and fought frantically to get free, but the arms that had grabbed him from behind were way too strong to break free from. He thought about biting, but that seemed like maybe going too far. So instead he thrashed as hard as he could. He really didn't hold back, but it was still useless against the iron-clad hold he was in.

Matt snarled, "You son of a bitch! You're going to regret whatever it is you think you're about to do! I swear to God!" He could see Mope off to the side, in his usual crouch, unmoved by Matt's plight and letting it happen.

Petey's voice huffed through the effort of keeping Matt in his hold while moving him forward, "Christ, Cornhole! You're harder to hold onto than a greased up Japanese prostitute!"

In a move that they were obviously trained for and had practiced quite a bit, Baya grabbed Matt from the front in a tight bear hug long enough for Petey to let go. This way, they could force him down into the folding chair they had and Desantos resumed the hold on Matt from behind.

Matt was grinning, but still not willing to give up so easily. He fought against Desantos, but was now firmly held down in the chair in their staging area of the hangar deck. Several of the crew were pausing to see whatever the SEALs were about to do to Matt.

As soon as Matt had finished talking to the captain of the ship, he made his way down to the hangar as Randall had suggested. The staging area they had used there over the last few days was empty except for the chair and he didn't see the team anywhere. But then he was suddenly ambushed from behind. Whatever it was they had in mind, Matt was sure he wasn't going to like it.

He decided to try and turn the team against itself. He yelled at Mope, "Mope, dammit, you can act like you're not a part of this, but if you don't help me, so help me God, I'll hold you responsible for whatever these guys are about to do!"

Mope swaggered over to Matt slowly and said, "Well, if I'm going to be held responsible, I might as well go ahead and help them."

Matt redoubled his fighting in the chair and shouted, "Shit! That's not how you're supposed to respond to that! You asshole!" Petey, Baya and Desantos all laughed at Matt's efforts to get loose and to turn themselves against one another.

Petey moved to plant himself directly in front of Matt, and the grin on his face couldn't possibly bode anything good for him. He said, "Calm down, Tinkerbell, or it'll turn out much worse!" He pulled out from a cargo pocket on the thigh of his pants a battery powered set of hair clippers.

Matt realized what they were about to do. He yelled, "Uh uh! Hell no!" He started fighting back harder than ever, but still couldn't shake free of the steel grip Desantos had him in.

Petey looked thoughtful for a moment while Matt tried to pull free. He said, "You know what? Mope, I think you should take the honors."

Desantos put Matt in a headlock so Matt could no longer move his head. Mope took the clippers from Petey and turned them on.

Matt said, "You'll regret this, Mope!"

Even though Matt had been fighting them, he knew it was inevitable. But just because it was inevitable didn't mean he couldn't make them work for it some. Mope stepped forward with a broad smile on his face and used the clippers to shave one big clear swath across Matt's exposed head. If getting his head shaved was the cost of seeing a smile like this on Mope's face, it was well worth it. Once the first cut had been made, Matt stopped fighting entirely. He said, pretending to sulk, "You guys are such douchebags."

Petey, Baya, and Desantos all took turns shaving Matt's head, leaving probably only an eighth of an inch behind, just like a new recruit. To make it all the more humiliating, they took pictures of the entire ordeal.

Matt told Petey as he was trimming off the last bits of Matt's hair, "Colorado, if you want a lock of my hair for under your pillow while you sleep, you could just fucking ask for it!"

When done, they released Matt, who just shook his head at them and felt his head where he used to have hair. Matt had never in his life had a haircut this short. He felt naked and exposed and bald.

The SEAL team all stood in front of Matt, finished laughing at him and letting Matt laugh at himself some, too.

Baya said, "We took a vote this morning, Matt. And with the haircut formality out of the way, you are now an honorary member of this SEAL team. Congratulations, uh... Cornhole."

Matt suddenly stopped laughing and treating this like it was all a joke. It was all in good fun, but at its heart was something much more. It was their way of celebrating the results of the night before, and it was their way of letting Matt know that he had earned their faith and trust, just as they had so easily earned his. His mind once again turned to Mope and how he had guided Matt to this point. To make him see honor and courage and trust and faith as far more important than he had ever understood.

Matt nodded and said, "Thanks. You guys are... are... great. And I just want to say... and I mean this from the bottom of my heart... you'd all better sleep with one damn eye open after this." He ran his hand over his head to emphasize what he meant, which got the team all laughing again.

They all came up to Matt, each one rubbing on his freshly shaved head.

Baya said, "Yeah, we're not done, though," which made Matt groan.

"But this next bit is just for you," said Mope.

They took Matt over in front of one of the helicopters in the hangar for some photos.

They had one of the Marines nearby in the hangar deck take a few pictures of Matt with the team in front of the helicopter. Matt liked this very much. Everything they were doing made him feel much better after what he had been through.

Petey said, "Okay, it's gonna be a stretch, but we're gonna let you pretend you're a man for a few pics. Take the shirt off."

Matt looked at him like he was crazy.

"Take the goddamn t-shirt off, Cornhole, or *I'll* take it off you!"

While Matt was taking his t-shirt off so he was wearing only his cammies and boots, Mope told Desantos, "Hey, Desantos, grab those bandoliers out of that bag and hand me my M4 in that bag there."

Desantos grabbed a few runs of machine gun ammo and Mope's rifle out of the bag. They crossed the bandoliers across Matt's bare chest, put Mope's rifle in his hands and posed him for a few ridiculously macho shots in front of the helo. Baya took several shots with Matt looking ready to take on the Taliban single-handedly.

Petey shook his head and said to Matt, "Don't get your hopes up. You still look like a fruit. Maybe we should try the M203 instead."

While Desantos was looking for the grenade launcher, and Petey and Baya were laughing and reviewing the pictures they had already taken on the camera, Matt glanced down at Mope's rifle and noticed something. On the stock of the rifle were scratches. But not scratches from heavy use and abuse. These were orderly and intentionally placed, in groups of five. It took Matt a second before he realized what he was looking at. He swallowed kind of hard — there were twenty-seven scratches on it. Twenty-seven.

Matt gave Mope a stunned look. Mope saw what he was looking at and saw the look on Matt's face, but all he could offer back to Matt was a gentle, apologetic expression. Desantos came up to Matt and said, "Here, try this grenade launcher." He had Matt swap out the M4 rifle for the grenade launcher instead.

It wasn't like he didn't know what Mope, or any of them, sometimes had to do in the line of duty. He had even seen Mope do it in front of his face. It just came as a shock to Matt to see it quantified this way. Twenty-seven. Matt didn't want to spoil the good time, and he put it out of his mind before any of the other guys saw what was going on. Instead, he tried to figure out how to best hold the grenade launcher for a few photos with it, and prayed it wasn't loaded.

After a few photos with the grenade launcher, Matt decided that, if he was going to be bare-chested, then fair was fair. He made them all take their shirts off for a few photos.

Matt watched as they shucked their shirts off. He had a hard time believing they were letting him do this to them. Petey stood there, his lean body, and abs so sharp you could grate cheese on them. Baya, thin and lithe, his caramel colored skin corded with muscles. Desantos, stocky and thick, like his wide face and white smile was sitting on top of set concrete covered in soft leather. And then there was Mope, his body as strong and finely tuned as a racehorse, a fine layer of gunpowder hair covering his chest and stomach.

Petey sneered, "I guess you undressing us with your eyes wasn't good enough anymore, huh?"

Matt flipped him off and said, "Petey, when I undress you with my eyes, I get blinded by that fluorescent orange crab-trap you call your bush and immediately dress you again. And where the hell does anyone get hair that color, anyway? What exactly did your mom screw to have you, huh? Carrots? Or pumpkins? Maybe a traffic cone? Is your dad a traffic cone, Petey?"

Baya handed the camera to a maintenance crewman and cackled, "Heh! Fluorescent orange crab-trap!"

Petey shot him a dirty look, "Shut it, camel jockey!"

Once they had taken a few photos like that, Matt decided to go ahead and push just a little bit farther. He grabbed the camera from the maintenance crewman and told the team, "Now grab your dicks through your cammies for me!"

They groaned and Matt commanded, "Do it! Petey, I'll give you a few extra seconds to find that puny thing of yours." They all obliged Matt and let him take a photo of them with their hands in their crotches grabbing their dicks.

Petey said, "Hey Desantos, this is practically beating off for you! The Pope's gonna come kick you in the nuts for this!!"

They wound down with taking the photos just as Randall showed up to give Matt details on his ride home later that evening. Matt wanted to get home, but he didn't want to leave the team, either. It was going to be harder than he thought for all of this to end now that the dangerous part was over.

Mope, Petey, Baya and Desantos needed to get back to the ready room to finish packing their gear up and told Matt to come along. Matt said he'd be there in a few minutes, but that there was something he needed to go do first.

As they walked out, Petey grabbed Matt's arm and slowed him down for a second. Petey had been in a very good mood all day, but Matt saw a very serious look on his face now.

"You're going to call him, aren't you?" asked Petey.

"Yeah," said Matt, nodding. "Now that I know exactly when I'll get home, I need to let Brian know. Well, Brian, Bret and Jim."

Petey looked like he had just swallowed a shot of cheap tequila, and like he had something else he wanted to say, but was struggling with whether or not to say it.

He finally couldn't stand it. Petey pushed Matt up against the wall, pinning him there with his forearm across Matt's chest, his breath coming in huffs like a bull about to charge. Petey held Matt like this, up against the bulkhead, for few moments, his eyes darting over Matt, studying him. Matt was about to ask him what was going on when Petey said, "You know what, Matt? You're a slut!"

Matt said, "I am not a slut! I've never..."

"You're a fucking slut! But not like with sex. It's worse than that. It doesn't take anything to see what's going on here. You've given this guy all of you, and you've gotten nothing back. You gave your heart away. You gave it away to some asshole that doesn't even deserve it! And for nothing. You're giving it away to some chump that hasn't earned jack shit from you!"

Matt was stunned. He had no idea what to say to Petey. If it had been anybody else saying these things, Matt would have gotten seriously pissed and told them to fuck off. But this was Petey. And Matt was finding out just how much he really cared. Matt remembered Mope saying that once Petey was on your side, he was *really* on your side.

Petey let go of Matt. "C'mon, man," he said, "You're a good guy. You deserve more than what you're getting from this guy. I'm no damn expert on solid relationships, and maybe I'm just a manwhore who just wants to get laid by any bitch that comes along with a tight enough pussy. But, Cornhole, I think you're giving it up for nothing here."

Matt knew if he wasn't careful, Petey was going to turn into one of the best friends he could ever have. Hell, he was probably already past that point. But Petey just didn't understand Brian and what Matt had in him.

Matt ran his hand across his almost-bald head and tried to figure out what to say. He put his hand on Petey's shoulder and said, "Petey, I swear to God... despite you being the most offensive person I've ever met, you're going to settle down one day with some really lucky woman, and you're going to drive her bat-shit insane. And... make her *very* happy."

Chapter 23 – A Million Miles Away

After having helped the team get their duffel bags and equipment loaded on the Chinook helicopter on the flight deck, Matt stood with them in the evening sun to say goodbye. They couldn't tell Matt where they were going, but they did assure him it was an easy mission, and then they'd be back in the US for a round of survival training with the rest of their platoon. Matt didn't like not knowing, but he knew it wasn't their decision. It just made him feel like a mother hen and worry about them.

The large rotors in the front and back of the helo spun idly, waiting for them to finish their goodbyes.

Matt had spent all afternoon with them, and now that he was down to his last few moments with the team, he didn't want to let go. These men had become like close family in an incredibly short period of time and he didn't want to say goodbye.

He stood looking at the four of them, in their battle dress uniforms, and threw caution to the wind.

Matt grabbed Petey and hugged him hard. To his surprise, Petey let him do it, and even put one arm around Matt, half-hugging him back. But the words out of his mouth were, "Awww, Jesus! You and your fucking asswipe Hallmark moments! Will you knock it off?" He pushed Matt away and messed with his shaved head one last time.

Baya and Desantos both came up to Matt for their turn. Baya said, "We'll get you your photos soon, Matt. It's going to suck only having Petey to play video games against."

Baya looked thoughtful for a minute and added, "It's going to feel different, not having you around." Matt nodded in complete agreement with that.

Desantos said, "Yeah, it is." He paused a minute, then added, "I'm glad I got to know you, Matt. You've made me think a lot about things. No matter what any religion says, you're a good guy and I'm glad to have you as a friend. The fact that you're gay... it completely doesn't matter. It just doesn't matter compared to the things that do. We'll be in touch, man."

He studied Matt a moment more. They weren't making it easy on Matt to let go of them.

Desantos nodded at Matt and added, "I'd be willing to put my life in your hands, Matt, and I don't think I'd regret it one bit."

And to Matt's surprise, Desantos came up to him and gave him a rough bear hug, followed by a rub on his head. Baya came over, too, and followed Desantos with a hug. He rubbed Matt's head, as was somehow becoming the accepted thing to do. Matt was starting to choke up, and he still had one person left to say goodbye to. The one it would be hardest to say goodbye to of all of them. Matt wasn't sure he'd be able to hug Mope, though. Not without making a serious emotional idiot of himself.

Mope stepped up and grabbed Matt roughly, holding him tightly and leaving Matt no choice in the matter. Mope started to whisper in his ear, "I... I... uh..."

Before going any further, though, he pushed Matt away, his hands holding onto Matt's shoulders. He was squinting, but looked directly in Matt's eyes and finally said, "I'm really proud of you, Matt." And he placed his hand on Matt's head for only a moment before turning to get into the helicopter without looking back.

The flight ops guy nearby made Matt back up to a safe distance and he watched as the helo lifted off the deck of the *Iwo Jima* and into the early evening. If Matt had been able to get on the helicopter and go with them, he probably would have.

~~~~~

An hour later, Matt was seated in the helicopter that was going to take him to a nearby aircraft carrier. From there, he was on a Navy plane to a US base in Turkey, where someone from the embassy was going to meet him with his replacement passport and tickets for his commercial airline flight back home. Home. Once and for all.

He sat with his laptop in his lap, the only possession he had to take back with him. The helicopter lifted up, turned briefly into the sun as it sank lower in the sky, and then turned north towards his next destination. Matt looked out at the *USS Iwo Jima* for one last time, watching it retreat into the distance, thinking about everything that had happened to him. He was a million miles away from where he had started.

Chapter 24 — Off Balance

Matt was about one minute shy of asking someone if he could borrow their cell phone so he could call Bret or Jim to come pick him up. He had been waiting thirty minutes now from when Brian had said he'd be there to pick Matt up at the airport, and he was tired and ready to be home. Brian had insisted he'd be there on time. Someone surely would have been happy to let him use their cell phone. There had been multiple people on the flights back that had stopped Matt and thanked him for being a service member. He had just played along rather than try to explain why he was wearing an authentic BDU without actually being in the military.

Just as he was about to reach the end of his patience, he saw Brian, who would have walked right past him if Matt hadn't grabbed his arm and stopped him. His impatience to get home and impatience with Brian for being late evaporated as soon as he touched his arm.

It took a second before Brian realized who it was that had grabbed him. Brian gawked at Matt, and then finally found his voice. He said, "Matt! I didn't even recog... why the hell are you dressed like that? What the hell happened to your *hair*?"

Matt ignored his questions for a moment, instead pulling Brian to him and hugging him close, so glad to really be home. He kissed Brian right on the lips, which probably drew more than a fair share of looks from passers-by in the airport.

They made their way through the airport and all the other travelers. They got back to Brian's car and Matt started to finally answer some of his questions.

He explained, "These are all the clothes I have. I lost everything else while in Latakia. So I had to wear a BDU while on the ship. And as for the hair, well, some of the guys were horsing around before I left and decided I needed to look more like a real Navy recruit. They held me down and shaved my head." Matt loved thinking back over that last day he was able to spend with the team.

Brian looked at him, disgusted. "They held you down? You let these *assholes* shave your head?"

Matt could tolerate a lot of Brian's attitude, but not this. He turned on Brian in a way that he was clearly not used to hearing from Matt. "Ok. We're going to get something straight right here and now. You will NOT talk about these guys that way ever again. These are good guys, Brian. Better guys than you can imagine. I got to know them pretty well, and... and... just don't ever talk about them like that ever again. I mean it, Brian. Is that clear?"

Brian looked at Matt like he was crazy. He said, "Ok... sorry... jeez, Matt."

Trying to move past Matt's sudden outburst, Brian asked, "Ok, so you've got nothing that you went over there with, except your laptop, obviously. So what the hell happened, Matt? This whole thing has me freaked out and I'm tired of waiting to understand this."

Matt said, "As much as I really do want to talk about the details, Brian, I can't tell you much. I was kind of abducted while I was over there. And the Navy happened to be in a position to get me out of the situation I was in. They got me over to the *USS Iwo Jima* and let me stay there until they could arrange for me to get back to the US. For reasons I can't go into, and under specific instructions from the Department of State, I can't talk about it more than just to say that."

Brian almost lost control of his car and yelled, "WHAT!? Abducted? ABDUCTED, Matt? Abducted by who? How did they get you out? Why would someone abduct you? Jesus, Matt! You never said anything about being fucking kidnapped!! What the *hell* are you talking about?!"

Matt realized this was going to be much harder than he thought it was going to be. He sighed and said, "Brian, I know you want to understand what happened. But there are real reasons why I'm not talking about it, even above and beyond the strict instructions I got to not talk to anyone under any circumstance."

Brian asked, "Was it these people at that university you were at? Did they kidnap you? What did they do to you?"

Randall had been right that people would immediately start the game of twenty questions, trying to triangulate into the story from his answers. Matt recognized this. He said, "I'm sorry, Brian. I can't say any more than I have."

The rest of the car ride back home was very strained. Brian kept trying to probe in various directions, hoping to get anything out of him, but Matt refused each attempt until Brian finally gave up. Brian grew increasingly mad at Matt, and Matt was tired of having to tell Brian he couldn't answer his questions. The last few minutes before arriving at Matt's apartment, Brian spent in sullen silence.

When Matt walked in the front door of his apartment, he noticed the lights were already on. And before he had a chance to even look around, he heard someone yell "Matt!" and practically tackle him in a violent hug.

Matt backed up a step from the force of the person holding onto him. He relaxed and hugged back. "Chiliburger! God, Bret, it's good to see you, too!"

Bret finally let go, and Matt was able to give Jim a hug as well. Jim came up and grabbed Matt tightly. He could feel Jim's anxiety in his embrace, and that he was glad to have Matt home. Jim whispered in Matt's ear, "Please, Matt, please... don't ever scare me like that again. I'm serious, Matt."

Matt stepped back and said, "Believe me, I have no intention of doing this to you guys or myself ever again!" He thought to himself what an understatement that was.

Bret wrinkled up his nose and said, "What... is all this getup? And look at your hair, or *utter* lack thereof! You're almost butch all of a sudden!" He pointed at Matt's clothes and head and had his hand over his mouth in shock.

Matt laughed and said, "Ok. I want a beer. It's been two weeks, and I just want a beer right now. Then I'll explain the little bit I can."

Bret and Jim sat down on the sofa while Brian went to get beers for everyone. Brian handed out the bottles, then sat sullenly in a chair while Bret and Jim eagerly awaited getting real answers. Matt began his explanation, knowing it would leave a lot to be desired from his audience.

"This isn't going to be what you want to hear, and you're going to have a million more questions than you started with, but here goes. While I was over in Latakia, I was abducted, and the Navy..."

Bret immediately shouted, "ABDUCTED?! Abducted, like as in, what? Fucking *abducted*?!"

Matt said, "Yes, that kind of abducted. Let me finish, Bret, please. The Navy was in a position to step in and help me out. They got me back to the ship, the *USS Iwo Jima*, and I stayed there until they could make arrangements to get me home."

Bret immediately said, "Ok, so that's..." but Matt walked over to him and literally put his hand over Bret's mouth to shut him up.

Matt continued, knowing his next statement was just going to inflame Bret even more. "Guys... that's it. That's all I can say. Yes, it was scary. Yes, I'm glad to be home. But under strict orders of the Department of State, I can't say anything else. Please don't make this harder on me than it already is by demanding a lot of answers I can't give."

Bret and Jim sat in shocked silence for a moment. Bret recovered first and demanded, "Is this some kind of a joke? You're just pulling a joke, right? The hair, the weird military-fetish outfit, it's all just an elaborate joke, right?"

"No, Bret. I wish it was. I wish it was..." Brian, Jim, and Bret could all see the look on Matt's face as he said this, and knew that Matt wasn't joking.

Jim asked, "So, was it like terrorists or something? That kidnapped you?"

Matt said, sadly, "I can't talk about it."

Bret asked, "Did the terrorists shave your head? Is that what they're doing these days? Bad hairstyles?"

Matt laughed and said, "Chili, I swear to God... I got to know some of the guys on the ship. Before I left, they were horsing around with me and shaved my head."

He explained that the only clothes he came back with were the ones he was wearing. Then they started with questions along the lines of those Brian had asked, trying to get Matt to give them even oblique clues as to what happened.

To get them off of that, he spent a little time giving them safe details. He described the *Iwo Jima*, Vulture's Row, the chow hall, the flight deck, the hangar deck. He even mentioned how his friends had let him target practice with a submachine gun a little. This seemed to work pretty well, at least for Jim and Bret, who seemed very interested in these details.

Brian sat over in Matt's overstuffed chair, not saying much. Matt pretty much expected this as this was Brian's usual way of sulking when forced to be around Bret and Jim. Matt knew Brian didn't care for them very much, and if Brian had had his way, Matt would only really associate with Brian's friends. But Matt had been particularly obstinate about this and didn't give up on his good comrades.

Matt said he wanted another beer, and as he went to go get one, he noticed Bret starting to text people on his phone. He stopped and said, "Bret, seriously, do me a favor and just keep this between us. I can't talk about it, and having to tell a hundred people I can't talk about it will be exhausting."

Bret looked very disappointed, but put his phone away.

Jim followed Matt into the kitchen to get another beer as well.

Matt said, "You're pretty quiet, Jimmy Bob."

"What's there to say? If you really can't talk, you can't talk. Of course, my imagination is conjuring up all sorts of horrible things that would wind up with you being instructed by the US government to not talk about it, so that's a little upsetting. But, I'm just glad to see you here, in person, safe and sound. In the end, that's all that matters to me." Jim frowned, moved by the thought of what might have happened to his best friend, and made Matt hug him again.

Jim finally probed a little more, "I saw on CNN, there were explosions in Syria the other night, in Latakia. Not accidents, but like bombs. Please tell me that had nothing to do with you."

Matt clenched. He didn't like outright lying to Jim, but he couldn't leave this open-ended either. He couldn't leave Jim wondering if he was somehow involved in that kind of danger. He said, "No, Jim. I never left the ship." He hated saying it, but re-assuring Jim was more important.

Jim glanced down at Matt's arm, studying it for a moment. Matt caught the glance and immediately became self-conscious that he was looking at the still very fresh cut from the piece of glass in the explosions at Café Lucien. Matt knew Jim well enough to know that he might not be buying Matt's story.

Jim stared at the cut a moment, his concern over what his friend had been through growing, and almost spilling out as his lip started to tremble slightly. Jim fought it back and said, "I don't know what I'd do if you hadn't come home safely, Matt." Matt hugged him again, feeling so glad to be home and to have friends like Jim.

Matt called out to Bret in the other room without even looking to see what he was doing, "Bret! What did I say about sending texts? Put the phone down!"

"Ugh! How do you know these things? You're worse than my mom!" yelled Bret back to Matt.

~~~~~

Brian said, irritably, "Baby, I've got to be up early for work tomorrow, and it's already pretty late. I know you want me to stay, but I need to go."

Matt could feel his face flush hot, and he was flustered and disappointed. He was really looking forward to being with Brian all night, not just long enough to have sex. He really wanted to have Brian next to him all night. He needed it.

Matt said, "Please, Brian, it's like you don't seem to care that much about what I went through. Please stay!"

"What do you want from me, Matt? You can't talk about it at all, or just won't talk about it at all, but then expect me to be all over you like I understand what it is that you went through. I feel like I'm supposed to leave you alone about it, but then I get blamed because I *am* leaving you alone about it."

Brian leaned his forearm up against the open door jamb of Matt's apartment and put his head on it.

Matt stood there confused. Was that what he was doing to Brian? That didn't seem like what he was doing, but he couldn't figure it out.

Brian finally said, "There's just more and more of this lately. It's like you want to keep me off balance in this relationship, Matt."

Matt knew that wasn't the case at all. "Brian, no, you're the one thing I want more than anything else. I... I don't know what I'm doing that makes you say that."

Brian ran his hand over his face. "Can we just talk about this tomorrow? I'm really tired, Matt. I'm sorry for whatever you went through, and I'm glad the Navy got you home to me safely. I missed you, baby. Just keep that in your shaved head." He reached out and rubbed Matt's velvety head.

And with that, Brian left, leaving Matt alone with his thoughts, but at least safe at home.

After Jim and Bret had left earlier, Matt practically pounced on Brian, wanting to feel him next to him so badly he could taste it. Wanting to be the best boyfriend in the world. He had cheated death barely a week earlier, and he intended to keep his promise. So, they had had sex, but Brian still seemed a little uninvolved, like he was still disgruntled that Matt wouldn't tell him everything. Like he was just

160

going through the obligatory motions. Matt guessed he couldn't blame Brian for feeling that way. What really hurt was that he refused to spend the night. That was more important to Matt than the sex. Matt wanted Brian to be there for him, and he was disappointed that he couldn't seem to get even just a little solace from Brian.

Matt sat down on his sofa, feeling a little lost now that he was alone.

Just two nights earlier now, he had somehow had the most harrowing night of his life, and at the same time, one of the warmest and most peaceful. How could those things exist together? Even as bad as it was, just knowing that Mope hijacked a motorcycle to come after him, steadied his nerves and calmed his panic, put his arm around his shoulder to comfort him, told Matt that Brian was the lucky one, made Matt feel good. It made Matt feel... something he almost couldn't describe. How could a night so terrible feel so wonderful at the same time? Would he ever feel something like that again? Mope was such a set of contradictions to Matt. This person could plant himself in front of a speeding van, take aim with a rifle, and blow a person's head off without flinching. He could drive a knife into a guy's neck, killing him, then calmly take the knife out, wipe it off, and put it back in its sheath. Matt didn't know people like that, let alone gay people. And then this same person could hold Matt's head gently in his hands, make him look into his eyes, and slow his breathing and bring his nerves back down to earth.

He had the email addresses of Mope, Petey, Baya, and Desantos, and he thought that maybe he should send them an email letting them know he was home safe. He wanted to know they were safe, too. Any kind of contact with them would feel good. But he didn't want to be clingy, either. He felt lost, caught between two worlds and not really a part of either at the moment. He didn't know what to do.

He finally decided he'd wait and send emails to the team the next day. He needed to focus back on the life he had come back to, and he knew Brian would move past this. And he would help him. Matt was committed to really appreciating what he had in Brian. And daydreaming about other things would just result in broken promises. And honoring promises was an important thing to Matt, more so than ever before.

Matt crawled into his bed, wanting sleep, and hoped he didn't have the dream about being alone in the empty room.

Chapter 25 – Sincerity Sucks

"Ugh! Stop that! Why are you doing this? Don't give me that scolded puppy dog look! You know I *hate* when you do that!" said Bret, putting his sandwich back down on his plate.

Matt couldn't help it. Bret had never been quite so blunt in his remarks regarding Brian before. Sure, he had always tried to get Matt to feel like Brian was the one dragging their relationship down, but he always approached it much more indirectly or softly. Suddenly today, Bret wasn't being very gentle or indirect about it.

Matt said, his shoulders slumped and feeling hurt, "But what you say I should do, I just don't think I could, Bret. I'm lucky to have Brian, and more than ever, I want to be the best boyfriend for him I can be."

Matt had met Bret for lunch on the Friday after getting back from Syria before taking the afternoon off to go shopping. During their lunch, Matt decided he needed a little moral support and finally mentioned how he was a little disappointed that Brian hadn't stayed with him the night he had gotten back. That he kind of needed Brian's support that night, but hadn't really gotten it. To make matters worse, Brian had been grumpy all week.

It was at that point that Bret went off like a firecracker, pointing his fork at Matt and attracting the attention of nearby tables he was so wound up. He described Brian as completely not worth it. As someone that even *he* wouldn't go out with, despite his pathetically loose standards and morals. But he surely didn't expect Brian to change. *Matt* needed to fix the situation. Matt had to get some balls, stop being a doormat, and demand more from Brian, or find somebody who *would* give him more.

Matt could almost see the steam coming out of Bret's ears.

At the risk of making matters worse, Matt said, "You know how miserable I was before I met Brian. And who's to say all that wouldn't make matters worse? We've talked about this before, Bret. Even Brian says leaving him would be the stupidest thing I could ever do, that I'd just wind up with some douchebag who'd use me."

Bret looked like he was about to tear his own face off he was so frustrated with Matt.

Bret stood up from the table, stepped around to Matt and motioned at him impatiently with his hand. "Stand up," he demanded.

People were still staring and Matt was hurt and a little nervous about what Bret was going to do. Bret could draw from a deep well of drama when he wanted to, and that was worrying Matt right at this moment.

"STAND UP!" Bret yelled.

Matt stood up, and Bret grabbed him and hugged him tightly. He hugged Matt like he was never going to see him again for the rest of his life. Matt felt better and hugged him back, glad that Bret really cared and glad that it was just a hug. Bret didn't say anything and didn't let Matt go for what felt like forever.

Bret finally stood back from Matt and they sat back down. Bret's eyes were red like he was about to start crying. He said, more calmly, "Ok. You're now making me say something heartfelt and sincere instead of sarcastic and bitter, which I much prefer. Soooo... fuck you for that."

Bret had to take a second to pull himself together to say what he had to say.

"Matt, you are one of the best people I've ever known, and there are precious few men out there that deserve someone as wonderful as you. And frankly, *you* are so far out of *Brian's* league that it's downright comical... and sad. You want to think the best of Brian so much. You want to think the best of *everyone* so much. You want to give everyone the benefit of the doubt, always seeing the very best in them. So much so, that if you ever do seem to doubt someone, then that person is, without doubt, a douche extraordinaire. If you think it's easy for me to see you being treated like a dishrag, you're miserably wrong. But I know how much Brian means to you, having convinced yourself he's the best thing that's ever happened to you. And I just couldn't hurt you by speaking my mind. I just couldn't do it, Matt, not to you. I've hated holding back, but I did. But I can't do it anymore. It just kills me that you won't give yourself any more credit than you do. It just kills me how you don't see how you're worth so much more, and yet it's one of the most beautiful things I've ever seen."

Bret's lip quivered before he took a sharp breath and said, "Ok. There. I've said it. Christ, sincerity sucks! Alright... now... back to your regularly scheduled programming... that haircut looks much better on you when you're in that butch military outfit you came home in. You should wear that until your hair grows back out a little. I require you to wear the sexy military getup from now on."

Matt sat stunned. He had no idea how to react. He had never seen Bret being so unguarded and unequivocal with anyone. It hurt to hear him say these things and it made him feel deeply loved at the same time. It was a slap in the face and the tightest embrace. He knew Bret cared, in his own way, but he never realized how deeply. But still, Bret didn't understand. Brian was important to Matt, and having that connection with someone was important. Bret just didn't understand the give and take in a relationship. To think it wouldn't be there was naïve. Plus, Matt had made a promise to himself. And honoring that promise was important to the person he had become. Bret just didn't understand how important the promise was.

Bret pulled out his phone and punched at it some, sending a text.

He said, "You need to see this, Matt."

On Matt's phone, the text arrived with a picture attached to it. Matt opened it up and saw a picture of a really drunk Brian and his really drunk ex-boyfriend, Greg, sitting together on a couch out at some club. Brian's hand was down the front of Greg's shirt.

It hurt Matt to see it, but as easy as it would be to assume the worst from that picture, he didn't want to damn Brian for something that could so easily be innocent. Matt wondered what kind of person he'd be if he insisted Brian never have contact of any kind with an ex-boyfriend, including out in public.

Matt said, "They're just drunk, Bret."

Bret said, impatiently, "People have *sex* when they're drunk!"

"And sometimes they're too drunk to have sex," insisted Matt.

Bret looked like he didn't know what to do — push harder or let it go. He looked miserable, like he was destroying something rare and beautiful. But Matt had had this conversation with Bret, and Jim for that matter, before.

Matt said quietly, "Bret, I know you're looking out for me. You and Jimmy mean more to me than you can imagine. And after what I've been through, you guys mean more to me than even before."

Bret seemed to relax a little.

But Matt added, "But after what I've been through, so does Brian." He waited for the inevitable outburst.

Bret heaved an enormous sigh. He said, "I give up. You are the sweetest, most hard-headed person I know, and you look damn fine in a military uniform, and I could absolutely strangle you sometimes, and I could absolutely hug you the rest. I hope Brian makes you feel something no one else does, because it would be the only reason to put up with his shit."

Bret pushed his plate away from him at the table. He said, "I so totally wish I could take the afternoon off and go shopping with you. I could spend the entire time telling you how infuriating you are and shopping for clothes. Two of my most favorite things in the whole world. Well, after internet porn, anyway."

Matt was actually a little glad he couldn't go with him. Spending all afternoon with Bret being this intense would wear him out.

Instead, Matt made sure that Bret was going to come watch their first softball game on Saturday, and they went their separate ways.

~~~~~

Matt browsed through the sport coats hanging on the racks, but he wasn't focusing on them very well. His mind was still at lunch with Bret, hearing so many things put very bluntly that, for over a year, Bret had only tiptoed around out of concern and compassion for Matt.

He had already picked up most of the clothing he really needed. Since he had lost everything he had taken to Syria, he had to put a little concerted effort into rebuilding his wardrobe. He had gotten enough things to cover his needs, and now he was just passing time browsing through the men's department at the Macy's that he sometimes went to.

He ran across a sport coat he really liked, but he hadn't lost one of those in Syria, so buying it would be just buying it because he liked it. His mind drifted back to his lunch with Bret. Bret meant well, but he just didn't understand what he had gone through in Syria. How he had changed while he was over there.

Randall had been very right. It was hard not talking about everything that had happened over there. He wished he could talk about it. He had sent emails to Petey, Mope, Desantos and Baya, telling them he was safe at home. Wishing them all good luck and to be safe. And to please, please, please let him know they were ok. He wished he could talk to them. Hear their voices. Remind himself, remind them, of how much they meant to him. None more so than Mope. He went to bed every night thinking about how it felt to have Mope's arm around him, leaning against an olive tree in the middle of the night in the Syrian countryside. He went to bed every night with that thought and the guilt it caused. But he hadn't heard anything. None of them had replied. He tried to tell himself it didn't mean anything and that they were safe, but his own consolation wasn't much.

Matt decided to go ahead and buy the sport coat. He took the coat up to one of the register stations where he saw a clerk bent over and digging around for something under the counter.

He put the coat on the counter, and then about jumped out of his skin when he saw the person behind it stand up.

Greg was clearly just as surprised seeing Matt on the other side of the counter.

He recovered and said, "Hey, Matt!"

And before Matt realized what was coming out of his mouth, he said sarcastically, "Well, Greg, funny seeing you! I hope you and Brian have been having a good time with each other."

Greg turned slightly pink, but smiled and said off-handed, "I know. It's a little strange, but I'm really glad you're so cool about it."

Matt looked at Greg, not expecting quite that reaction. How could Greg be so boldfaced to admit it this way?

He said angrily, "Jesus, Greg, I can't believe you're this flagrant about it!"

Now it was Greg's turn to look confused. He said, "What's your problem, Matt? Why are you acting surprised by all this?"

"What the hell are you talking about?"

"Me and Brian. Brian said you *knew* we were, you know, messing around some. He said you guys had an open relationship and you were ok with it."

"*WHAT?!*"

Chapter 26 — When You Come Crawling Back

The drizzly rain seemed to be slowly stopping. Matt didn't really care, though. It matched his mood pretty well to have it. He had been sitting out on the front step of his apartment on East Broad Street, under the front portico, ever since he had gotten home from Macy's. If it hadn't been for the rain, he probably would have walked over to Chimborazo Park like he often did when he needed to think. Instead, he sat looking at the street and townhouses up and down East Broad, the damp road and sidewalk as miserable as he felt.

He spent the entire time thinking, crying a little, thinking some more, watching the rain, and thinking. But despite all that thinking, he didn't feel like he had arrived at any strong conclusions. Shouldn't he have, though? Why was it that everything regarding Brian always felt so disorienting? Nothing ever seemed clear cut with respect to Brian, even after bumping into Greg a few hours earlier.

For a little while, Matt was in denial. He had fled the department store pretty quickly, not bothering to grill Greg for details. For a brief period, he thought that maybe what Greg meant by "messing around" wasn't what he thought it meant. But even Matt had to finally realize he was being ridiculous with that defense on behalf of Brian. Was that why he had fled so quickly? Just so he could cling to the tiniest thread of doubt that he could give Brian the benefit of?

So instead, he sat broken-hearted. In fact, Matt found that it felt as bad as being in the empty room, bound and dying of thirst. There, it had been fear and physical pain. Here, it felt like betrayal, by the one person he should be able to trust above all others. There was that word again. This time, the thought of faith and trust made him feel emptiness, as far down inside as it could go. At the moment, it was hard to say that one was much worse than the other — the betrayal or the empty room. At least in the empty room, he had believed there was someone that loved him and was true to him and wanted him home.

It hurt so much to realize the person he had devoted the last year to, the person that was the central figure in his life, was capable of this. He had tried so hard to not be pessimistic about Brian, and, as Bret put it, to see the good in everything. But now he just felt like a dupe. Had he been the only one to not realize it? The discouraging answer to that was... probably.

Bret and Jim had been right. He'd been a fool the whole time. God, it hurt to realize that. Then the dagger dug deeper and twisted harder. Even Petey had seen it. He *was* a slut. He *had* given his heart away and gotten nothing in return.

So what would he do about his promise? Where was the honor in tossing the commitment aside? Honor was sticking by the commitment, no matter the personal cost. Matt made the mistake of wondering what would Mope maybe do in this situation. What advice would he give Matt? But the instant he thought of Mope, the pain seared through him and he thought he would get physically ill. Oddly enough, what came to his mind wasn't something that Mope had said. It was Petey. Petey had said that he was giving his heart away to someone that hadn't earned it. Maybe honor and commitment could be misplaced if it hadn't been earned.

He didn't know what to do. Well, he did. But it didn't make it any easier. He had spent a year practicing turning a blind eye to these signs, and continuing that would be so very easy.

Matt stayed outside and waited. Brian would arrive soon for their Friday night plans together. Actually, Matt had expected to get a call from Brian already, who he would have thought would have gotten a heads-up text or call from Greg. But Brian hadn't called. So he waited, looking up at the gray sky blanketing a gray world.

~~~~~

Matt watched as Brian parked his car down the street a little, where he managed to find an available spot. He steeled his nerves for what was about to happen.

But as soon as he saw Brian walking up the sidewalk to his apartment, he started to lose all the nerve he had built up. What if he had driven Brian to all this? If he had maybe been better all along, maybe Brian wouldn't have done this.

He cursed himself for falling into this trap already. But it was so easy to do.

Matt said, "We need to talk," as Brian walked up the front steps to where he was.

Brian sat down next to Matt, his arm pressing against his boyfriend's, which didn't make things easier. He said, "Good. You finally going to let me know what the hell happened? This cat and mouse game with you is getting old and you know you're going to tell me sooner or later."

Matt felt like his mouth was full of sawdust, and the only way to speak was to swallow all of it. Why was it so hard to say such basic words? Why was he so afraid of putting the truth out there?

"You've been seeing Greg, Brian. I know."

Without missing a beat, Brian rolled his eyes and leaned harder against Matt. "Greg? You're joking, right? There's a *reason* I broke up with him before I met you, you know?"

Matt thought, God, he can be so convincing. But what if he was right? What if Greg was just lying to stir shit up and get at them? The doubts crept in. Matt could turn and say he was sorry and make it up to Brian. He could earn Brian back, yet again. The thought of his world without Brian was frightening. He stared straight ahead at the wet street pavement in front of his apartment. Why was it so easy to look the other way?

Matt felt like it was inevitable to give in. Why was he fighting this? What would it be like to be without Brian?

Even as he thought this, a memory popped into his mind. Randall had taken him up to Vulture's Row and remarked that he had had his doubts about Matt, but that he was glad to be wrong. He called Matt remarkably brave. And then the captain of the USS *Iwo Jima* had said that what he had done took a lot of courage, and that it wasn't easy to earn the respect of the SEALs. And then one more memory showed up, a little painful but far more precious. More important than any other. He was standing on a deserted road outside of Latakia, covered in blood. Mope had put his hand on Matt's heart. And he told Matt that he had more in him than he could possibly imagine.

Matt decided he didn't have to cave in. He might not know what it would be like without Brian, but that wasn't an excuse to be afraid of it.

"I ran into Greg today at Macy's. He said he and you had been fooling around because you told him I said it was ok, that we had an open relationship."

This time, it took Brian a moment to respond, and Matt could tell it was because he was caught off guard and had to formulate an answer that might work. He finally could tell what this was now. It had taken him a year to see it, but now he could see this technique of Brian's as clear as day.

Brian forced a grin and said, "Oh, dear God, you're not going to listen anything that liar Greg says, are you? Why do you think I broke up with him?"

Matt didn't respond.

"The only time I've even seen him since we broke up was when I've been with you and we've just bumped into him. Christ, I can't believe he'd pull shit like this. Wait... actually... I can."

Matt sighed, pulled out his cellphone and showed Brian the picture of him and Greg all over each other. Matt felt empty, but brave enough to handle it, and it didn't really matter what Brian said any more.

Brian looked up from the phone, flustered, and Matt looked directly in his eyes. He didn't flinch this time. "I don't want to see you anymore, Brian."

Brian looked aghast. He looked at Matt like he didn't know who was sitting there.

He finally said, furiously, "Well, so what, Matt? What was I supposed to do? You've been picking fights with me for weeks now. None of this would have happened, we wouldn't be right here tonight with this problem, if you hadn't been so fucking weird for months now!"

Matt said calmly, "I don't want to see you anymore, Brian."

Brian began to rapidly turn red in the face. He tried again, "Matt, this is ridiculous. You're lucky to have me and you're going to throw that away? You and I know you'll wind up with some loser just out to use you! Is that what you want?"

Matt realized how desperately Brian was grasping at straws now. Why was it so obvious only now?

"I don't want to see you ever again, Brian," said Matt.

Brian sat, his eyes darting over the person sitting next to him like he was a stranger, his breathing rapid and shallow.

He eventually stood up, "Fine. But when you come crawling back, I don't know that I'm going to want you back."

Brian waited to see if Matt would cave in, but Matt just stared at him, emotionless. He finally shook his head and waved his hand dismissively at Matt and walked off.

When Brian finally got in his car and drove off, Matt broke down and cried. Was this how a year's commitment wound up? Where was the honor in any of this? Everything in his life had twisted around so much since being in Latakia. Everything had been upended and scattered. Is this what borrowed time was going to be like?

Through his tears, he watched the haze gray sky above him and wondered what to do next.

Chapter 27 – Respect And Admiration

It didn't take Matt long to figure out what to do next. In fact, the next day at the softball game, he realized one thing he could do. Bret and Jim had been all over him for most of the game peppering him with questions about his breakup with Brian, what he'd do next, who he'd like to go out with (as if he could simply pick absolutely anybody), and making sure he was ok. Their support meant a lot to him, even if it felt a little suffocating at times. But at one point, they left him alone long enough for his mind to wander and it hit him. Just like anytime he let his mind free, he started thinking about the SEALs, particularly Mope. He liked being able to think about Mope now without the guilt, even though he had dumped Brian less than a day earlier. It was in this brief time that his mind was free that the thought struck him.

When the game was over, he wanted to get home to look around to see if he could make it happen or not, but had to first contend with Bret and Jim. They saw the job of supporting Matt only beginning at the softball game... that was just the warm up. Since they wanted to make sure he didn't have a chance to second guess his decision, they insisted they go out drinking after the game, and Matt spent the better part of the afternoon indulging them.

When he finally did get some time to himself at home, he was able to focus on his other task. He did a little searching on the internet and found what he was looking for remarkably easily. The harder part was the conscious decision to violate his promise to not talk about what happened in Syria to anyone. He knew he wouldn't need to give away anything that mattered. He wouldn't put the team at risk, or the rest of the process of dismantling what they could of Al-Hashim's world. But he had given an absolute promise nonetheless, and honoring that commitment was very important to him. But so was something else.

The other thing that bothered Matt was that he knew this plan could backfire on him. He prayed it didn't. He just had to show a little courage and faith that it wouldn't.

So on Sunday afternoon, Matt found himself on a beautiful residential street. The kind with large, mature trees that grew in a canopy over the road, lined on either side with expansive, well-kept lawns. He stood in front of a house he had never been to before in his life, ringing the doorbell of the front door. It was a large, well-kept brick house with black shutters and a wide front door with mullioned glass panes on either side of it.

He waited apprehensively. He might have come all this way only to find no one home, but at least he would have tried, and could try again if necessary.

He was about to decide if he should ring the doorbell again, or just leave, when he heard the front lock turn in the door and watched the door open.

The man that opened the door had to be in his sixties, but looked older than that. More worn down and moving slowly. He was well-dressed, though, and looked at Matt a little suspiciously, like Matt was going to try and sell him life insurance or a cable TV package. Matt instantly recognized the ears that clearly stuck out from the side of his head, though, like a taxi driving down the street with its doors open.

Matt asked, "Hi, uh... Dr. Thomason?"

The man squinted at Matt and answered, "Yes, that's me. Do I know you?"

"No, sir. You don't. My name is Matt Goodend. But I know your son, Travis."

Dr. Thomason squinted a little harder. "Oh."

"I know this may be a little strange, Dr. Thomason, but I felt a need to come and let you know that, recently... that I got to know your son as a result of some trouble I found myself in overseas. I can't talk about it very much, at the request of the Department of State, but you and I both know what your son does for a living."

Matt shifted nervously from one foot to the other as Dr. Thomason studied him. "But I wanted to tell you that your son is an amazing sailor. Getting to know Travis a little, I doubt he brags about himself, but I thought you'd like to hear it from someone with direct experience."

Dr. Thomason watched Matt, his mouth pulled into a slight frown. He said gruffly, "Hmmph. He's not what you think he is."

Matt immediately assumed that the gay thing must be playing into this a little. And it shouldn't. It would hurt Matt to hear anyone say this about Mope. But his own dad? It was heartbreaking.

Matt said, "Well, I mentioned I got into some trouble. And Travis, your son, saved my life. Twice. And I don't mean like pulling me out of a burning building or giving me CPR, Dr. Thomason. He put himself in serious harm's way to save my life both times. And then he made it seem like it was nothing and that he'd do it for anyone. And while I can believe he *would* do it for just about anyone — there's certainly nothing special about me — I can tell you for absolute sure, what he did definitely wasn't 'nothing'. And since he probably won't ever even mention it to you himself, I wanted to take the chance to tell you personally just how proud you should be of your son. Of Travis. I only got to spend a few days getting to know him due to a very odd circumstance, but I'm more proud to say that I know him than anyone else I think I've ever met. To be able to refer to him as a friend is a huge honor for me, even if it's one I probably don't deserve."

Matt reflected for a moment. "Mmmm... Dr. Thomason, you say Travis isn't what I think he is. I'm not sure what *you* think your son is that changes any of this. But it seems very strange to me to focus on what you think might be missing in your son instead of seeing what's actually there. Even if he had not saved my life, I think I would have more respect and admiration for Travis than any person I've ever met."

Dr. Thomason got quiet for a minute, his aged eyes distant. "He's not his older brother, though. Chris would have been even more than what Travis is," he said, attempting to be defiant, attempting to hold onto a way of thinking that had served him for the last thirty-plus years.

Matt had a hard time listening to this. Maybe this was all pointless. Maybe Mope's father had built the wall around himself so thick that nothing could get through. But he needed to hear it. He was *going* to hear it.

"Travis told me that his older brother had passed away... that you lost your son. I'm very sorry for that. But with all due respect, Dr. Thomason, Travis is the one that's here. And he's the one that actually has accomplished so much that few people in the world could. I don't think I knew what it meant for someone to be an actual hero in real life. But I do now. You son did that, Dr. Thomason. Travis did that. I came away a different person from everything that happened to me because of your son."

Matt stopped talking. He had had his say, and waited to see if it made any difference to Dr. Thomason at all.

Mope's father dropped his eyes from Matt, looking out past him into the manicured yard and quiet Baltimore street beyond. He finally nodded a few times and said, "Well... Matt? Right? Thank you, Matt, for coming by to tell me."

Dr. Thomason's mind seemed to be on Matt's words and he didn't wait for any response from him. He fumbled with the door, finally closing it and leaving Matt on the front step.

Matt turned around and looked at the young, green leaves shimmering in the spring sunlight over the yard and over the road. He wondered if this was all for nothing.

Chapter 28 — The Seven Word Statement

Matt sat in his living room, on the edge of his sofa, with the TV news mumbling in the background. He wasn't looking forward to the weekend alone and had spent a lot of the previous week wondering if he had really done the right thing breaking up with Brian. Deep down, he knew he had, but he still didn't like not having Brian in his life, either. That, coupled with the fact that he hadn't heard from any of the SEALs in two weeks, made him very depressed. Jim and Bret had been great about trying to support him, even if it was a little too much at times. Even today, for a Friday night, he knew they'd try and get him out and cheer him up. He knew they'd be scheming to get him to move past Brian, but Matt wasn't sure he was ready to start plowing through whatever set of guys they might be lining up.

He was about to turn the news off so he could answer his cell phone when he heard a name mentioned on-air that made him forget all about the call. He left the cell phone ringing in his pocket, forgotten, and actually turned the volume up so he could hear the CNN announcer more clearly.

The announcer said that the Pentagon had, earlier that day, announced a development in the war in Iraq. US Special Operations Forces had captured Shahrokh Al-Hashim, an Iranian national that was believed to be a significant player in the supply and coordination of insurgents within Iraq. At the same time, they were announcing that infrastructure Al-Hashim had put in place to ensure a steady flow of explosive materials, those typically used in IEDs in Iraq, had been disrupted after a long and careful intelligence gathering mission. The announcer mentioned that the Pentagon refused to give any details on how Al-Hashim had been captured, or where.

Matt sat on his sofa for a long time after the story was over, his mind thinking about that night in Latakia. He found it very surreal that he knew more about the intimate details of that capture than any other person alive, except maybe Mope. The news and the Pentagon had made it sound so generic and impersonal — *US Special Operations*

Forces had captured him. But it was Mope. It was a real person that had done that, that had risked his life. All of them had risked their lives. And this was just the one incident that Matt actually knew about. It made him think about all the news stories about things happening in Iraq and Afghanistan. All of these stories had real people behind them.

His mind had already been on the team all day, all week actually, but hearing the news story and knowing that the government was now acknowledging Al-Hashim's capture, put him in even more of a funk. He decided he needed to get out of the apartment and think through all the thoughts and feelings playing bumper cars in his head.

Matt suppressed a twinge of guilt as he felt his cell phone buzzing yet again in his pocket as he locked his front door, but he didn't answer it. He knew he wasn't going to answer it. He even had a very good guess as to who it was without looking at it. It was almost certainly either Bret or Jim, but even though this was surely another attempt by them to keep his spirits up and get him out where he could get his mind off of everything, he didn't want his mind off everything. He wanted to think about it. So, even though it was a Friday night, one week after he had dumped Brian, he wanted to be alone. He wanted to be alone to think and remember.

He stepped off of his front step out onto the sidewalk so he could walk the few blocks over to Chimborazo Park. It was already mid-April, and it had been a perfect spring day, so Matt had his favorite long-sleeve t-shirt on, plus new jeans and sneakers he had bought the week before. He put his hands in his pockets and headed out.

As much as he didn't want to feel disappointed, he did. Since he had said goodbye to Mope, Petey, Baya and Desantos the day he watched them leave on the Chinook helicopter, he had not heard from them. He really had thought he'd hear something by now. He had sent a couple of emails to them, but just short ones asking them to let him know they were really ok. He was worried that something had happened and he would have no way of knowing. He tried to tell himself that surely Dr. Thomason would have said something when he spoke to him a week earlier if something had happened to Mope. But still. It felt almost like part of himself was missing to not have any contact with them. The thought that maybe they had simply moved on to other things and forgotten about him hurt even worse. What if that was what had happened? He didn't know what he'd do if that was the case.

In the park, there was a band setting up on a temporary stage for one of the free concerts they occasionally held there in the warmer months. People were already starting to gather in anticipation of it, spreading out on the large lawn in front of the stage. They were setting up blankets and picnic dinners, having a few drinks, and having a good time while they waited.

Matt wondered, what if the guys had all moved on and forgotten about him?

He also thought about what he had done up in Baltimore the previous Sunday afternoon. Had that been the right thing? Was it meddling where he wasn't wanted? Would it just make things worse between Mope and his dad? The more he thought about it, the more he thought it had been a bad idea. Did he really expect to change Dr. Thomason into the loving father Mope had longed for in a five minute conversation? God, he felt how stupid an idea it was now.

He had wanted to do something, though. Anything that would reconnect himself with them. Help them. Especially Mope. He had meant every single word he had said to Dr. Thomason. Matt didn't think there was anything in the world he wouldn't do for Mope.

He wandered around the park for a few minutes and watched as more and more couples and groups and families arrived for the concert. It was a beautiful spring evening for some live music, and the grassy lawn was alive with people in love, people with friends, people with family. He had thought he wanted to be alone when he walked out of his apartment, but now it just hurt. He envied the carefree people around him.

Had he been too quick? Had he walked away too easily? If he had done more, could he have made things right between him and Brian? Matt wondered if he were to call Brian right then, would he be able to make things right? Could they maybe start over and get it right this time?

Matt's shoulders slumped and he wanted to kick himself. Why did he do this kind of thing to himself? It was depressing to think of how easily he wound up blaming himself yet again for what he knew were Brian's faults. He wanted to punch himself for actually considering calling Brian. He wound up feeling worse than when he had started out. He hated being like this.

Matt put his hands back in his pockets and started to walk back to his apartment, not wanting to be around even the crowd in the park.

As he came around the bend that led to the edge of the park closest to his way home, he saw a familiar face. But it didn't help his mood any. It made it much worse.

Brian waved and came up to him.

"Hey Brian. What are you doing here in the park?" asked Matt, his voice far more doleful than he would have liked it to be. He didn't seem to have the willpower to lift it up any, though.

Brian said, "Looking for you, of course."

Matt looked confused. "How did you know I'd be here?"

Brian rolled his eyes. "You always come here when you want to pout and wallow in self pity." The tone in Brian's voice wasn't nearly as harsh as it normally would have been when saying something like that. Matt didn't want to be happy to see Brian, and he wasn't. But, at the same time, it felt a little good having someone know him that well. The mixed up emotions were eating him alive.

Brian turned to walk with Matt as they continued back towards his apartment.

"So, Matt... I'm sorry. I shouldn't have done those things, and I'm sorry you got hurt. But look at you, Matt, you're miserable."

As much as Matt didn't want to believe that Brian had really changed, that kind of genuine apology from him was something he had never heard in the entire year they had been together. Maybe Brian *had* changed, after all.

Brian pushed his arm up against Matt's as they walked along. He said gently, "If you think that you can move past your overreaction, though, we could try again. Make this work. Make this relationship better."

Overreaction? Matt sighed. The new and improved Brian had lasted precisely three seconds. Brian had clearly not really changed at all.

Matt said, "Brian, I don't trust you and I don't have any faith in what we had, or *could* have, together."

They had turned onto Matt's street, and Matt started to say something else, but his voice trailed off when he looked down the sidewalk to where his apartment was. There was a crowd of people standing on his front steps.

Brian stopped when he saw the crowd, too. He asked Matt, "Who are all those people?"

Matt's brow creased. "I don't know."

They walked a few steps closer. Matt saw a group of guys, well over a dozen of them, standing on his steps. He didn't recognize any of them.

But then he heard a booming voice from inside the crowd, "Shit! I guess Richmond lets the queers run free range here!"

Brian stopped dead in his tracks, but Matt suddenly felt the world lift from off of him. He yelled, *"PETEY!"* and started running towards the crowd just as a tall, fire-headed Navy SEAL pushed his way through.

Matt hit Petey almost full speed and grabbed him with all of his might. He didn't care how queer it looked or how much grief he'd get from Petey. All that mattered was seeing Petey again, and knowing they were ok after all.

His collision didn't budge Petey one bit, though, and the tall SEAL put his arm around Matt and hugged him back slightly. He said loudly, as pissed off as usual, "Goddammit, Cornhole! You're getting your faggot stink all over me!"

Petey pushed back on Matt's shoulders so he could get a good look at him, and grinned widely. Matt felt like his own grin would have split his face in two if it got any bigger. Matt noticed Baya and Desantos walking up behind Petey, both of them clearly happy to see him as well.

When they got to Matt, they both gave him a hug and each rubbed on his head a little.

Brian had caught up to them at this point. He said to Matt, "You mean you actually know these assholes?" Brian looked like he had just stepped in dog shit.

Matt's grin never wavered. He punched Petey in the chest, hard, but it was like punching a concrete wall and Petey didn't even notice. "Know them? These are some of the finest assholes in the whole US Navy!"

Petey looked over at Brian, a cold scorn on his face that could have put out a roaring fire. He asked Matt with a slight sneer, "Am I interrupting your little pussy party? Oh... wait... is *this* your butt-buddy Brian?"

Brian took a slight step back, not quite sure he wanted this Petey person paying attention to him now, on reflection.

Matt was definitely ready for Brian to go away now that the guys were here, in person. He was happy and excited and didn't want anything bringing that down.

He said to Petey, knowing it would probably make him happy, "Well, not so much anymore, Colorado. We pretty much broke up a week ago."

Brian scowled and cut in, "We're not done, Matt. *You* may think we're done, but *I* don't think we're done. I still want to talk about this and we're going to..."

"No WE aren't, Brian. It's over. There's nothing else..."

"Yes, there is, Matt! Christ, you can be so *stupid* sometimes," said Brian, forcefully.

Petey had watched the interchange play out, his eyes narrowing and his fists clenching the more he listened to how Brian treated Matt. Brian obviously hadn't noticed or he probably would have shut up much sooner than he did. Petey snarled, "You heard the flamer, asswipe! Get lost! He doesn't need you anymore. He's got fifteen *real* men here lined up to butt-fuck him tonight."

Brian looked simultaneously terrified, and completely offended, and shocked.

Petey waited a second for Brian to get the unsubtle hint. But he didn't get it fast enough, so Petey said, "C'mere, dumbass." He put his large hand around the back of Brian's neck, making him flinch, and led him a few feet away. Petey had that severe, angry look on his face that had scared Matt so bad the first few times he was around him. This time, it was Brian that he had never seen looking so frightened.

Matt looked at Baya and Desantos nervously, wondering what Petey might actually do. Petey kept his hand firmly on Brian's neck so he couldn't get away. He leaned over and whispered a few words in Brian's ear. Brian jerked back away from Petey, and turned ashen-faced. Petey raised an eyebrow at him and said loud enough for everyone to hear, "Do you want me to show you?"

Brian started backing up, away from Petey, his jaw hanging open and his face horror-stricken. He didn't look away from Petey and wound up backing into a car parked on the street, almost falling over it. He finally turned and fled as fast as he could go. Matt didn't attempt to stop him.

Petey looked back at Matt and said, disappointed, "Cornhole, why would you ever go out with that fuckface?"

Matt felt like he surely had the absolute best friends in the whole world. "What the hell did you say to him, Petey?"

Petey said, "A simple seven-word statement of fact."

Matt grinned. "What? My dick is smaller than a housefly's?"

"I've got a rifle with a silencer."

Matt couldn't help but think what a terrible thing that was to say to someone, and he could have kissed Petey if he thought he could get away with it.

Matt looked at the three people he didn't expect to see in person so suddenly, but it made his heart leap to see them. To know they were safe. To actually have them there, right in front of him, was almost too much.

He said, "I've sent you guys emails! You didn't reply. I got worried about you. You have no idea how good it is to see you guys! God, you have no idea how good it is!"

Desantos said, "We had a short mission, after we left you, remember? Then we told you we had survival training after that. Survival training doesn't mean a shitty internet connection and continental breakfast at a Holiday Inn, dummy! We were out in the middle of nowhere the whole time!"

The other men, none of which Matt recognized, had all walked up now, standing behind Baya and Desantos. Petey had moved behind Matt and put his hand on Matt's shoulder.

Baya said, "We finished training this morning. And we just got back to Little Creek this afternoon. We all agreed to come and find you so the guys could meet you before we went our separate ways for the weekend."

Matt looked across the other guys, another dozen of them, all gathered around now. All as intimidating as Petey, Baya, and Desantos had been when he first met them. At least this time, they were all dressed casually, in jeans, t-shirts, knit shirts and so on... no BDUs, helmets, rifles or black masks. Actually, now that he looked, Matt realized that Petey apparently couldn't dress himself for shit. The ridiculously ill-fitting baggy jeans overwhelming his lean, muscular body. The dingy, dirty t-shirt looked like something he found while dumpster diving behind a crack house.

Matt was about to make a comment, but Baya said, "These are your brothers-in-arms, Matt. This is the rest of our platoon."

The comment made Matt forget about Petey's clothes. He looked at Baya, confused.

Baya laughed out loud and said, "Matt, when I said we voted and made you an honorary member of our team, it was the entire platoon that voted, not just the four of us. These guys all knew what went down almost as soon as it had happened. They wanted to meet the guy that helped bring Al-Hashim in."

Matt felt funny again. He didn't know what to do with the idea that this crowd of men, an actual platoon, had wanted to make the trip to Richmond to meet him.

But he also noticed the one that wasn't there.

"Where's Mope?" he asked.

Desantos and Baya glanced over Matt's shoulder at Petey. Petey put his hands on his hips and said, "His whiny daddy issues were flaring up again. His dad called and said he needed to come see him as soon as he got back in town."

Matt's insides clenched. He hoped again he hadn't fucked things up for Mope. He couldn't help but be a little disappointed that the one he wanted to see more than any other couldn't be there. He really, really hoped he hadn't made things worse for Mope.

Petey waved at the rest of the guys and said, "So, here's the rest of these pathetic losers, none of which can fight hand-to-hand for shit."

And at this point, Matt was introduced to the brothers he didn't know he had: Kennon, Wyatt, Wes, Fincher (also known as the other Wes), Crank, Rickey, Dillinger, Jonas, Marshall, Wasp (who was even bigger and more imposing than Petey), Geoff, and Ambush.

Matt felt completely outnumbered, and knew there was no way he'd remember their names. But he also found himself once again feeling something deep inside that all of these guys had felt him worth including in their platoon, even if informally.

Baya rubbed Matt's head again and said, "We're ready to go get drunk and get some chow, Matt. You got a place nearby we can go hang out and raise some hell?"

Matt couldn't wait. His Friday night had suddenly become the best one he could remember in a long time. They walked as a group over to Poe's, a pub near where Matt lived, and took over the outside patio area.

Matt spent the next several hours having a blast meeting the rest of the platoon. They ate a lot and drank even more, and Matt actually did learn all their names. They played darts, which Desantos understandably kicked ass at given his knife-throwing abilities. They all wanted Matt to tell the story of what happened, even though they already all knew it from Mope telling it to them. Matt was able to be the first to tell them it had been mentioned on the news earlier that evening as well.

Matt found out that the big guy named Wasp, who was another couple of inches taller than Petey and bigger all around, was one of Mope's best friends. Surprisingly, he was also the youngest guy in the platoon, only 22 years old, despite looking more mature than that. He had a boyish face, but looked older than 22 at the same time. His light brown eyes seemed to watch everything, taking in every detail, but he didn't smile and he didn't laugh hardly any, like he didn't know how. Wasp was a very quiet, very intense guy, the opposite of Petey's offensive, loud-mouthed personality. At first, Matt felt a little uncomfortable around Wasp, feeling like this might be the one guy that was a little put off by the fact that Matt was gay. That didn't seem to jive with him being such close friends with Travis, though, so Matt wasn't sure what to think of him.

It got cleared up for Matt later, though. Petey pulled Wasp over, they did a round of Southern Comfort shots, and Petey announced he wanted to tell a story about Wasp.

Wasp's lips clenched into tight lines and he told Petey, "No, man. Don't."

Petey said, "Relax, half pint. I'm gonna tell Cornhole how you got your nickname. Stop being such a damn woman!"

Wasp ran his hand over the dark gold buzzcut on top of his head nervously, but nodded at Petey, and Petey proceeded.

Keith, Wasp's real name, had been in a sniper position trying to knock off some insurgents that had pinned down Kennon, Rickey, Dillinger, and Jonas on a mission just outside of Kabul. His sniper rifle had jammed, though, and he hadn't even gotten a single shot off. So Instead, over the next ninety minutes, he managed to slowly sneak his way up on the insurgents' position and took out three armed guys with his bare hands. Petey started laughing at this point in the story, tickled by what was coming up, but Keith's face was fire red from the blush. Petey told how Keith started to swagger up to where the pinned down SEALs were, the big-fucking-deal for single-handedly saving their asses. But halfway up to them, he stepped on a wasp nest in the ground and started running around screaming that the wasps were after him, practically dancing in the desert to get away from them. The guys he had saved laughed themselves silly all the way back to the extraction point, and Keith was known as Wasp ever since then.

Matt got it then. Keith was still the young one on the team that needed to prove himself. He was just shy. His behavior wasn't about Matt at all, it was about himself. It made total sense to Matt now to find out that Travis would take him under his arm and be a good friend.

Wasp allowed a small grin to escape. He hated hearing this story told yet again, but knew there was no way Petey wasn't going to tell it. He laughed at it good-naturedly anyway, and Matt tried to make him feel better by telling him at least he didn't get the nickname Cornhole. Wasp shook his head and said, "God damn and god bless for small favors, you know?"

No sooner had Petey finished the story than he stood up, his eyes and nose flaring. He said, "That fucker! Excuse me while I go pound the shit out of Crank for picking this song out on the jukebox. I told him not to play this crap ever again." Petey stomped off, which sent Crank trying to hide behind a couple of the other guys.

Matt turned to Wasp. "Mope's a good guy. I wish he had been able to come tonight. I really look up to him. No way I would have been able to cause all that trouble in Latakia if it weren't for him."

Wasp nodded, warming up a little now, "Yeah. It's hard joining up with this group 'cause they've all got so much experience under their belt. I feel like an idiot around them. But Mope's always been there, encouraging me, helping me through it. I doubt I'd still be here if it weren't for him."

Wasp looked down at his big hands and didn't seem to want to look Matt in the eye for a moment. He picked at the label on the bottle of Coors he was drinking and looked like his dog had died.

Wasp's silence dragged on way longer than it probably should have, so Matt asked, "You ok?"

Wasp nodded, but still didn't look up at Matt for another few seconds. When he did, he said, "It's been hard fitting in with these guys. You get through BUD/S and feel like a world-class bad-ass, but then you get on a team like this one and feel like you don't know shit. I've been in the SEAL program for less than a year, but I... you know... I don't know."

Wasp changed the subject suddenly. "Mope really respects you and how you helped out in Syria. You did a lot more than we've got any right to ask from a civilian."

Matt wasn't sure what Wasp had been about to say, but he felt a little unwilling to press on it.

Wasp said, "Petey, too, you know. I mean, aside from him referring to you as queer and faggot and every other slur he can come up with, you can tell he likes you. So, it's cool to meet you in person. Petey can be kinda tough to get to know. It seems weird that you'd actually be friends with him given how he treats you. But I guess he treats everybody that way. He calls me pipsqueak all the time."

"It's just a game between us. I know he doesn't mean it. He's just a big softie inside and doesn't want anybody to know it," said Matt, watching the drunk Petey still trying to get his hands on Crank, who was now holding Baya in front of him like a human shield.

Petey shouted, pissed, "Stop hiding behind Prince Falafel, Crank, and take it like a damn man!"

Wasp said as he squinted at Petey and grinned again, "You sure we're talking about the same guy?"

Eventually, the group wound down as some of the guys started to go their own ways for the weekend. All too soon, Matt was left with just Petey, Baya and Desantos. It didn't escape Matt's attention that Petey had hardly left his side all evening. All of it, all of them, was just exactly what Matt needed that night. He felt like a new man getting to spend the time with them.

Petey, Desantos and Baya finally had to take their leave as well, a little before 11pm. They walked back towards Matt's apartment, but stopped to say goodbye where the three of them would need to split off to get back to Desantos' car.

Desantos told Matt, "Keep the emails coming, Matt. We love getting the emails, as many as you want to send. We'll be at our home station in Little Creek for the next few weeks, so we'll be able to reply this time."

Baya handed Matt a disc and said, "And, here's your photos, from your last day on the *Iwo*. They're pretty good, I gotta admit, even that embarrassing one where you made us grab our junk. We even added a couple extras for you."

Petey said, "And you're not off the hook with just tonight, you little butt-suckin'-nut-nudger. You'll be coming over to see us in Little Creek in the next few weeks, so you might as well just get used to the idea. You can bunk with me. I'll let you do my laundry since you'll probably be rooting around in my crusty underwear when I'm not looking, anyway."

Matt was sorry for the night to end. But at least he now had something really good to look forward to.

Matt said goodbye, giving Baya and Desantos a hug and letting them rub on his head as was becoming their tradition, as every other member of the platoon had done that evening before leaving. When he got to Petey, though, he merely extended his hand out to shake his.

Petey shot Matt a scalding dirty look. "What? You too fucking good to give me one of your fucktard hugs now? But these dickheads get one? Is that how it is?"

Matt wrinkled up his nose and said, "You smell kind of like cheap beer and possum roadkill, Petey."

Petey snarled, "FUCK YOU!" and grabbed Matt, throwing him up over his shoulder like a sack of potatoes.

Matt started laughing and Petey eventually put him back down. He gave the SEAL a hug, and Petey roughed up his head a little.

Desantos turned to Baya and said, "Would you look at that? Whaddya think, Baya? You think Petey will start in with buying a bunch of Streisand CDs first, or you think he's more of a Celine Dion kinda guy?"

"Celine Dion. No contest," said Baya.

"No way, man," said Desantos. "He's got Streisand written all over him."

Baya gave Desantos a fist bump and said, "Twenty dollars and you're on, D."

Petey flipped both of them his middle fingers and told Matt, "You let me know if that asswipe of yours gives you any trouble. We can put an end to that shit in about two seconds, and nobody will ever know."

As Matt made his way back to his apartment after watching the three of them drive off, he could still hear the concert playing faintly a few blocks away in the park. He was a little high from the drinks and shots, and a lot high from just being around the guys again. He felt better than he had in weeks, and he couldn't wait to see the photos and show them to Bret and Jim. Of course, for those two, Matt would only describe the team as some of the guys he had met on the ship and became buddies with, but he knew they'd get a kick out of the pictures no matter what. Especially Bret.

As Matt turned onto his street, he looked down and saw yet one more person sitting on the front steps of his apartment. He wondered if Brian had come back and his heart sank a little. Maybe he'd take Petey up on that offer after all.

But then he noticed that the figure wasn't sitting. He was crouching.

Chapter 29 — The Back Of Your Hand

Matt's feet slowed a little as he approached his apartment. If the person crouching on his front steps turned out to *not* be who he hoped it was, he was going be devastated. And if it *was* who he thought, he was going to be nervous. What if he had made things worse between Mope and his father? How would he face Mope? Even more than that, now that he had broken up with Brian, and knowing how Mope didn't seem to share the feelings that Matt felt that night outside of Latakia, it was going to hurt.

Matt got about twenty yards away when the figure's head turned, and Matt could see the ears sticking out in silhouette. There was no doubt who it was.

Mope stood up as Matt stepped up on the first step to his apartment, and then waited quietly in front of him, as serious as always. He was wearing a tight gray t-shirt that said Hilton Head Island, plus jeans, and a pair of seriously old sneakers. And it looked like he hadn't shaved the entire time they had been out on survival training. Even after having seen Petey, Desantos, and Baya in casual civilian clothes, Mope looked a little odd to Matt in jeans and a t-shirt, but that was only because he wasn't used to it. In reality, the tight t-shirt showed off Mope's finely-tuned torso and broad chest really well.

Mope's expression was serious, but his voice was more cheerful when he said, "Hi, Matt."

"Hey, Mope. I... uh... shit, it's just so good to see you. All the others just left. It was such a huge surprise to have them show up. A good one! Why are you here? I mean, Petey said you had to be somewhere. Why didn't you come with the rest of the guys? Do you want to go inside?" Matt felt like he was blathering, and he wanted to turn and run, and grab Mope and hold onto him for all he was worth, all at the same time.

"Ehh... do you mind if we walk a little bit?" asked Mope.

Matt said sure and they walked back down the street, Matt aimlessly leading them back towards the park.

"I did go see my dad, Matt, for a little while, at least. And as for the rest of the guys, I'm glad they got some time with you. But me? I kind of wanted you all to myself. So I waited. How are you?"

"Are you kidding me? A helluva lot better now that I know you guys are ok, and now that you're here. I got worried when I didn't hear anything."

Mope said, "No, I mean, how are you doing? A lot of people would wind up with PTSD after what happened to you. Are you ok? Are you having bad dreams? Panic attacks? I worried about you the last few weeks."

Matt felt a bittersweet thrill knowing Mope had been thinking about him. Maybe it was just out of concern for how he had fared since getting home, but it felt good.

Even though Matt had thought about what happened that night in Latakia a lot, he was ok with it. It had been scary, and he was still a little troubled by the fact that he had killed a guy, but he was coping as well as could be expected. He felt that a lot of that had to do with Mope getting him out of the van and making him focus on his eyes and his breathing instead of what had just happened. Matt was sure that he had Mope to thank for not being a post-traumatic disaster.

And he hadn't had any bad dreams, either. He had been having the dream about being in the empty room, with the door open. Sometimes, while in the room, he would hear whispers that he couldn't make out, but it had never seemed like a nightmare. He had always just felt sad in the dream and a little helpless despite the door being open. And now that he thought about it, he couldn't remember having that dream in probably a week now.

"I've done ok, Mope, I think. Thanks to you. But I've really been alright."

They had arrived in the park at this point, the concert still playing nearby. Matt felt like he needed to get it out in the open. It was tearing him up to not know.

"Uh... Mope? How did your visit with your dad go?"

Mope considered the question for a moment. "He told me you came to see him, Matt."

"And?" Matt's hands were shaking and Mope's expression hadn't veered from serious.

Mope seemed to have trouble answering, and his hand wiped nervously at his nose. He said, "And... and... Matt... for... *shit*... for the first time I can remember, he didn't compare me to Chris. He... uh... he said I had done well." Mope wiped his eyes with his sleeve quickly. "He said I had done well, Matt."

The rockabilly song the band was playing sang out through the park.

The relief that washed over Matt was almost too much. He felt so lucky that he hadn't fucked things up. He felt so glad that Mope's father had listened, even just a little. Nobody in the world deserved it more than the man in front of him.

"It may not seem like much to most people, but that's more than I've ever gotten from him before," said Mope.

Mope suddenly stopped and turned to Matt. His face got even more serious than it was and his brow furrowed. "I need to know the truth about something, Matt. I don't doubt that you'd be truthful with me, but you don't know how important it is to me that you give me an honest answer right now."

Matt waited, and Mope asked, "Is it true that you told my dad that even if I hadn't saved your life, you'd have more respect and admiration for me than anyone you've ever met?"

Once again, Matt was incredibly relieved. He wondered why this was even a concern. He said, like it should be obvious, "Well, yeah, Mope."

Mope's lips tightened and he looked past Matt again.

Matt said, "I mean, you showed me what it means to have courage and to be brave. You showed me what it means to have people that you trust at your back and what you can do when you know you've got that. I don't think I could even have imagined that on my own. It would be easy to say that what happened in Latakia changed me, Mope. But the truth is that you changed me. I may still be Matt Goodend, but I'm a different person than who arrived in Syria a month ago."

Mope continued looking off in the distance, almost like he wasn't paying attention, but Matt knew he was.

"As a matter of fact," continued Matt, "it was because of what you helped me see in myself, and knowing I had my friends Bret and Jim there for me, that I broke up with Brian last week."

Mope's eyes snapped back to Matt. "You what?!"

"I broke up with him. I was an idiot for staying with him as long as I did. But better late than never for growing some balls, I guess. It's still hard, though. I got weak and I almost thought about calling him, and then Brian came crawling back to me earlier tonight." Matt chuckled lightly, "But he got scared off by a bunch of asshole Navy shiprats that don't know how to call before dropping by."

Mope seemed like he wasn't quite listening again. He suddenly looked at Matt with a strange expression that Matt couldn't read. There was a long silence between them that stretched out while Matt tried to figure out what Mope was thinking. Matt was about to ask when Mope said, "Look up, Matt."

Matt looked up. It *was* a nice night. The band was playing nearby, people were in the park enjoying themselves, the moon was out, the air felt good. He said, "Yeah, it's ok tonight. The moon's nice, but you can't see the stars like..." He had started to look back down at Mope just as Mope grabbed his head with both of his rough hands and kissed him hard.

The ground started spinning under Matt and he kissed Mope back, their tongues intertwining, the taste of Mope on Matt's tongue, and the stubble on Mope's face burning just slightly. Matt smelled Mope; the dark, masculine smell of the sea and cedar wood filled his nose and permanently fixed itself in Matt's memories. Mope's hands slid past until his strong arms fully wrapped around Matt's head, completely encircling his every sense. There was nothing in Matt's world but Mope's lips, his stubbly chin, his nose, his thick arms, his breath, and that amazing smell. Matt wrapped his arms around Mope's back, feeling the hard muscles underneath the thin t-shirt. Mope finally pulled back, put his hands back on Matt's head, holding it gently, holding Matt's eyes locked to his own. Mope held Matt's gaze, searching to make sure he hadn't overstepped a boundary with the kiss, wanting to see if Matt felt the same thing he was feeling. Only when Mope saw in Matt's eyes that the feeling was fully returned to him did he relax.

Around them in the park, the music had changed. The band was starting a new song, one with a slow, gentle, pulsing beat. It had an almost haunting, ghostly quality to it. The steel guitar and fiddle and piano complemented each other as the singer sang of finding your way back.

Mope whispered, "Dance with me, Matt."

Matt grinned shyly and said, "Here? Now?"

Mope almost begged while the singer crooned intimately behind him, "Please, Matt."

'Cause even in the time I've known you
It's like you're the back of my hand
And the time is short

To find your way through
But you're the back of my hand

Matt put his arms around Mope's midsection and they held each other. Mope's cheek against Matt's. They started swaying to the song, and Matt closed his eyes and marveled at how the world worked. Could he ever ask for anything more in his life than this moment?

Lord knows, it's hard enough to toe the line
When you feel like you've lost your mind
Think of me and look up at the stars
And you'll be fine
Just look at the stars and the sky they span

They lost themselves in the gentle sound of a song that felt like it was theirs alone. Matt felt Mope's hand move up to the back of his head and hold him tightly. They swayed to the beat together underneath the springtime moon.

And you look up at the stars
And the sky they span
You'll see that you understand
You'll find your man
You'll find your way home to me
'Cause I'm the back of your hand

Mope's stubble slowly dragged across Matt's face until their lips were touching again. They floated on the kiss and the feel of their bodies pressed together.

As long as the stars
Occupy the sky
I'll be here
I'll be your man
Mmm... mmm... I'll be here...
I'll be the back of your hand

The song finally wound down to a stop and the crowd applauded and cheered appreciatively in the distance. Matt and Mope eventually realized the song had ended and found they weren't even dancing anymore. All there had been was the kiss between them, the rest of the world put on pause and in their pocket for a while.

Mope continued to hold Matt, their faces merely inches apart, but a sheepish smile spread over his face. Mope said, "Sorry, I really can't dance."

His eyes sparkled and he added in a rough whisper, "But, dear God, you make me want to."

The light brush of Mope's breath across Matt's lips made him feel like he could fly around the park. Matt's insides felt all tied up and tingly. The night had started out so bad, but had wound up somewhere completely unexpected. Somewhere wonderful. They walked back to Matt's apartment, but Mope stopped him just outside.

"I've got something to give you. But I don't want to give it to you inside your place. I'm not sure if it'll be a good thing or not. You might not like it, and I'll take it away if it bothers you."

Matt had no idea what Mope was talking about and watched him curiously.

Mope reached into the back waistband of his pants and pulled out a handgun. He held it out to Matt, resting flat on his open palm.

Matt looked at it, the recognition hitting him.

Matt had killed another person with the gun held out in front of him now. It had been that very gun.

He started to reach out to touch it, but his hand started shaking, and he left it in Mope's palm instead.

Mope frowned. "I knew it might be hard for you to see it. I'm sorry I brought it. I'll get rid of it, Matt."

"No, wait. Don't," said Matt. "You're right. It's not easy to see it. It still scares me that I... killed... that guy so easily. I feel like there's a part of me that I don't know. Something bad. But at the same time, I'm not going to have any other day in my life more important than that one. I need the reminder."

Matt studied the gun, still in Mope's hand. Mope said, "It bothered you, seeing the hash marks on my M4, didn't it?"

Matt thought back to the day they took the photographs and he saw the scratches on the stock of Mope's rifle. He scratched at his chin for a moment, trying to figure out exactly how he felt. "Kinda. No. I mean, I had just watched you kill several guys the night before that, but you did it for me. I just hadn't thought about how many others there had been over time."

Mope said, "You know there's nothing I wouldn't do for you."

Matt tore his eyes from the handgun and looked up at Mope. "Will you keep it for me?"

Mope nodded. "Of course I will. I know that you see it as something a little scary and dark. But I see it as something that shows just how brave you really are. I hope one day you'll see it the way I do."

He put the gun back in his waistband, then put his hand on the side of Matt's head. He leaned in and kissed Matt again lightly, their lips barely brushing against one another's.

~~~~~

Matt and Mope sat cross-legged and facing each other on Matt's bed. They had gotten down to their boxers and had spent several minutes studying each other up close, their fingertips gently exploring the other, along the tips of noses, tracing eyebrows, down chins, across the tips of ears, along shoulders, following chest muscles, and brushing across stomachs.

Matt studied Mope's eyes with the dark eyebrows, his crooked nose, strong chin, protruding ears, and slightly off-kilter smile with the deep smile lines, which hadn't left his face since they had danced in the park. The whole was far more than the sum of the parts; the whole came together in the most handsome and masculine form Matt had ever seen. He ran his fingers across the layer of smooth, dark hair that covered Mope's chest and stomach, feeling the chiseled muscles underneath.

Mope admitted, "I feel like such a perv."

Matt asked, "A perv? Why is that?" He had to chuckle at the thought.

"When I first found you in that room, and even in the bad shape you were in, I went to cut the ties off your hands and feet. I was so busy looking at those green eyes of yours I was afraid I was going to cut you. I'm lucky I didn't."

Matt smiled and said, "God damn and god bless for small favors."

"You've been talking to Wasp, I can tell."

Matt laughed and continued to run his finger over Mope's body. "You're the most beautiful man I've ever seen, Mope."

Mope grimaced and said, "What? With these flappy ears..."

Matt slapped his hand across Mope's mouth and said, "Shut up, dipshit! I'm not asking for your opinion!"

Mope nodded and Matt removed his hand.

"You're the most beautiful man I know. Inside *and* out. And... and can I call you Travis instead of Mope? Mope seems like a stupid nickname to me."

Mope — Travis — laughed softly and said, "I never liked Mope that much, but you try and get the rest of the team to quit it and they just dig in that much harder. And thanks. Thanks for saying that. And thanks for talking to my dad. You have no idea what that means to me."

Travis added, "And I guess I owe some thanks to Brian, too. Thank God he was enough of a dick to blow it with you, and I could be here with you tonight instead."

Matt said the single word, "Travis," and leaned forward to touch his lips to Travis' again, kissing deeply. Travis pushed forward until Matt fell back on the bed and he lay down on top of him, both of them ready for the night to really begin.

Chapter 30 – Muster

Matt woke the next morning to find he had kicked most of the covers off of himself during the night, for once not needing them for warmth. He looked down and saw Travis' head resting on his bare stomach, his arms wrapped around Matt's midsection snugly. The steady rise and fall of Travis' wide shoulders let him know that he was still sound asleep. He could feel the soft-yet-sandpapery prickle of Travis' beard on his stomach.

As much as Matt wanted to reach out and touch Travis' head, to verify this wasn't some mirage, he didn't want to wake him up, either. Just being able to see him like this was good, too. He thought what a nice problem it was to have.

It was strange for Matt to look at Travis like this. This person was capable of what seemed to be almost super-human things. But here he was, lying on Matt's stomach, clutching at him like a five-year-old clutches at a favorite plush toy. It made Matt feel very warm and secure inside.

The sex the night before had been very good. Better than Matt had had with Brian in a long time. In fact, Matt couldn't think of a better night in his whole life. Seeing Petey, Baya, and Desantos and finding out they were safe and sound was a huge relief after all of his neurotic worrying, and an unexpected thrill. Watching Petey get very protective and putting the fear of God into Brian. Meeting the rest of the platoon and finding out he had twelve other guys that all considered him their friend without even having met him before. Finding Travis on his doorstep. Suddenly finding himself dancing in the park in front of whoever may be walking by, wrapped up in Travis' arms with their cheeks pressed together. Feeling Travis' warm breath on his neck. He thought how that dance would be a special memory the rest of his life. Even seeing the gun that Travis had saved and brought to him - a tangible reminder of a night that was simultaneously horrible, and a turning point in himself as a person, and possibly the start of something that would be the best thing in his life. Matt looked at Travis' head on his stomach. It was all because of him, all of it.

After about fifteen minutes, Matt couldn't stand it anymore. He reached down and stroked Travis' head, running his fingers across the inch-long dark hair carpeting it.

Travis stirred and stretched like a cat waking from a nap in the sun. He rolled over on his back and looked up at Matt, smiling that crooked, magnificent smile, his body halfway wrapped up in the white quilt and white sheets on Matt's bed.

The first words out of Travis' sleepy mouth were, "This has been the best twenty-four hours I've ever had in my life." Matt wondered who would ever be stupid enough to argue with that?

Matt smiled back and traced a finger along Travis' disjointed-just-exactly-right nose. Travis sat up and moved up next to him, pushing his back up against Matt's chest, pressing his ass up against Matt's still-sleeping dick. He said, "I want to feel your arms around me." So Matt wrapped his arms around the man, spooned up against him, and held on tightly. He ran his hands over the bare chest he held in his arms, feeling the layer of silky chest hair covering the raw, rough muscle beneath.

They lay like this a while, Matt's nose buried in the back of Travis' neck, feeling his skin against his lips and smelling the scent he so strongly associated with Travis now.

Travis said, "This feels so good, and I'm glad I'm here with you. I can actually relax around you and be myself. I don't have to hide myself from you and you understand. You *know* me. God, this feels so good."

Matt traced an index finger across a four-inch scar he found along Travis' left arm, near the elbow. He asked, "How did you get this scar?"

Travis rolled over to face Matt. He said, "Firefight with some Somalian warlord thugs near Oddur. We had been warned they might have a grenade launcher, but I wasn't paying attention. I will say, I'm lucky that's the only permanent damage I came away with, and even luckier they're crappy shots with the launcher. I was a young, dumb, inexperienced SEAL back then. Don't tell anybody I talked about that; we weren't officially there. I'd have to kill you if you did." A goofy, sleepy, grin spread across his face.

"What about this one, the one over your eye?" asked Matt, tracing the scar that cut through Travis' right eyebrow.

"That one?" asked Travis, smiling again. "You'll like this. I got it when I was about seven years old. Turns out that razor blades glued together make pretty dangerous ninja throwing stars. That was probably the only time I really saw Chris get into serious hot water with our dad. He was furious with Chris, throwing those things at me!"

Matt cringed while grinning, "You threw razor blades at each other? Really?"

Travis nodded and laughed. He said, "I think Chris and I are where that old saying about 'Stop that or you'll put your eye out!' comes from."

Travis asked with the face of a three year old eager for an ice cream, "Can we go out, Matt?"

"You mean, like on a date? Sure. I was kind of hoping you'd spend the weekend with me if you can." Matt loved how his morning was turning out even better than the night before.

"No. Wait, I mean, yes, I'd be crazy not to spend the weekend with you. But no, not like a date. I mean, I'm asking if you'd... you know... date me. Jesus, that sounds corny."

Before Matt could answer, Travis' face clouded and he said, "Maybe I shouldn't do this. It won't be fair to you."

Now it was Matt's turn to feel like the three year old, this time one that had just had his ice cream stolen from him. "Wait... what? Travis, don't you fucking offer me that and then turn around and try to take it away. Why do you say that?"

"It's too much to ask, Matt," said Travis, the sparkle in his eyes dwindling. "It's too much to expect of anyone. I'll be gone for stretches of time. Some of those times I won't be able to tell you where I'll be. Sometimes I won't even know when I'll get back. It's too much waiting and worrying to put you through. It'll be hard on you, Matt. It'd be hard on anyone. It'll be hard on me knowing what I'm doing to you."

Matt said, "And so it's better to give me the best night of my life with the promise of more of this, and then take it away? Knowing I'd be worried sick about you anyway? Uh uh. Hell no. I want you more than I've wanted anything else in this world, and we'll work the rest out."

Travis smiled again, feeling better and the sparkle started to return to his dark eyes, but he was still a little leery of what he was asking of Matt.

He said, "There is one other thing, though."

Matt waited for whatever other shoe was about to drop.

"No boyfriend of mine is going to be afraid of the water, Matt. I practically live in the water, and you're going to have to get used to it."

Matt felt like he had swallowed a bucket of ice cubes at one time. He cringed and asked, pleading, "Awww, shit. You wouldn't really make me do that, would you?"

"I surf. I swim. I ski. I scuba. You're going to have to get used to some of this. But I promise you, I'll be there and take it one step at a time with you, and we'll go at your pace. Are you willing to try?" asked Travis.

"Fine. When I wind up drowning, and I will, it'll be all your fault," said Matt, teasing him, but secretly apprehensive. But if he couldn't trust Travis, who in the world could he trust?

Travis' eyes peered intently at Matt, seeing past Matt's teasing and superficial bravery. He put his hand behind Matt's neck as they lay face to face. "There's no way I'll ever let anything happen to you. You know this."

"I know," said Matt. "I just like hearing you say it."

Travis asked, "And speaking of this kind of stuff, how do you feel about jumping out of airplanes?" The corner of his mouth almost imperceptibly twisted up into a smile.

Matt's eyes narrowed. "You just don't know when to quit, do you?"

~~~~~

Bret said, "Ok, I get it! You *dog*, you! You let Brian hang himself so you could ditch him knowing you had this Navy *hottie* waiting in the wings. Matt! I didn't think you were capable of this kind of stuff! I'm so proud of you!" He pretended to sniff and wipe away an imaginary tear from his eye.

Matt turned a little red and said, "Chili, that's not the way it happened at all. I knew Travis was gay. He trusted me with that when I met him on the ship, but nothing happened until last night."

Bret looked over at Jim, pretending to not buy it, "Shit, he's become a good liar! Jimmy Bob, our little boy is all grown up now!"

Jim laughed, and Travis did, too.

Matt and Travis had met Bret and Jim in Byrd Park for the softball game scheduled that afternoon. They were almost seriously late for it, because as soon as Matt had put his softball uniform on, Travis had gotten totally turned on by how he looked in it and they wound up getting undressed again and having sex before they could get their clothes back on and leave for the game.

Matt had introduced Travis as one of the sailors he had met on the *Iwo Jima* and become friendly with, but left it at that. Bret and Jim could tell how happy Matt was, which made them very happy for him. They had been worried about Matt from the night before when he hadn't answered his phone, so Matt explained to them how he ran into several of the other guys from the ship, and then found Travis waiting on him at his apartment.

Jim was the one that pressed Travis a little bit, wanting to know what he did in the Navy, and was it the *Iwo Jima* he was assigned to. The questions had made Matt a little nervous because he had not thought about people asking these kinds of questions. But Travis had good, generic answers for exactly these questions. He explained to Jim that his platoon was stationed in Little Creek and didn't have a specific ship they were assigned to. They filled in gaps as needed on different ships at different times. Travis explained how happy he was to find out he wasn't really that far from Matt, because he planned on seeing a lot of him.

Travis had been watching Bret study him through the conversation, and finally called him on his ogling. He said to Bret, "You know, Bret, my eyes are up here."

Bret shot back, his eyes never leaving Travis' chest, "Hey! I didn't make you wear the tight t-shirt!"

"It's just a t-shirt."

"It's a *tight* t-shirt. In all kinds of right ways. And don't dangle a catnip toy in front of a cat and not expect it to become fascinated and start pawing at it."

Travis grinned and looked over at Matt, who gave him a whatya-gonna-do shrug.

Even Jim scratched at the back of his head, blushed a little and said, "I kinda have to go with Chili on this one."

Blake, the coach of the team, called Matt over for a moment before the game started. As Matt walked over, he looked back and could see both Bret and Jim leaning in on Travis and talking to him rather intently. Matt suddenly worried about leaving Travis alone with those two, even for a few minutes. He answered Blake's question as quickly as possible, and ran back over to them, but Bret and Jim seemed to already be done with whatever third degree grilling they were giving Travis. Travis didn't seem too concerned, though.

A few other team members, including Lane, Tommy and Sal, all wanted to meet Matt's new friend, so he introduced him around some. Tommy and Sal wound up chatting with Bret and Jim, distracting them, so Matt leaned over to Travis and asked him what they had talked about when he had stepped away.

Travis smiled and said, "Nothing, really."

"It didn't look like nothing," said Matt, "and I know those two pretty well. And don't try that '*I can't talk about it*' bullshit you love hiding behind."

Travis said, "They're looking out for you, Matt. It's obvious how much they care about you. But they said you had been treated pretty rotten by your last boyfriend. Bret said I'd better not hurt you or he'd cut my nuts off."

Matt turned white. "Sorry, Travis. I guess they're a little over-protective."

Travis leaned back a little and said, "It's fine. I told Bret that if I ever hurt you, I'd give him the knife to do it with."

He added, "Speaking of protective, I got a text from Petey a little while ago." He held out his phone for Matt to see it. It said:

Met Matt's ex-BF last night. Guys a tool. If I see him again, I'll probably kill him.

Matt chuckled and said, "Petey's too much sometimes. He cracks me up!"

"Mmmmm," murmured Travis doubtfully, "I don't think he's completely kidding. You probably really ought to make sure he and Brian don't run into each other again. You know how Petey feels about you now. He talked about you constantly during our training last week."

Travis slapped Matt on his knee and said, "I've gotta run to the bathroom. Back in a minute."

He headed off and Bret and Jim pounced on Matt.

Bret said, "Are you sure he's in the Navy? I've seen Navy guys and he doesn't look like Navy. He looks more like one of the guys out of *Soldier Of Fortune* magazine. And I know what those guys look like because I spend thirty minutes a week at the grocery store flipping through it and ogling the pictures."

Matt rolled his eyes and said, "Yes, Bret. He's really in the Navy."

"He's hot. If you get tired of him, I'll take him off your hands," offered Bret.

"If you like him like this, wait till you see some of the photos I got of him and the other guys from the ship. You'll *really* get a kick out of those," teased Matt.

Jim said, "I like him, Matt. I can tell he's really crazy about you. And he is good looking. Really masculine. He's probably got the sexiest voice I've ever heard."

Bret got pissed at Matt and spat at him, "And what the fuck is with you anyway? That you can go to Syria, get fucking *kidnapped*, and wind up on a Navy ship where you happen to meet a fucking hot, butch, gay Navy guy that's now all over you? Huh? What the *fuck* is that? I *hate* you."

"Sorry, Chiliburger," said Matt, pitifully.

Travis came back from the bathroom just as the game was ready to start. Matt stepped out of the stands to go to his position in the outfield, but Travis stopped him before he could take his place on the field.

"So, did I pass muster with Bret and Jim?" asked Travis, a knowing grin on his face.

"You've got absolutely nothing to worry about. Bret's pretty furious with me for trading so far up above Brian so quickly."

Matt glanced back at Bret in the stands. He said, "Trav, if you can't handle being alone with Bret the whole time, you can come sit with me in a few minutes."

Travis got a slightly funny look on his face and just stared at Matt.

"You ok?" asked Matt.

Travis' lips pulled down slightly. He said softly, "Trav... You called me Trav."

Matt tried to understand. He asked unsurely, "Is that... bad?"

"Chris... he was the only person to ever call me Trav." Travis' eyes were distant as he thought back over things he hadn't thought about in many years.

Matt felt bad about stepping on something that was special between Travis and his older brother, Chris. "I'm sorry, Travis. I didn't know. I won't…"

Travis grabbed Matt and hugged him tightly. "No, I like you calling me that. I've missed it. God, I've missed it."

He kissed Matt deeply and without regard to the crowd in the stands watching the two of them. The kiss was intense enough that even Matt's hat got knocked off his head, and both of them forgot all about the game trying to start.

When they stopped, they realized the mostly-gay crowd was cheering and hooting at them. The umpire walked over to them and told them the make-out area was clearly marked behind the stands and to take it back there. Travis bowed for the crowd and smacked Matt on his ass to send him out to start the game.

Chapter 31 — Ironsides

What Ironsides, or The 'Sides as the locals called it, lacked in cleanliness, polish and general upkeep, it more than made up for in authenticity. Newer places, such as The Eight Bells, were right on the beach, cleaner, better advertised, more popular with tourists, definitely more expensive, and every bit as fake as most of the people in them.

The 'Sides, though, was as real as it got, and the people that went there routinely did their best to keep the tourists away. It wasn't too far from the beach proper, but still a little bit off of Pacific Avenue and very poorly marked, which helped the secret stay secret. The Marines, sailors, and other locals often on their way to The 'Sides might be stopped and asked by tourists where the best bar in Virginia Beach was — you know, the authentic nautical one. Invariably, those poor souls would be given the name of any place other than The 'Sides. And if the Marine, sailor, or other local was feeling particularly mean-spirited, they'd get directed to the Red Lobster that was nearby.

The bar was dark, often a little too smoky, loud, and usually packed. It was frequented a lot by the Marines and Navy personnel stationed nearby, but also by crews of the local fishing and charter boats. This place had as much maritime history to it as the waterfront towns surrounding it. The beat up tables and booths were made of heavily varnished teak wood, sticky and thick feeling. Around the circumference of the entire bar, up along the ceiling and hanging down, were examples of every imaginable knot known to sailors anywhere in the world. It was a huge honor for any ship crewmember to bring in a knot and have it deemed worthy of hanging up in The 'Sides. The more obscure and difficult the knot was, the more prominent position it would get on display. Some of them had to be twenty-five years old if they were a day. The bronze ship's bell occupied a spot on a pitted, split post near the cash register at one end of the bar. It only got rang when somebody passed out drunk in the bar. Which is to say once, maybe twice, a night. More on the weekends.

Given the popularity among the Navy and Marines, and plus the presence of cheap alcohol, it wasn't unusual for the rivalry between the two branches to manifest itself a little too physically. Most of the rest of the patrons took it in stride and ignored it. Tug, the current owner for the last fifteen years, would usually throw a hot pot of coffee on whatever two might be thumping their chests at each other and tell them to get the fuck out. Tug wasn't easily intimidated, despite the fact that he was overweight, probably only about five foot seven, and walked with a limp due to a failing hip.

All of this wasn't to say that there weren't people from out of town there. On the contrary, if you came to Virginia Beach and knew someone that was local, it was often a point of pride that you were taken to The 'Sides. Family and friends were welcome, and tourists could go to hell.

Matt decided he loved this place. They had come there the Saturday night of Matt's first weekend visiting the guys on their home turf, and they were well on their way to getting drunk. Just one week after the guys all came back from what Matt now referred to as their "boy scout jamboree" and surprised him in Richmond, one week after he and Travis started... whatever it was they had started... Petey had insisted Matt come spend the weekend with him and whoever else in the platoon was around. Most of the guys lived in or very near Virginia Beach, which was convenient to the Little Creek Amphibious Naval Base where they were stationed.

Matt had desperately wanted to stay with Travis, but Petey was a pit bull about how the whole weekend would go. Travis had laughed it off, saying he'd be there with him and Petey the whole weekend, but both knew it would be incredibly frustrating to be that close and not be together.

Matt's first night in Virginia Beach had been... odd. Petey had gotten several of the guys, including Travis, Wasp, Desantos, Fincher, Dillinger, and Geoff, together and they had gone out to a Mexican restaurant for dinner and too much tequila. That part was fine; he was even able to sit next to Travis and brush his leg up against Travis' occasionally. But later, when Matt was back at Petey's, getting ready to crash for the night, Matt had assumed he'd sleep on the couch. But to Matt's amazement, Petey pointed at the far side of his bed and told Matt that was his side. Definitely not what Matt was expecting from the guy that called him "faggot" and "cocksucker" pretty much every chance he got, even if it was just roughhousing. It was like it never entered Petey's mind that Matt would sleep anywhere else. That part was only a little odd, but then it got odder. Matt stripped down to his boxers and got in bed, and then watched as Petey stripped down buck naked and crawled in next to him. It caught Matt off guard and he wasn't quite sure what it meant. Petey, though, just rolled over and promptly fell asleep, so Matt didn't overanalyze it. It was good, though, to know that Petey really was that utterly comfortable with him, like he had known him all his life. So Matt lay there in Petey's bed, with a six foot four Navy SEAL naked and conked out next to him, as if it was something that happened all the time. Matt started to agree with the other guys... there was just no explaining Petey most of the time.

Now on his second night in Virginia Beach, close enough to smell Travis but not touch, Matt was handling it by getting lit. It wasn't helping that Petey was partial to shots of Southern Comfort, and insisted Matt come along for the ride.

By 11:30 that night, Petey was totally wankered. Matt had stopped doing the shots earlier when Petey was too gone to notice he was doing them alone, so he wasn't as bad off. Travis had done a shot or two at first with them, then kept it to light beer after that, so he was still mostly in his right mind. Baya and Fincher were there, too, but had wandered off to talk to a few other guys they knew for a little while. They probably had smelled trouble brewing with Petey getting drunk and decided distance was a good thing.

Petey said to Matt, "I don't like the way that faggot's looking at me."

Matt knew who Petey was talking about. There was a Marine nearby that hadn't looked at Petey a single time that night. But drunk Petey had made up his mind that the guy was scoping him out.

Petey added, "It's these clothes. That homo's macking on me because of these clothes."

Before Matt could even respond, Petey said, "That's it! He's going down!"

Petey put his drink down on the table he and Matt were leaning against and started over towards the Marine to cause some trouble. Matt looked at Travis, giving him a what's-up-his-butt look. Travis calmly put his own drink down and went after Petey. Petey roughly shouldered his way through the crowd, rolling the sleeves up on his new shirt in anticipation of a fight. And in a bar full of men that didn't mind a scuffle, even they took one look at Petey pushing them out of his way and let it go. Travis caught up to Petey before the hapless Marine had any idea he was in the crosshairs, hooked his fingers in his jeans and stopped him from going any further.

206

Petey looked back at Travis in a slight fog. Travis didn't even try to explain that the Marine hadn't looked at him a single time all night. He said, "Colorado, you know what Tug said about you picking fights in here. You're gonna get banned if you keep this up. C'mon, Matt'll buy you another round. He's been macking on you all night and it doesn't seem to bother you at all."

Petey grinned like he was just learning how, sloppy and uncoordinated. "Yeah, he's got it bad, dudden he?"

Travis dragged Petey back to their table, pointed his finger at Petey's shoes and commanded, "Park it!"

Petey put his arm on Matt's shoulder. "Whats-his-Mope over there said you'd buy me a drink."

Matt held up the drink Petey had just put down a moment before and said, "Here you go, champ. You showed that faggot who's boss!"

He smiled at Travis, who smiled back. Matt was feeling pretty mellow given the amount of alcohol he had tossed back, but even so, he could tell Travis seemed a little off. He pulled out his phone and sent a text message to him:

You know I'm here with you. I'm pathetic but I wanna kiss you so bad I cant stand it!

Travis checked his phone a second later when the text came through, smiled more fully this time and gave Matt a tiny wink. It sent a shiver through Matt.

"Is that dude wearing a fucking Florida Gators t-shirt in here? Those sons of bitches aren't allowed in here!" Petey was getting riled up again.

Matt looked around but didn't see anyone wearing a Florida Gators t-shirt. He did briefly notice a cute girl with curly brunette hair smiling at either him or Petey; he wasn't sure which.

Matt leaned over and asked Travis, "Is he always like this when he's drunk?" He put his arm on the table behind Travis so he could lean in to ask the question over the noise of the bar, touching his arm to Travis' in the process.

Travis shook his head in resignation, "He's the most belligerent drunk I know. He'll be picking a fight with you any minute now, so be ready."

Matt hated moving his arm when he stepped back. Even just that tiny touch made him feel like he was floating four inches off the floor.

He moved back next to Petey, wondering when Petey would finally focus his inebriated anger on him.

"I'm getting a water. You want one? Another drink?" Travis asked Matt.

"Nah, I'm ok right now," he replied, and Travis wandered off through the crowd to chase down a bottle of water.

Petey turned to Matt and poked him in the chest. Matt braced himself for whatever Petey was angry about now.

"You like this, don't you, Cornhole? I like this." Petey asked, sounding for all the world like he was seeking Matt's approval. This wasn't what Matt was expecting.

"You like this?" Matt asked. "You mean hanging out with a queer? Going and buying some clothes and new sheets today?" Matt had seen how Petey lived and decided that if Petey was going to have a queer friend, he was going to make sure he put himself to good use.

"Yeah. Well, no. Don't like that stuff very much," said Petey, his arm back around Matt's shoulder, Matt straining to keep Petey's large frame upright. "Y'know, like, I like having you as a buddy. I'm knee-deep in assholes like Mope and Baya, Kennon and Wyatt 'n Wasp alla time. I think it's cool to have a buddy like you."

Matt wasn't sure if this was meant to be kind or offensive. He certainly wasn't being belligerent to Matt like he had been warned about.

Petey leaned in close. Matt could smell Petey's boozy breath, but his eyes seemed pretty sharp. Maybe Petey wasn't as far gone as Matt had thought.

"I don't have friends that make me buy better clothes, like these," he said, indicating the new shirt and jeans Matt had made him buy earlier that day. "Or decent sheets. Shit like that. Makes me do something to improve myself. The pussy herd will appreciate it. Not my favorite shit to go do, but I need to, you know?"

Matt decided he meant it all nicely.

Petey was still leaning so closely against Matt that his nose was almost touching Matt's face. "We're good buddies, right, Matt? Like brothers? I never had a brother. I mean, the platoon's like my brothers, you know? But it's cool having someone like you. Jeez, I suck at explaining this."

Petey looked at Matt a little helplessly, his extremely pale blue eyes locked onto Matt's green ones.

Matt did like it. He liked Petey. Petey had actually explained it better than he thought he had. Matt *did* feel kind of like Petey was the brother he never had before.

Matt nodded at him and said, "Yeah, Petey. It's good. We're brothers. I like it, too, you know?"

Petey hovered up in his face a moment longer, making sure Matt wasn't just saying so to make him stop being such a needy bitch. He stood back up a little straighter and said, "Good! I like that. Don't hold out on me now. I don't want my brother holding out on me. You can tell me anything, ya know?"

Matt wasn't sure how to handle Petey like this. This wasn't the Petey he was used to. It wasn't the fight-picking Petey everyone else seemed to get.

"I mean it, Matt. You're my brother now. You're the brother I never had. I don't want you hiding shit from me. I can talk to you about anything, and I want that from you, too. Got it?"

Matt said, "I know what you're fishing for, Colorado, and I'm not telling you I want to suck you off. So forget it."

Petey grinned and beat Matt in the chest a few times. "Yeah you do, but that's ok. You can sleep with me in my bed again tonight. I'll be drunk and passed out. I won't even notice if you grind my axe for me."

"Not gonna happen," replied Matt. It never ceased to amaze Matt just how comfortable Petey actually was with him.

Travis had taken his spot back right across from them and was swigging out of a bottle of water. He was watching the two of them intently.

Petey watched Matt, put his hand on his shoulder and said, "Brother."

Matt nodded in reply.

Matt looked at Petey's clear liquid eyes and he could tell. He could see it. In the blink of an eye, their relationship had fundamentally changed. This didn't feel like some mindless drunk-speak that would be forgotten the next morning. Petey had meant every word he said. Petey had chosen Matt to be his brother, his family. He may be all arrogant bluster and hard-shell around everyone else, but he had chosen Matt to be the one he'd open up to, to talk to about things he'd never talk to anyone else about. And he wanted Matt to do the same with him. Matt wasn't quite sure why it was him, but he wasn't going to question it. Maybe one day he'd ask Petey. And it felt good to know, really know, that Petey would give him an honest, no bullshit answer. For the first time in his life, Matt had a brother, and he didn't think he could pick a better one than Petey.

Matt got caught for a moment trying to understand the steps that had led him to this place right here, right now. He was an only child, and his mother and father had already passed away, but suddenly, he had a brother. Settled and done. No take-backs. No second guesses. Petey was one of the strangest, most amazing bastards Matt had ever met. He was now his family. In a way, Matt felt honored. He *was* honored by it.

He glanced up and saw Travis trying to read his face, but all he could manage was a what-the-hell-just-happened look.

Petey leaned over to Travis and asked if he could have a little of his water and held out his empty glass.

While Travis was pouring some for Petey, the pretty brunette girl showed up in front of Matt and said, "Hi!"

Matt smiled at her and she asked, "So, are you one of the Navy guys, too?"

"Nah, these guys are shiprats, but I'm just a friend." He pointed to Petey and Travis. As he glanced at the two of them, he noticed with amusement that Travis suddenly looked jealous. Matt floated four inches off the floor again.

"The haircut looks Navy, but the goatee doesn't. I couldn't figure it out." She reached up to touch Matt's fuzzy chin lightly. Matt wasn't used to getting hit on, and definitely not by women. Travis looked like steam was about to come out of his ears.

Matt said with a smile, "It's a long story, but the short version is that these guys are assholes and they have clippers. I'm Matt."

The brunette said, "I'm Claire" and they shook hands.

Matt asked, "You live in Virginia Beach?"

Before she could answer, he heard Petey say, "Fucking Gators fans!" as he started off towards the unsuspecting guy with the orange t-shirt and Gators logo on the back. He was rolling up the sleeves again on his new shirt, ready to start something. Travis was busy glaring a hole in Claire's back.

Matt said to Claire, "Whoops, hang on one second."

He took a step or two and grabbed Petey by the belt and pulled him back. He said, "Go Vols and all that, Petey, but there's no law against being a Gators fan in here. Kinda neutral ground, you know."

210

Petey let Matt drag him back and he finally noticed cute Claire standing there.

She looked up at the tall Petey towering over her, her eyes smiling at the both of them.

Her eyes shifted back to Matt, amused by what she saw. "Norfolk, actually. Here with friends for the weekend. You?"

"I'm from Richmond, but here babysitting." He nodded over towards Petey with a grin.

Petey was staring at Claire and said, "Wrong tree, honey!" Matt realized that Petey suddenly didn't look or sound nearly as drunk as he did just a few seconds ago.

Claire looked confused.

Petey slapped his hand on Matt's shoulder and explained it for her in very simple terms. "This one's a bigger flaming faggot than Elton John in a pink satin dress."

Claire looked horrified at what Petey said. She shifted her glance to Matt, her mouth hanging open.

Matt looked abashed and scratched at his forehead with his thumb, but laughed, too.

Petey made it even simpler. "He's as gay as my dick is long."

Matt laughed out loud now. Claire's expression shifted to a confused smile as well, but looked at Matt, questioning.

Matt nodded and said, "Yeah, I'm gay."

Claire looked at Petey, truly offended, and said, "That's a terrible way to describe your friend!"

Petey ruffled Matt's head. Matt smiled and leaned against Petey and said, "He's just horsing around. He's a good friend, one of my best. He's a good guy."

Claire seemed to relax a little, finally feeling good that the two of them were just kidding around.

Petey put his arm around Matt and pulled him close. He leaned over and planted a big, sloppy kiss on Matt's forehead. "This guy... this one... more than a good friend. He's my brother."

Matt caught the look that Petey gave him, the one that said absolutely nothing less than "brother" would do from now on. Matt fully accepted that.

As they chatted, Matt noticed how Claire shifted her attention slightly more towards Petey. It was fine with him. Petey, now that there seemed to be a chance he might hook up, suddenly didn't seem nearly as messy drunk. Claire asked him what he did in the Navy and Matt heard the usual line they gave about filling in here and there where needed, the same one Travis had given Bret and Jim.

Matt decided to help out a little. He asked Claire, "Hey, you're running low and I'm about out of cash. You mind if Petey here buys you another?"

Claire happily nodded her approval and Petey sauntered off to buy the lady a drink.

Claire turned back to Matt, concerned, and asked, "Does he always treat you like that? Calling you faggot?"

Matt laughed and shook his head, "Usually? Way worse. He's behaving tonight. But, the big rascal, he's good, really. Once you get past that... spectacularly... offensive exterior, he's got the heart of a lion. Petey's right... for better or for worse, he's my brother. Hell, he even made me sleep in the bed with him last night so I didn't have to sleep on his couch."

"Really?" Claire bit her bottom lip like she thought that had to be the sweetest thing she had ever heard. Or maybe she thought the sound of both of them in bed together sounded like something she wanted to be in the middle of.

Matt pushed just a little further. "Nothing happened of course, but between you and me, Petey does have one really amazing body."

"He does look pretty good. Especially that fire red hair and smooth skin next to that cream colored shirt."

"You have me to thank for the clothes. He can't dress himself for shit, so I made him go shopping today and picked a few things out for him."

"Awww... that's just the cutest thing!" Claire seemed to eat up the whole image of the big Navy guy with his best gay friend.

Petey returned with a fresh drink for Claire, and Matt was relieved to see that Petey had switched to a bottle of water for himself. She started to ask Petey about his shopping trip with Matt, and so Matt excused himself to go check on Travis.

He leaned up against the same tall table Travis was against, their arms pressed together. Travis was talking to someone on his mobile phone.

He was saying, "Just don't make a decision you can't take back." There was a pause as he listened to whoever was on the other end.

He looked frustrated and said, "I think we need to talk more about this first. You're the only one that's hung up on this, and I understand why, but you've got to hear me." Travis' strong shoulders slumped and he glanced at Matt next to him.

While he listened to the other end, Travis' eyes opened wide and he said, "Look, I want to talk in the morning, ok? You promise to give me until then?"

He listened a moment more and said, "Ok, tomorrow morning," and hung up.

Matt didn't feel like he should press about the call, so he said, "If I didn't know better, I'd think you maybe didn't want me talking to that girl."

Travis looked distracted for a moment, before realizing what Matt had said. "Fuck! I'm not used to this! I wanted to punch her in the back of her curly-haired head!"

It gave Matt shivers to hear Travis say that. "Relax, Trav, it'll be ten years before that happens again. I *never* get girls coming on to me."

Travis pushed up a little closer against Matt possessively. It was easy to do in the crowded bar without attracting any attention. And just like that, Matt was floating again.

"You and Petey seemed pretty deep in conversation there for a second," said Travis. "Has he not tried to pick a fight with you yet? That's his thing when he gets drunk. He's been a hair's breath away from being banned from The 'Sides for a year now."

Matt said, "No. No fight. Actually, it's strange, not like Petey very much. He's decided I'm his brother now. He didn't seem to be kidding around, but it's probably just crazy liquor talk. He's pretty drunk."

Travis looked confused momentarily. He told Matt, "Huh... that doesn't sound a lot like Petey. But he usually only seems drunker than he really is. And he definitely likes you a lot, Matt. Who knows, maybe he really means it. I hope you wanted a brother, because I think you've got one now."

Travis added through a smile, "Ha ha! Good luck with *that*!"

"You jealous?" asked Matt, halfway joking, halfway serious.

A wry smile spread over Travis' face and he said, "If it had been anyone else, I would. Jesus, I'm totally not used to having jealous feelings like this about anyone. But with Petey? Nah. I'm glad. You know how much I like Petey, despite him being... Petey. I like how he is with you. It's funny, but I can totally see you two as brothers. I've seen Petey take a liking to people here and there, but Matt... nothing like with you. Beats anything I've ever seen. I think that if I was going to trust you in anybody's hands other than mine, it'd be Petey's."

Claire had stepped away from Petey to go back to her friends, and Petey came up behind Matt, thumping him in the ear.

"Hey Cornhole, she wants to go back to my place! You wanna come? We can tag team her! You'd like that, right? You can pick whichever hole you want and I'll take the other!" Petey was a kid on Christmas morning before his parents let him rush the living room.

"Colorado, didja ever stop to think for a minute that maybe she could be more than just a hole to fuck?" asked Matt.

"Mmmmmmm... like what? You mean like fucking her between the tits? I dunno if hers are big enough for that."

Matt rubbed his eyes. Petey wasn't going to be led anywhere other than where he wanted to go.

"Hey, you wanna suck my balls while I'm fucking her? That'd be kinda cool!" said Petey, his imagination and his face lighting up.

"Gee, Petey. Hot red pepper balls. That's sooooo tempting... No."

Petey feigned indifference. "Meh. Your loss. You gotta key to my place, so get Prudy McPissyDaddy here to drop you off whenever you guys are done drinking."

Suddenly, Petey's eyes narrowed and he poked Matt in the chest. "But if I find out Mope here hooks up and you wind sucking *his* balls while he's banging some chick, there's gonna be problems."

Matt glanced at Travis out of the corner of his eye, almost feeling a blush across his face.

"But I ain't gotta worry about that," corrected Petey. "Mope never hooks up. It's those radar-dish ears."

Claire came back and Petey put his arm around her and they made their way through the crowd. Matt and Travis watched as he held her small hand in his and led her out of the bar.

The grin that appeared on Matt's face was epic, and he said, "God, that worked out great! So, Trav, do you think I could maybe crash at your place tonight?"

"Maybe. I gotta see if I can score one of the leftover bitches in here so I can get you to eat my nuts while I'm porking her. How about the one with the tattoos and nose-ring over there?"

~~~~~

When Matt set foot in Travis' apartment for the first time, it wasn't quite what he expected. But that was only because he didn't know what to expect. It was a small one bedroom apartment, but very close to the beach. It was sparsely furnished and a little messy, but it wasn't anywhere nearly as bad off as Petey's. Petey's place looked like he shared his apartment with four or five feral hogs. Travis had a nice TV hanging on one wall, surrounded by bookshelves on either side with movies and books filling them.

Travis immediately apologized, "I didn't think I'd be able to get you home with me, so I really didn't clean up any."

Matt said, "I'd rather see it how it really is. And believe me, after spending the night with Petey, the slums of Calcutta would seem like a Ritz-Carlton. Petey actually had a peanut butter and bologna sandwich for breakfast!"

Travis asked, "Did he put mustard on it?"

Matt wrinkled his nose in disgust. "No."

"He adds mustard a lot of times. It's like a secret Tuttle family recipe or something. He must be out."

They stood just inside the door of Travis' apartment for a moment, neither quite sure of how to make the next move now that they were both alone together. It was Matt that couldn't stand it anymore and broke the stalemate. He shoved Travis against the closed door of the apartment and pressed himself against him, kissing him hard after going a week without it. Matt loved the feel of Travis' tongue against his, in his mouth. He loved the taste of alcohol on his breath. He loved the feel of Travis' eleven o'clock shadow against his face. Travis' arms went around Matt and they kissed long enough to confirm that what they had started the weekend before wasn't just a fluke. Matt was aroused like he couldn't ever remember before. He was in *his* place. He'd be in *his* bed. He pressed his face into Travis' broad chest and inhaled deeply. Salt air and cedarwood.

Travis finally invited Matt into the apartment proper, rather than just standing and making out against the front door all night. Matt went ahead and sent Petey a text letting him know he was going to crash at Travis' place and would see him in the morning. With that out of the way, Travis gave Matt a quick tour of the apartment, which mostly consisted of pointing at the living room, accompanied by the words "living room". Matt took note of the two sticker-plastered surfboards up against the wall near the door to the apartment, one taller and reaching almost to the ceiling, the other shorter and narrower. Travis pointed in another direction and said, "kitchen". Travis would have been just as succinct with the bedroom, but Matt insisted on lingering for a moment. There was a metal cabinet on the wall opposite Travis' bed with the door hanging open and a collection of guns neatly stored in it, both rifles and handguns. Something that would have freaked him out to see in anyone else's bedroom was somehow reassuring to see in Travis'. The closet door was open and Matt could see several of the BDU's he had seen Travis in before, as well as his civilian clothes.

Matt wanted to pay more attention to the bed than anything, though. Travis' bed was an unmade mess, and he tried to move Matt out of the room quickly for the rest of the tour. But Matt was fascinated by it. It was like a nest of navy blue sheets and pillows and a wadded up white cotton blanket. There was no headboard or footboard, just a simple, unadorned bed. He wanted to be in *his* bed so bad it almost hurt. But, he let Travis lead him back into the living room. Travis lay down on his couch and pulled Matt down on top of him.

"I didn't think I'd be able to get this close to those green eyes all weekend," said Travis, one hand stroking Matt's soft hair, the other pushing down into the back of his pants to feel his ass.

"Thank God Petey hooked up!" said Matt.

Travis thought about it and said, "This is all going to wind up sucking. You were the perfect wingman for him tonight. Now every guy in the fucking platoon is going to want you to wing for them. I'll never get you to myself!"

Matt asked through a grin, "You a little jealous?"

"I didn't like that Claire bitch coming on to you. I didn't like that Petey got to spend all afternoon with you. I *really* didn't like that! I didn't like how Petey got to hang all over you all night, right out in the open. It's all driving me a little nuts here! If you weren't here with me now, I'd probably have to go find an all-night firing range just so I could go blow big holes in things for a few hours!"

Matt stared into Travis' dark eyes sympathetically.

Travis asked, "Will you do that stuff with me? Help me buy clothes? Help me pick out better stuff for this apartment? It's a shithole. It's embarrassing."

Matt thought about it for a moment. "Probably not."

Travis looked hurt. And jealous, again.

"Petey needs the help. You don't. I want *you* to dress like *you*. I want *your* bed to be *yours*. I want to be in *your* bed."

Travis softened, understanding now.

Matt added, "And it's not a shithole. Petey lives in a shithole."

Travis finally admitted, "This is actually a little harder than I thought it would be. For the first time ever, I don't like hiding. I don't like hiding you and I don't like hiding us. Too many secrets. Stupid secrets."

Matt didn't want this. He didn't want to put Travis in this position. "Trav, I'll not come to Virginia Beach again if this is going to be hard on you. Or, if I do, we won't tell any of the guys and you can keep me locked up in your bedroom." He wagged his eyebrows at Travis suggestively.

Travis ran his thumbs across Matt's eyebrows. He didn't like that answer very much.

"You would, wouldn't you? You'd wind up sacrificing what you've got with Petey, with the other guys, for us, wouldn't you?" Travis was asking a question he already knew the answer to.

Matt's answer was to bury his face in Travis' neck and hold on tighter.

Travis held Matt on top of him and stroked his hair gently again. He sighed, "No wonder it was so easy for someone like Brian to take bad advantage of you."

Chapter 32 – Friendly Fire

Matt inhaled deeply, not even opening his eyes. Fresh salt air and cedarwood. God, how he loved that smell. He lay on his stomach and kept his face buried down in the warm pillows and sheets of Travis' bed, allowing himself to wake up slowly. If it was left up to him, he'd never get out of this bed.

Matt had no idea what time it was and was about to fall back asleep when he felt it. It started as a slight tickle, but then he felt it more distinctly. He felt something brushing lightly in the small of his back, just above his ass. He shivered at the sensation, then groaned out loud when he felt the soft lips kissing and brushing around in that spot. Matt felt Travis' strong hands plant on either side of him as the lips pressed down a little harder and he could feel a tongue start to lick in soft circles at the base of his spine.

The licking stopped and Matt felt warm breath on his back, slowly moving farther up along his spine until it stopped at the base of his neck. He could feel the heat coming off a body suspending itself just a few inches over him, watching him, smelling him.

And then with a lion growl deep inside a chest, the body lay itself down on top of Matt, pressing him down into the sheets and mattress. With all 225 pounds on top of him now, strong, rough hands ran along Matt's arms to his hands, until their fingers laced together.

The breath above him tickled his left ear and he heard a guttural whisper in his ear say, "Mmmmm… you like this, don't you?" It was a statement and not a question.

Matt felt the body on top of him. It felt like an animal, muscle and sinew and hair, on top of prey it had been stalking, now pinning it down for the kill. In the cleft of his ass, Matt felt something pressing insistently there, grinding into him.

Matt nodded a weak reply. There was an animal bite on his earlobe, tasting him. He felt hot breath on his face and the stubble on a muzzle rub against his ear and cheek.

The animal voice whispered low again, "There's something I need…"

Matt groaned and shivered again. He moaned, "Yeah."

The grinding continued, and with the full weight on him, he wouldn't have been able to stop it if he wanted to. But stopping it was absolutely the last thing on his mind.

The voice purred, "Something you know you want…"

Matt smiled to himself and hummed into the sheets, "Mmm hmmm."

The animal on top of Matt reared back a little and Matt felt bared teeth biting lightly into the back of his neck.

He felt a rough shock as the animal on top of him suddenly lifted all the way off, exposing him fully, and he felt a sharp smack on his bare backside.

Travis said brightly, "Good! A five mile run on the beach it is!"

Matt groaned again, in complete exasperation this time.

Travis rolled over onto his back next to Matt. Matt shifted over, and put his head on the cruel animal's chest, the dark chest hair grinding into his face and tickling his nose. "You've got to be kidding. And you're a son of a bitch. Not necessarily in that order."

One of Travis' arms reached down along Matt's back to play with his ass while the other reached up and ran through Matt's hair. He kissed Matt's head softly.

"C'mon. I'm getting flabby. It's the best time of the day for a run on the beach."

Matt didn't move, and he didn't grace the suggestion with a response.

Travis decided to bribe him. "And when we get back, you can do," he kissed Matt's head, "absolutely," kiss, "positively," kiss, "anything to me your sick mind can come up with."

Matt turned his head over on Travis' chest so he could look right into his dark eyes under those dark eyebrows and said, "Put it in writing and get it notarized and you're on."

Travis gently kissed the tip of Matt's nose, which would have to serve as a notary seal for the day, but it was good enough for Matt.

Travis pulled Matt up and out of bed. The sun was up and filtering through Travis' windows, but Virginia Beach was still quiet outside. For a Sunday morning, it felt way too early. Travis let Matt borrow some clothes to run in since all of his stuff was still over at Petey's apartment for the weekend. As he watched Travis get ready, though, he couldn't understand what Travis was doing. He had put running shorts on, but then had put on a heavy Navy sweatshirt. That was odd since it was warm outside, even in the morning. When he pulled his running shoes on, he grabbed a spare rucksack and went into the living room. Matt followed him and watched as Travis filled up the rucksack with as many heavy books off the bookshelf as he could cram in it.

"What the hell are you doing?" he finally asked.

"Five miles is a pretty short run, so I'll load up a little bit to make sure I get more of a workout," replied Travis.

Matt looked at the bag. There had to be forty pounds of books in it.

"I'm not even going to tell you how much of a jerk you are."

Travis grinned unapologetically as he lifted the bag up onto one shoulder. He came over to Matt and kissed him on the cheek. He pointed at the kitchen and said, "There's a cereal bar in the cabinet to the left of the stove if you want one before we go." He trotted back into the bedroom without waiting for a reply.

Matt went into the kitchen to get one of the cereal bars or he knew he'd be cramping before the end of the first mile. As he was eating it, he could hear Travis on the phone in the bedroom talking to someone.

Travis came back into the living room a few minutes later, bubbling with energy, and kissed Matt again. He said happily, "I like having you here!"

~~~~~

Matt and Travis made it up to a low stone landscaping wall in front of one of the hotels facing across the boardwalk to the beach and ocean beyond. Matt collapsed panting on the wall, laying down on it and staring straight up for a little while. He had started sweating buckets by about the second mile of the run and was thoroughly exhausted now that it was done. The smirk on Travis' face was digging into Matt and irritating him. Travis had only barely begun to break a sweat in the last ten minutes or so of their run and was barely breathing heavy. And the only reason he was sweating at all was because of the heavy sweatshirt he was wearing under the book-filled rucksack.

Travis took the bag off his back and put it down on the ground. He sat down next to it with his back against the stone wall where Matt's feet were.

Matt said, between huffs and puffs as he watched that misaligned grin on Travis' face that he loved to see so much, "You're just showing off, aren't you?"

The grin expanded across Travis' face a little bit more. He looked out across the ocean and people on the beach, "Maybe. A little."

He glanced at Matt sideways, shrugged, and admitted, "I want you to like me."

Matt said after a pained groan, "I want to shoot you."

Travis laughed at him.

After a moment of catching his breath, Matt got up off the wall and sat down on the ground next to Travis so he could look out over the beach, too. Virginia Beach was waking up and the people out and about had increased since they had started their run. There were walkers and beachcombers, people riding their bicycles and rollerblading, and families claiming their sovereign patch of sand for their day at the beach. There were also a group of surfers out in the water trying to catch some waves before the crowds got too thick and pushed them out. The sun inched its way up in the sky, poking through wispy feathers of clouds, but the sea breeze had not cranked up for the day yet.

Matt said, "Tell you what, let's stop on the way back and buy some things and I'll make you my world famous French toast for breakfast."

Travis nodded, "Now *that* sounds great! I love a man that can cook!"

"Heh! I hope you like French toast then, because that's about all I can cook."

Matt was very much looking forward to having some time alone with Travis before he had to catch back up with Petey later.

"And when we're done with breakfast, I've got some ideas for the syrup."

Travis laughed again. "I said anything you could come up with, and I meant it. But you're making me a little nervous now!"

"That's *your* problem. You ready to go?"

Travis glanced down at his watch and looked around a little. He said, "Gimme a few more minutes. I might want to go jump in the water before we head back. Is that ok?"

"Sure."

Travis leaned forward and pulled his sweatshirt off so he could cool off more easily. He asked, "You wanna try getting in the water with me a little?"

"Nuh unh! No way! I'll get eaten by a shark or attacked by some rabid jellyfish or mugged by stingrays or something."

They sat watching Virginia Beach waking up for a few more minutes. Matt would steal glances over at the man sitting next to him occasionally, liking the view of a bare-chested Travis better than the beach and ocean and rising sun in front of him. Everything about him was more than he might have hoped for, and he had never felt about anyone the way he felt about Travis. Not even when he first met Brian, when he was totally smitten with him, did it feel like this. It wasn't just a puppy-dog crush on Travis, though. At least, it certainly didn't feel that way. Their personalities meshed well. They could joke together, be serious together, talk, be quiet. Travis seemed to fit him in every way he might want. Matt found himself wishing his parents were still alive. He would have liked for them to meet Travis, something he had never even thought about with Brian. They would have liked Travis.

"How's your dad doing, Trav? Did you talk to him this week?" asked Matt.

"Yeah, I've talked to him. He's doing pretty good. He didn't even mention Chris this time on the phone. And he always mentions Chris when we talk. It might not seem like much of a change to anybody else, but I know my dad. It's good to get even small steps from him, Matt. It really is."

"Does your dad know you're gay?"

Travis sighed. "Yeah, he knows." He rubbed his hand across his unshaven face. "I handled that like an asshole. I got tired of him, got really mad actually, after I became a SEAL and still got no respect or... anything really... from him. And so I told him. But I did it because I wanted to hurt him. I wish I could take it back and handle that differently, but that's how it was. That's how hurt I was. I wanted to hurt him back. To my surprise, he didn't freak out or tell me he hated me or anything like that. Maybe he just expected it because he expected me to be a disappointment in every possible way. But he doesn't talk about it, either. I tried a couple of times to get him to talk about it, but he won't. So I eventually just dropped it."

Matt was quiet, feeling bad about Travis' relationship with his dad. Getting so little when he deserved so much.

"It means a lot to me, you know," said Travis, his voice barely a whisper over the sound of the waves, "what you did. Talking to my dad and making him actually see *something* in me. It may not seem like much changed to most people, but for me, even that little bit is a lot. It means something. It means something to me."

He squinted at the beach in front of him. "I'm learning about you, Matt, through this kind of stuff. The fact that you're willing to go do something like that for someone that you barely know."

Matt shrugged, "You *did* kind of save my life. I felt like I should do something."

Travis pulled his knees up to his chest and wrapped his arms around them. He looked over at Matt and said, "I don't believe that. And... I think you're a pretty shitty liar. I don't like thinking that the only reason you'd do something like that is to pay off some debt you imagine you have. Like I said, I'm figuring you out a little. I think you would have done it anyway. I don't think for one minute you did it because I saved your life."

Matt didn't know how to reply to that. He felt a little awkward at Travis making him out to be something more than he was. He would have done it for Travis, just out of admiration for him. But Travis made it sound like it was *something*.

Travis grinned and said, "You're just a big fat liar. But the best possible kind, Matt. At first, I thought the best thing about you was those pretty unbelievable green eyes. But it's that heart of yours. That huge heart."

Matt really felt warm and awkward and even a little nervous now. He wondered if this was how it felt to have someone say things like this to you. He guessed it must.

Travis glanced past Matt, down the boardwalk. He said, "So, actually, I need to ask you a question... Do you trust me?"

"Completely," said Matt.

"If I asked you to help with something you might otherwise be a little uncomfortable with, would you trust me enough to do it?"

Matt wasn't sure what Travis was asking, but it didn't matter. "Yeah, the answer's still yeah."

"Ok, good."

Matt waited a moment to see what it was that Travis wanted to ask him to do, but Travis didn't say anything. He just squinted out at the water.

Just as he was about to ask Travis what he wanted, he heard footsteps behind him and turned to see Wasp walking up to them, as huge as always. He was dressed in long white shorts and a faded orange t-shirt that was too big for him. But what Matt noticed was that Wasp looked awful. He hadn't shaved in a couple of days, and he didn't look like he had slept, either. The bags under his eyes stood out like dark clouds.

"Hey, Matt," he said dolefully. "Didn't expect to see you here." Wasp cut a glance over at Travis as he said that.

Travis said, "Petey hooked up last night, so Matt crashed at my place."

Matt got the feeling that Wasp's arrival had been planned.

Wasp said, "You guys go running?"

"Yeah, five miles," said Travis.

"That's all?"

Travis nodded his head over at Matt as an explanation.

Matt said, trying to lighten the suddenly gloomy mood, "Ok, you guys are going to give me a complex here." He really didn't know Wasp very well, but he was a little worried about him.

Wasp didn't even smile. He stood looking at them uncertainly for a moment, then said, "Yeah, so, it's good running across you guys. Nope, I'll catch up with you. Later. I guess."

Travis said, "Keith, wait a minute and do me a favor, ok? Keep Matt company for a little bit." He swung his head around, looking, "I've gotta go run take a leak in the hotel there. I'll be back in just a minute."

Wasp nodded and sat down on the other side of Travis from Matt. He crossed his legs and rested his chin in his hands, looking out at every single other person in the world having a good time and in a good mood.

Travis stood up and grabbed his sweatshirt. He opened up the rucksack and dug around for a moment while he told Matt, "Be right back. You guys talk."

He pulled something out of the rucksack and put it down between Matt and Wasp and immediately trotted off to find the bathroom.

When Matt saw what he put down, he immediately looked after Travis to see if he was insane.

Wasp looked over. His blue mood was overcome by curiosity all of a sudden and he asked Matt, "Mope brought a gun out here? Why did he leave his handgun sitting out?"

Matt didn't say anything.

Wasp picked it up and admired the gun for a moment. He popped the clip out before shoving it back in. He squinted and checked the sight on it.

"A Caracal, 9 millimeter. I didn't know Mope had one of these. Don't see many of these in the US."

Matt watched Wasp work the gun. He stared at it in Wasp's hands. His chest tightened some when he realized that he could still see a little bit of blood still on it along some of the crevices of the gun. In his mind, Matt was assaulted with the burning image of the flash of the gun and a person's head twisting and tearing apart right in front of him.

Wasp realized Matt hadn't said anything, so he looked over at him. Matt's eyes didn't leave the gun. Wasp asked, "Mope brought a handgun with him on your run?"

Matt understood what Travis wanted, even if he didn't understand why, even if it didn't make it easy. But he trusted Travis. Completely.

Wasp noticed the funny look on Matt's face. He asked, "Matt?"

Matt finally snapped out of it and realized Wasp was talking to him. It was Matt's turn to pull his knees up to his chest and put his arms around them. He said, "It's not Mope's gun. It's mine. I guess."

Wasp gave Matt an impressed nod. "Cool. I didn't know you were into guns."

Matt's mouth felt a little dry. He had only talked to Travis about this before. He said, "I'm not. I'm not even comfortable with them. Mope's keeping this one for me."

Wasp looked a little lost. He put the handgun back down on the cement between them and stared at Matt curiously.

Talking became harder. Matt could talk to Travis about what happened, about killing that person, but he wasn't as sure about talking to any of the other guys about it. They wouldn't understand, especially since it was one of the bad guys. They'd think he was being silly and weak. Matt said, his voice unsteady, "This is the gun I killed one of Al-Hashim's guys with. Mope brought it back as kind of a souvenir. He thought I'd be proud to have it." He scratched at his nose a little. He still didn't feel very proud.

"You know the story of what all happened that night. All you guys seem so proud of the fact that I took one of them out. But... I don't know. Even though I guess I had no choice, I don't like what I did. Mope wanted me to have it, but I asked him to keep it for me."

Matt expected Wasp to laugh at him, to tell him he did good, he should be proud, that he was a man for what he did. All that. All the things he didn't feel. But instead, Wasp watched him intently, very respectful of what Matt was saying, almost sympathizing with him.

Wasp's face turned very cloudy again and they sat in silence for a long time.

Wasp eventually said to Matt, "I've killed a guy, too, Matt."

Matt thought about the twenty-seven hash marks on Travis' rifle. The thought hit him that it might actually be more at this point. They had been on another mission since they left Latakia.

"That's kind of your job, right?" said Matt. "Part of it, anyway. You guys are trained."

Wasp frowned and didn't dare look Matt in the eye.

"No. I killed one of our own."

Matt didn't know what to say. He didn't know if he should press it or not.

Wasp took a second, but then started to explain.

"We were coming back from a mission and headed to the green zone in Baghdad. We were passing through this neighborhood that had a little bit of a spotty reputation. There was a group of Iraqis crowding around a guy, a local, and suddenly the local pulled out a rifle. I was the first one to see it and thought we were heading into an ambush, so I reacted and shot the guy. Just one bullet. And he was dead."

Wasp stopped for a second before clearing his throat uncomfortably.

"But he wasn't a local. It was a Marine. One... one of ours. I killed one of our own guys."

Matt felt terrible. Wasp... Keith... was so young. To have that happen must be terrible. But he kinda knew the feeling.

"I'm sorry, Keith," he said.

Wasp said, "It turns out the guy wasn't supposed to be there. He had left the green zone to go find some prostitute he had heard about. He broke all kinds of regs being out there, and definitely shouldn't have been dressed like he was. The locals got a little antsy when they noticed him and he pulled the gun. Anyway, that's what I was told. There was an inquiry, and they said it was his fault and cleared me of any wrongdoing."

"When I joined the SEALs, I felt like I could do anything. But I let it all go to my head. And now, there's some poor Marine's parents in Eugene, Oregon whose son won't be coming home because of me. I killed a good guy, Matt. I'm the failure on the team. Responsibility is always placed where it belongs, and this was all me. And now I'm becoming a liability. I'm second-guessing every response I have now. I'm dragging the team down. Worse, one of these days I'm going to second-guess at the wrong time, when I should have acted, and get a team member killed. I don't know which way to go any more. All I can think about is that guy from Eugene."

"I'd have thrown my helmet in a few months ago already if it weren't for Mope. He's the only one that's kept me going. I don't know why he does it. I'm just dead weight at this point. But he made me promise to talk to him every time I felt like I couldn't keep going."

Matt felt overwhelmed. At his own guilt that rose up in him as soon as he saw the gun again, and now also for seeing a good man, so young, but so weighted down with the blame he put on himself. Neither of them quite knowing where to turn to unload the guilt pressing on them so heavily. At least Matt knew he wouldn't likely have to face something like that again. Poor Keith had to face it almost every day.

Matt said, "It's funny, but I think I kinda know how you feel. The guys all said I killed this person because I had to, and I guess I did, but this isn't me. I sit in an office every day. I don't shoot people in the face. It's been hard on me, too, at times. And for better or worse, there's this reminder sitting right in front of me of what I did."

Wasp smiled grimly. "I guess we're kind of a pair. You regret shooting the bad guy and I regret shooting one of the good ones. At least there's someone around that I know can relate to it some."

They sat in silence for a few moments, their regrets sitting in-between them in the form a handgun.

Matt said, "Tell you what, Keith. For what it's worth, we can help each other, maybe. I'll forgive you for shooting the good guy if you'll forgive me for shooting the bad guy. Maybe we can do for each other what we can't quite seem to do for ourselves."

Wasp thought about it hard for several moments. "Yeah, maybe that'd be good. Maybe that'll help. Thanks, Matt. Thanks for forgiving me."

Matt felt better, too. He wasn't quite so alone in how he felt about something he had done. And for the first time since he had pulled the trigger and killed another living person with it, Matt picked up the gun between them. Carefully, like it might go off again. It felt so strange and foreign to hold it in his hands. He hadn't realized that what he needed was forgiveness for what he had done, no matter how right many people thought his actions were. He hadn't realized what he needed until he found someone that could rightfully understand what he felt.

"Yeah, you too, Keith. Thanks."

"Thanks," he repeated.

Wasp reached over with his hand to shake Matt's, sealing the exchange. Absolution passed through pressed palms.

Wasp suggested they put the gun back in the rucksack before someone walking or jogging by noticed there were two guys sitting out on the boardwalk waving a gun around.

They started making small talk, but Travis showed up just a moment later, soaking wet and his sweatshirt and sneakers in his hand.

Wasp said, "You can't stay out of the water, can you?"

Travis said cheerfully, "Nope." He gave Matt a quick, curious look and Matt smiled back at him, letting him know it was ok.

Wasp asked, "How far out?"

"Ahhh, little more than a half mile, I think."

"You're getting lazy, Mope. And old." Wasp had a half a grin on his face. His mood seemed to be improving.

Travis said, "Yeah, yeah, I know. C'mon, I got a hankering for some French toast."

Wasp lit up a little. "Man, I haven't had French toast in ages!" He looked at Matt and Travis hopefully.

Matt gave Travis a hidden look of benign frustration. He had really wanted to get back to Travis' apartment, get in the shower with him, and together use up every drop of hot water he had. It seemed like he'd never be able to get Travis alone again at this rate. But he wasn't about to not let Wasp come along, either. No way.

Matt could tell Travis felt the same way. Hiding in plain sight was always going to weigh on them. But you had to be prepared for the sacrifices.

Matt said, "Well, it's my one and only specialty. Let's go. I guess we'll stop by the ATM first. I'll need extra money to buy all the food I'm pretty sure you can put away, Wasp. Am I right?"

Matt entirely missed the tender, admiring look that Travis gave him.

Chapter 33 – Memorial Day

On the Saturday night about a month later, Matt was out at the vodka bar called Kremlin for the start of the Memorial Day weekend. The place was fairly packed for the start of the holiday, and the mixed gay and straight crowd was definitely in the mood for a holiday weekend. The DJ was spinning a down-tempo mix of sophisticated club music to provide a soundtrack to all the people looking to see and be seen. Matt was there with Bret and Jim, but his mind was elsewhere and he didn't care a whole lot about seeing or being seen.

Travis had been off on one of his missions that he couldn't talk about for more than a week now. He had told Matt he'd be back on Friday afternoon and would have the long weekend to spend with him in Richmond. And then Friday had come and gone with no word from him.

It wasn't the first time since they had started dating that this had happened, and he knew it definitely wouldn't be the last. But it still was hard on Matt. The training missions were no big deal. Matt usually knew where they were, whether it was out in San Diego or in the desert out west, or the other typical places they often trained. But these missions where he knew nothing were harder to deal with; Travis had been very right about that. He never knew when he'd get word back from one of the other guys in the platoon that maybe something had gone very wrong and something terrible had happened. Matt had made the guys solemnly swear that if anything happened to any of "his" platoon that they would let him know as soon as possible. He meant it, too. It wasn't just Travis that he worried about. But it was far and away Travis that he worried the most about.

So on Saturday night, since he still hadn't heard from Travis, Matt agreed to go out with Bret and Jim to pass the time until he hopefully heard something. Bret and Jim could tell Matt was distracted and worried; it wasn't the first time they had seen him like this since he had started seeing Travis.

Jim swirled his vodka martini around a few times and said, "Matt, look, Bret and I both like Travis a lot. God knows he treats you incredibly well when he's around. But what's the deal with these periods when he just disappears? It seems odd, and it's clearly not easy for you."

"We've talked about this. You know there are some assignments he can't talk about," said Matt.

"Yeah, but it seems like there's a lot of them. He's gone a lot. You have no idea what he's doing. Or... you know, who he's doing it with. How do you know he's even actually on some kind of assignment? How do you trust him? Are you sure you can?"

That was the last thing in the world to cause Matt concern. "I trust him more than you can possibly imagine." His friends were getting close to stepping over a line in how they talked about Travis, and Matt's response had something of a steel edge to it to warn them.

Before this conversation could go any further, and to put Matt in an even worse mood, the bad penny turned up.

Brian came up to the three of them, along with a young new boyfriend on his arm. Matt had not seen Brian or talked to him since the night that Petey had scared him off. None of them had. Nonetheless, it was a disappointment to see him now. He did feel sorry for the young guy taken in by Brian, though. Brian had apparently shifted his target demographic younger to find someone a little more easily misled; the fellow looked barely old enough to get in the bar. Matt hoped the young guy would learn his lesson about Brian a lot more quickly than he had.

Brian had this arrogant look of superiority on his face. He leaned over and conspicuously kissed his trophy boyfriend on the cheek in front of the three of them. He said to Matt, all happiness and bitter light, "Hi Matt! So I hear you've got a new boyfriend, but I don't see him around. Seems like no one I've talked to has actually seen him. You sure you're not making this guy up? I would have thought that six weeks after I dumped you, you would have found *somebody* by now."

"No, Brian. I'm not making him up. And thanks, Bret, I can handle this." Bret had opened his mouth to give Brian a piece of his mind before Matt stomped it shut for him.

"So, if he's real," said Brian, "then what I told you would happen is true. You've got some loser that's just using you. You had your chance to come back to me and have a real man. And you blew it."

Bret and Jim both now looked like they were on the verge of beating the shit out of Brian.

231

Matt knew that Brian was trying to hurt him, but it almost made him laugh at how pathetic the attempt was. The idea of Brian being a real man was laughable. Matt replied, "When you say the words 'real man', do they sound like meaningless foreign words to you?" It was strange how transparent Brian was, but only now, on the other side of the breakup, did Matt see it this way. He felt ashamed for how easy he had made it for Brian to be this way for an entire year.

Brian looked at Matt stupidly for a second before his eyes darted to a spot just over Matt's shoulders.

The entire universe melted into a puddle around Matt's feet as he felt two strong arms wrap around him from behind and a face bury itself in the side of Matt's neck, kissing him. He knew the scent of the man behind him instantly — the smell of salt air and cedarwood. Just that scent alone made Matt feel at home and at peace.

Matt said, "Brian, you have no idea what it means to be a real man. No idea at all."

Travis spun Matt around and they kissed, Travis lifting Matt off the ground a few inches in the process. Matt said, "You fucker! You had me worried again!"

Travis smiled sheepishly. He said, "I know. I just wanted to surprise you a little this time. So, this is Brian?" He looked over Matt's head at Brian curiously.

Brian stood irritated as he watched this display. Matt's new boyfriend actually showing up didn't line up with his plans very well, especially when the boyfriend was as imposing as Travis. He recovered quickly, though, and said with a sneer, "I can't believe you put up with this shit from Dumbo here, but I wasn't good enough for you!"

Matt could and had put up with a lot from Brian, but this time he was tipped over the edge. No, he was shoved violently across it and someone was going to pay. He pushed back from Travis, spun around, and punched Brian awkwardly in the nose, causing a loud crack. Pain ripped through his fist from the impact and Matt cursed and shook his hand. Bret and Jim cringed and put their hands to their own noses just from the sound. Brian fell back a step from the impact, and his nose started bleeding a little, dropping dark crimson spots onto his crisp, white shirt and the hardwood floor below. He touched it gently, realizing in horror he was actually bleeding. Travis' eyes got real big and he couldn't help but grin, his mouth gaping open. Everyone in the bar had started watching what was playing out, shocked that a bar brawl seemed to be about to break out somewhere as tony and hip as Kremlin.

Brian screamed at Matt, blood running across his mouth and all over his hands, "You fucking cunt! You deserve this jerk!"

Bret and Jim started laughing quietly, thrilled to see Matt really put Brian in his place once and for all. Brian and his boyfriend stormed off and Matt put his arms back around Travis and said, "God, I hope I do!"

"Look at you, defending your man!" said Travis. "I feel safer just knowing I've got a bad-ass motherfucker like you here next to me!"

The inside joke wasn't lost on Matt one bit. He said, "Really?"

Travis cocked an eyebrow at Matt and said, "No. You hit like a queer, you know? We're going to have to work on that."

Matt laughed. "You think Colorado'd teach me how to fight, Trav?"

"Be careful what you ask for. How do you think Petey'd react if you asked him to man you up?"

Matt laughed even more when he thought about what Petey would become if he was set loose on that kind of a life mission with his gay brother.

Matt buried his face in Travis' chest and pulled him tight, so happy to have him back, safe and sound once again. There was nothing in the world that made him feel like he did when Travis came back to him. Without him, everything felt a little off, about to spin out of control at any moment. When he was there, with Matt, everything felt solid and grounded. Travis kissed Matt's head, brushing his lips affectionately across the soft kitten-fuzz there. Travis had mentioned at one point how much he liked how it felt, so Matt had kept the buzz cut that he had gotten on the *Iwo Jima*.

Travis glanced over Matt's shoulder at Bret and Jim, finally nodding hello to the two of them.

Bret was in a feisty mood, though, and wasn't ready to let Travis off the hook so easily. "Nice of you to show up. I guess you were off on one of your mysterious disappearances, pulling relief janitor duties on some ship in dock in San Diego while playing grab-ass with the gay guys who can't wait to get their hands in some Navy guy's pants. Good for you."

Matt had had enough of people picking at Travis, though. He said, some heat definitely in his voice, "Hey Bret, that's totally not..."

"I've watched you put up with this kind of shit once before, Matt," hissed Bret. "I don't want to watch it again! Don't you fucking make me watch this all over again!"

Matt looked to Jim for a little support, but could instantly tell Jim felt the same way even if he was going to let Bret be the one spelling it out. Matt felt a little helpless. He knew they were trying to look out for him, but they just didn't understand.

He didn't know what to do.

There was an awkward minute of silent tension between all of them. Travis, though, put his hands on Matt's shoulders and said, "Guys, let's go outside and talk a little."

Bret and Jim looked at Travis a little skeptically, and he had to jerk his head in the direction of the enclosed patio area at the club to get Bret and Jim to follow him.

Matt whispered in Travis' ear as they headed through the crowd to the outdoor bar, "Are you about to come out of the closet? Are you sure you want to do this? You don't have to do this, Trav."

"It's time. I trust these guys. And they're my friends, too, now. I should treat 'em like that." Travis shook his head and looked down at his feet as they made their way through the festive crowd to the outside. He said, almost to himself but Matt caught it, "Just too many secrets on both sides. Too many."

Matt said, "They'll start to figure other things out. Stuff that happened. How we met."

Travis put his arm around Matt's shoulders and said, "But we won't be telling them directly. You definitely won't. I can't help it if they're smart and can figure things out a little bit."

It had turned into an unseasonably cool evening, and so the outdoor bar at Kremlin was not very crowded. It was an enclosed courtyard area, set up with a sleek outdoor firepit that most of the people out there were gathered around while sipping their flavored vodkas and martinis. Travis found an empty table as far away from the rest of the bar crowd as possible and they sat down.

Bret and Jim waited for Travis to say whatever he had to say. Bret's expression was clearly daring Travis to say *anything* that might change his mind about him.

"First of all," began Travis, "I want you to know that, absolutely, positively, I have not and will not cheat on Matt." His hand was on Matt's back, but he lowered his head and gave Bret and Jim a stare with his dark eyes that instantly showed how deadly serious he was.

"Matt knows this, but you guys need to know it, too. I don't want this causing friction between the three of you because you mean too much to Matt for me to let that happen. And... and... you mean too much to me, too. Bret, you and Jim can almost take for granted the kind of friendships that you guys have, but I haven't had much of a chance for this in my life, and it does mean a lot to me. I don't blame you for being a little mistrustful of me right now. But... I need your word that you'll keep this between us."

Travis gave Jim the pointed stare, his eyes boring into him, looking for any duplicity that might come back to haunt him.

Jim said, "I give you my word, Travis." Travis was satisfied with this.

He shifted his gaze to Bret. Bret rolled his eyes. "Fine. Whatever. I'll keep quiet."

That response was definitely *not* what Travis was looking for. Travis leaned across the table aggressively at Bret, eyes narrowed to fiery slits. He pounded his fist on the table once to emphasize what he was saying, practically growling his voice was so serious, "No! Not to me. I want you to give *Matt* your absolute word you'll keep this to yourself. This isn't play-acting, Bret."

Matt watched with interest as Bret actually drew back a little. Travis had always held back around Bret and Jim, and this was probably the first time he had let his more forceful leadership style show through, and it caught Bret off guard. Bret's mouth pulled down into a frown while he tried to decide if this was all really worth it, or if it was just a pile of bullshit. He finally sighed and said, "Fine. Matt, for you, I promise not to talk about this."

Travis accepted Bret's promise this time. He continued to lean over the table and said, "As much as I'd like to be able to talk freely about what I do all the time, I can't. I'm a platoon lead for SEAL Team 8, US Navy, and so I can't."

Bret and Jim stared blankly at Travis for a moment. Whatever they were expecting to hear, it wasn't this. The silence dragged on, with no one even breathing the entire time.

"Hole. Lee. Shit!" Bret finally said.

Matt asked, not quite believing that this would mean anything to Bret, or maybe even Jim for that matter, "Do you know what a SEAL is, Bret?"

Bret looked at Matt sharply, "Dammit, I'm not a complete airhead, Matt! I told you I spend every week rooting through the hot guys in *Soldier Of Fortune* magazine. Yes, I know what a fucking SEAL is!"

Bret cocked his head slightly to one side and looked back over at Travis, like he was a museum curiosity out of Ripley's Believe It Or Not.

He said, to no one in particular, "I'm sitting at a table right now with an honest to god US Navy SEAL."

Jim was looking at Travis with the same odd expression as well, his mouth hanging open slightly. He added, "A gay Navy SEAL. A gay Navy SEAL that's dating our best friend."

"Jesus H. Chrysler!" exclaimed Bret.

Matt watched them closely. Bret's mind had stopped with the fact that Travis was a SEAL, but Matt could immediately tell that Jim's mind was already beyond that. He could see the wheels turning furiously in his mind, putting two and two together.

Matt asked, "Jim? Do you understand?"

Jim nodded slowly, not taking his eyes off of Travis, "I'm beginning to. I mean, I get the SEAL part. I'm just figuring out the rest of how this fits together. It's starting to make sense."

Bret looked at Jim, confused and unhappy that there was something he was missing. "How the rest of what fits together?"

Jim looked at Matt with concern. "I'll talk to you later about it, Bret. Matt and Travis can't talk about it and I'm not putting them in that position."

Bret looked impatient. He didn't like being the only one left out of the loop suddenly. He started to verbally poke at Jim to get him to talk, but Jim just said, "Seriously, Bret! Later!"

Bret gave up and asked Matt, "So, all these other Navy buddies of yours? They're SEALs too?"

Matt looked to Travis to see how he wanted to answer and Travis nodded.

Bret lit up a little. "Shit, this is awesome! Are they all gay? Can I meet them?"

Travis looked panicked, but Matt shut this down quickly. "No, Bret! They're not. And they don't know about Travis. This isn't some joke. I mean it, Bret!"

The disappointment in Bret was palpable. He sank down in his chair. "Fine. You take the one good one for yourself and leave me and Jim empty handed."

Travis relaxed and even managed to smile at Bret.

Matt put his hand on the back of Travis' neck and said, "This is why Travis goes away. These guys get into some seriously dangerous stuff. Classified stuff. They can't talk about it most of the time, not even to me."

Jim looked like he didn't know how to act around Travis all of a sudden. Finding out what Travis really did in the Navy, thinking through what that implied about how he and Matt met given Matt's abduction, and the now-clear seriousness of it almost stole the words from him. He turned red and couldn't look Travis in the eye for a moment. Finally, Jim admitted, "Ok, it makes so much more sense now. Travis, man, I'm sorry I ever doubted you. It seems so obvious now. Really, man, I am sorry I ever doubted you."

Travis reached across the table and grabbed Jim's hand, trying to reassure him that he was still the same person. He said, "Thanks, Jim."

Bret looked physically pained. "Fuck! Here's that sincerity shit again. I'm sorry, too, Travis."

Travis smiled and said, "Thanks, Chiliburger."

Bret added, "Not as sorry as I am that Matt got to you first instead of me, but I am sorry. I hate you, Matt. I *really* hate you!"

Matt grinned, happy to have Bret back to normal.

Travis pushed back from the table and said, "I hope you guys don't mind, but I'm taking this one home since we've got some catching up to do."

They got up to leave, and Travis turned to Bret and gave him a hug and kiss, lifting him up off the ground and spinning him around once, giving Bret a huge thrill. He turned to Jim and gave him a hug and a kiss as well, plus a playful slap on his ass. Jim held onto Travis for just a second longer and Matt saw him whisper something in Travis' ear.

Travis smiled warmly, winked at Jim and said, "I have no idea what you're talking about."

Bret shook his head and said to Matt, "I can't believe you get to take that home! You fucking lucky bastard!"

"It's Memorial Day. I've got to show our armed forces just how much I appreciate them," said Matt through a dirty grin.

Travis hooked a few fingers in the waistband of Matt's jeans and pulled at him. "C'mon, Cornhole, I can't wait to get you home."

As they walked out, Matt couldn't stand the curiosity prickling his skin any longer. "What did Jim whisper to you?"

"He said, 'Thanks for getting Matt home safely.'"

As soon as the two of them left the bar and stepped out onto the sidewalk outside, the cool night air around them, Travis grabbed Matt and pulled him tight against him.

He said to Matt, "Have I told you how good it is to have you to come back to?"

Matt couldn't help but blush a little and grin a lot. "Every single time you come back!"

Matt studied Travis, whose off-balance smile and bullet-hole dark eyes were trained on him and dancing. It came to a head — worrying about Travis all week, watching Brian pick at him, watching Bret pick at him, all of it. Before he knew what was happening and before he could stop himself, his mouth opened and the words fell out.

"I love you, Trav."

Matt immediately winced inwardly. It was too early, even if it was what he felt. He was going to make Travis uncomfortable. Put him in an awkward position. Who knew what danger he had been in for over a week now, and here he was, dumping this on Travis suddenly, too. He wanted to take it back, and at the same time yell it out louder for everyone to know how he felt about this amazing man in front of him.

Travis flashed his eyes upwards once and said to Matt, with the voice that sounded like distant whispered thunder, "Look up!"

Chapter 34 — An Almost Imperceptible Distance

"How's your dad doing? You haven't said much about him lately."

"Open 'em up."

"What about Keith? How's he handling things?" asked Matt.

"Open your eyes, dummy."

Matt paused before trying a different approach. "This was a bad one this time, wasn't it? It was a dangerous mission, right? I can tell, you know."

Matt heard the firm and gentle command come from behind him. "Eyes open, Matt."

"Bret and Jim asked about coming to visit again. They want to come see you surf."

Matt scrunched up his face at the silence that followed, only the sound of lapping water reaching his ears for a moment. He was being unfair with Travis now.

The voice behind him was softer this time, "Please, Matt."

Matt shouldn't have made the comment about Bret and Jim. He knew that Travis felt guilty for not being comfortable having the two of them come visit him in Virginia Beach. Travis had gotten rather attached to both of them, and now that they finally understood Travis better, all of their initial doubts about him had evaporated like mist in the morning. Matt knew that Travis struggled with keeping the two major aspects of his life separate, and the certain sacrifices he made in the process. He felt lucky he got to spend time with Travis the way he did, but his relationship with the entire team made it easier for him to be a public part of Travis' life. And it had made it harder, too, since it had to appear to be only a friendship, like he had with the rest of the team. But a little was better than none, and Matt was thankful for that.

Matt couldn't leave his statement about Bret and Jim hanging out there like that. He couldn't use something like that against Travis, even flippantly.

Matt said, his eyes still tightly shut, "But you know what they're really after, Trav. Bret just wants to see you with your shirt off. You can do that in Richmond."

Travis was distracted now, and it took a few seconds before he grunted a "Hmm..." in reply.

Matt sat a moment longer. "Ok, my eyes are open now. Happy?" he fibbed.

There was some shuffling behind Matt, rocking him and making him clutch harder to the handles next to where he was sitting.

The voice came again, right next to his ear this time, sing-songing to him, "You're lyyyyyying, Matty... You're a shitty liiiiiiarrrrr..."

That voice was so low that Matt almost felt the vibrations travel through him instead of actually hearing the words. He felt the slightest tickle of Travis' ramshackle beard against his ear, feeling like a crackle of electricity between them. God, how Matt loved the sound of that voice. It drove him crazy, even when it was calling him a shitty liar. A shiver literally ran up his spine at the sensation.

Matt felt Travis' thick arms snake under his own and around his chest from behind, followed by the rough beard pressing up against the side of his face.

Travis whispered, "I've got you, Matt. Nothing can happen. I won't let anything happen to you."

Matt gritted his teeth and opened his eyes. If it weren't for the arms around him, he would probably be freaking out. Even with them, his heart clenched in his chest tightly.

He looked around and couldn't see any land anywhere. None. It was like dry land didn't exist anymore. There was only the tiny CRRC they were in and an infinite amount of ocean spreading out from them in all directions.

Matt's breathing started to get faster and shallower, until he felt Travis behind him again, gripping him tighter. Travis said, "Shhh, Matt... It's ok. Relax. I've got you. You're perfectly safe. Just relax."

Travis rubbed his lips across Matt's ear, just above his life vest, biting and kissing him lightly there, reassuring him that he was safe.

Matt said, "You didn't warn me we were coming out this far. It's getting late. How do you know where land is? What if we go back in the wrong direction? Are we going to run out of gas? We don't even have a radio in this thing, do we? Are there sharks out here?"

Travis started to say something, but Matt tensed up and cut in, "It's hurricane season. What if there's a hurricane?"

"It's only about 7pm, Matt. And you see where the sun's getting low? That's west. Not even I can miss the eastern coast of the entire United States of America as long as we follow the sun."

Matt looked back at Travis, who was grinning at him through two weeks' worth of rather wild beard growth. Matt had gone straight to the base to meet up with Travis, who had just barely gotten back from a two-week mission and was still wearing his cammie pants and a tan t-shirt. No lifejacket at all. He envied how completely comfortable Travis was near, around, in, and under the water.

Travis said, "Sheesh. I am in the Navy, you know? Give me a *little* credit."

Travis' dark eyes studied Matt and said, "Give me your hands and turn around and face me."

Matt didn't like letting go of the handholds on the CRRC, but as long as Travis had him, he could do it. He swung his legs over the seat on the small rubber boat and faced towards Travis.

Travis made Matt lock his eyes to his own. "I'm here. Just keep your eyes on me. Nothing's going to happen. If you get nervous, just focus on me. We'll head back in a few minutes, but just relax for now. It's really peaceful out here tonight. It's beautiful."

The sound of Travis' voice, the sight of him after being gone for two weeks, the words he spoke, all made Matt feel more at ease. It *was* a beautiful evening, even if it was also a little nerve-wracking at the same time. But Travis was right, as long as he focused on him, he felt like he could handle anything.

Travis eyed Matt a little suspiciously before asking, "So, smartypants, what makes you think this was a dangerous mission this time? Is it the bruise?"

Matt glanced at the large bruise and scabbed up scrape peeking out from under Travis' t-shirt sleeve on his left arm. He said very seriously, "Kinda. But not really. You're pretty clumsy, so I expect you to come back looking like that even if you've just been out to check your mail."

Travis grinned crookedly. "Kiss my ass! I'm not clumsy! Come on now, seriously, what makes you say it was a bad one?"

"You were gone for two weeks, no communication at all. You come back earlier today and you've clearly not shaved at all for the entire time. You don't come back like that unless it was a bad one."

Travis nodded, his eyes sparkling at Matt as he continued to grin at his boyfriend. He scratched at the beard covering his face and growing down his neck almost to the top of his t-shirt. "You got me there, I guess. Yeah, the last two weeks got a little intense a few times. I bet I do look like crap."

Matt said, "I didn't say that. I kind of like the beard, even if I know you can't keep it. Stupid Navy. How do you get to use this boat for something like this anyway?"

Travis said, "Oh, midnight requisition. I know some of the guys. They don't mind if they look the other way and a zodiac disappears for a few hours."

Apparently, Travis had taken advantage of this "midnight requisition" multiple times. They'd been out several times now, getting Matt used to being on a boat and out in the water. Each trip, they went further and farther out.

Matt nodded, then asked, "Seriously, though, how is your dad?"

"About the same as always. Well, not totally. Ever since you talked to him, he's been better about not comparing me to Chris."

Matt nodded.

Travis looked at his boots in the bottom of the boat.

"The last time I talked to him on the phone, though, he called me Chris a couple of times. Not just a mix-up, but like he really thought I was Chris. I wonder if maybe he's getting a little... I don't know... not senile. Maybe early Alzheimer's. He seems a little different. A little foggy. I worry about him..."

Matt hoped it wasn't that.

Travis frowned slightly, his face lit by the slowly sinking sun. "Are Bret and Jim mad that I haven't invited them over to the beach this summer?" His shoulders slumped a little.

"No, not really," said Matt. "I mean, they'd like to come visit and I think they'd love to watch you out in the water. I certainly do. But they actually do understand. Plus, they really like showing you off in Richmond when you come. The big roughneck Navy guy and all that."

That finally managed to get a smile and laugh out of Travis, which made Matt feel much better. It was the truth. Bret and Jim did understand about Travis' situation in Virginia Beach and respected it.

But Matt knew it weighed on Travis anyway, having to hide friends of his just to hide something about himself. It took its toll on him.

"Look at your hands, Matt."

Matt looked down at his hands clasped together casually in his lap. He looked back over at Travis and shrugged a "what about them?" at him.

"You're not white-knuckling the handholds. You're getting much more comfortable. You're getting there, Matt!" Travis seemed genuinely proud of him.

Matt realized that he was right. When he had been out in the small boat previous times with Travis, he almost always clung to the handholds for dear life. Today was the first time they had gone so far out from land, into open water. But he was feeling more relaxed than ever in the boat now that his mind had wandered off it a little bit.

Travis said, "So, since you're not so wound up this time..." He looked expectantly at Matt.

"What?" said Matt.

"You think I could go for a quick dip? The water looks really good right now."

Matt's heart hitched and grabbed in his chest at the thought of Travis getting out of the boat and leaving him alone, but he also knew how much Travis loved being in the water. "Sure, frogman. I'll be ok. You just won't go swimming way off or anything, will you? No two-mile endurance swims right now, got it?"

Travis grinned and said, "No. No endurance swims. I just wanna get wet." He was already taking his boots off as fast as he could.

He stood up in the boat and shucked his t-shirt off and started taking his cammies off, shaking the boat slightly in the process, which made Matt grab the handles next to him again.

Travis stripped down completely naked and dove effortlessly into the water. At least that sight could distract Matt some more. He loved seeing Travis' body, and the late-day sun seemed to highlight the peaks and valleys of every muscle in his arms, back and legs. Matt watched where Travis had dived into the water, knowing he could stay under for lengths of time that could make him panic. But to his relief, Travis surfaced just a few seconds later about twenty feet away from the boat, the blue ocean rippling around his neck and sparkling in the late daylight. Matt couldn't comprehend how it would be to feel more at home in the water than on land, but that was Travis.

Travis groaned, "Ohhhh, God, this feels soooooo good right now!"

He swam back towards the boat lazily, reassuring Matt, "This is going to be you one day, Matt. I'm going to get you to where you're this comfortable in the water, too, one day. One step at a time."

Matt did kind of wish he could be in the water with Travis right now. The two of them there, naked, not another boat or person in sight, surrounded by the warm water of summer. Except if he were to get in there right now, he'd be screaming his lungs out in terror and clawing rabidly trying to get out of the water. Maybe one day. For now, though, Travis had focused on making Matt comfortable in boats. Travis had decided that actually getting in the water and learning to swim could come later.

Travis swam up to the side of the boat and put his arms up on it, the water running over his face and out of his full beard. "So, tonight's video games with Petey, huh? And Baya, too, I guess?"

"Yeah. Maybe Crank or Jonas, too, if they don't have anything else going on."

Travis pushed back off from the boat, floating on his back, his naked body fully exposed as he drifted away from Matt slowly. He teased Matt, "I guess I'm lucky, as usual, to get this little bit of you to myself before you 'officially' show up here in Virginia Beach. I suppose I could start playing those dumb video games just so I can have more time with you."

Matt shrugged his shoulders and said, "Hey, I'm out here in a boat with *you*."

Travis nodded and gave Matt a wet grin. "Okay, point taken. Maybe I'll come by. For what it's worth, I know what you and Petey are like when you're together. I do like for you guys to spend time together, you know. I like what you guys have become."

"Petey's a shithead. I can't believe I let that dick hang out with me," said Matt. Travis smiled broadly at Matt's sarcasm. Matt very much appreciated that Travis wanted to give them space to become the close friends, the brothers, that they had become.

Travis pushed himself up against the side of the boat, his wet arms flexing as he lifted himself up. Matt grabbed the handles again as Travis got back up into the boat with a grace that came with going through that particular motion probably hundreds of times.

He stood in front of Matt, naked and dripping wet, golden in the warm light, with that proud, goofy grin on his face.

Matt said, "You know, even with two weeks of totally unchecked beard growth, I can still see those smile lines around your mouth."

Travis immediately stopped grinning and tried very consciously to smooth the lines out. He said, "I hate those things."

"They're handsome. One of many things about you. There's so many things like that about you, Trav. You're incredibly good-looking."

Matt almost started laughing as he watched the struggle play out across Travis' face — the grin forcing its way back to the surface after Matt's comment versus Travis' desire to not let the smile lines show.

The grin finally won out and Travis asked, "Really?"

"Really."

Travis taunted, "You'd ditch me for Petey if you had the chance. Admit it!"

Matt guffed in disgust at the thought. Travis planted his wet hands on either side of Matt and leaned over him, dripping seawater onto his shirt and jeans. He said, "I'm just a consolation prize for you."

Travis leaned further over Matt, pushing him back and off the inflated seat until he was trapped in the bottom of the boat under him. He lay his body down on top of Matt, getting him all wet in the process, and started kissing Matt.

Matt kissed him back, feeling Travis' wet beard all over his face, their tongues slipping around each other. He didn't care how wet he got, just as long as he could feel Travis on top of him. He put his arms around Travis and grabbed his ass as their kissing became deeper and more intense. Matt thought maybe he didn't mind boats so much after all.

When Travis finally pulled back, his dark, rifle-shot eyes only inches from Matt's, Matt whispered to him, "I love *you*, Travis."

Matt ran his hands up Travis' damp back, and stared into his dark eyes in anticipation. Travis leaned in and kissed Matt hard again, done teasing him about Petey. Everyone else, everything else in the world could just fuck off for a little while. For now, it was just sea and sky and warm sun and the two of them.

Despite the brief moment of disappointment Matt felt at what had just happened, he let it go. Instead, he let the looming Travis have his way, beautiful, crooked smile, non-aerodynamic ears and all. Without any witness from one horizon to the other, in the heat of the late summer sun and the gentle rocking of the small craft, Matt found that a tsunami-inducing orgasm went a long way towards getting him past his fear of boats and his fear of water. Especially if it was brought on by a large, wet Navy SEAL that was clearly glad to be home after having had a rough few weeks.

Matt slowly floated back down into the bottom of the CRRC when Travis was done with him, the ocean-sized whirlpool swirling the boat around and around, but for once in a good way. Matt let go of the minor discouragement that had swept over him and just let the moment be what it was, and it definitely was a good moment.

Matt gave Travis a stupid, satisfied grin and said, "You know, for someone that claimed to stink at being gay once upon a time, you sure are good at it."

~~~~~

Matt twisted around trying to get a better angle, firing up wildly. But the guy above him had too good of a position, and the next thing he knew, his head was blown off, leaving Petey completely exposed.

Petey kicked at him with his bare foot while they sat next to each other on the floor, game controllers in their hands.

"You useless cocksucker! What the hell's wrong with you tonight? You've left me exposed and gotten me killed, like, seven times tonight!" yelled Petey. Petey glared over at Matt while Jonas, Baya, and Crank laughed at them from the couch. Wasp was his usual quiet self in one of the other chairs.

And in the split second distraction, Petey was riddled by bullets and reduced to a greasy, bloody smear on the TV screen.

Petey was sitting there with nothing but a pair of running shorts on, his pale, bare chest lit by the glow of the video game.

"You're too busy trying to look up my shorts at my cock, and it's gettin' me killed, dipshit!" grumbled Petey. "I went commando for you tonight, but if you're gonna play the game, then play the damn game, Cornhole! You can perv on me later!"

Matt stood up and pulled his own shorts down and shot a moon at Petey. "Eat it, Colorado!"

Petey shot one of those looks at Matt that could singe hair. He rubbed his middle finger up and down the burning red stubble that had been growing on his face for two weeks, a fiery bird aimed right at Matt. But Matt knew Petey was right. He *was* distracted. Just not by trying to see Petey's dick. Crap, he had to look at that thing way more than he cared to. Every time he slept over at Petey's place, in Petey's

246

bed, Petey was nude. As much as Petey ragged about Matt perving on him, it was all just bluster and show. He knew that Matt wasn't ogling him, or didn't care. And he was never the slightest bit shy around Matt and didn't care at all what Matt saw. Hell, half the time, Petey didn't bother to close the bathroom door when Matt was bunking there with him.

What was distracting Matt, though, was Travis. He had gotten that feeling again, earlier that evening on the CRRC, the one that he had started feeling little by little over the last month or so. In the boat, he could feel Travis holding back, keeping a little distance. It was almost imperceptible, but he could feel it there, the gap between them. He was pretty sure he knew why, but it made his heart heavy nonetheless.

He sensed how Travis struggled with keeping the two sides of his life safely separated, and felt more and more like one was going to have to be sacrificed at some point. How could he not feel sad at that?

He didn't blame him. Travis had said right up front that being a SEAL was everything to him, and that he was willing to sacrifice for that. And at some point, Matt was going to be that sacrifice. He could feel it in how Travis held back from him. He felt sure that was why Travis kept that slight bit of insulating distance between them.

Matt just really loved Travis. He had meant it every time he had said it to him. He loved the connection they had, on all the different levels. He loved Travis' smile lines and crooked nose and finely tuned body, even with the scars of a tough profession. He loved that voice that felt like it could move heaven and earth. He loved Travis' gentle, quiet sense of humor. He liked the vulnerable side that Travis only showed to him. He liked how sometimes Travis used his stomach as a pillow and held onto him tightly when sleeping. He liked how Travis could instantly and aggressively take charge, but yet was never, ever that way with him, preferring instead to respect what they had as a partnership. He liked how he felt that he could trust Travis totally and never be disappointed for doing so. What he had with Travis really felt right to Matt, and that feeling was really important since he had such a recent bad relationship to compare it to. But Travis was in a different place in his life, and was holding back as a result.

Jonas said, "Yeah, Matt. What's up with you tonight? It usually doesn't take anything for you to beat Petey's ass raw at this game. Tear him a new one, Cornhole, or he's gonna be impossible to live with for weeks!"

Matt was about to reply when Jonas corrected himself, "Sorry, even *more* impossible to live with."

Matt picked up the controller, pointed it at the TV, and said, "Start it up again, bitch, and get ready to get that hick ass of yours paddled."

Petey snarled, "You wish!"

They played a little longer, but Matt was still not up to the challenge that evening. He finally reached over and tried to push Petey to distract him. But Petey rarely would let a physical challenge like that go, especially from Matt.

He dropped his controller, spun around Matt in a flash, grabbed him from behind and fell back with him, then rolled over on top so that Matt wound up in a headlock. It was shocking how fast Petey could pull shit like this.

Petey dug at Matt, "Who's your fucking daddy now, cunt hair? Huh?"

Despite all the other guys constantly telling Matt to not get in a physical match with Petey, it never stopped him. Maybe everyone else had something to actually worry about when it came to instigating something like that with Petey. But not Matt. Matt could tell that Petey was barely holding onto him. It was all just for fun. If there was one person he could trust equally to how he trusted Travis, it would be the red-headed SEAL holding him in a headlock at that moment.

He said, "Shit, Petey, all you're doing here is making my dick hard."

Petey started laughing and let Matt go. "You disgust me!"

Matt flipped him a bird and sneered, "You love me!"

"I might as well be playing this game by myself!" griped Petey. "Hell, the way you're getting the good guys killed off, I might as well get Wasp down here on the carpet."

Petey grabbed his game controller again and continued without batting an eye at what he said. "Crank, why don't you get your hippy ass down here?"

Matt had already glanced back up over at the guys behind him. Crank and Jonas both shifted around on the couch uneasily, and Matt looked over at Wasp sitting in the chair. Wasp's lips were pulled tight, and he was totally still, but he didn't react. Matt could tell, though, even if Wasp would never let it show; Wasp wasn't about to let it show. But Matt could tell what was behind those unblinking, unmoving eyes.

Matt wanted to beat the crap out of Petey. But instead, he got up to go have a shot of Southern Comfort since it was the only hard liquor Petey kept in his apartment, stepping over the trash bags sitting out in the kitchen. He was pretty sure they were the same bags of trash that had been sitting out the last time he had stayed at Petey's. Inexplicably, there was now a stuffed armadillo sitting on the kitchen counter that *hadn't* been there the last time he had been over.

Matt called out, "Colorado, why is there a dead varmint on your kitchen counter?"

"Family heirloom!" was the only explanation that came to him from the living room.

"And why is there a dirty pair of boxer shorts sitting in here? On a plate, for God's sake!" Matt was getting seriously close to hiring a nanny for Petey.

Petey hollered, "Oh yeah, I know you're into that shit, so they're for you. I wore 'em three or four days in a row while we were training. Enjoy!"

Matt picked up the boxer shorts and shoved them down into the trash bag. He decided to not even ask about the dried-up condom he spotted on the floor next to the trash bag.

Back in the living room, Crank slid down off the sofa to take Matt's place.

"Good!" said Petey. "Someone with a little bit going on! Crank, if I win, I get to arm wrestle you."

Crank frowned and said, "Hell no! No fucking way! You've been drinking and Matt's got you wound up. I know what your 'arm wrestling' turns into. Even worse, you're not wearing any underwear. No fucking way I'm getting all tied up in that shit tonight! You hear me? I swear to God, Petey, keep your hands to yourself!"

~~~~~

Matt lay in bed, unable to fall asleep. His mind had been spinning for probably over an hour now. He had started out thinking about Travis, wishing he was with him, but also thinking a lot about that slight distance that Travis seemed to be keeping in place. But it wasn't just that. He had been stewing over Petey's comment earlier in the evening, too. Petey dished that kind of shit out to everyone, so it wasn't anything personal about Wasp. But still, Petey could cross over a line sometimes, and this one bothered Matt. He couldn't decide if he should get in the middle of it, or butt out.

Matt figured he wasn't actually a part of the platoon, despite how well he had gotten to know the guys. On the other hand, he cared about them, especially Petey and Wasp. But, realistically, it wasn't his place to try and "fix" anything about these men, or between them. He didn't really fully see the total context of how they were around each other. There were boundaries around his place among them that he should probably pay heed to. He told himself he needed to just butt out.

Which is why, a few minutes later, he was pushing himself right in the middle of it.

Matt started poking at Petey next to him, trying to wake him up. "Petey! Get up!"

Petey didn't budge. Matt learned a while ago that he could make all the noise he wanted to in the room with Petey sleeping, and he wouldn't wake up. But let there be the tiniest sound that wasn't supposed to be there, and Petey would be instantly wide awake. Even in a dead sleep, Petey had this crazy sixth sense about sounds around him.

The second time Matt had stayed at Petey's place, he woke up in the middle of the night, only to see a naked Petey calmly loading a magazine into one of his personal handguns, a big one. He had asked Petey what the hell was going on, only to have Petey shush him while he looked out the bedroom window. Petey had heard a noise outside that wasn't supposed to be there, and was instantly wide awake. It had turned out to be a false alarm, though; Petey's neighbor, three apartments down, had gotten locked out of her place in the middle of the night and she and her boyfriend were getting back into the apartment through the bedroom window. Petey had heard them, several apartments over, while he was in a deep sleep.

Matt shoved hard on the big, worthless lump next to him. He practically shouted, "Come on, you red-assed hillbilly! Get your white-trash ass up!"

Nothing. Matt scratched at his head for a few seconds.

Petey hadn't gotten that drunk while playing video games, and it shouldn't be this hard. He turned sideways and put his bare feet up against Petey's side and pushed as hard as he could. He yelled, "Peter Andrew Tuttle, wake the FUCK up!!!"

He finally shoved all 215 pounds of Petey right out of the bed. Petey landed on the carpet and dirty clothes next to the bed in a dull thud, taking the sheets with him. But at least it finally woke him up.

"Dammit, Matt! What the hell is the matter with you? What the fuck do you want?"

Matt said, "We gotta talk."

Petey groaned on the floor next to the bed. "Christ, Cornhole, you woke me up in the middle of the night so we can fucking talk? You are the *only* bitch I sleep with that I don't fuck."

Petey stood up and said, halfway between asleep and aggravated, "Start talking. I'm taking a piss, and when I'm done, I'm going back to sleep whether your whiny vagina has had its say or not." He headed towards the bathroom.

Matt glared at him as he left the room.

"You stepped over a line with what you said to Wasp tonight."

The light in the bathroom flipped on and Matt could hear Petey say, "Shit, you're not really gonna start in on this bullshit are you? Wasp needs to suck it up and take it like a man, or get out." The sound of a stream of piss hitting water made its way back into the bedroom.

Matt said, "This isn't about Wasp, though, dickhead. It's about you."

Petey didn't reply, but the piss stream continued unabated.

"Everyone expects you to be the hard-ass," said Matt. "But there's a difference between being tough, and being cruel. No one's going to see you as weak if you respect the difference."

Petey had finished taking his leak and stepped back into the bedroom, his naked body illuminated by the bathroom light. His face had that hard edge it almost always carried.

"Fuck you!" Petey said. "You don't know me! That has nothing to do with what's going on. If Wasp, or any of the guys, can't take a fucking joke, then they can kiss my red-headed ass."

Matt gave the hard edge look right back to Petey. He wasn't about to let him off the hook with this. "Petey, save your bullshit for everyone else. I expect more from you than this. You're not this clumsy. You're not this person. You gotta respect that there's a fine line here."

"If you think I'm gonna start holding his damn hand, and telling him it's all gonna be ok, and that he's just a swell guy, then I must have had you too tight in too many headlocks," said Petey. "That shit ain't happening!"

"I'm not asking you to baby him. Or me. Or anybody. There's being tough and hard, like you are, and there's being stupid and clumsy. Learn the goddamn difference!"

Petey started to say something, but then stopped. He continued to glower at Matt.

Matt continued, "I expect more from you than this, Petey. Give me more than this, or you're not the person I thought you were. You know I love you, you asshole, and you're better than this. You're my brother. I know you, Petey. I *know* you."

Petey kept glaring at Matt, leaning against the doorway to the bathroom. He held like this for a long time, and then in the half light from the bathroom, Matt thought he could just barely see a shift in Petey's expression. Petey spoke, and for the first time ever, Matt got the unmistakable impression that Petey was choosing his words very, very carefully, and the edge in his voice had dissipated just a little.

"You sure this is about me?"

Matt said coolly, "Yes, Petey. This is about you."

Petey stood there, his face set in the same stone-like expression, but his gaze drifted off to the side a little bit. After what felt like forever, Petey looked down at the dirty carpet in his bedroom, his running shorts crumpled up at his feet. He reached back into the bathroom and turned the light off.

He walked back over and sat down on the edge of the bed, his sharply defined back towards Matt. Matt couldn't see Petey's face and couldn't tell what he was thinking, but Petey sat like that for several long moments. Without looking back, and almost poking Matt in the eye in the process, Petey reached back behind him and rubbed around on Matt's head for a moment. Matt had been about to keep pressing Petey on it, but decided to let it go instead, a little relieved that Petey wasn't mad. Petey pulled the sheets back onto the bed and got under them. He said, "Move over. You keep hogging the whole damn bed."

Chapter 35 – A Tiny Handful / Lost At Sea

Maybe it's just my gay-bitch side, but, God, I love lying here with him like this.

The thought swam lazily through Travis' mind, following the same path in his head that Matt's finger was absently playing out on his chest as they lay together in his bed. He didn't think it was the margaritas from earlier talking… he felt like this about almost anything he did with Matt. Matt was the calm, normal, safe bedrock in Travis' very dangerous world. And Christ, he never realized exactly how much he needed that until Matt showed up.

He said to Matt, "I'm glad you put your foot down with Petey so you could stay here with me tonight."

Matt said, his breath and dark chestnut goatee tickling the hair on Travis' chest, "I've stayed with him plenty of times already. I actually told him if he wanted me to keep on sleeping with him, he'd better put a damn ring on my finger."

Travis grinned to himself. Matt had no idea the charmed life he had with Petey. He had seen Petey break bones for someone saying far less than that to him. Early on, he had not been totally honest with Matt about how hotheaded and, frankly, dangerous Petey could be if provoked. But that was because he didn't want Matt to back down from him. That had worked out better than he ever imagined it would, but he still felt a little bit guilty about it. Now it just seemed stupid to try and explain it to him. Matt probably wouldn't believe him at this point, anyway. But that was just because he didn't know the charmed relationship he had with Petey.

Other people had to watch what they said around Petey because of his volatility. He had seen him get in a fight with some UFC champion fighter out in San Diego one time, outside of a bar. The guy had made some stupid crack about Petey's hair being the color of Cheetos, and before anybody could react, the dude was on the ground with a broken arm and Petey's knee in his back almost snapping his spine, the guy screaming in agony.

Hell, two of the hash marks on the stock of Petey's M4 were for killing guys with a single punch each. One a Somali pirate on a hijacked cargo ship, the other a Taliban creep that had caught them by surprise. These idiots had made the mistake of getting within three feet of Petey, and wham! One hard fist, right in the face, and they were roadkill. Even the most experienced SEALs in DEVGRU would think long and hard before taking on Petey in close combat.

It had been Petey's and Baya's idea to make Matt an honorary member of the platoon after the capture of Al-Hashim. The whole platoon had voted to include Matt this way, with only Wyatt balking at the idea of giving this kind of respect to a "faggot." But after Petey asked him when was the last time he had actually done as much for the team as Matt had in helping to capture Al-Hashim, Wyatt shut up and voted Matt in. Travis had worried that Wyatt would give Matt a hard time, but he had kept it to himself and didn't seem to hold anything against Matt in the time since.

But even with these clues, and surprising everyone on the platoon with the ferociousness with which it had happened, Petey had taken to Matt. A sincere, protective side started to emerge that no one had expected at all. And then, just like Glenda The Good Witch had beaten him senseless with her wand, he had decided that Matt was his brother. As in *there's no place like home* and all that. And now, God help the person that ever so much as raised a finger at Matt. No one had expected how close they would wind up, but no one on the team was going to argue with it, either. Matt obviously totally loved Petey, and he seemed to do Petey a world of good. And everybody else got some shits 'n grins out of watching Petey and Matt go round and round the way they did.

The only real loser was Travis. But that was only because he had to share Matt with Petey when he came to Virginia Beach. Small sacrifice, though. But, one he was willing to make for Matt's sake. And Petey's, too, if truth be told.

Travis decided he had to tease him a little bit. "You're the only person in the world that can harass Petey like that, you know?"

Matt shrugged, still lying on Travis' chest. He said, "Psssh! He's just a pussy with an oversized ego. Besides, he's the one that wanted me for a brother, so he's gotta live with the consequences."

He added, "I'm thinking about buying him some pink polka-dot boxer shorts for his birthday and making him wear them under his BDU."

Travis started chuckling, shaking Matt violently in the process, which started Matt laughing, too.

I never want to get up from this bed with him. Fuck the boat tomorrow.

Matt was the hot burning coal inside him that made him want to get up every morning, that made him want to come home from every mission. Matt had done so much for him — Al-Hashim, his father, toning Petey's aggression down some, helping Keith come to terms with the death of the Marine — and all he ever seemed to think about was how much Travis had done for him instead. Travis might not have had a lot of experience dating a lot of guys, but he knew deep down that Matt was rare. And the red ember inside him burned all the hotter because of it.

He reached down and felt the faint hair at the base of Matt's spine. He loved that spot, right there in the small of his back. "You gonna be ok on the boat tomorrow?"

"As long as you guys are there. I did pretty good on that sightseeing boat two weeks ago, didn't I?"

"You did great, Matty," whispered Travis. Matt had done well, even when they were pretty far from land for the sunset.

"I think Chiliburger creamed in his pants a little when I told him you took me on a romantic sunset boat trip."

If Travis hadn't been a little nervous about having Bret and Jim right in his own backyard, he probably would have invited them to come along on that trip. But there were just too many people he worked with crawling all over Virginia Beach for him to take that risk. He didn't like hiding Matt and he didn't like hiding what they had together. It had never bothered him much before, but now he didn't like his life being split in two. It didn't feel right. But he knew there'd be sacrifices no matter what when he became a SEAL. Just because he could keep a secret didn't mean he liked them.

Matt had come a long way in a short time. Back before Memorial Day, Travis had started working with him to overcome his fear of the water, and they had spent time all summer long taking it in small steps. Matt had made much more of a serious effort when he realized the platoon expected him to be a part of their Labor Day boat and beach outing. It was a sacred Labor Day tradition among them - just the platoon, no support staff, no officers, no girlfriends, no outsiders. Except Matt had earned the right to be there in the team's eyes. It gave him a concrete goal to work towards, which made Travis' job easier.

Travis had started small with Matt. They'd gone out in CRRC's at the base, tooled around Little Creek Cove right up against land, then working up to being out in more open water. He had decided to get Matt used to just boats for now. Actually getting Matt into the water and teaching him to swim was going to take longer. Probably a lot longer. He had told Matt he wouldn't rush him, and if he wasn't ready to go out for the day of deep sea fishing (loosely translated as drinking on a boat), he didn't have to go. But it was really important to Matt to do it. God bless him, he seemed game for anything with the guys, no matter how hard it might be for him. And Travis really loved that.

Travis watched Matt's eyes in the pale light coming through his bedroom window. The low light made them a dark forest green instead of the brighter emerald green that the daylight brought out. He thumbed the slight dimple in Matt's chin, the one hidden behind the perfectly-groomed goatee. He liked knowing about that secret dimple on Matt. It felt like it was his alone. Travis never felt more content than he did in these moments — the two of them laying together, studying each other, no need for words.

Matt shifted up in the bed and buried his face in Travis' neck like he loved to do. A moment later, Matt said softly, "I love you so much, Trav."

Travis exhaled contentedly and kissed the top of Matt's head and pulled him a little tighter and a little closer.

Fuck the boat tomorrow.

Matt lifted his head up, just barely, and looked at Travis. And that's when Travis saw it. The faintest shadow of disappointment slid across Matt's face, like a gossamer cloud across a full summer moon. And then it was gone again. Matt snuggled back down into Travis' neck and kissed him there.

Travis waited a second, hoping to see if Matt would say anything. He didn't even realize he was holding his breath.

He finally asked, whispering into Matt's ear, "You ok?"

Matt lifted his head back up and smiled, "I'm good. I'm right where I want to be."

Travis looked for any kind of doubt in Matt's voice, any kind of equivocation, but there wasn't any. But he couldn't get the image out of his mind.

Travis shifted down and put his head on Matt's stomach and wrapped his arm around his midsection, clutching him tightly, feeling the warm reassurance of the rise and fall of Matt's chest as he breathed. It was one of his favorite ways of being close to Matt, from the very earliest part of their relationship. Normally, he did this to feel close to Matt, but this time he lay there feeling insecure and worried. He held onto Matt a little tighter and hoped that Matt didn't push him away. He wouldn't know what to do if that happened.

Matt fell asleep pretty quickly, but Travis lay awake for a long time trying to figure it out. He eventually fell asleep, too, though with no answer and no peace.

~~~~~

I'm fucking this up, and I don't know how.

Travis sat on the flybridge, next to Jonas in the pilot's chair at the helm. Geoff, Wes, Kennon, Desantos and Wyatt were lined up next to him along the white vinyl bench seats, a row of drunk, shirtless pirates, ready to pillage. Crank was out on the foredeck with some of the others, in his torn up cutoff jeans and faded tie-dyed shirt, playing his guitar like a wannabe pothead. Crank played, but they were all singing the old sailor song "The Holy Ground" at the top of their lungs, and shouts of "fine girl you are!" punctuated the air every few seconds. They were cutting up and laughing as they sang, butchering the lyrics, drinking their beer and whiskey, enjoying their day out on the brilliant blue water. Except for Travis. Travis wasn't singing. They had tried to drag him into it, but his mind was one hundred percent elsewhere. Right now, it was focused aft, right at Matt down on the deck below.

Travis watched him, seated below in the boat's fighting chair. Matt was working a large rod and reel with both beautifully sculpted hands. The toned muscles in his arms strained and worked, alternating between pulling hard and reeling in. He wasn't using the pole gimbal since whatever was on the line definitely wasn't all that big, but Matt was having the time of his life fighting to land it anyway. Petey was right behind him, coaching him, his shoulders bright red under the aqua blue tank top that Matt had picked out for him at some point over the summer. Fincher, Rickey and Dillinger were there, beers in hand, egging him on. Wasp was leaning back, up on the built-in fishing lockers, almost napping in the shade behind his blue-mirrored sunglasses. His broad, golden tan chest was rising and falling rhythmically, oblivious to everything going on around him. Travis knew that Matt probably had an image of some huge marlin or sailfish in his mind given the fight on the line, but everyone else was probably thinking more along the lines of a small mahi-mahi, maybe a tuna. It didn't matter. Travis was just glad to see that Matt was able to actually enjoy himself.

It was a beautiful day - light winds out of the southeast, a few snow white clouds dotting the crystal blue sky here and there from horizon to horizon, and not another boat in sight. The late afternoon sun glinted off the rippled water like camera flashes going off randomly just under the surface of the water. Travis caught a strong waft of cheap cigar smoke, one of the ones Marshall had been handing out earlier and was now a smoldering stub in the side of Petey's mouth. The smell of it briefly overpowered the more persistent smells of salt, fish, and alcohol. Normally, a day like this would be everything Travis could ask for. Open water and good friends. Beer and bullshitting. Rum and rods and reels. Tequila and team. But this time around, all he could think about was the night before.

Travis felt his body swaying slowly as the fishing charter they were on bobbed like a large marshmallow in the water. Wyatt clapped him on his shoulder, shouting "fine girl you are!" in his ear, but Travis ignored it. He had earned the nickname Mope today. Easily.

The brief look on Matt's face had consumed him, even though he hadn't seen a hint of it since the night before. Travis wanted to think it was all in his imagination, but he couldn't. Brief and unmistakable were *not* mutually exclusive.

I'm slowly losing him, and I don't know why.

In a way, he wanted to just ask Matt about it. But at the same time, he didn't want to be that kind of boyfriend — *Christ, honey, what the hell's wrong with you now?* There was no way in the whole damn world he was going to turn into that. He wanted to figure it out for himself and make it right. He owed Matt that effort.

But he just kept drawing a blank. And it was killing him. All day so far, it had felt like a hand was twisting his lungs around inside his chest.

Hell, why would he even want me in the first place?

Travis considered how Matt could have much more than what he had to offer him, how Matt deserved more. He didn't think Matt was doing it because he had saved his life. Travis wouldn't have liked that at all and wouldn't have even kissed him that first night without knowing for sure that Matt wasn't driven to him that way. But other than that, why? His heart sank thinking about all the time he had to spend away. Matt deserved someone there with him, way more than what he could be. And Matt was so good-looking, too: the dark brown-to-almost-black hair, the perfect goatee framing his mouth, the great build he had behind skin with such a magnificent complexion. And that wasn't to even mention those malachite eyes of his that wars should be fought over. Sure, Travis was muscular and he had stamina as his job absolutely demanded, but his body was scarred up from seven years of fighting, near misses and bad decisions, not to mention the ridiculous ears he hated and that broken nose. And then those damn smile lines etched in his face. Even with Matt telling him all of this was handsome and attractive, Travis had a hard time accepting that. Didn't Matt deserve better than all this? What was he really offering Matt in the end?

Travis put his hands on top of his head and sighed wearily. He wished he knew why Matt was slipping through his fingers. He wished he knew why someone as great as Matt was even bothering with him to begin with. He wished he knew what was going on.

After a full day of these mental gymnastics behind him, the only conclusion he had managed to arrive at was that he needed to remind the team about discussing classified information with Matt, yet again. He had spied Wes telling Matt a story about Crank earlier, then looking like a kid caught with his hand in a cookie jar when he realized Travis was watching him and knew what he was talking about. He couldn't hear what Wes was saying, but Travis knew exactly what it was anyway. The guys had gotten looser over the summer, sharing details of their missions with Matt, and he had warned them about it once already. It wasn't a trust thing, not by a long shot. Travis knew that Matt was every bit as trustworthy as anybody else in the platoon with the information, and would never take it outside the team. But he didn't like the guys doing this because he wanted to protect Matt. The more of these stories Matt heard, the more worried he'd be every time they left. He didn't want Matt to always be thinking the worst every time they went off; Matt did plenty of that already. Travis would do anything to keep Matt from getting hurt that way, even if he knew it was almost inevitable in the long run. It was the nature of the fucking job. He didn't like to enforce this little bit of separation, but it was for Matt's own good. It was Travis' dangerous world, not Matt's, and it was Travis' responsibility to protect him from it.

Aside from the episode with Wes, though, he didn't know what was going on. And the hand twisted the air up in his lungs in him tighter and tighter, to where he almost could no longer breathe. He downed the rest of his beer and tried to get his chest to loosen up some.

He's drifting away from me, and I don't know how to get him back.

Fortunately, Travis had been able to leave Matt to the team for most of the day, otherwise he would have been a neurotic wreck around him, which would have just worried and upset Matt in turn. Petey was always more than happy to monopolize Matt, to put a herculean effort into picking on him, who then picked back in just exactly the right way. Instead, Travis had watched Matt like a hawk from a distance, had a bead on him like a sniper, waiting to see anything that might give him a clue. He did notice that Matt stayed away from the gunwales if at all possible and absolutely didn't attempt the very narrow breezeways this boat had running to the foredeck. Matt was still a little nervous on this particular boat, but unless someone looked for it carefully, they'd never notice it. It was that important to Matt to be a part of today. Travis had managed to steal a few secret winks at Matt, a brief Morse code message reassuring him and making Matt smile, and safely hiding his own knotted up guts.

Suddenly, down below, the fish Matt had on the line breached the water's surface close to the boat. From what Travis saw, it looked like a mahi. Petey shifted the cheap cigar from one side of his mouth to the other and started shouting advice on bringing it in the rest of the way. Rickey grabbed a net to catch the fish in when Matt got it close enough. The guys up on the flybridge stopped singing to see what kind of massive sea monster Matt was going to finally reel in.

Matt pulled up on the rod, reeled in more as he lowered it, pulled up more, reeled in more, until the mahi was fully up out of the water and flapping around in the air just off the stern of the boat. Rickey chased it around with the net while Petey helped Matt steady the rod.

Rickey finally caught the fish in the net and brought it onto the boat. The mahi was only about four pounds worth, but mahi tend to be fighters, so even the small ones are a workout to land if you're not used to it. Travis couldn't help but smile at Matt's big trophy catch of the day. Rickey unhooked the fish and got it out of the net so Matt could hold it up for a picture, Petey right next to him, grinning like a fire-topped fool with a cigar stub.

Matt struggled to hold the fish while Dillinger snapped a few pictures. He actually looked offended by the fish.

"This is what I caught? All that fucking work for THIS?! What the hell?"

The guys around Matt couldn't help but start laughing at his reaction.

Matt added, "It smells bad, too."

Petey commented loudly, "I said the same thing about the fish I picked up last night at The 'Sides!" He took the cigar out of his mouth and added, probably more proudly than he had a right to, "She sure did taste good, though."

"Is there *anything* you won't fuck, Colorado?" asked Matt.

"You. Cornhole, that dude-cooch of yours smells worse than that fish there. My apartment always smells like sardines after you've bunked for the night!" said Petey, punching him in the arm.

Matt dropped the fish, which started flapping around by the base of the fighting chair. He chased it around trying to grab it again.

Matt said, sarcastically, "Yeah, yeah, I love you, too, pencil dick." He threw the fish overboard and back into the Atlantic Ocean.

Petey got this gentle, wry smile on his face as he watched Matt chasing the fish. He said, quietly, "Yeah, I love you, bro."

Fuck.

Fuck fuckity fuck fuck FUCK!!

How could I be so fucking brain dead STUPID?!

Wyatt took his foot and pushed in on the back of Travis' knee playfully, causing his leg to buckle and almost making him fall. Travis hadn't even realized he had stood up to begin with.

"You alright, Mopey?" asked Wyatt, trying to kick Travis in the other knee and finish the job.

Travis couldn't believe how dumb he had been. How obvious it was.

He turned and saw the boozy grin on Wyatt's face, his bare foot still buzzing around trying to make Travis' legs collapse under him.

Travis avoided Wyatt's foot and his gaze and said, "Huh? No. I mean, yeah, I'm fine. Just gotta get a refill."

He turned back and looked down on the deck below again. He never felt so angry and ashamed of himself in his entire life.

Matt stood down there with Petey, Dillinger, Rickey, and Fincher. And now Wasp had joined them.

Travis looked at Matt and wondered sadly if he'd ever be as brave as him. Matt, who had volunteered to be bait in a country where he almost died, who had trusted in guys he had no reason to trust, who had reached deep down inside himself for a courage he had no reason to believe was there, who would swallow his own deep fear to be on a boat with a bunch of guys that he cared about more than himself. Matt, who gave himself so openly and completely, whose fucking heart was big enough to park a goddamn aircraft carrier in. Who had told Travis he loved him more times than he could count now. And Travis hadn't said it back to him one single time. Not. One. Single. Goddamn. Time.

He had to get out of there or he was going to explode.

Travis practically slid down the ladder from the flybridge to the aft deck and flew through the door into the salon. He needed some privacy right now or he was going to make a grade-A ass of himself in front of a lot of guys he couldn't afford to do that with.

The boat, *Lucky Stars*, was a 45 foot Ocean Super Sport charter. Jonas had worked on it on his off days back when he was a Special Warfare Combatant Craft crewman. The owner of the charter company was pretty gung-ho patriotic and when Jonas made it into the SEALs, he was super excited. He let the guys have it at a very steep discount each year. It was equipped for fishing, with a fighting chair on deck for the sport fish, live bait wells, fish box, lockers, a sink and tackle center. Inside, the salon was well equipped with a comfortable couch, entertainment center, and galley. There was a separate stateroom with queen sized bed and a comfortable head, too.

Travis didn't want to stay in the salon, though. He needed to pull himself together and the salon was too open. The guys were in and out a lot since the ice chests and drinks were set up in there.

He passed through to the stateroom and was going to hole up in the head for a little while, but it was fucking occupied. He should've known that would be the case.

Fuck! What the hell is wrong with me? How could I be so miserably stupid?

He spun around next to the queen bed with the ugly brown bedspread, trying to decide what to do. He could feel Jonas crank the boat up and start out to find another fishing spot.

Travis gave up and plodded back into the salon, feet like boat anchors and feeling miserable. He could see Desantos, Crank and a few others out on the foredeck, and Matt and that whole crew on the aft deck. There was nowhere to really go. He sat down on the floor and leaned back against the cabinets in the dead end of the galley, hidden by the cabinets on three sides.

What made him want to punch a mirror just so he could hit his own sorry face, make it even uglier than it was now, was that he got it now. In one blinding flash like the mythical green flash of sunset, he understood the disappointment in Matt's face, and he understood why he hadn't said the words. Why he hadn't said the three fucking words that Matty deserved more than anyone he knew.

He had held back out of some stupid, misguided attempt to protect him. If he didn't say the words, then one bad day when he came home feet first, maybe Matt wouldn't hurt as bad. Maybe Matt would heal a little faster and move on a little more quickly. But he was hurting Matt now. His subconscious didn't take into account that he was hurting Matt a little bit every day right now. Slowly killing off the light in Matt that was there for him.

The agonizing thing was that he did love him. He loved Matt. Matty. Matt was everything to him. His safe mooring in a stormy sea. His flak jacket. His extraction point. Matt was... his. Travis might not have a lot in this world. But he had Matt. He just needed to say it. Matt just needed to hear the words. All that was missing was a tiny handful of words — *I love you, Matt.*

On this boat were sixteen men he trusted his life with. But there was only one he trusted his heart to. Matt just needed to hear him say it.

I love you, Matt.

Right on cue, Petey came busting through the cabin door to the salon. Travis sat up and tried to come up with an excuse for sitting on the floor of the galley, but Petey just belched and walked on past into the stateroom without even noticing Travis on the floor.

Travis rubbed his red, burning eyes a few times. He knew what he needed to do; he just had to find the first opportunity to make things right with Matt. To be the man Matt was and deserved. Travis thought that maybe he'd be able to get Matt alone for a few minutes at Chick's Beach later on, after a little dinner. Get him away from the team for just a few minutes so he could get down on his knees and tell Matt how he felt. And tell him how sorry he was. To give Matt the tiny handful of words.

Travis felt better, and his breathing finally slowed back down to normal.

Petey came back in from the stateroom and started poking around in one of the ice chests. Travis felt a little embarrassed and opened one of the cabinets next to him and started digging around, pretending to look for something.

Petey stood over the open ice chest and looked back over his sunburned shoulder at Travis in the galley behind him. He asked, "Whatcha lookin' for?"

Travis was about to make up some answer when he heard something pouring into the ice chest at Petey's feet.

"Petey, are you pissing in the ice chest?"

"Yeah, Baya's hogging the head again."

Travis shook his head. "Fuckin' hey, Petey! Were you raised by dingoes or something?"

The stream of piss continued unabated. "What, you'd rather I flop it out in the sink and piss there?"

"Shithead! Yeah, that'd be better! Our beers are in there."

Petey let out another small belch and expressed his opinion. "Whoever drinks this gay shit deserves to have my piss all over it. What are you lookin' for, anyway?"

Travis just picked. "A Corona, I think."

"Yeah, I'm pissin' on 'em right now. You want one?"

Travis didn't bother to answer.

Petey finally finished and zipped his cargo shorts up. He slurred at Travis, "And I have impeggable manners, I'll have you know, you crap stained taint hair."

Travis was about to respond and tell Petey that he had the manners of a son-of-a-dingo, but he heard a sound. Over the growl of the boat engines, it barely registered, but he had picked up on it for some reason.

As he listened, Jonas gunned the engines a little more to put on some speed and Travis heard some of the guys on the aft deck start laughing and clapping.

Then he heard Rickey's voice yell out, "C'mon, Matt, catch up!!"

The blood in Travis' veins turned to sharp ice crystals, stinging and stabbing every inch of his body. He flew up off the floor, glancing at Petey just enough to see the terror in his face, too.

Travis' hands felt like slippery ice, almost unable to work the latch on the cabin door as he tore it open, trying to get outside. The instant he was outside, he could see Rickey, Dillinger and Fincher looking off the stern of the boat.

Travis yelled, "Where is he?!?"

Rickey and Fincher laughed good-naturedly and pointed out in the water. Travis felt like he had been cut in half and could no longer move his legs. Matt was already forty agonizing yards off the stern since Jonas had gunned the engines, and getting farther away every split second. He stole one more glance at Petey, who was as white as a ghost.

Travis screamed at them, "HE CAN'T SWIM!!!" His body finally reacted, jumping up on the gunwale and his powerful legs launched himself hard, out as far as he could go. It was a dangerous thing to do with the engines churning the water at full power, but he sliced into the water and swam like he had never swum before.

He swam five or six strokes, then looked for Matt. Another five or six strokes, checked for Matt again. He noticed that Petey was in the water with him, trying to keep up. Six strokes, check for Matt.

I've fucked it up, and I've lost him.

Travis screamed in the water he was swimming so hard. Six strokes, check for Matt.

I waited to tell him, and I might as well go down with him if I'm too late.

Six strokes, check for Matt. Six strokes, check for Matty.

I let him down in every way.

After a tortuous eternity, Travis got to within a few yards of where he knew Matt last was. He instantly dove under to find him. He spotted him, another ten yards away, underwater and not moving. He screamed "Matt" underwater, even though he knew it was a pointless thing to do.

Travis reached Matt, swam up behind him, put his arms around his chest, and pushed his way up through the water harder than he ever had in his life. He broke the surface, and Petey was there, waiting to help.

Drowning victims will reflexively fight and claw to get their head above water to get air. Often, they can wind up drowning the very person there to help them because they can't control the desperate response of the body to get oxygen.

Travis prayed for Matt to fight. He could handle it, and a fighting Matt meant he was still conscious.

But Matt didn't move in Travis' arms. Petey and Travis both treaded water, keeping Matt's head up. Jonas had turned the boat around and brought it up alongside them as fast as he could, throwing the engines into reverse just long enough to stop the boat on a dime before cutting them off entirely.

Petey and Travis hauled Matt's body through the water to the side of the boat near the ladder. Together, they went under and pushed Matt up by his ass, lifting him out of the water as high as possible. Fincher and Wasp leaned over the side of the boat far enough to grab Matt's unconscious body by the arms and haul him into the boat. They laid him down next to the fighting chair.

Travis flew up the ladder of the boat like a man possessed. He threw himself onto Matt's prone body, screamed at the guys, "Get back!! Give him room!!" and started an emergency response. They had all been trained extensively in this, but Travis would be damned to hell before he let anyone else near Matt right now. Even as he checked Matt's pulse, the thought that he might be damned to hell anyway tore violently through his mind.

Matt's pulse was extremely weak and he wasn't breathing. Travis opened his mouth and started rescue breathing, forcing air into his lungs. He switched to chest compressions to keep Matt's heart beating. The tears in Travis' eyes mixed with the saltwater of the Atlantic Ocean and fell onto the limp body under him. He had to be Matt's heartbeat, his breath. But he could do that.

Everything else faded away, and Matt's quiet, still body was all he saw, needing Travis to be his heartbeat for him. Needing Travis to be his breath. Needing Travis.

Travis sobbed as he pushed on Matt's chest. He cried, "Don't you leave me, Matty."

He put his mouth to Matt's and breathed for him a few more times. His promise to Matt had been "last bullet, last breath." He had meant it. God, how he meant it. He'd gladly give his last breath right now to bring Matt back. He'd gladly sacrifice his life to do something... anything... everything... to save the person limp and lifeless under him right now. All he wanted was a goddamn chance. The agony spread through him like a wildfire, consuming him.

I'll be a better boyfriend. I swear to God, I promise.

His eyes stung with the tears, his face contorted with the pain. "You're all I got, Matt! Please, Matt. You're everything to me!"

He breathed for Matt again, and then pressed on his heart.

"I love you, Matt. I should have told you. I'm sorry I didn't tell you. I love you more than anything, Matty."

Travis put his mouth to Matt's again and breathed one more time. Travis felt saltwater push out of Matt's mouth and into his own. He sat up a little and ocean water heaved out of Matt's mouth.

Matt's eyes finally opened. Travis started crying and sobbing. Those beautiful eyes opened for him.

He lifted Matt up into a sitting position and held him. His green eyes were open, but still flat and lifeless looking. Matt's chest spasmed hard, still frantically trying to get air. Matt violently twisted over onto his hands and knees, finally able to vomit up all of the salt water in him. Finally able to let it drain out of his lungs. He pulled a long rattling breath into his chest.

Travis kept crying, and rubbed Matt's back. Anything to make this better.

Matt coughed and spit out as much as he could, panting violently to get air in his lungs again. And when he turned to sit back down and look Travis in the face, his face was pale, but Travis could see the life back in those beetle green eyes.

Travis put his hand on Matt's neck, tears still streaming down his face, and said, "I love you, Matt! God, you have no idea how much I love you! I'm sorry! I'm so sorry!"

He leaned forward and kissed Matt on the forehead. Travis thanked God for giving him Matt back, for giving him the chance to tell Matt how he felt. Travis sat down facing towards Matt and wrapped his arms around him, pulling him close, rocking him gently with his hand on the back of Matt's head, like a protective mother rocking her child to sleep. He whispered in Matt's ear, over and over, "I love you, Matt. I love you."

He stroked Matt's head and looked him in the face. He ran his thumb gently along Matt's eyebrow and asked him, "Are you ok?"

Matt nodded to him, weakly, but his breathing was slowing down now. He was going to be ok.

Matt coughed again a few times. He nodded his head again and rasped through sandpapered vocal cords, "I'm ok."

Travis' eyes were damp and red at the thought of what he had almost lost, almost let slip away from him, and his throat felt raw and rough. Together, Travis and Matt looked up at fifteen pairs of eyes gathered around, watching them in deafening silence, save for the sound of seawater slapping against the side of the boat.

Chapter 36 — Two Halves Collide

Matt wanted to try and walk into the salon, but Travis insisted on carrying him all the way into the stateroom. He put Matt down on the floor, leaning against the foot of the bed. Travis pulled out his rucksack and got the change of clothes he had brought for himself and insisted that Matt change out of his own wet, vomit covered clothes. Travis' shirt and shorts were a little bit big on him, but at least they were clean and dry. Travis pulled his own wet shirt off and threw it on the floor, dried himself off with a towel some, and left it at that.

That accomplished, Travis didn't know what to do next. So many things had gone wrong so quickly here, and he didn't know where to even begin. It was one of the few times in his adult life where he felt completely powerless.

Travis could tell Matt was a little shell-shocked still, and glassy-eyed, but not paralyzed by the trauma, either. He asked Matt, "You doing ok? How's your breathing?"

Matt coughed some again, but nodded. "I'm ok. Just a little scared, I guess. You ok, Trav?"

No, I'm a fucking basket case right now.

Travis sighed, "I've been better, but I'm ok."

With his immediate concern about Matt settled a little, his imagination started kicking in on how everyone outside was reacting to what they had seen. Every single guy in the platoon now knew about him. The job he loved was going to be stripped from him. His career in the Navy was chum in a bucket now. Might as well throw it overboard since the sharks were circling around, ready for a frenzy.

Some noises came into the room from outside. It quickly escalated into a heated exchange of unintelligible yelling and scuffling. Travis mostly ignored it. He was entirely focused on taking care of Matt right then, and his own fears about his career.

Matt started to try and get up, clearly worried about what was erupting outside on the deck of the boat. Travis grabbed his arm, probably a little more roughly than he intended, and growled at Matt, not angry, but balanced between worry and begging. He said, "You're not going anywhere! Don't you even think of leaving my sight! I'm never letting you more than four feet away from me ever again."

Matt looked at him weakly and sat back down on the floor. The angry shouting and scuffling up top got worse, even rocking the boat from side to side.

Matt looked utterly defeated and couldn't seem to look Travis in the face. He said, "I'm sorry, Travis. I shouldn't have come today. I've kind of ruined things for you, I think." He coughed a few more times, still trying to get the last of the seawater out of his lungs.

Travis' anger boiled up, all right, but not at Matt. There was no chance in the world of that. He had put Matt's life in danger, again, and now was staring down a dishonorable discharge, too. He had no one to blame but himself, and that's exactly where he directed his fury. Travis paced back and forth a moment, and then couldn't contain it. He turned and punched a hole in the bulkhead of the stateroom, straight through to the fiberglass hull of the boat.

Matt said again, "I'm sorry, Travis."

Travis came over and flopped down next to Matt, pressing up against him. He turned and held Matt's chin in his hand and kissed him as gently as he could on the lips. "*I'm* sorry, Matty. *I'm* the one that let *you* down. One of us fucked up way bad, and it definitely wasn't you. I love you, Matt. Please forgive me."

Matt nestled in more closely against Travis' bare side. "You saved my life again. Another one to throw on the pile," he said through a pale smile.

Travis felt his anger defuse a little and allowed a tiny chuff of laughter escape, making Matt laugh, too. Matt said, "It's getting to be a pretty big pile."

"To be fair," said Travis, "Petey was right there, too, swimming right next to me and pulling you up out of the water."

Travis felt his heart sink a little more. He put his arm around Matt and kissed the top of his head. "You're all I've got now. My Navy career has crashed and burned in a pretty spectacular way, but at least I've got you."

"Trav, give the guys a chance," begged Matt. "I don't think it's going to make a difference to them. I think they're better than that."

Things outside the stateroom had gotten quiet again. Travis wished that what Matt had said was true. Maybe there was a small chance it might be. But there was a big difference between Matt being open versus himself being openly gay around the team. Matt wasn't actually on the team; he was kind of like the team mascot. He had never hidden what he was around them, and they accepted him as he was from the beginning. The guys liked him plenty, even respected him for how he had handled himself in Latakia. They definitely liked how he had helped make the platoon look good on what wound up being a high profile mission.

But Travis was an integral part of the team. He was the senior enlisted member, the leading petty officer for the platoon. How many times had they come to him for advice on everything? Sex, money, girlfriends, drinking problems, stress, fear, all of it. They were going to see him differently now. Like they didn't know who he was any more. He'd become a stranger in their midst. God, that was gonna hurt like hell. To see *that* look in their faces. And sure enough, the respect he had earned over time would crumble away. They'd grumble about orders. They'd question his judgment. They'd question his fitness to lead.

And at some point, it'd go beyond just the platoon. It was fifteen guys, for Chrissake! No way that was gonna stay contained. And then he'd be out. Proud recipient of a great big dishonorable discharge he could frame and put on his wall to look at every day. If this had all happened just one fucking year from now, he might have legal grounds to stay. Everyone knew Don't-Ask-Don't-Tell was gonna drop pretty soon. Exactly when was just a detail. But shit, even legal grounds didn't matter. If he couldn't command the respect of his team and maintain leadership, he'd be pushed aside for someone that could. And they'd be right to do that. Lives depended on it.

Travis' breathing got labored the more he thought about it.

How had he wound up here, stuck in a no-win situation? He had put off saying the words to Matt, telling him he loved him, for whatever bullshit reason he had invented in his mind. Maybe too much damage had already been done with Matt. Maybe Matt wouldn't forgive him in the end. Maybe Matt had already drifted too far from him in the time he hadn't said it. And now it had all spilled out at the worst possible time. Either his career or what he had with Matt was gonna be wrecked, if not both. Gay Travis and SEAL Travis had lived separately in a peaceful, carefully maintained separation ever since he had joined the military. But now, today, the two sides of his carefully delineated life had suddenly smashed together and exploded like uncontrolled fireworks.

Fuckin' goddammit motherfucker!

Travis' breathing reached a fever pitch. He stood up again and punched another hole in the bulkhead, right next to the first one. His knuckles were starting to bleed now, but he didn't even notice.

He looked back over at Matt, now drawn up into a ball, with his arms around his knees. He didn't like seeing Matt like this. It was how he had laid eyes on Matt for the very first time, and he didn't like being reminded of what Matt went through, of what those filthy motherfuckers had done to him. Those green eyes of his were watering again and he looked scared. The poor guy had almost just drowned and here Travis was thinking selfishly about his shitty career path.

Damn it! Can't you do anything right, asshole? What are your priorities here?

He turned and smashed his bloody fist into the wall a third time, getting it out of his system once and for all.

Travis sat back down again next to Matt. Needing to feel Matt against him. But Matt actually drew away just the tiniest amount.

I deserve that. I deserve for him to pull away from me.

Travis turned to Matt and started trying to fix at least one half of his life. "I love you so much, Matt," he said, his deep voice cracking and his eyes stinging. "I have since the moment you told me to look up at the stars in the night sky outside of Latakia. I just couldn't say it. I was afraid of what it would do to you if you lost me one day. When I got on the helo the next day, leaving you behind on the *Iwo* was one of the hardest things I've ever done. I talk about courage, but I'm chickenshit about you. About us. And here I am scaring you to death when you've already been through hell. I love you, Matt. This whole fucking ocean can't hold what I feel for you, but I was just too chickenshit to say it. Forgive me, Matt. Please?"

Matt asked him, timidly, "You're not mad at me? You don't blame me for what happened today?"

Travis closed his eyes hard and had to stem the anger at himself for what he had allowed Matt to feel.

"I'm pissed as hell, Matt, at myself. Not you. Never you. I'm supposed to be watching over you and protecting you and almost totally blew it today. And worse, despite feeling it every day we've been together, I hadn't said the words. You deserve better than that, Matt, and I'm sorry. I love you. I'll never be able to say it enough. But I love you, Matt."

"You really love me, Trav?" asked Matt.

Travis leaned over and gently pulled Matt's face towards him. He touched his lips to Matt's, for a brief moment, almost unable to do it at the thought of what he had almost lost. But when they did kiss, it was one of relief. A gentle confirmation that what they had was still there, despite it almost all being lost at sea.

"I love you more than you can possibly imagine, Matt. Forgive me for not saying it."

Matt looked at Travis, the pain in those green eyes. Travis knew it wasn't pain for what Matt had been through, it was pain for what *he* was going through. Matt hurt for others more than he did for himself.

Matt blinked and sniffled. "I love you, too, Trav." He pushed back up against Travis' arm. Travis leaned over and kissed Matt lightly again, glad to be able to resume breathing again. Glad to have his breath back. Glad that his heart could start beating again.

They sat quietly for a few minutes, next to each other, not quite knowing what to do next. Travis wasn't sure what his next step should be, and Matt, bless him, was just waiting to follow his lead.

But the next step came to them. Travis and Matt heard a light knock on the stateroom door. Travis stiffened, immediately knowing it was now time for the other shoe to drop. Once that door opened, it would be the beginning of the end for him in the Navy.

It turned out it was Baya that stuck his head in the door.

"You guys ok?"

Travis looked at the floor in front of him and didn't answer. He didn't have the willpower to look Baya in the eye.

Matt nodded, though, and Baya came on into the room, a little nervous about interrupting them.

"Here, Matt. I brought you a bottled water. I thought you might like it, you know, to get the taste out of your mouth some." He handed the bottle to Matt, who twisted the top off and took a swallow.

Baya said, "I, uh, rinsed it off for you." He glanced back towards the main salon. "Someone took a leak in the ice chest. Fucking animals!" he said with a laugh, trying to break the tension.

Matt swallowed some more of the water, and Travis stole a quick glance at Baya, trying to get a read on him.

"You sure you're ok, Matt?" asked Baya again.

"Yeah, I'm ok. Thanks for the water."

"Everybody feels really bad about what happened, you know. Especially Rickey and Fincher. They didn't know, Matt. They had no idea you couldn't swim. We get a little carried away and assume everyone's as comfortable in the water as we are."

Matt nodded again. "It's ok. I know they didn't mean it."

Baya scratched at his wavy hair, glancing back again towards the stern. "Petey went nuts. Completely insane. I think he was going to kill them, and you know he probably could have. They all went over the side and Petey kept wailing on them even out in the water. It took Wasp, Marshall, and Ambush to pull him off of them. We finally got Petey calmed down, but now he won't talk to anyone. He's sitting up front in the pulpit."

Baya looked over at Travis, who had to look away again when he did. They all ignored the pink elephant in the room until Baya spoke up.

"Travis, look… you know it doesn't make any difference to me."

Travis refused to look at Baya. Instead, his bloody knuckles had become the most interesting thing in the world.

Baya said a little more firmly, "Mope! You're gay. Big deal. It doesn't change anything. You're still Mope. You're still the guy I stood back to back with and held off twenty insurgents outside Najaf for three hours until the cavalry showed up."

Travis, on hearing the word said out loud, looked up. Baya stepped over to Travis and slapped him on the shoulder reassuringly.

Travis almost didn't know what to say. So he kept it simple, "Thanks, Baya. Thanks."

Baya left and was immediately replaced by Fincher, Rickey, and Dillinger in the room. They looked like soaking-wet shit. Fincher had a black eye. Rickey's lip was busted open and bleeding down his wet shirt, and Dillinger had a cut and bruise over his right eye. For three big men that were normally fearless, they looked nervous as hell coming into the room with Matt.

Fincher was the one that spoke. "Matt, dude… shit… Matt, you got no idea how sorry we are. You know we never would have horsed around like that if we had known you couldn't swim, right?"

"I know," said Matt. "I played it down because I didn't want to be a downer today. It's more my fault than anybody's."

Dillinger's jaw set firmly. "No, it's not. Matt, you're as much a part of this team as anybody else at this point, and we always put responsibility where it belongs. Rickey, me, and Fincher… we're not stupid kids and we shouldn't have assumed you knew how to swim. We are sorry, though."

Rickey stepped into the head and spit out a mouthful of blood into the lavatory. He grabbed some toilet paper while in there to hold against his lip. When he came back out, he grinned and said, "We got our asses handed to us for doing it, though. And Petey doesn't have a scratch on him, the bastard. I gotta say, I don't want to get in a fistfight with Petey in the water again. I'll probably be asking his permission next time I even want to shake your hand, Matt."

Matt laughed a little. "Sorry. Yeah, I guess somewhere along the way he turned a little protective."

Dillinger took some of the toilet paper from Rickey and held it on the cut over his eye. "A little?!" he exclaimed. "Your little brother is as mean as a fucking wombat!"

Fincher shuffled his feet and said, "Mope, thanks for pulling Matt through. We all owe you for that one, man."

Travis nodded at them.

"But, I guess you got a good reason to save him, don't you?"

Travis flinched slightly at the comment, but nodded again.

The conversation paused uncomfortably, and Travis' heart started to sink a little.

Dillinger was the one that eventually said, "We'll keep it quiet, Mope. We need you on the team and don't want some pissy two-star bringing in someone that we don't know, don't want, and that doesn't fit with us."

That made Travis feel much better, and he even managed a feeble smile at them. They each stepped over to give Travis a fist bump, and then rubbed Matt on his head before leaving the room again.

Over the next thirty minutes, the guys came through, a few at a time, to check on Matt. And they all, without exception, reassured Travis that it didn't matter to them that he was gay. Kennon, Marshall, and Geoff came in, followed by Ambush and Wes. Then Crank.

Travis found out that Crank practically grew up in a gay household. Both of his uncles were gay and had long-term partners. Growing up, they were always his babysitters and the family he stayed with when his parents went on trips. Crank was downright enthusiastic to find out about Mope, even wanting to know if he and Matt were going to get gay married at some point. Travis looked nervously all around the room before saying it was a little early to be picking out china patterns and toaster ovens, which made Matt laugh.

Wyatt and Jonas came through after Crank. Jonas was more concerned about the boat. He took one look at the big holes in the wall and put his hands on top of his head and panicked. "Jesus, Mope! Did you have to go punching your fist through the damn hull? Man, look at those holes! Broussard is gonna poop himself when he sees that! We're gonna have to start putting down a security deposit! Couldn't you have punched one of the pillows or Wyatt or something?"

Wyatt, though, was one of the ones Travis worried about. He had heard Wyatt say some annoying things about gays in the past. It had been a while, and he had been pretty good to Matt, but he still worried about Wyatt's reaction.

Wyatt said, "You know. Back earlier this year, I woulda probably had a problem finding out about you, Mope. But Matt's softened me up, I think. It was good to see a gay guy that didn't fit my mold of what gays were like. Made me think that it wasn't what all I had been taught growing up. You ain't gotta worry about me, Mope. We gotta look out for our own, and you're still a part of this team."

Desantos was the last one Travis worried about. He finally came through by himself. He didn't have a lot to say, but he got right to the point.

"Mope, I'm still not sure what to think about homosexuality, and I don't pretend to understand where it comes from. But I guess if I had to pick two guys that I think are pretty decent for each other, I suppose it would be you two."

Travis didn't want to beat around the bush any more, with any of them. He asked him, "You gonna rat me out, Desantos?"

"You know me, Mope. I have my beliefs, but I don't judge."

Desantos left and Travis expected Wasp and Colorado to make some kind of appearance. He especially expected Petey to come in and check on Matt. But after a few minutes, they were still in the cabin alone. In a way Travis was glad to just sit quietly. Everything today had wound up happening so fast late in the day, and he had a lot to think about. Matt was ok, sitting next to Travis on the floor holding his hand, occasionally coughing to get rid of the last of the seawater, but otherwise quiet. And now the bulk of the team had seemed to accept a gay Travis, even after what they had witnessed up on deck. Travis didn't know what forces worked in the world to bring him this kind of luck, but he felt like he was using a lifetime's worth in one day. But if he was going to use it all up, today was the day.

A change in heading and engine noise let Travis know that they must be pulling into the marina. He felt a little bit of an obligation to go up top to help secure the boat, but then there were fifteen sailors up topside already that knew what they were doing. Plus, Matt seemed to be content to just sit and rest quietly after almost being lost at sea. He didn't want to leave Matt alone, so he stayed right where he was.

Eventually, after the engines stopped completely, Jonas leaned into the stateroom and said, "All ashore that's going ashore. We've still got the shrimp boil, so we'll see you guys over there."

He glanced again over at the holes in the bulkhead and said, dejected, "Man, Broussard is gonna kill me!"

Once alone again, Travis told Matt, "Let's go back to my place. We don't have to do this tonight. You've been through a lot, and honestly, so have I."

Travis stood up to get his rucksack put together, stowing Matt's wet clothes in it. He put his own damp shirt back on.

Much to Travis' surprise, Matt said, "No."

Travis' eyes raked over Matt, sitting on the floor, his legs stretched out in front of him. Matt's eyes were firm, but Travis saw the care and love behind them. He stared at Matt a moment, trying to understand.

"No, we're going to the beach."

Travis couldn't believe Matt wanted to make this day any longer than it already was.

"Matt, you've probably had the second worst day of your life today. Let's just be done with it."

"No, we're not finished with this. You're not finished with this and we need to go. Something's still not sitting right, and we need to see this through. I'm fine and I'll be on dry land."

Travis wondered if there was any end to how much Matt could amaze him. But the beach trip was unnecessary. He knew Matt was worried about Petey, but the three of them could talk tomorrow.

Matt seemed to know Travis was about to open his mouth, so he said, "We're going, or I'm going without you."

Travis couldn't argue with that.

Chapter 37 – Sea, Air, Land, Fire

There's something intrinsically peaceful about sitting out on a beach at night with a warm breeze, a crackling fire in front of you and the eternally repeating sound of tidal water just out of the reach of the dancing firelight. Sea, air and land. It's hard to worry about the future when you've got a moment like this surrounding you and the rest of time can be put on hold for just a little bit. It's like taking the rest of the world, holding it in the palm of your hand and putting it down in your pocket. You'll pull it back out at some point, but until then you can forget about it and just *be*. Be in the sand, in the sea breeze, in the flickering fire, under the starlight.

After the day he had had, Travis felt much calmer. After the night before, seeing the disappointment in Matt's face, he was regaining the peace he had slept without. He just wished it was complete.

All seventeen men had sprinkled themselves around the fire, having had their fill of a huge pot of the shrimp boil that was their tradition for many years running now. Crank was noodling softly on his guitar again, but not any particular tune. Beach guitar jazz, he called it. Some were talking and laughing in low voices, smoking on the shitty cigars that Marshall always seemed to be pushing on all of them. A few others were roasting marshmallows over the open fire, like big kids. That is, after giving Ambush a hard time and telling him the marshmallows were way better than the stringy possum and rabbit he usually caught for them to cook and eat while out on survival.

Travis lay in the sand, legs stretched out and facing towards the fire, and leaning against one of the logs they had pulled around for the evening on their favorite quiet spot on Chick's Beach, down near Lynnhaven Inlet. He could see the lights from a few boats dotting the darkness, out off the coast. Matt was right next to him, side to side pressed up against him, comfortable, warm, and safe. He had kept close to Matt all night, partly because he didn't want to let Matt out of his sight anymore, and partly because he didn't quite know how to act around the team. For such a little thing, it felt very strange to Travis to be able to do this openly now in front of these guys. But, none of them seemed to really even notice. None of the guys focused on them, but they didn't avoid or ignore them, either. They all seemed to be keeping their promises from the boat earlier.

Travis felt like the rest of the world could be safely put away in his pocket for a little while. Except, not quite. He didn't know what to do about Wasp and Petey. What had come to light on the boat earlier was still between them, like a scab. It kept bothering him, and he didn't know if he should pick at it or leave it alone.

Neither of them had barely been able to look at Matt or Travis since getting off the boat. Both had come to the beach, but they had stayed to themselves, not really interacting with anyone, their minds occupied with the day.

Travis was tired and wanted to finish it. He wanted to know where he stood with Keith and Petey. He just didn't know if should pick at the scab or not.

He was a little surprised at how tired he was. He wasn't used to feeling exhausted like this. Travis could endure a tremendous amount, but the emotional toll of the day had left him drained. Two weeks earlier, he had stood completely motionless on a pressure-release trigger attached to a bomb for nearly three hours, in a dark cave, near Asadabad, in those god-forsaken mountains of Afghanistan. He and some of the others were checking a cave network the Taliban had recently been routed from. The things were rife with booby traps and Travis felt the trigger as soon as he stepped on it. If he moved just the wrong way, the trigger would trip and he'd be blown to chowder. None of the other guys were nearby, and it took an hour and a half for Wasp to finally hear him yelling and locate him. Then another hour for Wasp to get Crank so he could disable the bomb. Most of them could have probably done it, but Crank was the best at it. Travis stood motionless until Crank showed up, whistling a tune and casually asking why he had stepped on it, as if Travis had done it on purpose. Travis would have smacked him upside the head if he could have reached him without moving his foot. This was the kind of stuff he didn't dare tell Matt about. But now, after the last couple of days, he might change his mind. He trusted Matt, they all did, and trying to insulate Matt was starting to seem like a bad decision.

He could handle that kind of stress well, but today had been entirely different.

He wondered why it was that Keith and Petey seemed to be the ones that wound up having a problem with him being gay. Something felt broken with them now. He lay in the sand, fretting about it. Trying to decide if he should pick at the scab or not.

He glanced over and could tell Petey was watching the two of them, probably also trying to decide if he should pick at the scab or not.

When he looked back, he started to get a little nervous again. Wasp had now walked over to them and was hovering nearby, stubbing his big bare foot into the sand and looking everywhere except Travis and Matt.

Wasp's round face finally settled on the two of them and he cleared his throat a little uncomfortably.

Matt sat up some against the log and said carefully, "Hey, Wasp."

Wasp took a step closer and looked for everything like a ten year old kid in a hulk's body.

"Hey... uh, Matt. You doing ok?"

Matt nodded and said, "Still on borrowed time." Travis grinned grimly without looking over at Matt.

Wasp said, "Good. I guess." His brow was deeply furrowed, his hands were shoved down in the pockets on his dark plaid shorts, and he was still nervously toeing the sand.

Matt looked up at Wasp looking at Travis and said, "I'm gonna go see if Jonas needs any help putting stuff up." He got up to go help. Travis growled quietly, deep in his chest, at Matt being that far away from him, but let him go.

Wasp came over and sat down in the sand next to Travis, his thick legs crossed in front of him. Travis decided to let him have his say since he had come over, but he found it hard to look Wasp in the eye. So, he stared at the crackling, spitting fire instead.

Wasp didn't say anything for a while and the only sound was Crank's soft guitar, the ocean and the sound of insects.

Wasp said, "I won't be able to stay on the team, you know."

Travis' heart sank. It sank like a chunk of lead thrown overboard.

Why do you have to do this, Keith?

It disappointed Travis so much to hear this, made him feel like a failure. He had put a lot into trying to get Keith past the death of the Marine. Keith had an amazing soldier inside of him if he could just get his confidence back and let that soldier out. But now, to have him wind up wanting out because Travis turned out gay? Travis didn't think he could stand by and watch that kind of talent go to waste. Travis thought that maybe, despite how it hurt deep down, he needed to get out of the way for the sake of the team. They'd be better off without him, without the disruption and distraction.

"Keith..." Travis tried to speak through the cotton-mouth he suddenly found he had.

"Keith... I'm ready for the sacrifices I need to make. And the team is important to me. I'll back out."

Wasp picked at a shell in the sand next to his feet.

"It was good while it lasted, I guess," said Wasp in tired surrender.

Travis started to feel an odd peace. It started in the pit of his chest, and worked its way out from there. It had been foolish to get his hopes up that he might be able to make it work. That maybe the only person on the team afraid of him being gay, in the end, was himself. But if that wasn't to be, then he'd bow out and wish the team luck. He'd find something else, somewhere.

Travis agreed. "Yeah. I can't complain about the good run I had."

Wasp looked over at Travis, still turning the small shell over and over in his thick, tan hands. "The stupid thing is that I think I was finally kind of accepting it. The thing with the Marine. You... Matt... you guys had helped me turn a corner with it. Well, that and the fact that, for whatever reason, Colorado's stopped grinding my ass about it. I... well, never mind."

Travis couldn't help but think this felt a little like Wasp was twisting a knife in him now. All the support over the friendly fire incident was great, until Wasp found out Travis was gay.

Travis scratched at his nose, uncomfortable even talking to Wasp any more. "Well, now I'll be out of the way, and you can be the SEAL you were meant to be."

Wasp looked over at him oddly. He looked confused, but Travis wasn't really looking at him anymore. He stared at the heart of the firelight and wanted to be alone. Well, no. He didn't want to be alone. What he really wanted was for Wasp to go away and for Matt to come back.

Wasp said, "I said, I wouldn't be able to stay."

Travis wondered if Wasp was just trying to rub it in. He looked over at Wasp, about to tell him to just leave, but he saw the confusion on Wasp's face instead.

"Yeah, I know, so I said I'd be the one to leave instead," explained Travis.

"And if you go, then I go, too."

That hadn't been what he said earlier.

"Huh?" said Travis.

"Mope, if you leave, then I don't think I have it in me to stay on the team. You're the only reason I've been able to hold on this long."

Travis suddenly felt like they were having two completely different conversations.

"I thought you were saying that since you found out I'm... gay... that you'd didn't want to be on the team," he said.

Wasp shook his head. "No, I thought... what the hell are we talking about?"

Travis started to speak, but Wasp interrupted him. "I thought you were going to leave because you didn't want to be on the team, you know, having figured out you're gay. That you'd want to be with Matt or something. And if you go, then I go."

The vise grip on Travis' insides started to let up. He couldn't help but laugh at how badly they seemed to have gotten their lines crossed. "I don't want to leave. I mean, I am with Matt, but he and I are working that out. I love being a SEAL. And... I love Matt. I don't want to give either up." There - he had said it out loud, intentionally, to one of the team. He felt himself blush slightly when he said it, but it was getting easier. He added, "I thought it had freaked you out. And I'd rather get out than ruin the bonds on the team."

"Why would you being gay freak me out?" said Wasp. "Matt doesn't freak me out. I like Matt. Hell, he helped me come to grips with the Marine probably more than even you. But Mope, I don't know... you've done so much for me. You've been my mentor about everything."

He took a deep breath. "I would've failed out of this program a long time ago if it weren't for you, Mope."

Travis felt the need to lay this out on the line before they made any more stupid assumptions. "I'm not going anywhere as long as the team is ok with me staying. And I want you to stay, too. You're a part of Team 8, Keith. You've hit a rough spot, but in the end, you're gonna be much better for it."

The haze gray frown on Wasp's face gave way, and he started to smile. "I'm glad we had this fucking talk!"

Travis said, "Shit! Crisis averted, I guess."

Wasp nodded and said, Travis joining him as he said it, "God damn and God bless for small favors!"

When Matt finally saw that their conversation was done and they were both smiling, he came back over, handed a fresh beer to Wasp and one to Travis, and sat back down next to his man.

"Wasp? Trav? You guys ok?"

Wasp grinned, "Yeah, barely!"

Travis held out his beer bottle and Wasp clinked his against it, drinking to his mentor.

Wasp started to ask questions. He wanted to know when Travis and Matt had started seeing each other. He wanted to know how long Travis known he was gay. Now with the misunderstanding out of the way, he was curious about all of it. And when Matt reached over to hold Travis' hand, Wasp didn't bat an eye at it.

The three of them talked for a few more minutes before, out of the corner of his eye, Travis saw Petey down the rest of his beer and stand up. Petey must have noticed that Travis and Wasp had figured out their way through this and it was his turn to make or break. Out of fifteen guys, it was going to be Petey that was going to make or break his chance to stay on the team.

Petey walked over and stood in front of Travis and Matt. He crossed his arms over his chest and looked pissed. The look on Petey's face said it all. Make or break... and all Travis could see was break.

Before Petey had a chance to jump all over him, Travis sighed and said, "Petey, why do you hafta be the one with a problem? Huh? Out of all the guys..." Travis' voice was almost pleading. Why did it have to come down to him?

Petey looked at him. "What?"

"Wigging out about me being gay."

Petey looked at Travis with that patented sneer of contempt on his face. "Jesus Christ, Mope. I don't give a good goddamn about you being a fudge-packer. Hell, all y'all on this team seem like a bunch of queers except me."

Wasp sat up a little bit and said, "Fuck it, Petey! We're all *right here*, you know?"

"You stay outta this, half-pint. Jesus, Mope! It's not always about you!" Petey shifted his pissed-off gaze a little bit and looked squarely at Matt.

"You! I got a bone to pick with you, asshole."

282

~~~~~

Petey stomped off into the night, down the beach a ways to get away from the rest of the team. Matt looked back at Travis and Wasp behind him as he followed Petey. Both were watching him pretty closely, wondering what Matt could have done to get Petey like this. As he glanced back, he realized that it wasn't just Travis and Wasp watching. The whole platoon had pretty much stopped to see what was going to happen.

He caught up to Petey, dimly illuminated in the distant firelight. He could barely make it out, but Petey looked like he could bite a grenade launcher in two he was so angry. He was looking at his bare feet and his lips were pulled tight and down into a hot grimace that could have boiled the large pot of shrimp that they had had earlier.

Matt started, "Petey, what the hell did I..."

"You held out on me, asshole!"

"About Travis?"

Petey interrupted him again, "You fucking promised me! This is important!" He repeated, "This is important to me."

Petey wiped his hand across his forehead and glanced around him.

Matt stood there, unable to follow what Petey was getting at.

"Do you love him?" Petey's voice was still angry and accusatory.

"Travis?"

Petey hit Matt in the shoulder, and his voice hitched up a notch. "DO YOU FUCKING LOVE HIM? Or is this just some rebound thing after that worthless piece of shit Ryan or Brian or whatever his name was? I gotta know, Matt! This is fucking important!"

Matt rubbed his shoulder. Petey had actually hurt him a little when he hit him. "What the hell is this about, Petey?"

"Answer the goddamn question, Matt!"

Matt replied angrily, "Yes! Fuck you, Petey! Yes, I love him! No, it's not some stupid rebound thing."

Petey's large hand shot out and grabbed Matt by the throat, not strangling him, but holding him in place where he couldn't move.

Despite how pissed Matt was at Petey, he was taken by surprise at how effortlessly Petey could immobilize him with just one hand.

"I mean really fucking love him, Matt? Huh? Love him enough to take a fist in the face for him?" Petey pulled his free arm back, like he was actually considering punching Matt in the face.

Matt was unable to move. But he didn't want to. What the fucking hell was wrong with Petey? If Petey wanted to punch him in the face over Travis, then fine. Fucking do it. He had already drowned today. He might as well get his nose smashed in, too.

Matt spat at him, "YES!"

Petey's fist flew out at a speed that Matt wouldn't have thought possible, but Matt didn't flinch. And to Matt's complete surprise, his face didn't get smashed in; Petey's fist sailed right past his left ear. Petey had intentionally pulled the punch.

Matt said, "Petey, what the hell is going on here? Are you ok?" Petey's hand was still at Matt's neck, but it was only resting there now. Matt was getting worried about Petey, trying to understand what all this meant.

Petey's mouth was still contorted into a frown, but it was totally different than before. Matt could see it in his eyes. Petey looked dangerously close to crying.

"I gotta make sure, Matt. I gotta make sure you're taken care of! This has gotta be real."

Petey was shaking with the massive effort he was putting into keeping it all in check. And damned if, even in the feeble light, Matt didn't see a tear finally break free and trail down Petey's face. Matt would have far rather been punched in the face than see Petey like this.

"I need you here, Matt. What happened today can't happen! I need to make sure you're gonna be here." Petey's voice was breaking up and the tears were starting to drop regularly now.

Matt started crying, too. He begged, his own anger now replaced by a desperate need to know what Petey was trying to say, "I don't understand, Petey. What are you talking about? What's going on with you?"

Petey couldn't talk for a moment. He looked out at the ocean, and finally back at Matt. "You're my brother, asshole. You gotta talk to me! Because... one... one of these days..."

Petey's voice dropped off and he put his hands on his hips and tried to get control again, and didn't do very well.

He sobbed even worse than before and croaked, "One of these days my luck's gonna run out, Matt! It's gonna run out and I'm gonna come home in a fucking zip-lock bag. I need you *here*! Somebody's gotta talk to my parents when that happens. You're gonna have to go do it, Matt. Please. You need to tell them that I wasn't just some cold-hearted, selfish, violent son-of-a-bitch. That's what everyone sees. I don't want to be... that... You're my way out, Matt. But I gotta know you're taken care of! You *gotta* talk to me."

Matt couldn't hear this anymore. Anybody else... fine. But not Petey. He had started hitting him in the chest even as Petey was trying to explain. "Shut up, Petey! Don't you *fucking* talk like this to me! I can't stand here and listen to this! No way you're coming home... like *that!* You're gonna be around to aggravate the hell out of your grandkids, you fucking asshole!"

Petey shook Matt. "PROMISE ME! Promise me, Matt! Don't hold out on me, and don't let something like today happen again."

Matt grabbed Petey and held him tight, and Petey hugged him back.

Petey said again, begging, "Promise me that if anything happens, you'll be here and you'll go see my parents, Matt."

Matt nodded, his head against Petey's chest, his tears soaking into Petey's shirt. Petey had hugged Matt before, but this was different. He was clinging to him this time. Petey was clinging desperately to Matt. It was almost impossible for Matt to push the words out of himself. He could barely croak, "Yeah, Petey. I promise. I promise."

Petey sniffled, finally satisfied that Matt got it and was taking him seriously.

Matt stood back and wiped the sleeve of Travis' t-shirt across his own eyes, drying them. He understood now. He understood.

Matt suddenly punched Petey in the chest as hard as he could. Petey just looked at him blankly, unfazed by Matt's fist.

Matt glared at him. "And I swear to God! If anything happens to you, I'm gonna kick you so hard in the ass you'll start spitting out shoelaces. So you just think about that, you bastard!"

Petey sniffed one more time, then grabbed Matt, and hugged him again, rocking back and forth with him. He kissed his brother on the forehead, for a long time, finally satisfied that if something happened to him, some good part of him would still be around.

They took a few steps back towards the team, but Petey stopped Matt and studied him one more time. Matt thought he looked almost unsure.

"Mope... You really love him?" he asked calmly.

Matt nodded and said, "Yeah, I really do."

"And he loves you? Really loves you?"

Matt nodded again, the nagging doubts he had had about Travis fully chased off. "Yeah."

Petey was quiet for a second. He put his hand on Matt's shoulder and said, "Good. Alright. Travis is a good guy. I trust him and he'll take care of you."

Petey kept his hand on Matt's shoulder a moment more and looked out into the dark at the sound of the water. He said softly, "Today scared the shit out of me." Somehow, Matt knew he was probably the only person in the world Petey would say words like that to.

Matt stepped up to Petey and hugged him again, and Petey put his arms around Matt and hugged back.

They started to walk back towards the firelight and the rest of the team, their differences aired and settled.

As they got near the team again, Petey got a little of the fire back in him and he said, "And you're a disgrace to the Tuttle family, you know? I gotta teach you how to throw a punch and you're gonna learn how to fucking swim. I'm not jumping in to save your sorry ass every time you can't figure out how to lift your fat head up out of the bathtub."

Matt said, "Fine."

Petey nodded once and said, "Good."

Matt growled, "Whatever."

"Yeah."

"Done."

"Fuck you."

And everything was good between them again.

~~~~~

Travis watched, his nerves completely frayed and shot. He once again cursed himself for letting Matt out of arm's reach. When he saw Petey rear back to punch Matt, he just about lost his head. He had jumped up and started running, knowing there was no way in the world he'd be able to stop Petey from crushing Matt's face in if he wanted to. But before he even got a few yards towards them, he realized Petey had already thrown the punch, and that Matt was fine.

He stopped, his heart beating a million times a second, and he unconsciously dropped into his preferred crouching position in case he needed to move quickly again. But otherwise, he left the two of them to work it out the rest of the way. He watched the interchange between them, wondering what the hell they could be flaring up like this over. But when he saw Petey grab Matt and kiss him on his forehead, he knew all was fine between them. More than alright. Travis had seen Petey give Matt a kiss before like this, but that was usually Petey's secret weapon to get his dick in some girl's pants. Tonight, this one was just for Matt, and it was one of the truest, purest things he had ever seen Petey do.

Matt got back to where they were and sat back down next to Travis. Travis grabbed his hand and held it in an iron grip, like Matt was a bad child that got into all kinds of trouble the instant he let go of his hand. He wasn't going through any more tonight, the stuff that seemed to happen when Matt was more than an arm's length away from him.

The rest of the team was still all transfixed by what was happening between Petey and Matt. Petey stopped by his bag to grab a bottle out. He glared at all the eyes that had been watching him and Matt, and said angrily, "The fuck are y'all looking at? Family discussion and you shitheads can mind your own fucking business."

Petey plopped down in the sand next to Matt, his orange hair practically glowing in the red light of the fire, and really joined the group for the first time that night. He eyed Matt and Travis sideways and said, "Fucking fags," then handed them the bottle of Southern Comfort so they could all start drinking.

Matt laughed, which made it ok for Travis to smile, too. Even Wasp had to shake his head and laugh a little.

Petey said, "If either of you hurt the other, you're gonna have me to answer to for it. Just so you know. You've been warned."

"Fair enough," said Travis, swallowing from the bottle.

Petey looked across Matt at Travis and said, "You given Matt a Dirty Sanchez yet?"

Matt shoved Petey up against the arm and grumbled, "Petey, stay the *hell* out of my sex life!" He took the bottle from Travis, drank a quaff and then handed it over to Wasp.

Travis said nothing. He couldn't believe this conversation was happening.

The contempt rolled off of Petey again, "I didn't think so. You call yourselves perverts? You guys are pathetic. Buncha fucktards."

Petey looked around, noticing a lot of the team was still watching what was going on. His attitude turned slightly more contemplative, but not much, and he spoke to Travis again, "You need to kiss him, though. Now."

Travis said, "Petey, can you lay off?" If Petey was now going to be riding Travis' ass constantly about being queer, then this was a problem. Travis didn't care if he did it around the rest of the team since they now knew, but Petey needed to keep it there.

Petey insisted, "No. You need to kiss him. Here, in front of all of us. Intentionally. You don't, dumbass, and next week, it'll all be back the way it was. Back in the closet. Is that what you want? Matt's gonna be around, so you might as well get it out in the open. For real, this time."

Jesus, when did Petey get an IQ higher than his shoe size?

Travis thought maybe Petey wasn't actually going to constantly give him a hard time after all. He looked at Matt, who was watching him expectantly. He swept his eyes around the rest of the team in the firelight. Some had gone back to their conversations, but they all seemed to be keeping a corner of one eye tuned to Matt, Petey, Wasp, and himself.

It turned out to be harder than Travis thought it would be. He was still nervous about all of this. But then, the hardest things to do were usually the most worthwhile. He reminded himself that the only easy day was yesterday.

Travis took a deep breath. He turned to Matt and put his hand behind Matt's neck, pulling his face to his own. Their lips met and Travis relaxed into the kiss. He hadn't realized how much he had needed to kiss Matt all night. Their faces pressed together, their tongues met and slipped against one another, and Travis felt the familiar crunch of the facial hair around Matt's mouth pressing into him. Inside him, the hot ember burned brighter and hotter, its warmth spreading out through his entire body. Travis pulled back, his face only an inch away from Matt's.

He could see the orange firelight dancing in Matt's eyes. He ran his hand along the back of Matt's head.

Matt grinned and said, "I love you, Trav."

Travis nodded and said, "I love you, too, Matty."

When he leaned back against the log, nothing had changed. No one had stormed off, disgusted. There were no MP's waiting to arrest him for conduct unbecoming. The insects still hummed and chirruped. The waves still rolled in. Even Petey laid off the taunts for once. Anticlimax never felt so good to Travis.

Dillinger, Rickey, Marshall and Wes started stirring around, pulling their things together to go. The long day was winding down, and soon everyone would go their separate ways.

Wasp stood up, too. But he looked down at Travis. He said, loud enough to get the whole team's attention, "Call us, Mope."

Travis got nervous again. They were all putting him through the wringer on this whole thing and he was so tired.

The team stopped what they were doing to see what would happen. Dillinger, Rickey, Marshall, and Wes stopped packing up to watch as well. They wanted to see how Travis would handle this.

Travis said, "C'mon, Wasp. We're on a holiday here. This isn't the time..."

Wasp said again, "Call us, Mope! You want to know if you're still in charge or not? Find out rather than waiting. Call us!"

Travis heard Baya say from the other side of the fire, "Do it, Mope. If you lose your leadership over this platoon, it's only because you're unwilling to maintain it, not because you're gay."

Travis gritted his teeth. This is what it would come down to. This moment. This would re-establish the team, or show that things were not going to hold. Travis stood up, his hands suddenly clammy and his heart starting to pound in his chest.

He snapped to attention, not quite as crisply as he usually did, and his insides felt like they were twisting around. All the "what if's" cast doubts into him. But Wasp and Baya were right.

Travis barked out at the team, as best he could, "SEAL Team 8!"

His shoulders slumped just a little, and his face twisted just slightly, daring the team to show him that something had changed irrevocably.

But every team member, all fifteen, with no arguments, discussion, confused looks, or hesitation, jumped up and into the same position of attention as Travis, all facing towards him.

He shouted again, his confidence gaining, "Platoon! Who are we?"

All sixteen men responded in exact unison, "We are SEAL Team 8!"

Travis shouted, his deep voice booming across land and sea, "Team! SEAL Team 8 has a creed! What is that creed?"

All sixteen shouted the response in the same practiced unison, "We are SEAL Team 8! We exist to serve our mission, to fight for our brothers, and to defend our country! Even with our last bullet! Even with our last breath! *We do not fail!*"

And if Travis wasn't mistaken, he could swear there was just the tiniest bit of extra emphasis on the word "brothers" in the creed tonight. He stood there, locked at attention, but he could feel his hands shaking at his sides. He let his eyes slide to the side just enough to steal a glance at Matt, who was looking up at him with pride and love.

If I can make it through this day, there's nothing in this world I can't handle.

He held the team at silent attention a minute longer than usual. He wanted to feel it between them - the bond that they still shared even when one of his deepest fears had come to light. He felt ashamed that he had doubted them, hadn't trusted them more than he had. Matt had been right about this, too. It was a fundamental thing he had kept from this team, always an invisible wedge between them. He hadn't understood the impact of it until it was gone. The secret had fallen away and they would all be the stronger for it. He felt like there was nothing he couldn't do.

Travis nodded to the team and said, "Thanks, men."

The team relaxed, and Travis sat back down next to Matt. He looked over into those green eyes and felt like he was going to burst inside. Matt shifted slightly, putting his head down on Travis' shoulder.

Travis felt lucky to have the sea, air and land around him. Now he had the fire, too. The darkly glowing ember deep inside him, burning for the man pulled up close to him, the one that brought the two parts of his life together so they could now be seamless. So that he could feel complete.

Travis leaned his head over and kissed the soft, kitten-fuzz on the top of Matt's head.

"Thank you, Matt."

Matt said, "Why are you thanking me? You're the one that saved my life today. *Again*."

Travis said softly, his lips brushing lightly through Matt's hair, "You know, I'm kinda wondering who saved who here."

Travis shifted around so he could change places with Matt. He wanted to put his head on Matt's chest. He wanted to hear Matt's heartbeat. Make sure it was still there. He thought about the close call and how he had been Matt's heartbeat today, his breath. If he was lucky, he still was. And if he was honest, as far back as a lonely night on a road outside of Latakia, Matt had become *his* heartbeat and *his* breath.

Travis now felt like he could completely be *there*, fully at peace. Matt had been right on the boat - they needed to finish this evening and make sure everything was sitting right. Everything was so different. And nothing was different. How could he ask for anything more than that? Come next week, who knew what shitstorm they'd drop into the middle of next. But for right now, he could relax, the rest of the world tucked in his pocket. The person he loved more than anything beneath his head, and the brothers he fought with surrounding him, supporting him. The men he trusted his life to and the man he trusted his heart to. Sea, air, land, and now the fire, too, all come together and completing him.

There's something intrinsically peaceful about sitting out on a beach at night with a warm breeze, a crackling fire in front of you and the eternally repeating sound of tidal water just out of the reach of the dancing firelight. It's hard to worry about the future when you've got a moment like this surrounding you and the rest of time can be put on hold for just a little bit. It's like taking the rest of the world, holding it in the palm of your hand and putting it down in your pocket. You'll pull it back out at some point, but until then you can forget about it and just *be*. Be in the sand, in the sea breeze, in the flickering fire, under the starlight with the people that mean absolutely everything to you. Sea. Air. Land. And fire.

A log shifted in the fire and dropped down, disturbing it.

Travis watched it and told Matt, "Look up."

And together they watched the sparks, the thousands of brilliant microscopic red stars, swirling up and into the limitless night sky above the both of them.

~~~ THE END ~~~

Other Works by JF Smith

Falling Off The Face Of The Earth

After his big-shot life in New York tragically falls apart, James Montgomery returns to his small hometown in south Georgia a defeated and broken man. All he has left is his mother to help him heal and regain his confidence before he's ready to get back out and re-conquer the world.

But being big-city gay in a small southern town has its own challenges. In addition to coming to grips with what happened in New York, his hometown of Lawder throws its own curveballs at him. James is confronted with a bitter enemy from his school days, and frustratingly can't seem to avoid the guy. His mother suddenly wants to expand the family. The one guy James takes a liking to and starts dating has a lot of hang-ups about being gay. And he watches almost helplessly as a new young bully starts to repeat the kind of abuse he suffered during his own school days.

Here where he grew up, the one place he should feel safe, James feels maddeningly off-balance. He starts to think that maybe going home was a bad idea after all. Maybe he'd be better off moving on and really starting over, completely from scratch. Maybe he should walk away from Lawder, just like he walked away from his life in New York.

But maybe, if he'd give it a chance, he'd re-think everything he ever thought he wanted out of life. And maybe what he thought was important, isn't so important after all. Maybe he could have everything he never realized he wanted, if he just looked around himself for a moment.

The Sticks (A Short Story)

Percy's given up. He's given up and wants to be as far away as possible from the place that has been the source of his troubles all his life. But to his disappointment, he finds himself in the last place he expected. And a chance encounter with a redneck and a stubborn hound dog aren't helping, either. That is... until they do.

Invincibility can be found in the strangest places.

The Last Day Of Summer

Rett's done some running away in his life, from family and from boyfriends, and he's not above doing it again. His current boyfriend wants to take their relationship to the next level, which makes Rett hesitant and doubtful. Luckily, a job offer in a new town solves his problem for him, giving him the perfect excuse to run away yet again from the uncomfortable feeling of someone trying to get close to him, even if it means picking up after seven years of school and starting over.

Most guys would kill for his new job, and Rett's certainly desperate for the paycheck. But the irony of the new position isn't lost on him — he's never cared a whole lot for sports, and even far less about the world of professional sports, which is right where he's landed. Then he finds out he's not the only one that's new to pro sports, and he gets closer and closer to one of the players as they try to make sense of the whole crazy thing together. And things seem good!

But when his family, whom he had long since left behind, shows back up with a family crisis, his life starts to unwind and Rett allows everything around him to painfully self-destruct. It's only then that he realizes he's got to get back up, stand his ground, and teach himself the one thing he never truly learned growing up.

He's got to stop running away and finally learn what it really means to be a man.

The Fence And Then The Trees

What would you do?

Jack Carber was in a bad spot. Betrayed and thrown in prison, he had to figure out fast how to survive, and with no idea who to trust and who not to trust. To make matters worse, he had already gotten on the bad side of The Kennel on day one. But his biggest threat was the vacant psychopath named Adder, whose cell he found himself sharing. And with this one, his best tools for survival, his skills as a con man, had no effect at all.

How would you survive?

Jack faced dangerous enemies, an indifferent prison administration, and an inmate advocate with his own twisted agenda. He was determined to keep himself alive and sane, even as he began to slowly give up on himself.

As long as he kept his head down and didn't fall prey to the fatal mistake of trusting anyone ever again, he'd eventually get out alive... in body if not in spirit. And that seemed like the most he could expect.

What would keep you going?

A sudden revelation and the resulting puzzle, though, throws his world into a wildly different light. He's unexpectedly clutching at a glimmer of hope, something more than mere survival, and yet fighting to not repeat the mistakes of his past again. But something deep inside him begs him to take that risk one more time.

Because, exactly how far would you be willing to go to protect the best thing that ever happened to you, especially when it hadn't even happened?

The Gully Snipe (Book One of The Dual World)

"A very many trickster moons ago," said Tony's grandfather, "and very, very far away... way past where our real world ends and your imagination begins, things were different than here. There was a proud kingdom that had fallen on darker days."

"The kingdom was known as Iisen, or the Iisendom as it was sometimes called. It was a prosperous and peaceful kingdom, but for years, a cloud had been forming over the land and was worrying the people that lived there."

"People were disappearing... not many, but when they did, it made the people afraid. There were rumors, of course. Rumors of gypsies and monsters in the woods, but no one seemed to know what was happening for sure. And the people of Iisen, the merchants and hostlers and iron mongers and farmers, couldn't very well hide in their homes and farmhouses. They still had to earn a living. All they could do was hope they weren't the next to vanish one day."

"But the tale doesn't really start with that. The tale starts with a thief. A thief who had just been caught and was about to be in very deep trouble..."

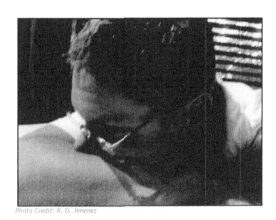

Photo Credit: R. D. Jimenez

About The Author

*The author, when not writing, spends a little too much time staring vacantly into space. You may contact him at **jfsmithstories@gmail.com** if you feel that you'd like to. He kind of likes that, actually.*

www.facebook.com/jfsmithstories

Made in the USA
Las Vegas, NV
24 February 2023

68073978R00184